P9-BBU-225

JUN 1 4 2012

BOOKS BY TIM LaHAYE

The Babylon Rising® Series

Babylon Rising
The Secret on Ararat

Tim LaHaye Prophecy Books—Nonfiction

Are We Living in the End Times?
Charting the End Times
Charting the End Times (study guide)
End Times Controversy
Perhaps Today (90-day devotional)
Merciful God of Prophecy
Revelation Unveiled
The Rapture
These Will Not Be Left Behind
Tim LaHaye Prophecy Study Bible: NKJV & KJV
Understanding Bible Prophecy for Yourself
Understanding God's Plan for the Ages (chart)
Bible Prophecy: Quick Reference Guide (booklet)

Tim LaHaye Fiction

Left Behind® (volume 1)
Tribulation Force (volume 2)
Nicolae (volume 3)
Soul Harvest (volume 4)
Apollyon (volume 5)
Assassins (volume 6)
The Indwelling (volume 7)
The Mark (volume 8)
Desecration (volume 9)
The Remnant (volume 10)
Armageddon (volume 11)
Glorious Appearing (volume 12)

Babylon Rising® (book 1)

Left Behind®: The Kids—Youth Fiction Series (volumes 1-40)

The Soul Survivor—Youth Fiction Series

The Mind Siege Project
All the Rave
The Last Dance
Black Friday

Additional Bestselling Books by Tim LaHaye

Spirit-Controlled Temperament
How to Be Happy Though Married
The Act of Marriage
How to Win over Depression
Mind Siege
How to Study the Bible for Yourself

NOV 1 4 2012

BABYLON RISING

THE SECRET ON ARARAT

TIM LaHaye
AND BOB PHILLIPS

BANTAM BOOKS

NEW YORK TORONTO LONDON SYDNEY AUCKLAND

Sycamore Public Library
103 E. State St.
Sycamore, IL 60178

BABYLON RISING: THE SECRET ON ARARAT

A Bantam Book

PUBLISHING HISTORY
Bantam hardcover edition published September 2004
Bantam trade paperback edition / August 2005

Published by
Bantam Dell
A Division of Random House, Inc.
New York, New York

All rights reserved
Copyright © 2004 by Tim LaHaye
Cover design by Craig DeCamps
Art copyright © Royalty-free/Corbis

Library of Congress Catalog Card Number: 2004056064

Bantam Books and the rooster colophon are registered trademarks of
Random House, Inc.

ISBN: 0-553-38350-7

Printed in the United States of America
Published simultaneously in Canada

www.bantamdell.com

10 9 8 7 6 5 4 3

Sycamore Public Library
103 E. State St.
Sycamore, IL 60178

DEDICATED TO *the memory of famed astronaut Colonel James Irwin, who walked on the moon in 1971. His faith in Jesus Christ and the Bible caused him to search diligently during the 1980s for the ever-elusive Ark of Noah, which many believe will one day be found high in the rugged mountain peaks of Ararat, where it has been preserved in ice for about five thousand years—waiting for someone like him to locate what many expect will be "the greatest archaeological discovery of all time."*

FOREWORD

Even before the Great Earthquake of 1840, which blew out close to a third of the upper regions of Mount Ararat, sightings of the remains of Noah's Ark had been reported. Scores of credible people claim to have seen it, from mountain people who live in the area to professional explorers. There is credible evidence that at least one hundred fifty White Russian soldiers saw and examined it in 1917, just prior to the Bolshevik Revolution. The evidence for the preservation of that irrefutable proof of the Bible story of Noah and his family preserving humanity could well be the most important archaeological discovery of all time.

Yet when all the stories are assembled there is a frightening thread that weaves through them. There must be a sinister force that has opposed all the searchers' valiant efforts up to the present from seeing the light of day. But we believe the tempo of exploration is heating up and that we may indeed be the generation that will finally reveal Noah's Ark for all the world to see.

Michael Murphy, noted archaeologist of *Babylon Rising* fame, will, in this book *The Secret on Ararat*, lead the most perilous expedition to date. One that could provide another exciting step in the fulfillment of prophecies of the end time . . . which Jesus Christ predicted would be like "the days of Noah." Can anyone seriously doubt that society today is very similar to the pre-flood days of Noah?

BABYLON RISING

THE SECRET
ON ARARAT

ONE

BREATHE. He desperately needed to breathe. But he knew instinctively that if he opened his mouth to try and suck in a breath, he would die.

Gritting his teeth fiercely, Murphy opened his eyes instead. And a pair of yellow, animal eyes stared back. Then a wildly gaping jaw came into focus through the greenish gloom, pointed teeth bared in a silent snarl. Murphy reached out, expecting the teeth to clamp down on his hand, but the dog face had disappeared, sucked back into the watery darkness.

It was no good. He had to get some air into his lungs before they burst. He turned his face upward, toward the feeble light, and after an agonizing few seconds during which he had the horrifying sense that he was sinking, not rising, his head broke the surface.

He sucked in a huge, spluttering breath, simultaneously

grabbing on to the narrow stone ledge that projected from the side of the pit. Resting his head against the jagged rock, he could feel something warm mingling with the freezing water. Blood. As the pain suddenly hit him, a wild carousel of thoughts started racing round his brain.

Laura. He would never see her again. She wouldn't even know he had died here, in this remote, godforsaken place. She would never know his last thoughts had been about her.

Then he remembered. Laura was dead. She'd died in his arms.

And now he was about to join her. With that thought, his body seemed to relax, accepting its fate, and he felt himself slipping back into the surging torrent.

No! He couldn't give up. He couldn't let the crazy old man win at last. He had to find a way out.

But first he had to find those puppies.

Clutching the ledge with both hands, Murphy took a series of quick, deep breaths, hyperventilating to force as much oxygen as possible into his lungs. He'd done enough cave diving to know he could stay under a full two minutes if he had to. But that was under ideal conditions. Right now he had to contend with the effects of shock, blood loss, and bone-shaking cold— all the while trying to find two little dogs somewhere in a swirling maelstrom. As he let himself slip back under the freezing water, he wondered—not for the first time—how he managed to get himself into these messes.

The answer was simple. One word: *Methuselah.*

Murphy had been making his way carefully through the cave, fanning his flashlight across the dank black walls, when he found himself standing not on loose shale but what felt like solid wooden planks. Ever alert to tricks and traps, Murphy instinctively reacted as if he'd just stepped onto a tray of burning coals—but before he could leap aside, the trapdoor sprang open. As he felt himself plunging into the void, a familiar cackling laugh shattered the silence, echoing crazily off the rock walls.

"Welcome to the game, Murphy! Get out of this one if you can!"

As Murphy cartwheeled through space, his brain was still trying to come up with a suitable response. But all that came out was a grunt as he slammed into the ground like a bag of cement and the air was punched out of his lungs, before the impact flung him sideways and his head connected with a boulder. For a moment all was black, buzzing darkness. Then he raised himself up on his hands and knees and his senses returned one by one: He could feel the damp grit between his fingers; he could taste it in his mouth; he could smell stagnant water; he could dimly make out the shadowy walls of the pit he'd fallen into.

And he could hear the fretful whining of what sounded like two cold, wet—and very scared—little dogs.

He turned toward the sound and there they were, shivering together on a narrow ledge. A pair of German shepherd puppies. Murphy shook his head: He always tried to prepare himself for *anything* where Methuselah was concerned, but what were a couple of puppies doing in the middle of an underground cave complex miles from anywhere? Could they have gotten lost and somehow wandered this far from the surface? He didn't think so. Much more likely they were there because Methuselah had put them there.

They were part of the game.

Fighting his natural instinct to gather the bedraggled pups tightly in his arms and tell them everything was going to be okay, he approached the ledge cautiously. They looked so helpless. But that didn't mean harmless. Nothing in Methuselah's games was harmless, and if he had put them there for Murphy to find, then something about the dogs was out of whack. He just had to figure out what.

Just then the steady dripping sound that had been nagging away at the back of Murphy's consciousness since he landed in the pit started to get louder. He turned in the direction of the noise and suddenly it became a roaring, as a huge wave of water surged through a narrow gap in the rocks. In a second a frothing tide was tugging at his ankles, pulling him off balance. Forgetting Methuselah's mind games, he pushed himself back toward the ledge, scooped up the puppies, and stuffed them under his jacket. His eyes darted round the walls of the pit, looking for anything that would help him find a way out, as the rising water swirled around his chest. The puppies were just a diversion, he thought bitterly, fighting to keep his footing. He hadn't spotted the real danger until it was too late. "Don't worry, fellas, I'll get you out of here," he assured them with more confidence than he felt. Then the torrent lifted him off his feet and the panicking dogs squirmed out of his jacket.

Fighting to keep his head above the surface, he grabbed for them, but his fingers closed on icy water and then he too was engulfed, spinning out of control like a bunch of wet clothes in a Laundromat washer.

He closed his eyes, and even as his lungs started hungrily demanding air, he tried to find a calm place in his mind where he could think. He checked through his options. The water would soon reach the level of the trapdoor, which was no doubt secured against escape. So, search for another way out under the water, or look for the puppies again before they drowned? If he tried to find a way out on his own, the puppies would be dead by the time he found it. If he tried to save the puppies first, he'd probably wind up too exhausted to find a way out. If there *was* a way out.

So much for his options.

The only shred of hope he could cling to was the fact that this was a game. And a game, however deadly, still had rules.

But there was no way he could figure them out while his lungs were screaming and his thought processes were beginning to go fuzzy due to lack of oxygen.

Get some air. Then go after those puppies. If he was still alive after that, maybe God would give him some inspiration.

When Murphy walked into the lab, he was greeted by the sight of a young woman bent over a workbench, her jet-black hair, tied back in a ponytail, making a stark contrast with her crisp white lab coat as she scrutinized a sheet of parchment. She didn't look up as the door clicked shut behind him, and he stood for a moment, smiling at the expression of fierce concentration on her face.

"What are you grinning at, Professor?" she asked, her eyes never leaving the parchment.

"Nothing, Shari. Nothing at all. It's just nice to see someone so absorbed in their work, is all."

She gave a short "hmph," still not looking up, and Murphy's smile broadened. Shari Nelson was one of the top students in his biblical archaeology class at Preston University, and for almost two years she had been his part-time research assistant. In that time he'd come to appreciate her passion for the subject, her limitless capacity for hard work, and her sharp intelligence. But most of all, he valued her warm and generous spirit. She might be pretending to ignore him right now, but they'd been through enough tragedy and heartache together in the past year, with the deaths of his wife and her brother still painful every hour of every day, for him to know that she would drop everything—even a fascinating ancient parchment like the one she was studying—if he needed her.

"So what's up, Shari? Did the results from the carbon-dating tests on our little pottery fragment come in?"

"Not yet," Shari replied, returning the parchment to the clear plastic container on the bench. "But *something* has definitely arrived for you." She gestured toward a large white envelope with the purple and orange lettering of Federal Express.

Shari watched eagerly as Murphy picked up the package. Clearly she'd had a hard time containing her curiosity while she waited for Murphy to arrive at the lab.

"Strange," he mused. "No return address. Just *Babylon*.

Doesn't look like it went through the usual FedEx mailing process." He heard Shari gasp. Babylon, she knew all too well, could only mean one thing: a whole heap of trouble.

Murphy carefully opened the envelope and shook the contents—a smaller envelope with the words *Professor Murphy* printed in heavy marker and a xeroxed page from a map—out onto the workbench. He glanced at the map, then opened the second envelope. Inside was an index card with three words typed on it.

Chemar. Zepheth. Kopher.

He handed it to Shari while he examined the map. A route had been marked in pink felt-tip from Raleigh, moving west, across the border into Tennessee. Where the snaking line stopped, there were an *X* and four barely legible words written in a spidery scrawl:

"*Cave of the Waters.* Mean anything to you, Shari?"

"It sounds like somewhere you definitely don't want to go," she replied firmly.

He winced. Exactly what Laura would have said. Same tone of voice, even.

"It's coming back to me. I've heard of this place. It's in the Great Smoky Mountains . . . past Asheville, somewhere between Waynesville and Bryson City." If he remembered it right, the cave was discovered in the early 1900s but had never been fully explored, because the high water table in the area—not to mention at least three underground streams that ran through it—caused the chambers to flood periodically. It was supposed to contain a vast labyrinth of passageways, but no one knew how far they extended. Caving expeditions had been officially discouraged after three cavers were lost without a trace in the early seventies.

"Okay, so we've got directions to a cave. Now, what about the message on the card? What do you make of it, Shari?"

She repeated the words. "*Chemar. Zepheth. Kopher.* It's Hebrew. No problem there. But beyond that it's got me stumped. Does it have something to do with Babylon?"

"It wouldn't surprise me," he said, stroking his chin thoughtfully. "But right now it doesn't mean any more to me than it does to you."

"And there's no signature anywhere, and no return address. So how can we find out who sent this?"

Murphy gave a half-smile. "Come on, Shari. A mysterious message in an ancient language? A set of directions to a remote spot? *Babylon?* He didn't really need to sign it, did he?"

Shari sighed. "I guess not. I was just hoping . . . you know, that it might be something else. Something innocent. Not one of these crazy games where you—"

She could tell Murphy wasn't listening anymore. He was studying the map intently, already halfway there. Her heart sank as she realized there was nothing she could do to stop him.

All she could do now was pray.

It had been a beautiful drive from Winston-Salem past Lake Hickory. He'd left before sunup and covered the 280 miles in good time. Now the bright sunshine at his back was giving way to a sharp chill as he made his way farther into the mountains with their thick covering of majestic oaks and pine. He stopped to check the map again and turned down a dirt road, which bumped along for a hundred yards or so before he reached a fork. He stopped again. This time the map didn't help. Frowning, he laid it on the dash and stepped out onto the sunbaked dirt. He looked in both directions. Both roads snaked into the trees in similar fashion. Nothing to choose there.

What was it Yogi Berra used to say?

When you come to a fork in the road, take it.

He shook his head. *Thanks, Yogi. You're a big help.* Then something caught his eye in the thick weeds at the side of the road. He knelt down and cleared away the foliage from a rusting sign. The yellow paint was almost gone, but he could just make out the words. CAVE OF THE WATERS. Then something else, in red paint this time. DANGER.

He carefully raised the sign and stuck it firmly back in the ground. It seemed to be pointing left. "I haven't even got there yet, and already you're playing games, old man," he muttered, getting back in the car and slamming the door shut. He revved the engine and turned up the narrow track.

It took another half hour to arrive at the cave entrance. At first, as the dirt track came to an abrupt stop in front of a huge oak, Murphy suspected another of Methuselah's tricks. Beyond the oak, the mountainside rose steeply, covered with dense undergrowth. There was no sign to tell him he was at the right place. Searching for a sign to indicate where he was supposed to go, he felt his scalp begin to prickle as the reality of the situation struck him. He was alone. Unarmed. Miles from the nearest habitation. At the invitation of a madman who had tried to kill him on several previous occasions and who was probably watching him from some hideaway on the mountain at this very moment. He could almost feel the crosshairs moving over his heart.

When you put it like that it didn't sound good.

But he'd come too far now to think of turning back, and he trusted in God that he was doing the right thing. After all, this might be a game, but the stakes were high. For a biblical archaeologist such as himself, they couldn't be any higher.

He scanned the mountainside, looking for any irregularity that would indicate the entrance to the cave, and his eyes caught a glint of metal amid the rocks and scrawny bushes. He squinted into the glare and tried to focus on the spot. There was something, definitely. Whether it was the cave was another matter, but what choice did he have? He hefted his backpack and started up the slope.

Twenty minutes later he was standing on a horizontal outcrop, wiping the sweat from his eyes and trying to catch his breath. In front of him was a tangle of wire—what had clearly once been a chain-link fence designed to seal off the gaping hole in the rock. This was what had caught his eye from the bottom of the mountain. He crouched down and gingerly eased himself around the wire, stepping into the mouth of the cave.

He pulled his flashlight out of his backpack and switched it on. The two cardinal rules of cave exploration came unbidden into his mind: Never cave alone, and never cave without three sources of light. *And, I guess you could add, never enter a cave when you know there's a psycho lurking in there somewhere,* he thought.

Although the cave entrance was relatively wide, it quickly narrowed, and Murphy soon had to crawl on his hands and knees over the floor of loose stones and grit. After a few minutes of gentle twists and turns, the only light he could see was the beam of his torch, and the familiar thrill, a unique mix of anxiety and excitement that all speleologists experience on entering a new cave system, took over. It had been years since he'd been caving, but the smell of damp limestone and the instant adrenaline surge reminded him of caving holidays with Laura in Mexico—and particularly the extraordinary Flint-Mammoth Cave System in Kentucky. It was said to be over 224 miles long—the longest in the world—and while they'd covered only a fraction of it, the sense of infinite depth was awesome. If you kept going, you could imagine you might eventually reach hell itself. But that wasn't the deepest cave. That distinction belonged to the Gouffre Jean Bernard in France, which wound its way 4,600 feet below the earth. Every year they'd planned on making the expedition, and every year they'd never quite managed to find the time in their hectic lives of teaching and digging for artifacts. And then . . .

Murphy shook his head and refocused on the task at hand. He could feel the humidity increasing as the temperature in the cave plummeted. Drops of water from stalactites on the ceiling started falling onto the back of his head and over his face, and he wiped them away with his sleeve. He pushed himself on, despite the soreness in his knees and elbows, hoping the cave wasn't narrowing further. After another ten minutes, he decided to take a breather, easing himself onto his back. Energy conservation was a key element of survival in this kind of unfamiliar environment. Something he'd learned from Laura. "You've got to pace yourself, Murphy," she used to tell him. "It isn't a race, you know."

And he needed to keep his wits sharp. He wasn't just dealing with an unmapped cave system where he might plunge off a sheer cliff into fathomless space, or which at any moment could narrow into a stone vise from which he'd never be able to extricate himself. At every step he had to remember why he was here. Methuselah had planned it all. And that meant there was some artifact of great value for an archaeologist—especially a biblical archaeologist—waiting for him at the end of his journey. But Methuselah wouldn't be content to see him rack up a few scrapes and bruises in search of his prize. For his own insane reasons, Methuselah required Murphy to risk his life. That was how you played the game.

And the game could begin at any moment.

Taking a deep, calming breath, he rolled back onto his hands and knees and crawled forward. Soon the cave walls started to get higher and the floor flattened and broadened out. After a few minutes he could walk easily without ducking his head, and then a sudden turn brought him to a large chamber. Playing his flashlight over the walls, he looked for some sign that someone had been here before him. Something out of place, anything that didn't look natural. But all he could see

was water glistening on sheer black walls and a cluster of stalactites hugging the roof over his head.

"No booby traps that I can see," he muttered to himself.
"Nothing here that God didn't create unless I'm much mistaken." So why was his scalp beginning to itch? Why was his
subconscious mind telling him something wasn't right?

Then it hit him. It wasn't what he could see. It was what he
could hear. Just on the very edge of audibility. A muffled keening, almost a whining sound. Like an animal—maybe more than
one animal—in distress. But how could that be? No animal
could survive down here—except possibly bats, and this was
too deep even for them, surely.

He moved slowly toward the sound, hefting his flashlight
like a weapon, every sense alert for danger. And that was when
his feet first touched the wooden planks.

His lungs full of air, Murphy had difficulty pushing himself
down into the icy depths of the flooded pit, but after a few
powerful strokes he managed to grab on to a rock projecting off
the bottom, and took a moment to get his bearings. He could
feel the rush of water at his back as it continued to power its
way into the cave. He figured that must be where the light was
coming from that turned what would have been pitch-black
into a ghostly, greenish gloom. And the puppies must have been
swept in the opposite direction. He launched himself forward,
hoping for a glimpse of thrashing limbs. Then suddenly he felt
rather than saw the two little bodies sweeping past him. He
reached out a hand but it was too late. But something about the

way the puppies seemed to be pulled through the water gave him hope. It was almost as if they were in a giant bath and were being sucked down the plughole. In which case water was going out of the pit as well as coming in.

Maybe there was a way out after all.

He followed in the direction the puppies had taken, and after a few strokes he could see them, their little bodies churning in the water as dirt and debris streamed toward a narrow gap in the rock wall. He thought of going back to the surface for another breath, then realized that this was his only shot. Either they managed to push their way out now or they were done for.

Scooping the puppies up and stuffing them back into the front of his jacket, he could feel them squirming in utter panic as the last molecules of oxygen disappeared from their lungs. Finding a handhold on the wall, he braced himself, then kicked his legs forward until his feet disappeared into the crevice. Every instinct told him to get himself back out, to get back to the surface, knowing that he was probably doing no more than wedging himself into a fissure from which there would be no escape, but he grimly forced himself farther in, his feet now above his head, the water pushing past him through the crack.

As his torso was squeezed into the fissure, he braced his arms across his chest, hoping he'd be able to protect the puppies from being crushed. By now he wouldn't have been able to force himself back out even if he'd wanted to. The force of the escaping water held him fast. There was only one way to go, and that was deeper into the crack. With a twist of his hips, he corkscrewed farther in, the jagged sides of the opening scraping deep lacerations into his thighs. But he hardly felt the pain. He was a machine now, with just one purpose: to get through to the other side.

As his head entered the fissure, he could feel his lungs about to give out. In the next five seconds he would take a breath and they would fill with water. For the puppies it was probably already too late. Their movements had become less urgent. Perhaps it was just the flow of water that made them seem alive. With his last scrap of willpower he kicked forward, and a giant hand suddenly seemed to be pulling him through from the other side. With a violent wrench, his head bumping roughly against the rock, he was spewed out onto the floor of another chamber. As the waters still surged over him, he managed at last to take a huge gulp of air—along with a large mouthful of water—into his lungs.

Choking violently, he raised himself onto his hands and knees, and for the first time in what seemed an eternity, his head was fully out of the water, caressed by an icy blast of precious air. And then it was being caressed by two eager pink tongues, as the puppies struggled out of his jacket, yelping with joy as they filled their little lungs. Murphy found he was gasping, laughing, and crying for joy all at the same time.

Once he had managed to steady his breathing and regain his composure, he tried to take stock of his surroundings. Behind him, he could hear the water still pouring through the gap in the rock, but thankfully this chamber was not filling up like the other one. The flood tide remained just a few inches deep and seemed to be draining away through a sinkhole at the other end. For now, at least, they were safe, and Murphy gave silent thanks for their delivery.

That was when he noticed he was shivering uncontrollably. Hypothermia. The chief cause of death among cave explorers. And the subject of a class on wilderness survival he himself had taught. He remembered the young man at the back who had raised his hand at the end of the lecture.

"How long does it take for a person to die of hypothermia?" he had asked.

"That depends," Murphy had replied, "on how fast your core temperature drops. When it drops to ninety-six degrees, you begin intense shivering. Between ninety-five and ninety-one degrees the ability to think is reduced. Your speech starts to slur and you become disoriented. As the core temperature drops to between ninety and eighty-six, muscle rigidity and amnesia kick in. Pulse and respiration slow and you get a glassy stare. Between eighty-five and seventy-seven degrees, death will occur."

That had seemed to impress the questioner. And it impressed Murphy now that he could remember it word for word. So amnesia hadn't kicked in yet. The good news was he was still in the intense-shivering stage. But it was nothing to get complacent about. The next stage was when you couldn't think straight, and thinking straight was what he needed to do right now. Especially since he didn't have a torch anymore and he somehow had to keep control of two surprisingly lively puppies, who seemed to have already forgotten their near-drowning ordeal as they splashed and yelped happily in the shallow, muddy water.

He gently pushed one of the pups away as it started gnawing at his wristwatch. How could he think straight when—of course! "You've got more sense than I have, you clever little pooch," he said happily, touching the button on the side of the Special Forces watch. A small blue light illuminated the chamber for a few feet around him. He switched it off again to conserve the battery and tried to think. The water was draining out of the chamber through one exit, but he'd had enough of water for one day. He certainly wasn't going to risk diving into the sinkhole in the hope that he'd emerge into another air pocket. But something else gave him a sliver of hope. The right side of his body was a little colder than the left, and that meant the air must be moving slightly. There was a breeze coming from somewhere and therefore maybe a route to the surface.

He switched the light on again and swung his wrist in a slow arc around his body. His eye was caught by a narrow pillar of rock in the middle of the cave. Something oddly shaped was perched on the top. He crawled over to it cautiously, herding the puppies in front of him. Reaching up, he ran a hand over the object. It felt like a chunk of some kind of very dense wood, the sort of sea-worn fragment you might find washed up on a beach. Had Methuselah put this here? Was this what he had come for? Was his prize for risking his life a worthless piece of flotsam?

There was no point speculating about it now. If Methuselah had finally cracked, that wasn't such a big surprise, and if this was the booby prize, then maybe Murphy deserved it for agreeing to play a madman's game by a madman's rules. He slipped the piece of wood into a pocket in his combat trousers and turned his face back in the direction of the gentle breeze.

"Come on, you guys. Unless you've got a better idea, I think it's time to follow our noses and see if we can get back home."

TWO

Jerusalem, A.D. 30

THE LANKY STRANGER ELBOWED *his way through the milling crowd. Even though he was taller than most, the constant jostling made it difficult to see who was speaking. But one thing was certain: Whoever it was seemed to have the crowd's attention. People were pushing against those in front of them to try and get nearer the front. Some were even trying to stand on baskets or bundles of cloth to get a better view. A child pulled at his mother's skirts, desperate to know what was going on, and the stranger hoisted him onto his shoulders with a smile. The boy clapped his hands in delight and the woman nodded her thanks, shyly. The crowd seemed to quiet all at once, as if on cue, and a man began speaking softly but clearly. Feeling the excitement of those around him, the stranger strained to hear. . . .*

It was his first visit to Jerusalem, and he had never experienced anything like it. In the marketplace the noise of people bartering with one
another was overpowering. Every now and then he would stop and
watch people who were yelling at each other so vehemently he thought a
fight was about to break out—until suddenly they slapped palms and the
deal was done. It was a far cry from his sleepy village in the hills,
where no one ever seemed to get excited about anything. And the multitude of stalls, with produce so various and exotic he found himself staring openmouthed like an idiot, was truly incredible. Open baskets were
filled with every kind of fruit and grain imaginable. Slaughtered car-
casses of sheep, goats, and cows hung from poles that held up the tent
coverings over the merchants, who cried their wares while lazily swatting at the flies that swarmed over the freshly cut meats. Women selling
brightly colored bolts of cloth called to him, gesturing to him to feel the
quality of the material—one even grabbed his arm roughly and tried to
pull him into her stall. Shiny jewelry and polished daggers dazzled the
eye, while the raucous din of ducks and geese in wicker cages assaulted
the ear.

He could quite easily have allowed himself to be pushed and pulled
this way and that through the market, like a leaf caught in an eddy, for
the rest of the morning, but he'd been told by his cousin—older and more
experienced in the ways of the world—that the city contained greater
wonders, things a man should see if only once in his lifetime. His journey from his village to Jerusalem, to offer the annual half-shekel of silver required of every adult male, might be the first of many. Maybe one
day he might even live in the city (though how a poor shepherd would
make a living there he didn't know). But it would be foolish to trust the

future in such troubled times as these, when the Roman occupation made everything uncertain. The wise thing would be to see all Jerusalem's wonders now, while he had the chance.

He strode purposefully out of the marketplace, and the walls of the upper city began to rise in the distance. As he climbed the steeply ascending roadway, he passed the Parbar, where the sacrifice animals were kept, and laughed to hear a sudden burst of squealing. Then the huge stone slabs of the Dung Gate loomed up before him, and he felt his pulse quicken as he stepped through into the city proper.

What he saw made his breath catch in his throat. The huge walls surrounding Herod's Temple dazzled with their whiteness. Some of the foundation stones were over sixty-five feet long and four feet high. He couldn't imagine how mere men could have fashioned such things from the bare rock. Their very existence seemed to speak of the majesty and omnipotence of God.

Then his eyes were drawn to the side, where the power of Rome boldly showed itself under the shadow of the great temple walls. A century of Roman legionaries, their oiled leather body armor gleaming, swords and spear points glinting in the sun, were marching toward the Fortress of Antonia, where they were quartered. The clatter of their iron-shod sandals over the ancient flagstones sent a momentary shiver through him. Then he pressed on eagerly toward his goal.

He had heard that the temple had seven entrances but that he must go up the arching viaduct ramp from the lower city. That was the most spectacular, his cousin had said. But what could be more spectacular than what he had already seen?

He walked through the arch to the courtyard, past the enormous bronze gates that he had heard it took twenty men to open and close, be-

neath the shadow of the great golden eagle Herod had placed there lest any forget who ruled here.

When he entered the temple courtyard, the vastness of the marketplace suddenly seemed cramped and feeble by comparison. As his eyes ranged over the expanse, he tried to imagine how many people it could hold. A thousand? No! Many thousands, surely. More than he could count! It must have been 1,500 feet long and 1,200 feet wide, and he had been assured that it could hold 250,000 people, but such a number meant nothing to him. He could not imagine what such a host would look like—if Palestine even contained that many people!

In the center of the courtyard was the temple itself, and for the first time his imagination was stirred not merely by scale but by beauty. No wonder it had taken ten thousand men and over sixty years for the temple and its surrounding buildings to be completed. He had no words to express what he was seeing, knowing nothing of harmony and proportion, but the graceful forms nevertheless spoke to something deep within his soul. He found himself giving thanks to God for the world and everything in it.

Suddenly he realized he was not alone. Many of the men milling around him were wearing prayer shawls. Some had phylactery boxes containing the Ten Commandments tied to their foreheads. Others were leading sacrificial sheep or carrying baskets containing turtle doves, the poor man's sacrifice offering. Over to one side he could see money changers bargaining with travelers like himself, while under the colonnades, rabbis were teaching little groups of a dozen or so.

Moving through the throng, he saw a marble wall almost the height of a man, behind which he glimpsed priests attending to various duties. As he drew closer he noticed a sign on the wall with an inscription.

No foreigner is to enter within the balustrade and enclosure around the temple area. Whoever is caught will have himself to blame for his death, which will follow.

He didn't think foreigner *meant him, but even so the words were intimidating. He resolved to watch his step, to copy the behavior of those around him in case he transgressed some unwritten rule by mistake. Trying to remember what else his cousin had told him, he recalled that the temple itself was divided into three chambers. The first was the vestibule. The second chamber was the Holy Place, containing the Altar of Incense and the golden candlestick with seven branches. The last chamber was the Holy of Holies, separated from the Holy Place by a curtain that hung from the ceiling and was said to be six inches thick. The Holy of Holies housed the most wondrous object of all—the ark of the Covenant. He had heard so many different descriptions of it that the image he had in his head was constantly shifting and blurring into the most fantastic designs. All he really knew for sure was that it was a wondrous piece of workmanship covered with gold.*

He didn't need a sign to tell him he was forbidden to enter the Holy of Holies, or that sneaking a look at the Ark of the Covenant would be taking his life in his hands—even if he was clever enough to do it. But it sounded so incredible, so awesome, that he felt himself being drawn toward the Holy of Holies like a moth to a flame.

That was when his attention was diverted by the growing crowd under the colonnades, and he found himself straining forward to hear what the speaker was saying. With the boy on his shoulders, people thought he was a young father bringing his son to the city for the first time, and the crowd parted good-naturedly to let him move forward—with the boy's mother bringing up the rear–until he was standing at the front, just a few feet away from the speaker.

Seated on a bench under the colonnades was a bearded man. He was wearing an earth-colored robe–the sort of rough woolen garment that might belong to a beggar–with a white prayer cloth around his shoulders. There was nothing at all remarkable about his features, but looking at his face somehow made you want to listen to what he was saying. He paused and looked the stranger directly in the eye, as if he was addressing him alone, before continuing.

"No one knows about that day or hour, not even the angels in heaven, nor the Son, but only the Father. As it was in the days of Noah, so it will be at the coming of the Son of Man. For in the days before the flood, people were eating and drinking, marrying and giving in marriage, up to the day Noah entered the ark; and they knew nothing about what would happen until the flood came and took them all away. That is how it will be at the coming of the Son of Man. Two men will be in the field; one will be taken and the other left. Two women will be grinding with a hand mill; one will be taken and the other left.

"Therefore keep watch, because you do not know on what day your Lord will come. But understand this: If the owner of the house had known at what time of night the thief was coming, he would have kept watch and would not have let his house be broken into. So you also must be ready, because the Son of Man will come at an hour when you do not expect him."

"Who is that man?" the stranger asked the person next to him.

"Do you not know?" said a short, beady-eyed man with bad breath. "Where are you from?"

"I just arrived from Capernaum, next to the Sea of Galilee. I came to pay the annual tribute."

"That's a man named Jesus. Some people think he is a prophet. Others say he is a rebel trying to start an insurrection against Rome."

"What's he talking about?"

The short man scratched his beard. "I'm not sure. It's some strange talk about judgment for sin and the end of the world. It doesn't make all that much sense to me."

The stranger felt compelled to question him further, even though the man didn't seem to have the answers. "What is he talking about when he says, 'As in the days of Noah'?"

The man merely shrugged. "Your guess is as good as mine. Perhaps the weather's going to turn nasty." He grinned.

The stranger persisted. "Who is this Son of Man he is talking about? And what does he mean 'So you also must be ready'?"

But the short man with the beady eyes had slipped away through the crowd and the stranger was left to ponder the mystery of the preacher's words on his own. He gently lowered the boy down to the ground and whispered quietly to himself, as if repeating the words would reveal their meaning: " . . . because the Son of Man will come at an hour when you do not expect him. . . ."

THREE

MURPHY PULLED INTO his reserved spot and got out of his car. The walk from the teachers' parking area up the winding path to the Memorial Lecture Hall always pleased him. The tree-covered walkways, beautiful flowers, and lush greenery of the South had a wonderful calming effect. But this time the familiar walk was more agony than ecstasy, as the pain from his various scrapes and bruises began to kick in.

"What happened to you? You look terrible!"

Murphy winced as Shari came bouncing down the path toward him. With Laura gone, Shari had taken up the post of chief worrier on his behalf, and he knew she hadn't really believed him when he told her he was going to look up an old acquaintance over the weekend. Well, Methuselah was certainly old, and *acquaintance* covered a multitude of sins, so he hadn't actually been lying. He'd just neglected to add that this acquaintance happened to be lurking in a dangerous underground cave system in the Great Smoky Mountains.

He had started to frame a reply that wouldn't get him into more trouble than he was already in, when he was saved by the two pups playfully nipping at Shari's ankles.

"Who are these little guys?" she asked delightedly, bending down to let them nuzzle her hand.

"Meet Shem and Japheth. Their owner wasn't really looking after them properly, so I decided to bring them back to Preston with me. I'm hoping we can find them a good, loving home. And in the meantime . . ."

Shari finished his sentence for him. "You want *me* to look after them. Now, listen, Professor, if you think I'm going to babysit these pups while you go off on some madcap adventure—"

Murphy held his hands up to interrupt her. "No madcap adventures, Shari. I promise. There's something I want you to take a look at. I want your professional opinion."

He grinned and she scowled back to show him she didn't buy the flattery. Nevertheless, it was hard to resist. "What is it?" she asked.

He steered her back toward the lab. "That's what I was hoping you would tell me, Shari."

While Shem and Japheth noisily emptied a large bowl of water in the corner of the lab, Murphy pulled the chunk of weather-beaten wood out of his briefcase. He knew that as soon as Shari had an archaeological puzzle to solve, she'd be so totally focused on it that she might possibly forget to interrogate him about his weekend activities. At least that was what he was hoping.

"Well, it's definitely old," she said, putting the wood under a powerful microscope. "It's practically fossilized. But there's something else—a layer of something that's bonded with the surface."

Murphy clapped her on the shoulder, almost upsetting the microscope on its stand. "I'm beginning to think I know what that is."

"You do?"

"*Chemar. Zepheth. Kopher.* Remember?"

Shari looked up from what she was doing. "Where did you get this, Professor Murphy?"

"Never mind that now, Shari. *Chemar* means to bubble up. *Zepheth* means to flow. And *kopher* means to cover or make watertight. Put them together and they form the biblical word for *pitch*."

"Pitch?"

"Bitumen. Asphalt. It bubbles out of the ground in liquid form, and shipbuilders used to spread it over planks to make them watertight. The Bible talks about tar pits in Genesis Fourteen: Ten. Apparently there were a lot of tar pits near Babylon."

Shari folded her arms. "Sounds like you've been doing some serious Bible study over the weekend, Professor. Anything else you can tell me?"

"Well, Shari, did you know that pitch was used to cover the papyrus basket that baby Moses was floating in when Pharaoh's daughter found him? Exodus Two: Three."

"I always wondered how a basket made of reeds stayed afloat."

"And the same stuff was used in the construction of the Tower of Babel. It says in Genesis Eleven: Three that they used tar instead of mortar between the bricks."

Shari was wide-eyed now. He definitely had her attention. "Is this piece of wood something to do with the Tower of Babel?"

Murphy rubbed his chin. "I'm not sure. The first thing we have to do is find out how old it is. Which means we need the best carbon-dating equipment we can lay our hands on."

"The Parchments of Freedom Foundation?" asked Shari excitedly.

"Exactly. If you wouldn't mind just handing me the phone, Shari . . ."

Murphy punched in the number and drummed his fingers on the workbench in anticipation. He didn't even notice Shem and Japheth chasing each other excitedly round his feet.

"Yeah, hi. This is Michael Murphy at Preston University. Can I speak to Isis McDonald—I mean, Dr. McDonald? Sure, I can hold." He drummed his fingers some more, wondering why he was so nervous. Was it just the excitement over a new archaeological find? Then he heard a familiar voice in his ear, and for a moment he was transported back to the ancient sewers of Tar-Qasir and the vision of a crazed fanatic coming at him with a butcher knife.

"Murphy, is it really you?"

He snapped back to the present, calmed by her soft Scottish

brogue. "Yeah, I think so, Isis. Long time no speak. How have you been doing?"

"You know me, Michael. Just poring over dusty old manuscripts in my little office. I haven't been in a life-threatening situation since . . . well, since the last time I saw you, actually."

He laughed, picturing her up to her ankles in old books and papers, pushing her red hair out of her eyes as she furiously scanned the chaos for some vital piece of parchment. "I'm glad to hear that, Isis. And I'd very much like to keep things that way."

"But?" she said good-naturedly.

"Well, I was hoping you could do me a favor."

"As long as it doesn't involve traveling halfway around the world and doing battle with a murderous psychopath."

"Absolutely. I promise." He laughed nervously. "You won't have to leave the building, let alone Washington."

"So what have you got for me?"

"A fragment of wood. Old. Very old."

"And you want to know exactly how old."

"That's right."

"And you want to know yesterday."

"If it's not too much trouble."

"Of course. Not a problem. Send it over and I'll get right on it."

"Thanks, Isis. I really owe you. Let me know if there's anything I can do in return."

After a pause she said, "Next time, don't wait six months before you call me. And don't wait until you need a favor."

He started to think of how to respond, but the line was dead. He turned to Shari with an awkward smile, suddenly feeling the need to get outside the lab again, to be doing some hard physical work that didn't require too much thought.

But Shari was gone.

He caught up with her in the cafeteria. She was sitting on her own in a corner, staring at a mug of coffee. Murphy slid in beside her and put a gentle hand on her arm.

"Are you planning to drink that, or are you just seeing if you can turn it to stone?"

She smiled wearily and brushed a tear from her cheek. "I'm sorry, Professor Murphy. That wasn't very professional, running out like that. I just needed to be by myself, I guess."

"Do you want me to go? I don't want to intrude, you know that."

"It's okay. I guess I need to talk to someone, and who better, right?"

"Right. So what's been going on?"

"It's Paul. We had an argument."

"What about?" He knew Shari and Paul Wallach had been seeing each other for a while, ever since Shari had nursed him back to health after the bomb explosion in the church. They seemed to be very close.

"Something stupid." She shook her head. "No, not stupid. I just mean it wasn't about us. It was about evolution."

"Evolution?"

She nodded. "I don't know who he's been talking to, but he's been reading some books. He keeps quoting someone called Dawkins. He had a copy of Darwin's *The Origin of Species* and wanted to show me these passages he'd underlined. Things about fossils and how they prove different kinds of animals evolved from one another and weren't all created at the same time the way it says in the Bible."

"I see. And what did you say?"

"I told him I didn't have all the answers, but if God created the world, and if God also created science, then the two would be compatible. I mentioned that my research into the early pioneers of evolution showed that many of them were simply trying to force science to fit in with their preconceived view that God didn't exist. So they came up with this theory that species somehow transformed themselves into other species, in order to take God out of the equation. Yet not one valid transitional fossil has ever been found, despite claims to the contrary. And with the discovery of the DNA code, which actually *prevents* one organism from changing into another organism, the theory of evolution today is in shambles. . . . Although I doubt you'll hear too many evolutionists admit it, especially after all the trouble they've gone through to get it taught in schools."

Murphy nodded. "That's a great answer, Shari. Paul's still unsure of where he stands. Knowing you has definitely brought him closer to God, but he's the one who's going to have to step over the threshold, and in his own time." He smiled. "But I think we just may have a little something that could help him on his way."

Shari looked up. "What do you mean?"

Murphy tapped his nose conspiratorially. "Let's wait and see what Isis McDonald can tell us about our little piece of wood. If I'm right, it could open Paul's eyes in a big way."

Over the next few days, Murphy concentrated on getting up to speed with his lecture notes, knowing that Dean Fallworth would be looking over his shoulder, just waiting for an excuse to boot him off campus. Shari, meanwhile, was becoming so infatuated with Shem and Japheth—who seemed to think the whole campus was their private playground—that she was beginning to hope an offer of a good home wouldn't turn up. She and Paul hadn't spoken since their argument, and having the little dogs around her apartment certainly made her feel less lonely. In fact, they had been so successful in distracting her from her problems that when Murphy burst into the lab, waving a letter with the Parchments of Freedom Foundation logo, she didn't at first understand what he was getting so excited about.

"The carbon-dating results, Shari. Isis has confirmed my theory. This could be one of the most amazing archaeological finds in the history of . . . well, the history of archaeology."

"That does sound pretty exciting," she laughed. "So what did Isis find out? How old is it?"

"Between five and six thousand years," Murphy declared triumphantly.

Shari shrugged. "Meaning?"

"Meaning," said Murphy, drawing it out, "that our little piece of wood might just be a chunk of . . . Noah's Ark."

Shari jumped out of her chair. "Are you serious? I was holding a piece of Noah's Ark?" She looked down at her hand as if it might be glowing with some special radiance.

"I can't say for sure yet, but the dates seem about right and it certainly could be a fragment from a boat of some kind. So . . ."

"So, where did you get it? I think you forgot to tell me that part."

Murphy held his hands up in mock surrender. "Where did I get it? Oh, sure. But listen, Shari, when I tell you, you've got to remember that this could be one of the most important biblical artifacts ever discovered. And I think it says somewhere in the Bible, 'No pain, no gain,' right?"

"Not in any Bible I've read," said Shari, folding her arms.

Murphy sighed. "There's no fooling you, is there? You remember that FedEx package?"

She frowned. "From Methuselah . . . the one with the map. Oh, my goodness—the Cave of the Waters! I thought you said you were—"

"I didn't want you worrying, is all. Listen," he continued, hoping to distract her from the uncomfortable facts of his ordeal in the cave, "the first clue was the three Hebrew words for pitch. God told Noah to cover the ark with pitch, inside and out. The second clue was the Cave of the Waters. After the Flood, of course, the face of the earth was covered by water, leaving only Noah and his family to survive."

"Don't forget all the animals," said Shari.

"Right. Shem and Japheth. Two little dogs. God told Noah to take two of every kind of animal into the ark so they'd be saved."

"But in case you hadn't noticed, Professor Murphy, Shem and Japheth are two little *boy* dogs," Shari said with a smile. "Didn't God ask Noah to take male and female animals with him?"

"You're right. Methuselah was cutting corners a little bit there. But he made his point. He was trying to tell us that the biblical artifact at stake had something to do with the ark. Which is why I named our two little friends Shem and Japheth—after two of Noah's sons."

"If it really is a piece of the ark, where on earth do you think Methuselah found it?"

"Not in Tennessee. I think we can be sure of that," said Murphy. "Traditionally, the ark is supposed to have finally come to rest on Mount Ararat, in Turkey. Plenty of people have looked for it over the years, but no one's ever been successful. Methuselah seems to be telling us to go get it."

Shari looked thoughtful. "Which leaves one more thing: Why did Methuselah write the word *Babylon* on the package?"

Murphy put his hands on Shari's shoulders. He couldn't hide the truth from her. They'd been through too much together. Sadly, Shari knew as well as anyone how evil was present and active in the world.

"I think it was a warning. He's telling us not to forget about the Seven."

FOUR

AS MURPHY DROVE into the church parking lot, the first thing he saw was the new sanctuary, gleaming pristine white against the blue sky. Its physical beauty struck him, but it was also a powerful symbol of community and shared faith. And yet, looking at it, he couldn't help remembering that terrible night when a massive explosion had turned Preston Community Church into a vision of hell.

He put his beat-up Dodge in park and stared off into space. He remembered with extraordinary clarity the moment before the bomb went off. That last fragile second of normality. He was sitting between Shari and Laura. Shari was agitated because Paul Wallach, a transfer student from Duke, was supposed to have met her at the church. She'd hoped it would be the first step in bringing him to a personal experience of Christ, and now she was worried that she'd frightened him off, that she should have taken things more slowly. Little did she know that he was in the basement of the church, right under their feet, lying injured. And there too was her wayward brother, Chuck. Already dead. But later found to have set the bomb.

For some reason he could never recall the moment of the explosion. Only the aftermath—the flames, the crashing timbers, the smoke, the screaming, and then Laura collapsing and the paramedics rushing her to hospital. In his mind he was there, sitting by her bed, surrounded by life-support machines, praying as hard as he knew how.

And then a word rose unbidden to his lips and he found himself whispering, "Talon."

The knocking at his window startled him out of his reverie.

"Hello, Michael. Admiring the new building?"

The tanned face of Bob Wagoner was smiling down at him. With his thinning white hair and his slacks and polo shirt, he looked as if he belonged more on the golf course than in the pulpit. And, in fact, Wagoner was often heard to say that you could learn as much about the frailty of human nature and the need to put your trust in a higher power while standing on the first tee with a driver in your hand as you could listening to preachers in church. He'd often tried to persuade Murphy to take up the game, but Murphy doubted he had the spiritual strength to survive a round without bending that driver round a tree. *God designed golf for saints like you,* he joked to Wagoner.

Murphy rolled down the window. "Good to see you, Bob. Thanks for agreeing to meet up. Are you hungry?"

Wagoner grinned. "Is the Pope a Catholic?"

———

Murphy hardly touched his chicken sandwich, but Wagoner finished up his cheeseburger and chili fries and wiped his napkin across his mouth before getting down to business. He waited until Roseanne, the gray-haired waitress who'd been at the Adam's Apple Diner as long as anyone could remember, refilled their coffee mugs and went back to reading her magazine by the empty counter, then fixed a concerned gaze on his friend.

"So, Michael. What's on your mind? You look a little beat up, to be honest. What's been going on?"

Murphy touched a finger to a laceration on his forehead. "Oh, that's nothing, Bob. A few bumps and bruises are par for the course when you're digging for artifacts. You know that."

Wagoner looked thoughtful. "I guess I'll take your word for it, Michael. So something else is troubling you. Would it help to talk about it?"

Murphy had so wanted to unburden himself. To pour all his feelings out to his friend. But now that the moment had come, he felt tongue-tied, uncertain how to begin.

Wagoner let him take his time. He knew the secret of good counseling was not to be afraid of silence. But as the silence stretched out, he thought Murphy would appreciate some gentle prompting.

"Is it Laura?"

Murphy nodded, then let out a deep sigh. "We've talked about all this before, Bob. And you gave me the best advice anyone could give. To give thanks for the wonderful life Laura and I had, to think about that instead of all the things we never got to do, all the years we wouldn't be spending together. And to remember all the good she did, which lives on every day in this community. And I do, Bob, I thank God every day for bringing Laura into my life and bringing me so much happiness. But the truth is, at the same time I just can't believe He let her be taken away. The pain and emptiness just doesn't get any less, whatever I do."

Wagoner waited until Murphy was finished, then he reached out and grasped his hand firmly. "I don't have any easy answers for you, Michael. You know that. But you know God will never leave or forsake us. It may not seem to be getting any easier now, but He will help you through this, Michael. And you've got lots of friends praying for you too. Every night Alma and I pray for you and for Shari and the others who were injured in the explosion or who lost loved ones."

"I know you do, Bob," Murphy said, tears welling up. "And I appreciate it." He wiped a hand across his face and attempted a smile. "Just don't slack off, y'hear?"

"That's a promise," said Wagoner, laughing.

Murphy hesitated. "There is one other thing. Talon."

Wagoner's face darkened. "The man who killed Laura. And all those others."

"I'm not sure you could rightly call him a man," said Murphy through gritted teeth. "And calling him an animal would be an insult to rats and cockroaches. I'll be honest, Bob. I feel nothing but hatred for that evil—" He stopped himself from blaspheming. "Hatred and a burning desire for revenge."

"I'll be honest too, Michael," Wagoner said. "If it had been my wife he killed, I'd feel the same. It's only natural. But I will say this. Don't let the hatred overpower and control you. If we focus on those we hate, we're in danger of becoming like them. Easy to say, I know. But it's the truth. The devil wants us to sink down to his level. We just can't let that happen. You've got to leave the Almighty to deal with the likes of Talon. I sincerely hope that's the last you ever see of him."

"I hear what you're saying, Bob. But I'm not sure I can guarantee our paths aren't going to cross again."

"What do you mean?"

"It's just a hunch. Maybe nothing. But I'm planning an expedition to search for an important biblical artifact, and I think somebody wanted to give me a warning. A little bit of a heads-up, if you know what I mean."

Wagoner knew exactly what he meant. Talon. The church bombing. Laura's death. It was all tied up with the quest for the Golden Head of Nebuchadnezzar, which Murphy had discovered near the ancient site of Babylon. And some very powerful—and evil—people had been determined to get their hands on it.

"All I can say is be careful, then," Wagoner replied. "You've never told me all the details of how you found the head, but I know it was a white-knuckle ride."

"Maybe one day I'll write a book about it," chuckled Murphy. "But right now I think I'm onto something just as big."

Bob reached into his pocket and pulled out a card. "Then I'll say no more—except may God be with you. And you might want to take a look at this some time. It's a quote from a famous preacher. I use it as a reminder. The next time you have a down moment, it might help."

Murphy slipped the card in his pocket without looking at it.

Wagoner looked over to the counter and waved to Roseanne. She nodded and reached for a pot of coffee. "Say, do you remember that FBI agent Hank Baines?" he asked.

"Sure. Wasn't he the one who worked with Burton Welsh, the guy in charge of the church-bombing investigation?"

Wagoner nodded. "That's the fella."

"What about him?"

"His family has been attending church for the past month and a half. They come every Sunday. They seem quite interested."

"That's great. What about Baines, does he come?"

"No, just his wife and daughter. I think their daughter has been in trouble with the law. I asked Shari Nelson if she might spend some time with her. What do you think?"

"That's a great idea. Shari's got her own problems with Paul at the moment. But focusing on someone else would probably be good for her. It must be hard to be a law-enforcement officer and have your own child in trouble at the same time. If I remember right, Baines was sort of soft-spoken. He seemed genuinely concerned for people. Unlike his boss. What an arrogant— We bucked heads on several occasions."

"Welsh is no longer working with the FBI."

"What did they do? Fire him?" asked Murphy with a smile.

"No, I don't think so. But I was told he's now working for the CIA."

"Good! Maybe I won't have to deal with him anymore!"

"Let's hope you have no reason to," said Wagoner. "Oh, by the way, I almost forgot. Back to Hank Baines. He gave me his business card two weeks ago. He asked me to give it to you."

"Me?"

"Yes. He was quite impressed with how you conducted your-self during the investigation. He was even more impressed with how you handled things with Laura. If you remember, he came to the funeral. He said he'd like to talk with you if you could spare him some time."

"What about?"

"I don't know. He didn't say. Here's his card. Why don't you give him a call?"

Wagoner glanced at his watch.

"Michael, I need to get going. Could you drop me back at the church? I have a three o'clock appointment."

"Sure. Thanks again for your time, and your advice. I really appreciate it."

Wagoner took Murphy's hand in a strong grip. "Remember what Paul the Apostle wrote in Romans: *We rejoice in the hope of the glory of God. Not only so, but we also rejoice in our sufferings, because we know that suffering produces perseverance; perseverance, character; and character, hope. And hope does not disappoint us, because God has poured out His love into our hearts.*"

Murphy dropped Wagoner at the church, waited for him to disappear inside, then got out of the car and walked around to the little cemetery. He tried to think about the good times he and Laura had had together. The thought of being near her overcame him. Soon he was looking down at a plaque in the ground.

LAURA MURPHY—SHE LOVED HER LORD

Murphy sat on the grass and began to weep. He wept until no more tears would come. He was not aware of time.

It was the sound of a bird singing in a nearby willow tree that caught his attention. He listened.

Think of the good times.

He reached into his pocket and pulled out the card that Pastor Bob had given him at the restaurant.

If finding God's way in the suddenness of storms makes our faith grow broad—then trusting God's wisdom in the "dailyness" of living makes it grow deep. And strong. Whatever may be your circumstances—however long it may have lasted—wherever you may be today, I bring you this reminder: The stronger the winds, the deeper the roots, and the longer the winds . . . the more beautiful the tree.

FIVE

IT WAS 1:50 A.M. when Shane Barrington climbed the steps from the tarmac to his private Gulfstream IV. He was greeted at the door by the copilot.

Carl Foreman touched his hand to his cap, uncertain whether to say anything. In the four years he had worked for Barrington, he'd learned to read his moods pretty well. Barrington demanded obedience, but he was irritated by obsequiousness. During those four years, Carl had seen as many people fired for overt sycophancy as for inefficiency or incompetence, and he put his own relatively long career as a Barrington employee down to knowing just what was required in any given situation. Right now, Barrington's default expression, an unpleasantly cynical scowl, had been replaced by a look that, on any normal person, Carl would have interpreted as fear. But

Barrington was a man who didn't fear anything. Which is why Carl was momentarily wrong-footed.

And why he made the first—and last—mistake of his career as an employee of Barrington Communications.

"Are you okay, Mr. Barrington, sir? You look kinda—"

Barrington whirled on him, teeth bared like an animal's. "What did you say?" he snarled, and for a second Carl thought Barrington was actually going to grab him by the throat.

"I just . . . I'm sorry, sir. It was nothing . . ." he stammered.

"Correct me if I'm wrong, Foreman," Barrington continued, more measured now, the initial impulse toward physical violence transmuted into a tone of icy cruelty, "but I don't believe I pay you to look after my health. Don't I pay you to fly a plane?" He smiled. "Or should I say I used to pay you to fly a plane. When we get to Switzerland, you're fired. But don't worry, they're always looking for ski instructors out there. I'm sure you'll make out just fine."

Carl stood like a statue as Barrington pushed past him to the interior of the plane. Four years up in smoke because of one stupid remark. Because for a moment he'd forgotten that Barrington was one of the world's most ruthless business operators and Carl had instinctively reached out to him like a normal human being.

As he made his way back to the cockpit, he wondered how he was going to tell Renee. They'd have to change their plans about moving to that big house in the hills, and maybe that would mean she'd change her plans about the two of them. The twenty-grand diamond engagement ring was definitely out of the question now.

For a moment he fantasized about deliberately crashing the plane into the Alps. That would show Barrington who was really in control. But he knew he didn't have the guts to do it. No, he thought with a wry chuckle, the only way the plane was going down was if the believers in Christ got snatched up to heaven in midflight, like in that book Renee kept telling him to read, and the bad guys like Barrington were left to fend for themselves. Assuming, of course, that he and the other pilot got picked for the angels' team. And that the devil didn't decide to help his own and take over the controls himself.

Stretching out his muscular frame in a padded leather seat designed to fit his body perfectly, and to allow him to relax on even the longest flights, similar thoughts went through Barrington's mind. How foolish to deliberately humiliate a key member of the flight crew before they were even in the air. The man's fate meant nothing to him, but it was never a good idea to have the pilot of your own plane plotting revenge against you, as he no doubt was at this very moment.

Although he had merely been exercising his ultimate power over the people he commanded, Barrington knew that it had actually been a moment of weakness on his part. He had lashed out at one of his employees because he was scared.

No, *terrified*.

Terrified of the people he was flying to Switzerland to see.

The Seven.

Because although they had helped to make him the world's richest and most powerful businessman, they could just as easily destroy him.

And he doubted they had summoned him to that grim castle of theirs in the mountains because they were pleased with him.

He spent the rest of the flight going over in his mind every detail of what he had been doing for the Seven, trying to find the weak points, the signs of failure, anything that might be interpreted as disobedience or lack of application. He refused all offers of food or drink—keeping a chef he had snatched from a four-star Parisian restaurant standing idle in the plane's luxurious kitchen—until he had exhausted every possibility, but by the time the wheels touched down with a bump at Zurich Airport, he was no nearer to knowing the truth.

He would have to wait until he was sitting facing them and they told him how he had messed up. And then they would tell him what they were going to do with him.

He laughed. A sharp, nervous sound like a dog barking. Carl Foreman would get to fly the plane back after all. Barrington was the one who was going to be fired. And when the Seven fired you, they fired you good.

They'd probably have that murderous psychopath Talon on hand to do the deed.

Barrington shuddered as he heard the door being opened. Then he stood up, adjusted his tie, shot his cuffs, and tried to muster as much dignity as he could. The limo would be waiting, he knew. With that creepy driver behind the wheel, no doubt. The roller coaster had started. There was no way he could get off until the ride was finished.

It was just a question of whether he had enough self-control to stop himself from screaming.

———

Driving out of the city, Barrington tried to focus on what he could see out the smoked windows. They crossed the Limmat River and passed the stately Grossmunster Cathedral, built by Charlemagne in the 700s. The Holy Roman Emperor. That was power, Barrington mused. In the Dark Ages, the Empire had been the nearest thing to a world government.

And if the Seven had their way, such a thing would be seen again. Only this time they would truly control every corner of the entire globe.

He thought of engaging the driver in conversation, just to see if he could pick up any hint of what was on the Seven's mind. Then just in time he remembered what was so odd about this particular chauffeur.

He had no tongue.

And Barrington was sure he'd be happy to remind him of the fact by opening his mouth in that awful, empty grin that had so shocked him during their first ride to the castle together.

Soon they were on twisting mountain roads rising higher and higher. The clouds on the mountains were low, and flurries of snow were beginning to stick to the tarmac. In such a landscape it was possible to believe you had left the real world altogether and were now entering some strange, fantastical realm of witches and demons.

"I guess we're not in Kansas anymore, eh, Toto?" Barrington muttered.

The driver started to turn his head toward the backseat, and Barrington quickly reassured him. "It's okay. I know you don't speak. I was just talking to myself."

Barrington had his eyes closed when the crunch of the

Mercedes's tires on gravel told him they were pulling up in front of the castle. He was glad he hadn't watched it loom out of the mist as they approached. The sight of those gothic spires rising like wraiths in a cemetery might have been enough to weaken his resolve.

Remember he told himself as he stepped out of the car and under the chauffeur's waiting umbrella, *get to the end of the ride without showing fear. Then they haven't completely beaten you.*

He looked at his watch. Right on time. Something about being in Switzerland encouraged punctuality, he thought. He glanced at his wordless companion as the chauffeur ushered him toward the giant wrought-iron door of the castle.

And something about working for the Seven, no doubt.

He had forgotten just how large the entry hall was. He was alone except for several suits of ancient armor standing like sightless and lifeless guards of the unknown in the flickering light of a dozen torches set into the walls.

I guess they assume I know the drill, Barrington thought.

As if he could forget.

Across the darkly lit hall, Barrington saw the large steel door, a sharp reminder of the twenty-first century amid all the medieval gloom. He took a breath and walked toward it. As he approached, there was a low hissing and it slid open. He entered, and the door hissed closed again. He looked at the two buttons in front of him. He pushed the down arrow, wondering if he would live to push the other one.

The sense of descending was almost imperceptible. Then the doors hissed open and Barrington stepped into a large, shadowy room. The only light was a beam from the ceiling, which illuminated a familiar shape—an ornately carved wooden chair with gargoyles on the arms. Twenty feet in front of the chair was a long table with a blood-red cloth covering it and hanging down to the floor.

Behind the table were seven chairs, occupied by six people—or, rather, six silhouettes. The center chair was empty.

"Welcome, Señor Barrington. It has been some time since we have seen you. Come and sit in the chair of honor," said a silky Hispanic voice.

As Barrington moved forward toward the chair in the center of the room, he heard a shuffling in the shadows to his right. As he glanced in that direction, he could see a figure emerging from the darkness and walking toward the center chair behind the table. Barrington and the darkened figure sat down at the same time.

Barrington gripped the arms of the chair and waited for the man seated at the center to speak. As the silence stretched, fear turned to frustration. After everything he'd done for the Seven—every lie, every criminal act, every betrayal—couldn't they treat him with some respect? Only one thing gave him hope: If they were still hiding their faces from him, then maybe they weren't planning to kill him.

Then again, maybe they were just messing with his mind. That seemed to be their specialty.

At last the icy voice Barrington had been expecting broke the silence. "You're a busy man, Mr. Barrington. And so are we—"

There was a feminine cough from his right.

"I beg your pardon. We are busy men *and* women. If you think we would have wasted your time and ours bringing you here merely to . . . eliminate you, then you still underestimate the importance of the great task we are all pledged to accomplish. No, since we injected five billion dollars into your company, you have performed well enough. We are still a long way from our goal, but our control of Barrington Communications is a crucial weapon in our armory."

A chuckle came from the speaker's left. "How else would we be able to fight the good fight?"

The voice resumed, now with a trace of annoyance. "Indeed. But now we need you to perform another task for us. One that will give full rein to your worst character traits—or should I say *skills*."

Barrington started to protest, but the voice cut him off. "You know who Michael Murphy is?"

"Of course," Barrington said. "The archaeologist. I seem to remember you wanted him dead at one point. Until you thought he'd be more useful alive. So, has he outlived his usefulness? You want him discreetly taken out? And you want me to do it?" He said it as if it would be a routine task. Just another item on his busy to-do list.

"Not at all, Mr. Barrington," responded the voice, in a tone that suggested he was speaking to a particularly dim-witted third-grader. "We don't keep you around for that sort of thing. Although I suppose you could say we want you to make Professor Murphy an offer he can't refuse."

Barrington was intrigued. "And what would that be?"

"Why, we want you to offer Murphy a job. A job with Barrington Communications."

Barrington was confused. "He's an archaeologist, not a TV reporter. What can I offer him?"

"Money, of course," came the reply. "Archaeological digs are an expensive business, and Murphy's thinking is so far outside the mainstream, he has a hard time attracting funds. If he felt he was on the trail of something huge—something irresistible—he might take money even from you, if it meant the difference between success and failure. With your silver tongue, I'm sure you'll be able to persuade him of the benefits of being Barrington Communications' archaeological correspondent."

Barrington stroked his chin. "Yeah, I think I could do that. I might need—"

"You'll get the necessary funds," snapped the voice. "Another billion dollars deposited in a special account should be enough to turn the whole of the Middle East into one huge archaeological dig, if that's what Murphy wants."

Barrington whistled. "It sure beats thirty pieces of silver. But what's in it for you? Why do you want Murphy on the payroll?"

A female voice with some sort of European accent cut in. "Yours is not to reason why, Barrington."

She let him complete the rest of the quotation for himself.

Yours is but to do and die.

"Quite so," agreed the icy voice. "But there's no harm in showing our friend here a little of the big picture. You see, Mr. Barrington, Michael Murphy has a knack for finding archaeological objects that are of . . . *interest* to us. It might make life a little easier if we were all on the same team. Even if Murphy doesn't know it."

There was an appreciative ripple of laughter around the table.

"Keep your friends close, eh?" Barrington said, and this time it was their turn to complete the quotation.

"*And your enemies closer.* Exactly," agreed the voice. "Now, get back to your plane and start planning exactly how you're going to corrupt Michael Murphy's soul."

Barrington rose to go, feeling the tension draining out of him.

"One more thing," barked the voice, freezing him in mid-stride. "In case you were worrying about that disgruntled employee—or should I say ex-employee—who might have some interesting things to tell the authorities."

"You mean Foreman?" How the heck did they know about him? "He wouldn't dare. He knows my reputation better than to try anything."

"Just to be on the safe side, we took care of him," said the voice, and just then Barrington noticed another figure, seated in a shadowy corner of the room.

Of course. Talon. So Foreman wouldn't have to brush up on his downhill skills after all. Barrington felt a chill go through his entire body, and he quickened his step to the elevator doors. He was sure he could feel those predator's eyes on his back all the way.

As soon as the steel doors had closed behind him, soft lighting illuminated the faces of the six men and one woman seated around the table. As one, they turned to the man in the corner, whose features were still obscured by shadow yet seemed to emanate a controlled ferocity.

"Welcome, Talon. I trust Mr. Foreman presented no problems?"

Talon sneered. "Swatting a bug would present more . . . *problems*." He turned to the man occupying the central chair. "So we're now trying the diplomatic approach with Murphy." He spat out the last word as if getting rid of something distasteful. "You're sure you don't want something more direct? Since I seem to be swatting bugs, I could easily squash this one for you too."

"Easy, Talon," the leader of the Seven soothed. "I know you and Murphy have unfinished business. And the time to conclude that business may not be far off. You recall our informer inside the Parchments of Freedom Foundation provided some intriguing information about a newly discovered and very valuable artifact? I'm beginning to think it may be more valuable than even they know. It could be vital to the unveiling of Babylon's dark power. And now, today, we hear from our agents in the CIA that there is something very secret going on in Turkey. I wonder if these two things are connected? What do you think, Talon?"

Talon knew he was being manipulated, skillfully deflected from his natural murderous impulses. But the Seven paid well, and he knew they would want him to bloody his hands again before too long.

"I guess I'd better see if I can find out," he said, rising to go. He walked to the elevator with the fluid stride of a beast of prey, then turned and grinned. "Who knows, perhaps my friend Murphy is involved. Perhaps we are fated to meet again. And this time, I think, only one of us will walk away."

SIX

"IT MUST BE SOMETHING pretty important for an FBI agent to come and talk to me in person," Murphy said warily. "Something you didn't want to talk about on the phone. Let me guess—you've uncovered a plot to overthrow the government, and you think it's all being planned from our little church."

Baines frowned. "Look, Professor Murphy. I'm willing to admit the bureau made some mistakes during the investigation of the bombing." He saw Murphy raise his eyebrows. "Okay, some *big* mistakes."

"And you've come to apologize on behalf of the FBI? After all this time? How nice," Murphy said.

Baines stopped and put his hands on his hips. They were walking on the path at the edge of the campus, where the woods began to climb up a gentle hill, and the tension between them seemed out of place in such a tranquil setting. Murphy faced him and crossed his arms.

"Professor Murphy, if there was anything I could do to make up for the pain the bureau caused you and your wife, I would. And if you want an apology from me, you got it."

"But that's not why you wanted to see me," Murphy said.

"No. There's something else I need to talk to you about. Not bureau business at all. Look," he said, indicating the place under his jacket where a shoulder holster would normally be. "I'm not even wearing a gun."

"So this is personal?"

"That's right." Baines looked down at the ground. He was tall, a couple inches over six feet, with broad shoulders and a rangy physique, but at that moment he looked weighed down with cares. Murphy decided to take pity on him.

"Okay, Agent Baines. Bob Wagoner told me you had some family problems you wanted to discuss. I'm sorry if I gave you a hard time. I'm not proud of it, but I still feel a lot of bitterness about what happened. Not that it was your fault. I'm taking it out on the wrong guy."

"That's okay," Baines replied, visibly relaxing. "If I was in your shoes, I'd still be churned up about a lot of things."

"So why did you want to see me?" Murphy asked.

"That's kind of the point," Baines explained. "The way you dealt with all that stuff. The false accusations, when the FBI thought members of the congregation had been involved in blowing up the church, and then . . . what happened to your wife. However much pain was thrown at you, you seemed to have an inner stability. Something was keeping you going, stopping you from giving in to total despair like a lot of people would have in that situation."

"Faith," said Murphy simply. "When everything in your life goes wrong, that's all you've got. But it's all you need."

"Right," said Baines, nodding. "Like I say, I was impressed. So when things started to go wrong in my life, you were the person I thought of."

Murphy's initial antagonism had completely evaporated now. Baines seemed sincere and was clearly willing to bare his soul. That kind of humility from a federal agent was rare enough to deserve his full attention.

"Come on," said Murphy. "Let's keep walking, since it's such a beautiful morning. And you can tell me what the problem is. If I can help you, I will."

"Thanks," said Baines. "You don't know how much I appreciate it. I've been going crazy these past months, and I just didn't know where to turn."

They walked on in silence for a couple minutes while Baines gathered his thoughts.

"My wife and daughter have been going to Preston Community Church for a while," he began. "It was my wife's idea. She thought it would be good for Tiffany, and since nothing else seems to get through to her, I thought, why not give it a try?"

"So Tiffany's the problem?"

Baines nodded wearily. "I'll say. The last straw was when she got arrested with some of her friends. They were riding in a car, drinking beer and tossing the empty cans at people on the sidewalk. For someone like me, who spends his time trying to catch criminals, trying to keep the streets safe for people like Tiffany and her friends, it's tough to deal with. And like I say, that was just the last on a long list of stuff—all sorts of misbehavior."

Murphy looked thoughtful. "So when did all this start? When did you first think there was a problem?"

"It sounds kind of trivial," Baines said. "But it started with her room. She wouldn't clean up, it was always such a mess. And if my wife, Jennifer, took her to task about it, Tiffany would curse her out. Overnight she seemed to become a different person—loud, excitable, argumentative, always changing her mind, never following through with anything, and angry all the time—almost like she was possessed, like that girl in *The Exorcist*."

Murphy laughed and patted Baines on the shoulder. "I'm not a priest, I'm afraid, so I can't help you with casting out demons. But I very much doubt things have reached that stage. It sounds like you've just got a somewhat strong-willed daughter on your hands."

"Then how come I can't get through to her? Why does everything we do just make things worse?"

"Let me ask you a question," Murphy said. "Does your daughter do anything right?"

He could tell the question knocked Baines back a little.

"Well, yeah, sure. I mean, she's creative, she does well in art at school. And she gets good grades in English. When she can be bothered to finish her assignments," he added.

"And what about you?" Murphy asked. "Are you the creative type?"

Baines looked a little confused. This was supposed to be

about Tiffany, not him. "No way. Why do you think I ended up an FBI agent? I like to deal with facts, logic. Everything in its right place. Details. Structure. Artistic people seem so messy and undisciplined to me. And they let their emotions take over. I like to stay calm, be in control of myself."

Murphy laughed. "Well, Hank, I think you just told me why you and Tiffany aren't getting along. You're just two totally different personality types, is all. She's spontaneous and creative, lets her emotions run free. You're logical and controlled. And I imagine you're a perfectionist too. Only the best is good enough. You two are bound to rub each other the wrong way."

Baines rubbed his chin thoughtfully. "So what should I do? Is there some self-help book that's going to tell me how to act around my daughter?"

Murphy smiled. "There's only one book that's guaranteed to help—whatever the problem. And that's the Bible."

"The Bible has stuff about parenting?"

"Sure. In the Book of Colossians, Chapter Three, it says, *Fathers, don't aggravate your children. If you do they will become discouraged and quit trying.* Do you think Tiffany has quit trying?"

"Yeah, maybe."

"And was your father a perfectionist? Was he critical of you, nagging all the time?"

"As a matter of fact he was," Baines admitted.

"Well, you were able to respond to your father's perfectionism by becoming a perfectionist yourself, by beating him at his own game, I'm guessing. For Tiffany—because she's got a different personality—it's not so easy. Maybe she gets discouraged because your standards are so high. When was the last time you encouraged her, told her she was doing great, that you liked her art or whatever?"

Baines looked crestfallen. "I don't remember. Not for a while." He turned to Murphy. "You've given me a lot to think about, Professor Murphy."

"Please, call me Michael. And don't hesitate to give me a call if you want to discuss anything we talked about. Look, my assistant, Shari Nelson, she's great at reaching out to teenagers with problems. She's had her share and she's wise beyond her years. Pastor Bob suggested she might introduce herself to Tiffany and your wife next time they attend church."

"That would be great." Baines nodded.

"And meanwhile, why not pick up the Bible and see what else you can find in it that's relevant to your life? It's never too late to start reading the Good Book. Start with the Book of Colossians."

Baines shook Murphy's hand, his spirits lifted. "I will," he said. "Thank you. Look, I won't take up any more of your valuable time. You've got classes to teach, artifacts to dig up, no doubt."

"Actually, I do," Murphy said. "But I'm always happy to help out if I can. You've got my number."

He watched Baines walk toward the parking lot, feeling his own spirits lift. Nothing like focusing on someone else's problems to get your own in perspective, he thought.

He didn't hear the soft clicking of a camera from behind the trees. He had no idea a pair of dark, feral eyes were watching him.

SEVEN

IT WAS TEN MINUTES TO NINE and the Memorial Lecture Hall was beginning to fill up. Which for a Monday morning was a somewhat unusual occurrence. Preston University students tended to play hard on weekends and sleep late the next day. Hence the first lecture of the week was known among the teaching faculty as the graveyard shift. Depressing if you wanted an audience that was going to eagerly soak up your words of wisdom. A relief if you were a little tired yourself and were glad the class wasn't too alert.

But this lecture was being given by Michael Murphy, and somehow the word had gotten out over the weekend that he wasn't going to be speaking on the designated topic: How to map out an archaeological site.

He was going to be talking about Noah's Ark.

As the rows continued to fill up, some of the students

laughed and joked together. But most were earnestly discussing the likely content of Murphy's lecture.

Wasn't Noah's Ark just a story from the Bible? Did it really exist?

One thing was sure: Whatever Professor Murphy had to say about it would likely change the way they thought about it.

Shari Nelson had arrived early to set up the PowerPoint projector for her boss. But she was as anxious as the rest to hear what he was going to say.

Paul Wallach was in the front row, wearing his typical pressed slacks and sports shirt. His dark hair was neatly trimmed, as if he had just been to the barber, and he was wearing one shiny loafer. His left foot was still in a walking cast, the explosion at the Preston Community Church having severely damaged his leg and foot. Finishing up with the projector, Shari left the stage and came to sit next to him.

She hadn't tied her hair back as she usually did. It was hanging long, its jet-black luster contrasting with the shining silver crucifix at her throat. The way her sparkling green eyes seemed riveted to him as he spoke, it was easy to see that she cared for him deeply. It was as if she was trying with all her being to bridge a chasm between them.

Then, at exactly nine o'clock, Murphy strode into the hall and the chattering ceased almost instantly. His magnetic presence was such that he never had to raise his voice or ask for quiet.

Murphy walked to the desk in the center of the room and placed his lecture materials down. He looked up at the silent crowd, quickly checking to see who was there, and launched straight into the lecture.

"Noah's Ark: Is it a fact, or is it a fable?"

For the next ten minutes Murphy talked about the Flood story and about Noah building the ark, quoting the Book of Genesis from memory and ending with the rainbow.

"The rainbow in the sky was God's promise to Noah that He would never again destroy the world by flood waters."

Murphy then clicked on the PowerPoint projector.

"As you can see from the following slides, there are many historians and scholars who, down through the millennia, have mentioned the ark as an actual stucture, and even talked of Noah. Keep in mind, these are all documented, non-biblical sources. So even without the Bible, there are plenty of pieces of recorded evidence in the historical record to conclude that a global flood did indeed occur on our planet more than five thousand years ago."

The Samaritan Pentateuch—5th century B.C.
   Talks about the landing place of the ark.

Targums—5th century B.C.
   Talks about location of the ark.

Berossus—275 B.C.
   A Chaldean priest: "It is said, moreover, that
   a portion of the vessel still survives in Armenia
   . . . and that persons carry off pieces of the
   bitumen, which they use as talismans."

Nicholas of Damascus—30 B.C.
   "Relics of the timbers were long preserved."

Josephus—A.D. 75

"Remains which to this day are shown to those who are curious to see them."

Theophilus of Antioch—A.D. 180

"And of the ark, the remains are to this day seen in the Arabian mountain."

Eusebius—A.D. 3rd century

"A small part of the ark still remained in the Gordian Mountains."

Epiphanius—A.D. 4th century

"The remains are still shown and if one looks diligently he can still find the altar of Noah."

Isidore of Seville—A.D. 6th century

"So even to this day wood remains of it are to be seen."

Al-Masudi—A.D. 10th century

"The place can still be seen."

Ibn Haukal—A.D. 10th century

"Noah built a village there at the foot of the mountain."

Benjamin of Tudela—A.D. 12th century

"Omar Ben Ac Khatab removed parts of the ark from the summit and made a mosque of it."

Murphy let the words on the screen speak for themselves. The class seemed stunned that what they had thought of as a Bible story was so well documented in other sources. Murphy turned off the projector.

"Any questions so far?"

One hand went up. It was right in front of Murphy and belonged to Paul Wallach. Paul had originally come to Preston to take a business-studies course, but partly under Shari's influence, he had become an enthusiastic archaeology student.

"I noticed on your slides, Professor Murphy, that several different mountain ranges were mentioned. There were the Gordian Mountains, the Arabian Mountains, and the Mountains of Armenia. Doesn't that prove that the information was made up and no one really knows?"

There was more than a touch of hostility and challenge in Paul's question, and Shari was now looking at Paul with annoyance.

Murphy smiled, as he usually did, even when challenged in front of others. You could have heard a pin drop in the silent lecture theater as the audience waited for his response.

"That's a good question, Paul. Thank you for drawing that to our attention. Present-day Armenia is just a few miles from Mount Ararat. Turkey is located in the continent of Asia, and this part of the world is often referred to as an Arabian area. With regard to calling it the Gordian Mountains, you have to remember that these writers each came from different areas and wrote in different time periods. The names of places change over time. Istanbul, Turkey, was once called Constantinople. Mount Ararat is also known as Agri Daugh, which means *painful mountain*. Most scholars believe that the writers were all referring to the same general area, calling it by the only names they knew at the time."

Paul looked a little disappointed, as if the question had been designed purely to needle Murphy and it hadn't worked.

Another hand went up in the back. It was Clayton Anderson, the class clown.

"Professor Murphy? What did Noah say to his sons while all the animals were entering the ark?"

Murphy could tell he was being set up.

"I give up, Clayton. What did he say?"

"Now I herd everything."

Some of the class laughed, most groaned, and more hands shot in the air.

"Terry!" said Murphy as he pointed to a tall thin student.

"Professor Murphy? What did Noah say to his sons when they wanted to go fishing?"

"What, Terry?"

"Go easy with the bait, boys—there's only two worms!"

Murphy didn't mind a little humor, but he didn't want to lose control totally.

"One more question. Pam, you're the last one."

"Was Noah's wife called Joan of Ark?"

Murphy raised both of his hands to quiet everyone down.

"The short answer, Pam, is no. But if you're interested in who Noah's wife really was, I think I can answer that. In the fourth chapter of Genesis there is the story of Cain and Abel. Cain had a son by the name of Enoch. Some Jewish scholars believe that Cain was the inventor of weights and measures and some types of surveying equipment. They believe that because of a great city he built and named after his son Enoch. Enoch had a number of sons and one of them was Lamech."

Murphy could see from the blank faces in front of him that he needed to get to his conclusion fast.

"Okay, hang on! Lamech had three sons: Jabal, known as the father of those who live in tents and deal with animals; Jubal, the father of musicians, and Tubal-cain, the father of all metallurgy. Tubal-cain had a sister by the name of Naamah, which means *beautiful*. Many ancient Jewish scholars believe that Naamah became Noah's wife."

It seemed like a good time to use the PowerPoint again. Murphy waited a moment or two and then turned on the projector.

"We left off looking at historical documents concerning Noah and the ark. The next slide gives you a list of a few other authors who have talked about the ark and its location."

> ### *Other Historical Authors Writing About Noah and the Ark*
>
> **Hieronymus**—30 B.C.
> **The Quran**—A.D. 7th century
> **Eutyches**—A.D. 9th century
> **William of Rubruck**—A.D. 1254
> **Odoric of Pordenone**—A.D. 12th century
> **Vincent of Beauvais**—A.D. 13th century
> **Ibn Al Mid**—A.D. 13th century
> **Jordanus**—A.D. 13th century

Pegolotti—A.D. 1340

Marco Polo—A.D. 14th century

Gonzalez De Clavijo—A.D. 1412

John Heywood—A.D. 1520

Adam Olearius—A.D. 1647

Jans Janszoon Struys—A.D. 1694

A hand was raised in the back of the room.

"Professor Murphy, I was told by someone that they have found pieces of the ark. Is that true?"

Murphy took a deep breath. For a moment he thought Shari had told someone about his adventures in the Cave of the Waters and his amazing find there. But he knew she was the soul of discretion. Even under torture she would have kept his secret.

"Well, there have been some very interesting discoveries. Mount Ararat is about seventeen thousand feet high. Most ark sightings have been somewhere between the fourteen-thousand- and sixteen-thousand-foot elevation level. In 1876, British Viscount James Bryce climbed Mount Ararat in search of the ark. He didn't find it, but he did find wood above the thirteen-thousand-foot level. Let me quote you what he said."

Murphy shuffled around on his desk and came up with a piece of paper. "Bryce stated the following:

Mounting steadily along the same ridge, I saw at a height of over thirteen thousand feet, lying on the loose rocks, a piece of wood about four feet long and five inches thick, evidently cut by some tool, and so far above the limit of trees that it could by no possibility be a natural fragment of one. . . .

"The question is, could that piece of wood have washed down from the ark, which was higher on the mountain? Along this same line, a man named E. de Markoff, a member of the Russian Imperial Geographical Society, found wood near the fourteen-thousand-foot level. Also, in 1936, a New Zealand archaeologist called Hardwicke Knight found waterlogged rectangular timbers protruding out of the snow. These pieces of wood were nine inches to a foot square. The wood was very dark and extremely soft. He concluded that they must have been submerged in water for a long period of time."

Murphy turned and grabbed another piece of paper off his desk.

"This represents probably the most famous wood find above the timberline. It was discovered by Fernand Navarra. In 1952, he and a search team were looking for the ark. They were walking over a clear ice field near the Ahora Gorge when suddenly they saw something.

In front of us was always the deep transparent ice. A few more paces and suddenly, as if there were an eclipse of the sun, the ice became strangely dark. Yet the sun was still there and above us the eagle still circled. We were surrounded by whiteness, stretching into the distance, yet beneath our eyes was this astonishing patch of blackness within the ice, its outlines sharply defined.

Fascinated and intrigued, we began straightaway to trace out its shape, mapping its limits foot by foot: two progressively incurving lines were revealed, which were clearly defined for a distance of three hundred cubits, before meeting in the heart of the glacier. The shape was unmistakably that of a ship's hull; on either side the edges of the patch curved like the gunwales of a great boat. As for the central part, it merged into a black mass. The details of which were not discernible.

"Navarra made two more attempts to discover what was under the ice. One in 1953 and the other in 1955. On the last expedition they found wood. In his own words, he says:

Once on the edge of the crevasse, I lowered the equipment on a rope. Then I secured the ladder and climbed down myself, assuring Raphael I would not be long.

Attacking the ice shell with my pickax, I could feel something hard. When I had cut a hole one and one half feet square by eight inches deep, I broke through a vaulted ceiling, and cleared off as much icy dust as possible.

There, immersed in water, I saw a black piece of wood!

My throat felt tight. I felt like crying and kneeling there to thank God. After the cruelest disappointment, the greatest joy! I checked my tears of happiness to shout to Raphael, 'I've found wood!'

'Hurry up and come back—I'm cold,' he answered.

I tried to pull out the whole beam, but couldn't. It must have been very long, and perhaps still attached to other parts of the ship's framework. I could only cut along the grain until I split off a piece about five feet long. Obviously, it had been hand-hewn. The wood, once out of the water, proved surprisingly heavy. Its density was remarkable after its long stay in the water, and the fibers had not distended as much as one might expect.

"Navarra had the wood carbon-fourteen-tested, along with other tests for lignite formation, grain density, cell modification, growth rings, and fossilization. His results suggested that it was about five thousand years old."

The bell rang and everybody jumped. Murphy had lost track of time.

"Thanks for your interest, people. I'm sorry we've got to end it there, but next time we're going to look at the stories of explorers who claimed to have actually entered Noah's Ark."

As he watched the students making their way out of the auditorium, he wondered if he would soon have a story of his own to tell.

EIGHT

IT WAS A BEAUTIFUL spring day on the Preston campus. Murphy had found a quiet table near where the lawn and small pond met. He got away, as far as he could, from the hustle and bustle of the students in the snack area. He was sipping a strawberry lemonade and thinking about the hand-size chunk of wood sitting in a locked cabinet in his lab.

Murphy was an archaeologist, not a biologist, by training. But lecturing on the ark had made him think about the incredible diversity of God's creation—everything that Noah had saved from the Flood. As he looked out over the lush green campus, he could see the flowering dogwood with its blossoms of four white petals. Interspersed were the maples and the tulip trees with their yellow blossoms. He could also see the deeply furrowed cinnamon-red bark of the loblolly pine.

His interest began to focus on the azaleas surrounding the

pond. The fragrant smell of the trumpet-shaped flowers filled the air. The bees were flying in and out, getting their fill of nectar. Then he spotted a Venus flytrap. It was growing on the damp edges of the pond in the direct sunlight. Its trap was lined with sharp bristles and was open, the sensitive hairs ready for its prey to come along and touch them. Murphy did not have to wait long. A small fly landed on the outside of the plant and began to work its way toward the center. Murphy watched as it got closer and closer to the trigger hairs. Then it happened. In a flash the plant closed on its lunch.

Murphy stroked his chin thoughtfully. Was someone trying to tell him something? That beautiful things can also be deadly, perhaps?

Before he had time to figure it out, his solitude ended.

"Professor Murphy! Could we ask you a few questions?"

Turning, he saw several students from his archaeology class. "Sure," he said, motioning for them to sit down. It was sometimes frustrating when he wanted to just sit and think, but he couldn't complain if his students were interested enough in his subject to track him down with burning questions. That was what being a teacher was all about.

"We've been talking about Noah's Ark," said a skinny young man with long, unruly hair. "Like, could it really have happened the way it's written in the Bible? How could Noah have gotten all the animals on the ark, for instance?"

"Good question," Murphy said as he reached for his briefcase. He opened it and took out a folder. He looked through it and pulled out a piece of paper.

"Here is a paper put together by Ernst Mayr. You may not

be familiar with his name, but he is one of America's leading taxonomists. He lists on this table the number of animal species. Here, take a look at it."

Murphy handed them the sheet, which read:

Total Animal Species

Mammals	3,700
Birds	8,600
Reptiles	6,300
Amphibians	2,500
Fishes	20,600
Tunicates, etc.	1,325
Echinoderms	6,000
Arthropods	838,000
Mollusks	107,250
Worms, etc.	39,450
Coelenterates, etc.	5,380
Sponges	4,800
Protozoa	28,400
Total	1,072,305

"Over a million species! No one could have built a boat big enough to hold that kind of number, could they? Especially if there were two of everything, right?" said one of the students.

"It does seem like a lot," admitted Murphy. "But, of course, many of those species didn't have to be on the ark to survive the flood. The fishes, tunicates, echinoderms, mollusks, coelenterates, sponges, protozoa, and many of the arthropods and worms would have been better off staying in the ocean. And many of the animals that did need to live on the ark were small, like mice, cats, birds, and sheep. If you look at the larger animals like the elephants and giraffes and hippos, they are the exception. Most animals are small, and many experts in the field do not believe that there were any more than fifty thousand land animals on the ark."

"That's still a lot of animals!" said another of the students.

"True, but there was more room on the ark than you realize. Let me see if I can help you visualize it. The average train stock car has a volume of 2,670 cubic feet. The ark was estimated to be about 450 long, 45 feet high, and 75 feet wide. That would produce a volume of around 1,518,750 cubic feet. Now, divide the 2,670 cubic feet of the boxcar into the volume on the ark and it would equal 569 standard railroad stock cars."

"That's a long train!" said one of the students, laughing.

"Keep following the illustration. If you double-deck a stock car, you can haul 240 animals the size of a sheep. Now multiply 240 animals times 569 stock cars and you get approximately 136,560 animals that could have been put into the ark. Subtract the estimated fifty thousand animals on the ark and you would have space for 86,560 more animals the size of a sheep. Only about thirty-six percent of the ark would have to have been used for animals. The rest could have been for food storage and living quarters for Noah and his family."

"I had no idea there was so much math involved in biblical archaeology," said the skinny student, shaking his head. But he wasn't beaten yet. "Okay, there's room on the ark for everybody, but where did they get water for all of those animals to drink? Weren't they on the ocean, which was loaded with salt water?"

The rest of the students nodded.

"You've got to remember that most of the Flood consisted of rain water. With water covering the highest mountains, the salt water of the oceans could have been diluted enough to drink. They could also have collected rainwater from the roof and stored it in cisterns on the ark."

They seemed convinced. But there was one more question. "Professor Murphy, why haven't they found more artifacts from Noah's Ark if so many people have seen it?"

Murphy smiled. He liked the way his students challenged his beliefs and his faith. It meant he really had to be sure about what he believed and able to defend it against all comers.

"We're not sure. One possibility may be tied to the Monastery of St. Jacob."

"Where's that?" asked one of the girls.

"The Monastery of St. Jacob was located on Mount Ararat. It is said to have been established in the fourth century by a monk named St. Jacob of Nisibis. The monks of St. Jacob's took on the responsibility of guarding the sacred relics of the ark. In 1829, Dr. J. J. Friedrich Parrot visited the monastery. Apparently he was shown ancient artifacts from the ark."

"What were they? And where are they today?" queried one of the boys.

"I wish I knew," said Murphy. "In 1840 a tremendous earthquake hit Mount Ararat. It caused a huge landslide. Two thousand people were killed in the village of Ahora below the Ahora Gorge, and the whole community, along with St. Jacob's

Monastery, was buried. All of the relics were buried with them. If Ed Davis's account of seeing the ark is valid, some of the artifacts are still hidden in a cave on Ararat. They may even still be guarded by people of faith."

A heavyset student named Morris spoke up and changed the direction of the conversation.

"Professor Murphy, you mentioned that Jesus talked about the days of Noah and the days of Lot in Sodom. What did he mean?"

Murphy was glad he'd been given an opening to talk to them about more spiritual things. "He was talking about how wicked society was. The Book of Genesis says: *The Lord saw how great man's wickedness on earth had become, and that every inclination of the thoughts of his heart was only evil all the time.* God was going to judge man for his evil by the Flood. When Jesus said, *As in the days of Noah,* He was referring to the fact that when He comes again in judgment, it will be to a world that is filled with people who do not care about the things of God. Just like the people didn't care in Noah's, or Lot's days."

Some of the students seemed a little stunned by what he was saying. Murphy smiled.

"Let me ask you a question, Morris. Do you think that society today believes in any absolute morals?"

Morris considered his answer carefully. He didn't want to get caught by some sort of trick question.

"I guess most of my friends and the people I know would say that there are no such things as moral absolutes. They'd say that we should learn to be tolerant and accept other people's points of view."

Murphy nodded. "The traditional definition of tolerance is living peaceably alongside others in spite of differences. But that view of tolerance has been twisted today to mean that everyone must accept the other person's viewpoints without question because truth is relative. What's true for one person may not be true for another person, right?"

"Right," said Morris, a little uncertainly.

"That was exactly what was happening in the days of Noah and in the days of Lot. Everyone was doing what was right in their own eyes. And it's the same today. Society preaches tolerance of every viewpoint and everyone—with one big exception: those people who have a strong religious faith. That's where their double-standard tolerance ends. Incredibly, people of faith are persecuted precisely because they do believe in absolute truth, in absolute moral values. That's exactly what Jesus was talking about." He paused and looked each student in the eye before continuing. "It makes me wonder if we are living in the days before the next coming judgment. That would be something to think about, wouldn't it?"

Murphy was worried that he'd come on a little strong, but he was a man of conviction and faith and he wasn't about to hide it from anyone. And what could be more important than getting people to think seriously about the next judgment? He did not want anyone to be left behind when they could be on the ark of safety, and if he could do anything about it, he would.

Murphy looked at his watch.

"Say, gang, it was good to talk with you. I need to head on to my next class. Keep thinking about all of this. It's important!"

No one spoke as he walked away.

NINE

"I'LL TAKE A CAFFÉ MOCHA, please."

The Starbucks next to the Preston University campus was one of Shari's favorite spots. It was always filled with faculty professors and college students, as well as many students from the nearby Hillsborough High School, but Shari still felt somehow she was getting away from it all.

Sitting at one of the umbrella-covered tables with her baseball cap low over her face, she could just watch the people and imagine she had no troubles. Or, as she was planning to do this afternoon, she could concentrate on someone else's.

"Excuse me, are you Shari Nelson?"

Shari turned and looked into the face of Tiffany Baines. With her golden shoulder-length hair and sparkling brown eyes, she looked like a cheerleader, not a delinquent. Dressed in her white sweatshirt with the large red cardinal emblem on the front, the words *Tar Heels* under it, it was hard to imagine her tossing beer cans out of a moving car.

"You must be Tiffany." Shari stood and shook her hand. "Sit down and let me get you something. What would you like?"

"Thanks. A latte would be good."

Tiffany was so different from what Shari had expected that, when Shari returned with her drink, she wasn't quite sure how to begin. "Have you been watching the Tar Heels this year?"

"Yes, I don't miss a game—except I have a question."

"Shoot."

"I was born and raised in Raleigh, and I watch games all the time. And I have a shirt on that says Tar Heels, but I don't know what Tar Heels means. Can you believe that?"

Shari smiled, not sure whether or not this dumb but sweet persona was all an act. "It all began back in the Civil War. North Carolina was under attack from the Union army. The Confederate army withdrew, leaving the North Carolinians to fight the battle alone. Those who remained to fight threatened to put tar on the heels of the Confederate troops so that they would 'stick better in the next fight.'" Tiffany nodded and Shari asked, "Are you sure you didn't know that?"

"Cross my heart," Tiffany said with a smile, and for some reason Shari believed her.

Having broken the ice, Shari decided to get down to business. "I was talking with Pastor Bob at the Preston Community Church. I know you've been going there with your mom for a while now. With that hair you're kind of hard to miss—even across a crowded church."

Tiffany sighed. "I guess I kind of stand out, don't I? Believe me, I'd rather just fade into the background sometimes." Suddenly she looked serious. "Pastor Bob just said he thought I might want to talk to someone my own age who attends the church, in case I thought it was all just old folks like him. But it's more than that, isn't it? I'm not as dumb as I look, you know."

Shari nodded. "Pastor Bob said you had some problems at home. And you might find it easier talking to me about them than to, well, some of the 'old folks,' I guess. But if you don't want to, that's okay."

Tiffany took a long sip of her latte, then put the paper cup down on the table. "No, I don't mind talking. You look like a good listener."

"I do try to listen." Shari nodded. "And not to judge. But if sharing my experiences helps in any way, then I'm happy to do that too."

"Fair enough," said Tiffany, and proceeded to tell Shari about her fights with her father and all the trouble she was getting in from hanging out with the wrong crowd.

When she finally finished, Shari didn't offer any comment. "You know, I used to be pretty rebellious too, when I was younger."

"You did?"

"You bet. My father and I had a lot of confrontations. It got pretty bad in my senior year of high school. I threatened to run away from home a number of times. I even began to experiment with drugs and alcohol."

Tiffany's mouth hung open in amazement.

"It was during my first year of college that things turned around and got better."

"How come?"

"Well, I met some college students who belonged to a Christian campus club. They asked me if I was happy. I told them that I wasn't. They then told me I could be."

Shari went on to tell Tiffany how these students reached out to her and became her friends.

"One day they asked me if I believed in God. They shared with me how everyone does wrong things and how our sins and wrongs separate us from a holy God. They went on to assure me that God loves me. He loved me so much that He sent His Son, Jesus, to die in my place. Jesus paid the penalty for me and rose from the dead to prepare a place in heaven for me. They asked if I would like to receive Christ into my life, and I did. From that day things began to change."

"What kind of things are you talking about?"

"Well, one of the first things I realized was that I had been hurt in my relationship with my father. I could never seem to please him. And I wanted to, desperately. My hurt led to anger. I then began to experience depression. I began to not trust people. Especially my father. I lost respect for him, and resentment and bitterness replaced the hurt. That's when I began to strike out in rebellion. I didn't realize what had been going on until I came to know Christ."

"What did you do?"

"I asked my father for forgiveness for my attitude. It was wrong. Even though he had done wrong, I had too. I apologized for my part. He began to cry and asked me to forgive him." She brushed away a tear. "That was quite a day."

"Are things good between you and him now?"

Shari took a deep breath. "My mother and father were killed in an accident not too long ago. We had about a year and a half of great times before he was killed. I just look back with such regret for all the wasted time. Life is so short, and we seem to hurt the ones we really love the most."

Shari unconsciously began to fondle the silver cross around her neck. Her father had given it to her as a reminder of their renewed relationship. She sat there for a moment looking into space, not seeing the people walking by. Another tear ran down her cheek, and this time she let it.

Tiffany was silent. When she felt that Shari was able to talk again, she said, "Thanks for sharing that with me, Shari. You've given me a lot to think about."

Shari smiled. "Any time. Do you want another coffee?"

"Thanks," Tiffany said, getting up, "but right now there's something I have to do. I really need to go talk to my dad."

TEN

MURPHY QUICKLY SURVEYED the audience. The amphitheater was filled and all eyes were on him. There were nearly one hundred fifty students in his controversial class on biblical archaeology.

Shari was in her usual spot in the front row. Her black hair was smoothed back into the familiar ponytail, but she didn't look like her perky self. There was an air of sadness in her green eyes. The seat next to her was empty.

Murphy's eyes went from Shari back to the audience. He then spotted Paul. He was seated about seven rows up on Murphy's left, in an aisle seat not far from the door. Why wasn't he sitting next to Shari? Had they had another fight? Or was his imagination just working on overdrive? Maybe Paul had arrived late and just took the nearest empty seat. He made a mental note to ask Shari about it later—but subtly, the way Laura would have done it.

"Good morning! It's good to see a full house. I guess I must have said something interesting last week! Okay, let's start right where we left off. When the bell rang on Monday, we were discussing the various men who had discovered wood on Mount Ararat. The last of the four men mentioned was Fernand Navarra. The wood he discovered was very ancient. We also reviewed twenty-six ancient and early writers who have written about Noah's Ark. Today, we will look at some individuals who claimed to have actually seen or climbed on the ark."

There was an audible buzz of anticipation as Murphy flipped on the first PowerPoint slide.

Those Who Claim to Have Seen Noah's Ark

Who:
George Hagopian and his uncle.

When:
During the years from 1900 to 1906.

Circumstances:
On two occasions—once when he was ten years of age, and the second when he was twelve years of age.

"George Hagopian's grandfather was an Armenian Orthodox minister near Lake Van in Turkey. He would tell stories about the holy ship on the mountain, and one day, when Hagopian was around ten years of age, his uncle told him that he would actually take him to see the ark—about eight days' journey away. He was told that the ship could be seen because it had been an unusually mild winter on Mount Ararat. In his own words, he says,

When we were there, the top of the ark was covered with a very thin coat of fresh-fallen snow. But when I brushed some of it away I could see a green moss growing right on top. When I pulled a piece off . . . it was made of wood. This green moss made the ark feel soft and moldy.

On the roof, besides one large hole, I remember small holes running all the way from the front to the back. I don't know exactly how many, but there must have been at least fifty of them running down the middle with small intervals in between. My uncle told me these holes were for air.

That roof was flat with the exception of the narrow raised section running all the way from the bow to the stern with all those holes in it.

Murphy paused and looked out over the audience. They seemed spellbound.

"The second time Hagopian visited the ark was when he was twelve years old. He was with his uncle again. In his own words:

I saw the ark a second time. I think it was in 1904. We were on the mountain looking for holy flowers, and I went back to the ark and it still looked the same. Nothing had changed. I didn't really get a good look at it. It was resting on a steep ledge of bluish-green rock about 3,000 feet wide.

The sides were slanting outward to the top and the front was flat. I didn't see any real curves. It was unlike any other boat I have ever seen. It looked more like a flat-bottomed barge.

"The next individuals to have claimed to see the ark were five or six Turkish soldiers. They also claimed to find wooden pegs that helped to hold the ark together. Here is part of what their letter said:

Those Who Claim to Have Seen Noah's Ark

Who:
Five or six Turkish soldiers.

When:
1916, upon their return from Baghdad.

Circumstances:
They wrote an official letter to the American Embassy in Turkey offering their services as guides for those who wanted to see the ark.

When returning from World War I, I and five or six of my friends passed by the Ararat. We saw Noah's Ark leaning against the mountain. I measured the length of the boat. It was 150 paces long. It had three stories. I read in the papers that an American group is looking for this boat. I wish to inform you that I shall personally show them this boat and I request your intervention so that I may show the boat.

Those Who Claim to Have Seen Noah's Ark

Who:
150 Russian soldiers.

When:
The summer of 1917.

Circumstances:
The Czar sends two research divisions of [150] army engineers and scientists on an expedition to Ararat to find the ark.

"The next sighting is even more interesting. A Russian pilot by the name of Vladimir Roskovitsky was flying his plane around Ararat in the summer of 1917 when he spotted the ark. He reported it to his superiors, and the Czar then sent research teams to investigate. I'm going to ask Shari to pass out two sheets of paper that relate their findings."

Shari started passing along a stack of printed sheets.

THE RUSSIAN EXPEDITION

The Russian investigators claim to have taken measurements of the ark. It was supposedly 500 feet long, about 83 feet wide at the widest place, and about 50 feet high. These measurements, when compared with a 20-inch cubit, fitted proportionately with the size of Noah's Ark as described in Genesis 6:15. The entire rear end of the boat, the investigating party [sic] able to enter first the upper room, a "very narrow one with a high ceiling." From here, "side by side to it, stretched rooms of various size; small and large ones."

There was also "a very large room, separated as if by a great fence of huge trunks of trees," possibly "stables for the huge animals," such as elephants, hippopotami, and others. On the walls of the rooms were cages, "arranged in the lines all the way from the floor to the ceiling, and they had marks of rust from the iron rods which were there before. There were very many various rooms, similar to these, apparently several hundreds of them. It was not possible to count them, because the lower rooms and even part of the upper ones—all of this was filled with hard ice. In the middle of the ship there was a corridor." The end of this corridor was overloaded with broken partitions.

"The ark was covered from inside as well as from outside," the story went on, "with some kind of dark brown color" resembling "wax and varnish." The wood of which the ark was built was excellently preserved except 1) at the hole in the front of the ship, and 2) at the door-hole at the side of the ship; there the wood was porous and it broke easily.

Page 1

THE RUSSIAN EXPEDITION

"During the examination of the surroundings around the lake . . . there were found on one of the mountaintops the remains of some burned wood 'and a structure put together of stones,' resembling an altar. The pieces of wood found around this structure were of the same kind of wood as the ark."

An eyewitness is said to have stated:

As the huge ship at last loomed before them, an awed silence descended, and "without a word of command everyone took off his hat, looking reverently toward the ark; and everybody knew, feeling it in his heart and soul," that they were in the actual presence of the ark. Many "crossed themselves and whispered a prayer." It was like being in a church, and the hands of the archaeologist trembled as he snapped the shutter of the camera and took a picture of the old boat as if it were "on parade."

Our guide, Yavuz Konca, reported that an elder Kurdish tribal chief remembered just such a Russian discovery in the summer of 1917. At the time, he was a young man of eighteen years of age. He recalled an unusual event that summer in which returning Russian soldiers came into the village throwing their hats in the air and shooting their rifles. When he inquired as to the celebration, he was informed that they had discovered Noah's Ark on Mount Ararat.

A detailed account stating the description and measurements of the ark, both inside and out, together with photos, plans, samples of wood, were sent at once by special courier to the office of the chief commandant of the Army—"as the Emperor had ordered."

Page 2

Murphy read out the story of the Russian expedition and let the incredible tale sink in. Once it did, he knew there'd be questions.

"Professor Murphy?"

Murphy looked into the center section of the amphitheater and smiled. Don West, one of his more serious archaeology students, had his hand raised.

"Yes, Don!"

"What happened to all the pictures and measurements that were taken by the Russians?"

"Good question, Don. The answer is, we don't know for sure what happened to them. Many believe that they were destroyed during the Russian Revolution. But I'd like to think they might be gathering dust in some forgotten archive. And there's an intriguing story that backs up their findings. One of the relatives of a member of the expedition worked as a cleaning maid in the Czar's palace. She testifies to having seen the pictures and reports. They were shown to her by the chief medical officer of the expedition. She says that the pictures show that the ark was three decks high, and on top of the roof there was a catwalk that was about knee-high with openings underneath."

Murphy clicked the projector again.

"There are a number of other people who have claimed to have seen or even climbed on Noah's Ark, but I would like to discuss only one more. His name is Ed Davis."

Murphy paused to gather his thoughts when the door to the lecture hall opened and he recognized the silhouette of Levi Abrams framed in the light. What could have brought him here, he wondered, before continuing.

Those Who Claim to Have Seen Noah's Ark

Who:
Ed Davis.

When:
The summer of 1943.

Circumstances:
While working for the Army Corps of Engineers, friends take him up Mount Ararat to see Noah's Ark.

"Ed Davis was working for the 363rd Army Corps of Engineers. He was working out of a base station in Hamadan, Iran, building a supply route way station into Russia from Turkey. His driver, Badi Abas, pointed to Agri Daugh, or Ararat, and said, 'That's my home.'

"The conversation turned to Noah's Ark and Abas told Davis that he could take him to see it. They drove to the foothills of Ararat and began hiking. On the way they passed a village whose name meant *where Noah planted the vine*. Davis said that the grapevines were very old and so big that he could not put his arms around them. Abas then told Davis, 'We have a cave filled with artifacts that came from the ark. We find them strewn in a canyon below the ark. We collect them to keep them from outsiders who would profane them.' Davis said:

> That night, they show me the artifacts. Oil lamps, clay vats, old-style tools, things like that. I see a cage-like door, maybe thirty by forty inches, made of woven branches. It's hard as stone, looks petrified. It has a hand-carved lock or latch on it. I could even see the wood grain.
>
> We sleep. At first light, we put on mountain clothes and they bring up a string of horses. I leave with seven male members of the Abas family and we ride—seems like an awful long time.
>
> Finally we come to a hidden cave deep in the foothills of Greater Ararat. The cave was at about the 8,000-foot level near the western wall of the Ahora Gorge. They told me

that T. E. Lawrence [of Arabia] hid in this cave. There's fungus there that glows in the dark. And they say Lawrence put it on his face to convince the Kurds he was a god and get them to join him in his war against the Turks.

Eventually we run out of trail for the horses. After three days of climbing we come to the last cave. Inside, there's strange writing, it looked beautiful and old, on the rock walls and a kind of natural rock bed or outcropping near the back of the cavern.

The next day we hike for a while. Finally Abas points. Then I see it—a huge, rectangular, man-made structure partly covered by a talus of ice and rock, lying on its side. At least a hundred feet are clearly visible. I can even see inside it, into the end where it's been broken off, timbers are sticking out, kind of twisted and gnarled, water's cascading out from under it.

Abas points down the canyon and I can make out another portion of it. I can see how the two pieces were once joined—the torn timbers kind of match. They told me the ark is broken into three or four big pieces. Inside the broken end of the biggest piece, I can see at least three floors and Abas says there's a living space near the top with forty-eight rooms. He says there are cages inside as small as my hand, others big enough to hold a family of elephants.

It began to rain. We had to return to the cave. The next day it was snowing so bad that we could not climb down to the ark. We were forced to leave the mountain. It took five days to get off the mountain and back to my base.

The lights were turned on and several hands were raised. Murphy could see Levi Abrams standing behind the back row smiling that big Israeli smile. Their eyes caught each other's and there was a barely perceptible nod of heads.

"Yes, Carl!" Murphy pointed to his right.

"Professor Murphy. In the Badi Abas story, Davis mentions that the ark is broken. In the other sightings the ark was all in one piece. Why don't the stories match?"

"We're not sure, Carl. It's possible the first sightings of the ark were when it was on a cliff above the Ahora Gorge. The movement of the glacier and/or an avalanche could have toppled it into the gorge and the fall broken it into sections. Ararat is known for earthquakes and avalanches."

Murphy glanced at the clock on the wall. He knew that the bell would ring in a few moments.

"We're almost out of time, but before the class is over, I want to give you an assignment."

Those who had already closed their notebooks anticipating the bell groaned and opened them back up.

"I want you to do a study and see what you can find in history about Noah and the Flood. Jesus even talks about Noah when He says in Luke Seventeen:

Just as it was in the days of Noah, so also will it be in the days of the Son of Man. People were eating, drinking, marrying, and being given in marriage up to the day Noah entered the ark. Then the Flood came and destroyed them all. It was the same in the days of Lot. People were eating and drinking, buying and selling, planting and building. But the day Lot left Sodom, fire and sulfur rained down from heaven and destroyed them all. It will be just like this on the day the Son of Man is revealed.

"Noah's Ark is a testimony that God will not let wickedness run unrestrained forever."

"Professor Murphy, I have a question," said a student named Theron Wilson.

"Go ahead, Theron."

"Do you think we will ever really find the ark?"

The question momentarily stopped Murphy in his tracks. Finally he said, "There's probably a reason it's been hidden all this time. And God would need a good reason to let someone reveal it to the world again. It could be that revealing it now would send a message, a message about how much evil there is in the world and how we have to do something about it. Maybe now would be a good time for someone to go looking for it."

There was a pregnant silence as his audience pondered his words. And then the ringing of the bell brought them all back to the present.

ELEVEN

VERNON THIELMAN WAS SMILING to himself as he took a deep breath of the cool night air. It was Friday night and he was glad he wasn't working the graveyard shift. He pushed the light button on his watch.

Ten-thirty. Almost done and the night is still young.

The full moon was making his job as night watchman a breeze. From the top of the roof of the Smithsonian, he could see anyone entering the parking lot that flanked the back two sides of the building. As he moved diagonally across the roof to the other corner, he could see 5th Street, which ran north and south, and Milford Boulevard, which ran east and west. The traffic was light for a Friday night.

After the violent death of two night watchmen and the theft of one section of Moses' Brazen Serpent from the Parchments of Freedom Foundation, a security guard had been placed on the roof. Despite the anxiety the deaths had engendered, the roof duty was regarded as relatively safe. His job tonight, after all, was to see and report, not to confront anybody or put himself in harm's way. Given that the security staff had negotiated extra danger payments, Thielman thought he had a pretty good deal.

It was hard to believe, but it appeared that the two guards had been killed by birds. Peregrine falcons to be exact. Birds of prey that had been trained to use their razor-sharp talons and beaks on man, instead of their usual quarry, pigeons and crows. It seemed pretty unlikely that such a bizarre incident could ever happen again, but Thielman was taking no chances. Every time he heard a squawk or a flutter of wings, his hand went straight to the security baton in his belt—ready to beat off any feathered attacker. And he had already checked the roof area several times for any lurking falcons.

Tonight, happily, he hadn't seen so much as a sparrow.

He did, however, see a dark-green Jeep drive slowly down 5th Street and turn right onto Milford. The Jeep stopped across the street from the foundation and a large man eased himself out. He looked in both directions as if he were going to cross the street, but then just stood by the Jeep. Then the man looked up at the roof and Thielman had the uncanny feeling he knew he was there. He couldn't see the man's face, but something about the situation sent a shiver up his spine.

Thielman stepped closer to the edge of the roof to get a better look, but the man's face remained in shadow.

Suddenly the man by the Jeep raised his hand, held it in midair for a few moments, then snapped it down against his thigh. Instantly Thielman heard an earsplitting shriek behind him and swiveled to see a dark shape arrowing down toward his face. Fumbling at his belt, he instinctively took a step backward and tripped over a taut monofilament line stretched between two steel air outlets. Turning awkwardly, he managed to break his fall by gripping the guardrail surrounding the roof.

For a second he congratulated himself on his swift reactions. *Not so bad for an old guy*, he thought.

And then the rail snapped in two like a stale breadstick and he was plummeting through space, spinning crazily as the ground rushed up to meet him in a crushing embrace.

By the time the stranger had ambled over to Thielman's body, with its crazy arrangement of limbs sticking out at odd angles, the last muscle spasms had finished their grisly dance, and everything was still. He paused for a moment to savor the pungent aromas of violent death, then dragged the corpse around to the back of the building and heaved it into the bushes.

He looked up as a starling gently settled on his shoulder and began to preen itself. He bared his teeth in a sickly smile. Starlings were mischievous birds and great mimics.

"You seem to have scared our friend here out of his wits, little one."

The bird gave a trill, cocked its head once, and flew off. The man moved silently to one of the large windows and removed a handful of tools from a backpack. First he held up what looked like a TV remote, pointed it at the window, and pressed a series of buttons. After a few seconds a red light winked on and a single beep told him the alarm system had been neutralized.

Next, he applied a suction cup to the window and attached an arm with a glass cutter.

Putting pressure on the glass cutter, he made an arcing circle around the suction cup, then tapped the circle once with a gloved hand and the glass popped out with the suction cup still attached. He set it on the ground, put away his tools, and slipped through the hole in the glass.

On the third floor of the building, another security guard methodically checked the doors as he walked down the corridor. So far everything was secure. Nothing out of place. Another quiet night.

He worried that maybe it was too quiet. He'd been experiencing problems with his hearing recently—his wife swore she had to shout to get his attention—and when he found himself wrapped in total silence, he couldn't be sure that he simply wasn't registering low-level noise. The kind of noise that could be significant in his line of work.

That faint grunting sound, for instance, gone as quickly as it had come. Did he imagine that? Or was it actually a shout—another guard in trouble somewhere in the building—and he should be rushing to his assistance, calling for backup, every lost second a matter of life and death?

He stopped. A thud. Definitely a thud. Like a bag of flour hitting the floor. Followed by more silence. But the silence was somehow eerier this time.

He quickly unlocked the door to one of the offices, slipped inside, and crossed to the window overlooking 5th Street. Nothing out of place. Still, better safe than sorry. He radioed to Thielman on the roof.

No reply.

Not good. He felt his skin go clammy. Then he punched more numbers into his walkie-talkie.

"This is Robertson to Caldwell. What's your location?"

"This is Caldwell. I'm in the basement."

"Okay. I'm going to the roof and see why Thielman isn't answering. Why don't you work your way up and join me?"

"I'm on my way."

Robertson headed for the stairs. But slowly. He'd give Caldwell plenty of time to catch up. No point taking more chances than he had to.

Talon heard the door to the basement open and quickly slipped into the shadows next to the stairwell. A few seconds later Caldwell jogged past him. Talon was momentarily startled by the security guard's speed. In his experience these rent-a-cops took their time over everything—especially investigating suspicious situations—but this one seemed determined to get to the source of trouble as quickly as he could.

In which case, Talon really ought to point out that he was heading in the wrong direction.

"Excuse me, sir."

Caldwell spun around, his hand instinctively going to the automatic on his hip.

"I seem to be a little lost."

Caldwell approached cautiously, unable to make out the features of the man lurking in the stairwell. "You certainly are, sir. Can you come out into the light, please?"

"Of course," Talon said, stepping smartly forward while simultaneously sweeping his right arm across Caldwell's throat. Before Caldwell could react, his larynx was severed, along with both carotid arteries. He slumped to the floor as twin fountains of blood painted the wall a garish red.

Talon carefully wiped the blood off his artificial index finger onto Caldwell's jacket and smiled. "Thanks for your help. I think I can find my own way now."

When Robertson reached the roof, Thielman was nowhere to be found. He walked over to the corner overlooking 5th Street and Milford. All was quiet except for a green Jeep parked across the street. As he walked along the Milford side of the roof, his flashlight illuminated the broken guardrail. He looked over the edge and could see something on the pavement that looked like a large oil stain. He then crossed to the corner overlooking the two parking lots. He swept his flashlight in a slow arc over the ground toward the bushes.

He gasped as he saw two black shoes sticking out.

He pulled his automatic out of its holster, slipped off the safety, and hurried back toward the roof door. He had one thought in mind. *Get to the fourth floor and set off the alarm.* Seven minutes later the place would be swarming with cops.

All he had to do was make it through the next seven minutes.

Isis McDonald's unruly mop of startling red hair was spread out on her desk, her pale face pillowed on a dusty copy of

Seagram's *Glossary of Sumerian Script.* The book lay open at the page she had been reading when she fell asleep. It was not so much that she'd been working for twelve hours straight (that was a common occurrence when a philological problem remained unsolved, and therefore a cause of mild but constant irritation); it was more that, since her sense of time completely deserted her when she was immersed in her work, she simply laid her head down for a nap whenever she felt tired.

She had been dozing softly for about twenty minutes and normally would have expected to remain asleep for another half hour or so before awaking refreshed, if a little stiff, and ready to attack the problem with renewed vigor.

But this time she was jerked awake by the sound of an alarm.

She sat up with a start, trying to get her bearings. Was there a fire? Had someone broken in to the foundation? Then she heard a series of loud noises in the lab next to her office. It sounded like things were being thrown about by a madman. Still not fully awake, she opened the door and turned on the light.

A man with black hair and gray eyes set in a long, pale face turned to face her. He gave her a look that chilled her to the bone.

She'd seen that look before. So had Laura Murphy.

She stepped back from the doorway, aiming for her desk, where a .32 automatic—as yet unfired—nestled in a drawer amid a clutter of stationery.

She didn't even manage a single stride before he caught her.

He grabbed her with his left arm and whirled her around, and her forehead made contact with a solidly aimed fist. Isis flew backward across her desk, knocking the computer to the floor and spraying papers everywhere. She didn't have time to scream before a numbing blackness descended on her.

Talon quickly moved to her side and circled his hands around her delicate throat. His thumbs began to move down on her larynx.

"Exquisite," he breathed.

There was nothing more pleasing than a face-to-face kill. Especially if one had the time to draw it out.

"Hold it right there!"

Talon knew without turning around that a gun was aimed at him, but he showed no sign of alarm. He let go of Isis's throat, letting her slump unceremoniously to the floor, and turned toward the remaining security guard.

"Put your hands up where I can see them."

Talon slowly raised his hands, locking eyes with the guard. The guard took his eyes off Talon for a moment to look at Isis, and Talon instantly appreciated his dilemma. If she was badly hurt and needed immediate medical assistance, how was he going to do that while keeping Talon in his sights?

In the split second provided by the guard's indecision, Talon put a hand behind his neck and slipped a throwing knife into his palm.

"I said keep your hands up!" shouted Robertson, a moment before the knife embedded itself in his throat with a sound like a cleaver chopping through ribs. He dropped his gun, and both hands closed over the hilt to try and pull it out, but the life force was already draining from him. He sank to his knees in slow motion, then toppled almost gracefully onto Isis.

Talon looked at Isis, then cocked his head at the sound of approaching sirens.

"Later," he said with a sneer.

The phone jolted Murphy out of a deep sleep. Shards of a shattered dream—Laura laughing on a mountainside, birdsong, the word *Jasmine*—fell away into darkness as he came fully awake. The ringing continued. Finally it registered that it was his phone.

"Murphy."

"Michael, it's Isis. I'm sorry if I've woken you."

During the ordeals they'd shared together, he'd seen the full range of her emotions, from elation to despair, but the sheer terror he could now hear in her voice struck a shocking new note.

"Isis. What is it? What's wrong?"

Isis started to speak, and then the words dissolved into crying.

"Take a deep breath."

Murphy waited until the sobbing subsided.

"Tell me what happened."

Haltingly, with several breaks for more crying, Isis related as much of her ordeal as she could recollect, though the blow on the head and subsequent concussion had jumbled the sequence of events in her memory.

A chaos of different emotions swirled through Murphy's mind. Sorrow, guilt, but most of all anger. "I'll be on the first plane out of Raleigh. I should never have gotten you involved in this. Are you sure you shouldn't be in the hospital? Did they discharge you, or was it that stubborn streak of yours—"

"No, Michael," she interrupted. "It's not your fault. And I'm okay. I'm just shaken up, that's all. The police asked me to go to my sister's in Bridgeport, Connecticut. That's where I'm calling from now. They have a patrol car guarding the house. They want me to stay here until they can figure out what happened."

Murphy gripped the phone so hard his knuckles turned white. "We know what happened, Isis. We know who did this—who killed the guards, attacked you. He would have killed you too if the police hadn't . . ." His voice trailed off as another thought struck him.

"The fragment of wood—is it still in the lab?"

Isis laughed through another sob. "I thought for a moment you were just concerned about me."

"I am, Isis," he protested.

"But there are other, more important things to worry about, aren't there? Don't worry, Michael, I understand. But the answer to your question is no. The wood is gone."

"So that's what he came for."

"Looks like it," Isis agreed. "But that's not all."

"What do you mean?"

"We did some further research. We discovered that the wood was not only about five thousand years old, but that it contained radioactive isotopes and almost no traces of potassium forty in it. What do you make of that?"

Murphy's brain started to go into overdrive. "Potassium 40 is found in just about everything. It's one of the things responsible for the aging process. For this piece of wood to have almost no traces of Potassium 40 could mean there was very little of it around in the pre-flood world. Which would make sense since it was normal for people to live for hundreds of years prior to the flood. After the flood, however, people's life spans were reduced to where they are today."

"How would you explain all this?"

Murphy thought for a moment. "There are some scientists who believe that at one time, there was a layer of water surrounding the earth called a water canopy. This could have filtered out harmful ultraviolet rays from the sun. That might account for the reduction in Potassium 40. It's also believed that when Noah's flood came, the water canopy collapsed onto the earth and that's what contributed to the floodwaters rising above the hightest mountains. With the water canopy gone, Potassium 40 would begin to increase."

There was a long silence on the other end of the phone. Then Isis said, "You want to find the ark, don't you, Michael? You want to prove once and for all that the Bible story is true."

"I do. No question. But maybe there are other reasons for finding the ark. Maybe the secret of extending life. Maybe other secrets too." Murphy paused, lost in thought. When he spoke again, his tone had changed.

"I don't have to tell you how important this all could be, Isis. But right now none of it matters. The only important thing is that you're alive and safe. You know, I don't think I could endure a second loss."

For a long time neither of them spoke.

TWELVE

LEVI SAT DOWN in one of the empty chairs in the lecture hall and watched as a handful of eager students plied Murphy with questions. He was amazed at the patience of the man. Most academics regarded the teaching of students as an annoying interruption of their own studies, but Murphy clearly cared about his students as much as he cared about archaeology. Levi knew his presence must have intrigued Murphy, but Murphy showed no sign of wanting to hustle the students away. Eventually, however, the last of them left the lecture theater and Murphy walked over to his old friend.

"I didn't know you were interested in Noah's Ark, Levi. If I'd known I would have saved you a seat in the front row."

"Maybe I know more about it than you think," said Levi coolly. "When I was in the Mossad there was always talk of the ark being on Ararat. Apparently the CIA took satellite pictures of the area. Very interesting, I'm told."

Murphy was hooked. "Did you ever see them?"

"It was all very top secret. I shouldn't really be talking about it. I could tell you, but then . . . I'd have to kill you."

He looked at Murphy with those intense, dark eyes, and Murphy could believe it. Then Levi suddenly laughed and Murphy realized he was joking. The killing-him part, at least.

"So, you haven't come for a lecture from me, then."

Levi shrugged. "I was in the area on business and thought I would drop by. I brought my workout gear. How about a little sparring? Then, if you're still alive, I'll buy you lunch," he said with a grin.

"And if I'm not?"

"Then you buy, of course."

When they had first met a couple of years earlier, Murphy had formed an almost instant liking for Levi. They came from different backgrounds and had different perspectives on the world in many ways, but at heart they were both adventurers. They enjoyed testing each other, physically and mentally, and Murphy always felt he came away from their meetings having learned something—usually some new martial-arts move.

At the gym, Levi and Murphy warmed up with stretching exercises to ensure no pulled muscles. They then both dropped into a "horse stance" and held that position while throwing five hundred right and left reverse punches. Murphy could feel the strain in his thighs almost instantly, while Levi looked as if he was relaxing in an armchair in front of the TV.

"Are you ready for something new?" asked Levi.

"Bring it on," grunted Murphy.

"We will practice a kata that has twenty-seven moves to it. It is called Heian Yodan. It was taught by Gichin Funakoshi, the master in Karate-do."

Levi was always the patient teacher, even in the midst of a high-intensity training session. He was a blinding combination of grace, speed, and sheer power. Murphy was always amazed at how quickly his stocky body could move—and with what lethal force.

Murphy knew that Levi had taken a job as head of security for a high-tech company in the Raleigh-Durham area. But he had suspicions that he still had strong ties to the Mossad and to other intelligence agencies in a number of countries.

For an hour Levi dragged Murphy through the unfamiliar kata, until Murphy could feel something new had been programmed into his aching limbs—a new way of moving and seeing. Just at the point where he thought he was going to collapse, Levi clapped his hands and dropped into a relaxation posture. Murphy gratefully followed his example.

He waited for his breathing to steady, then said, "Okay, Levi. Thanks for the lesson. But what's the real reason for your visit?"

"Your body may be slow but your mind is still sharp, I see," Levi laughed. "I got a call from Bob Wagoner last week. He was concerned about how you were dealing with the loss of Laura." He looked his friend in the eye. "How are you handling it?"

Painful as it was, Murphy didn't resent the question. Levi wouldn't have made much of a diplomat, but his directness was sometimes refreshing. Murphy hated it when people didn't mention Laura's name in case it upset him. He wanted people to talk about her and remember her, even if made the heartache more intense.

"Some days have been harder than others. I've been pouring myself into work, trying to do something positive and not dwell in the past. But every day I think about her, try to concentrate on the good times, try not to focus on—" He took a breath and tried to clear his throat, but the words wouldn't come.

Levi finished his sentence for him. "On Talon."

Murphy nodded, glad he didn't have to say the name. Then he suddenly realized that was why Levi had come.

"Listen," said Levi. "I heard about the break-in at the Parchments of Freedom Foundation. How your friend Isis was almost killed."

"You're always remarkably well informed," Murphy said.

"I have my sources, as you know. Anyhow, I was turning it over in my mind, thinking about the way the guards had been killed—"

"And you thought of Talon. Of course. I know it was him, Levi. He killed Laura, and now he almost killed Isis. It was a miracle he didn't."

He looked at the floor, suddenly overcome with emotion.

"Don't worry," said Levi. "I believe Talon got what he was looking for. He won't be coming back."

Murphy was amazed at how much information Levi already had. How much more did he know that he wasn't sharing?

"Look, Levi. If Methuselah is involved, and Talon is involved, something big must be going on. Something to do with the ark.

I just wish I knew what it was. But I think there's only one way to find out."

Levi scratched the iron-gray stubble on his chin thoughtfully. "If the ark exists, of course."

Murphy locked eyes with his friend. "I think you know more than you're telling on that score."

"Maybe," conceded Levi. "And what if the ark does exist?"

"I believe it does," said Murphy firmly. He gripped Levi's forearm. "And I want to try and find it. But I'll need help. The kind of specialized help I think only you can give me. If I set up a discovery team, I think the Parchments of Freedom Foundation might be interested in funding it."

Levi shook his head. "From what I know, Ararat is a very dangerous place. Not only do you have Turkish soldiers, Kurdish rebels, and wild dogs, there are also many rock avalanches and snow avalanches on the mountain. Even earthquakes. If you go to where everyone thinks the ark might be located, you will have to climb in high-altitude snow conditions."

"I know. That's why I'm asking for your help. We would need you to train us for all the kinds of problems we might encounter."

Levi continued to look doubtful but Murphy plowed on.

"I'm going to the CIA headquarters at Langley. I think they have information about Ararat that they've been sitting on for some time."

"You may be opening a big can of worms, Murphy. Are you sure that you want to do that?"

"You know me, Levi. I love an adventure. And I don't mind rattling a few cages in the government. Especially when it involves the possible discovery of the most important archaeological find in human history. If we can find the ark, it would be the greatest blow that could be struck against the theory of evolution. It would be a confirmation that the Bible is correct and that God created the world. And I have a feeling there may be other amazing things on the ark. Maybe then we could even convince an old skeptic like you, Levi!"

Levi didn't smile. "You are getting into areas that you know little about. There is more danger than you think."

"From what? I've already encountered Methuselah and Talon."

"Spooks," said Levi evenly.

"Spooks? Are we talking about ghosts?"

"We're talking about freelance, unofficial government operatives. They're no joke, Murphy, if you get in their way. I should know."

Murphy fixed him with an intense gaze. "Then I'm going to need all the help I can get, aren't I?"

THIRTEEN

50 miles from the great city of Enoch, 3115 B.C.

A SCREAM OF AGONY *filled the night air.*

Whirling around, eyes wide, Noah turned toward the noise. Down below the walls, through the flickering light of the torches, he saw Ahaziah. He was staggering backward, both hands gripping the arrow that had pierced his chest. He was gasping for air.

The men at the post near him ran to his aid. As Noah started to move toward his beloved servant he heard a tremendous noise, like a great wave crashing on the shore—the rushing cry of Zattu's attacking army.

"To your posts, men, to your posts!" he yelled.

Turning quickly, he shouted, "Japheth, the archers!"

Noah's archers began to take aim at shadowy figures on the ground below, some of whom were already climbing up the long siege ladders.

But the enemy archers were at work too, sending a blinding spray of arrows up toward Noah's men, killing or maiming many before they could loose their own shafts. But worse, many of the arrows had been dipped in pitch and set on fire to become flying torches, lighting up the sky before landing on the roofs of the buildings below.

Fire could soon be seen everywhere in the city, and no one could be in any doubt that Zattu's army was determined to capture or destroy it before another dawn rose.

On the walls, Ham and his men were pushing the ladders away with long poles, desperately trying to prevent the enemy from overrunning them. Everywhere there was shouting and yelling—a violent cacophony in which it was impossible to tell the screams of the dying from the bark of orders.

On the ground, inside the walls, women tended to the wounded as children drew water from the last remaining wells, trying to slake the fighters' terrible thirst.

Now Shem and his men began to pour scalding water on the attackers below from great iron pots, while others toppled large rocks down on the enemy holding the ladders. Soon all the ladders had been smashed, and the enemy's momentum seemed to have been halted. Suddenly, there was a mighty cheer from those lining the walls.

Zattu's men were retreating.

Once he was certain that it wasn't a ruse, that the enemy truly was in disarray, Noah gathered his sons and his chief officers beneath the walls.

"Shem, take some of the officers and see how many men we lost in the attack. See how many of the wounded can still fight. Japheth, gather as many of the enemy arrows as you can. Have your men move more rocks to the top of the wall and to the towers. Ham, have you gotten any signal from Massereth?"

"I sent him to the great city of Enoch for help, but he has not returned. He may have been killed by the enemy. Four days have passed."

Dawn was turning the horizon a muted pink as Noah began to walk through the city to survey the damage. Many of the homes were just smoking ashes. Some of his men were gathering the dead and carting them to the storage building next to the temple.

Every now and then he would stop to talk with the wounded, trying to encourage them and thank them the best he could. Women and children were crying. Some women were sitting on the ground, rocking dead loved ones in their arms and staring off into space.

Noah stopped and closed his eyes for a moment. How he hated war. How he hated the taking of another man's life. But a man must protect his family against those who threaten them. He had no other choice. And in recent years the threat of evildoers had become too much to ignore. Tears streamed down Noah's face as he began to search the crowd for Naamah. He wept for all the dead, for the widowed mothers, for the fatherless children. But he knew if he had lost his own wife his heart would break and he would not be able to carry on.

After an hour of increasingly frantic searching, Noah found her. She was with Achsah, Bithiah, and Hagaba, his sons' wives. Their once-fine clothes were filthy and stained with sweat as they tended to the wounded as best they could. Naamah stood to get another jar of water, wiped the hair out of her face, and turned to see Noah. They embraced without speaking for long moments and then she began to weep.

"Have you had word from Tubal-cain?" said Naamah finally, with a look of desperation in her eyes.

"No," Noah admitted with a heavy heart. "But I am hoping that Massereth was able to get through the enemy lines to your brother. He is our only hope. Supplies will only last for another day."

"What if he does not come in time?"

Noah looked away.

"Noah, what will happen to our people?" said Naamah with fear in her voice.

Noah held her shoulders firmly. He couldn't lie to her. "Zattu and his army are wicked men. They will take no slaves. They will kill the women and children."

Noah drew her into his arms as she dissolved into hysterical sobbing. "God will somehow protect us. We have trusted in Him since the beginning. He will not let us down."

It was noon when Japheth came to Noah with the bad news.

"We have about ninety men who can still fight. Our supply of arrows is low, and most of the water is gone. Our only weapons are rocks. We may be able to resist one more attack."

Noah sighed, then gathered his spirits as best he could. "Start organizing the men and take all of our supplies to the walls. Heat up the rocks in the iron pots. We must prepare for their next attack."

"Yes, Father," said Japheth with determination.

"I will have Ham gather any of the women who can fight, along with the older children. It is our only hope."

Noah mounted the wall and walked from tower to tower. He could see several thousand of Zattu's men spread out over the plain, readying themselves for another attack. They knew Noah was almost beaten. This time they would strike in broad daylight.

Noah called to his sons and officers, "We do not have much time left. Their army is beginning to form ranks! Gather the people!"

It was like being in an ill-omened dream, watching the enemy move slowly toward the city. They were coming like a swarm of ants ready to devour a juicy date. Noah knew that his people would not endure the next attack for very long. He began to pray.

Ham, Shem, and Japheth, along with Naamah, Achsah, Bithiah, and Hagaba, gathered around Noah as they watched the approach of the army. No one spoke. There was nothing to say and nothing to do until the final onslaught began.

Suddenly the silence was broken by a shout from one of the towers.

Noah and his family turned and looked in the direction the soldier was pointing. It took them a moment to register the cloud of dust on the horizon and discern the glint of armor in the distance.

Noah was infused with a new surge of energy. "Praise God! It is the great army of Tubal-cain! Massereth has succeeded! We must hold on until they arrive!"

The attack began in the heat of the day. Women, children, and even some of the elderly joined with the men. Some gathered stray arrows from the enemy, and the stronger ones dropped rocks. Everyone who could stand gathered on the walls in the hope they could somehow keep their city from being destroyed. They knew that once the walls were breached, they were as good as dead.

Zattu did not see Tubal-cain's approach until it was too late. With their rear unprotected, the slaughter was great. Tubal-cain's fighters were fierce, and they wielded weapons far more deadly than the curved iron swords of Zattu's army. Their swords made a high ringing sound when they clashed against shield or helmet—thus they were known as Tubal-cain's "singing swords"—and the metal seemed unbreakable and impervious to rust or decay. For many hours the swords did their deadly work, until, as the light began to fade, Zattu's army had finally been reduced to a pile of corpses. Tubal-cain's men roamed the plain, stripping the dead of anything of value. Their harsh laughter mingled with the groans of those not quite dead yet.

Against this grisly background, Tubal-cain was comforting his sister. "You and your family almost died," he said. "You must move out of this place. There is much wickedness here. Zattu's army of scavenging dogs is destroyed, but his brothers will seek revenge."

"But this is where we raised Ham, Shem, and Japheth," said Naamah.

"What does that matter! If you stay you will be killed. You have no army to protect you anymore. Many of your people are dead. The city of Enoch is too many miles distant." He shook his head. "I tell you, this is not a safe place for women and children. You and Noah and your sons and daughters must leave."

"But where should we go?" said Naamah.

"The forest of Azer," said Tubal-cain. "You would have everything you need. And no one has settled it yet. You would be safe from the evildoers."

"That is many miles distant," said Noah. "I need to stay here and instruct the people about the Great God of the Heavens."

Tubal-cain smiled and said, "These people don't care about your God talk. They will kill you for a few sheep. Even I do not believe in your God, Noah. I came only to save my sister, not to proclaim a victory for your God. And the next time evil strikes at you, I may not be able to help you in time."

"We must pray about this," said Noah firmly.

"What is there to pray about?" said Tubal-cain, spitting in the dust. "You either move or you will die!"

During the following months Noah and his family repaired the city as best they could. Many of the widows moved out of the city and went back to their relatives in distant villages. Others wandered out into the wilderness, fearing another attack on the city more than they did the threat of starvation or the predations of robbers.

The city began to dwindle before their eyes.

"Do you think Tubal-cain is right, after all? Should we move to the forest of Azer?" said Naamah one day.

Noah understood her anxieties.

"I have been praying about it. Of course, I know that it is not safe here any longer. But I do not know yet that God wants us to move. I will spend time today to seek His will."

"Where is Father?" asked Japheth later. "I have not seen him all day."

"He will return for the evening meal," responded Naamah calmly. She looked out over the plain. "See! Is that not your father coming now?" But her relief turned to fear as she saw that he was running. Soon the rest of the family had gathered, awaiting Noah's return. Could it be that Zattu's brothers were on the march? They clutched one another in fear as a breathless Noah finally entered through the gate and they shut the great wooden door behind him.

"Come, come!" said Noah when he had recovered himself. "I have something I must tell you all."

Soon the sons and wives gathered around their table.

"God has spoken to me today!"

A look of shock settled on their faces.

"No, no. It is true. God spoke to me today. He said, 'Take your wife, Naamah, Shem and Achsah, Ham and Bithiah, and Japheth and Hagaba, and build an ark of safety. The world is filled with wickedness and violence. The people have corrupted themselves. I am going to destroy them with a flood. But you and your family will be saved from destruction.'"

As his family listened in astonished silence, Noah went on to describe how the ark of safety was to be built. "We will be moving to the forest of Azer. We will need the trees there for the building of the ark of safety. I will travel to the great city of Enoch and let Tubal-cain know that we will be leaving."

A few days later, Noah was sitting in the cool shade of Tubal-cain's garden. "You have made a wise decision, Noah," Tubal-cain said. "The forest of Azer will be a safe place for you and my sister and your children. I will send some of my trusted men to protect you during your journey. Zattu's brothers may be lying in wait for you."

"I appreciate your kindness, Tubal-cain. You have protected us on more than one occasion."

Tubal-cain nodded. "I do have one suggestion, however. Don't tell anyone about your ark of safety. Or that God spoke to you. They will laugh you to scorn. Or worse."

"But it is true!"

"True or false, it will just stir up trouble. I don't want my sister subjected to any more danger."

Noah bowed his head. He was truly grateful to Tubal-cain, despite his lack of faith, and he had no desire to antagonize him.

Tubal-cain seemed mollified. "Before you leave, I have some spe-

cial gifts for you. The first is one of my singing swords and a dagger. They may be of some protection to you in the future. I also have a box with some things that may help you in your foolish plan to build the ark of safety that you talk about. You must promise that you will not share these secrets with anyone."

Noah nodded in agreement and bowed once more. When God had first told him what he must do, he had not known how such a task could be accomplished. Now, as Tubal-cain explained the nature of his special gifts, Noah believed for the first time that it really could be done.

FOURTEEN

"JUST A MINUTE THERE, Murphy!"

The harsh voice had an air of command in it, and Michael could feel a hand grabbing his shoulder and gripping hard. Turning instinctively, Murphy faced Dean Archer Fallworth. He was as tall as Murphy and had wispy blond hair, and his whitewashed face with his high eyebrows and long nose was set in a familiar scowl. You didn't need to be a mind reader to know he wasn't happy.

Murphy maintained a bland expression and willed himself to relax. It was a foolish and possibly dangerous thing to grab someone like Murphy from behind like that. Hundreds of hours of martial-arts practice had honed his reactions to a razor's edge, and the whole point of the exercise was that your body would counter a threat instinctively, before your conscious mind even knew the threat was there.

Luckily for Dean Fallworth, Murphy's sixth sense had told him that he was not about to be attacked.

At least not physically.

Realizing that he had Murphy's attention, Fallworth cleared his throat. "Got you at last, Murphy! You can be a hard man to track down, you know. And I have better things to do than chase around the campus after one of my professors because he can't stick to a timetable."

Murphy smiled. "Then why don't you go do them?"

Fallworth's pallor paled even further. "Watch what you say, Murphy. I think I've had just about enough of your disrespect."

"But you just keep coming back for more, don't you?" Murphy teased, almost beginning to enjoy himself.

Fallworth realized he was losing control of the situation. "Listen here, Murphy. We have an important issue to discuss. We could discuss it now, or . . . at a departmental disciplinary meeting." He smirked. "Up to you."

Murphy sighed. "I have things to do too, Dean. So why don't you just get whatever it is off your chest right here and now?"

"Fine. I hear reports that you have been lecturing about Noah's Ark, telling the students that it's sitting on Mount Ararat, as large as life. What next, Murphy—a seminar on Jack and the Beanstalk? Or are you going to mount an expedition to find the old lady who lived in a shoe?"

"I don't deal in fairy stories," Murphy said, his temper rising.

"Is that right? What would you call a tale of a big boat filled with two of every animal in the world? It certainly doesn't sound like history to me. I believe we have an agreement," he continued, jabbing a forefinger in Murphy's face. "You are at liberty to present your beliefs as just that—*beliefs*. This is a reputable university, and we cannot have ridiculous Bible stories presented to impressionable young students as if they are fact. Do you understand me, *Professor* Murphy? You've got to stop preaching religion in the classroom. This is a place of *higher learning*, not a church!"

Murphy waited until Fallworth was finished, then started counting on his fingers. "Number one, I am not preaching. I'm giving a class lecture. Number two, many reputable scientists believe Noah's Ark is on Mount Ararat. And number three, my students are free to question my presentations at any time. Nothing is being rammed down their throats. And besides that, you were not in attendance and have no idea what you are talking about."

Murphy could feel his Irish temper coming on strong. Fallworth's complexion was reddening too.

"Have you heard of the separation between church and state, Murphy?"

"Hold on, Fallworth. Where do you come up with this church and state stuff? Preston is a private university. It has nothing to do with the state."

"It's in the Constitution!"

Murphy made an effort to get a grip on his emotions.

"Really? Just where in the Constitution?"

"I don't have it memorized, but it is somewhere in the First Amendment!"

"Well, Archer, that's interesting. I do have the First Amendment memorized! It says, *Congress shall make no law respecting an establishment of a religion or prohibiting the free exercise thereof; or abridging the freedom of speech, or the press; or of the right of the people to peaceably assemble and to petition the government for a redress of grievances.*"

"See, what did I tell you? No establishment of a religion!"

"I'm not Congress, in case you hadn't noticed. I'm not establishing a religion. I'm exercising my free speech rights. You believe in free speech rights, don't you, Archer?"

"Certainly, but Thomas Jefferson said there is to be a separation between church and state!"

Murphy could tell that Fallworth was now just rattling off a well-worn phrase without a decent argument behind it.

"And in what context did President Jefferson make that statement?"

"He said it. That's the important thing," Fallworth blustered.

"Let me help you out, Archer. It was in a letter written to the Danbury Baptist Association on January 1, 1802. The Baptists were afraid that Congress might pass a law establishing a state religion. Jefferson wrote back and said there is a *wall of separation between the church and the state.* In other words, the state could not break down the wall and establish a state religion. It had nothing to do with keeping religion out of government. Most of our founding fathers were deeply religious men. If you read Jefferson's writings you will see many places where he encourages the free exercise of religion. It's just the opposite of what you are saying."

"There should be a wall *both* ways."

"You know, Archer, I gave a lecture to the Russian Archaeological Society last year in Moscow. I informed them that certain archaeological discoveries were made possible by information received from the Bible. I went on to say, 'I know that this used to be a communist country and many of you might be atheists and do not believe in the Bible.' The professor in charge said to me, 'Everyone in this lecture hall has at least a master's degree. There are twenty-two PhDs listening to your lecture. We are quite capable of hearing what you have to say and determining if it is valid for us or not. Aren't the educators in the United States capable of doing that?' I said, 'Sadly, many are not.' I think you have just proven me right."

Beaten back by Murphy's command of detail, Fallworth tried a different tack. "You're always talking about the Bible and Bible discoveries. The Bible is notoriously filled with myth and legend. How could Noah possibly get two of every kind of animal on the ark anyway?"

"When I find the ark," said Murphy with a smile, "I'll tell you."

FIFTEEN

MURPHY WAS DRUMMING his fingers on the table as the phone rang.

"Hello." A tentative female voice.

"Is Isis there, please?"

"I'm sorry, there's no one here by that name. You must have the wrong number."

Murphy was sure he had dialed the right number.

"Look, my name is Michael Murphy and this is the number Isis gave me. She said that she was staying with her sister in Bridgeport."

There was a pause at the other end.

"Mr. Murphy, I'm Hecate. Isis's sister. She said you might be calling. I'm sorry for the deception. The police told us not to let anyone know Isis was here. She's outside on the patio. Let me get her."

Hecate. Murphy smiled to himself. Old Dr. McDonald sure had a thing about those ancient goddesses. What was more surprising was that Isis had never mentioned a sister before. Then again, there were plenty of things he didn't know about Isis, and there was no reason for her to confide every detail of her personal life to him, was there? But for some reason the fact that she had kept her sister's existence a secret made him feel a little hurt.

He tried to put the idea out of his head as he waited for Isis to come on the line. When she did, he could tell from her rapid breathing that something was making her heart beat faster.

"Michael! I'm so glad you called."

"How are you feeling?"

"Still a bit shaken up. I feel so bad about the guards. The police said that I shouldn't go to the funerals—it's too dangerous—so I can't show support for the families. They must be devastated. And I feel somehow it's wrong I survived. It's my fault they're dead."

"That's crazy, Isis. Of course it isn't. I got you into this. If it's anyone's fault, it's mine."

"All right, Michael," she said with a deep sigh. "Let's just say it's no one's fault. We were doing our jobs, that's all. We didn't invite this . . . this . . ."

"Evil," said Murphy softly.

Murphy listened to the silence on the other end of the line. Since their adventures with the Brazen Serpent and the Golden Head of Nebuchadnezzar, Murphy had sensed a change in Isis's views about good and evil, and about faith. He wasn't sure exactly what she believed, or how close she was to accepting

Christ into her life. But no one could go through what she had without asking themselves the big questions.

He just hoped she came up with the right answers.

But he knew pushing her would have the opposite of the intended effect. Not for the first time where Isis was concerned, he found himself tongue-tied. Luckily Isis broke the awkward silence.

"Let's try and be positive, Michael. I'm a little battered, but I'm basically okay. And there is some good news. I got a call from the foundation. They wanted me to let you know that they are willing to fund an exploration team to search for Noah's Ark. They want you to head it up. Isn't that great?"

Murphy was caught off guard.

"What prompted them to make that suggestion?"

"Probably several things, I suppose. I think they want to follow the link between potassium forty and longevity. They also want to see if there are any other scientific discoveries on the ark. And there is something else."

"What's that?"

"They received a check from an anonymous donor to cover the entire search."

Murphy whistled. "That's a big chunk of change!"

"Yes. Harvey Compton, the chairman of the foundation, called me himself with the news. He said the check came from some offshore company that he'd never heard of before. The check was signed, and he cashed it, but he couldn't read the signature. The anonymous donor sent a note stating that he wanted you to lead the discovery team."

Methuselah! What was he up to now?

Murphy knew Methuselah had to be wealthy to finance his elaborate games, but if his guess was right, now he seemed to be willing to put all his resources into finding the ark. Why?

"There's even enough money to get a totally upgraded computer system. My old computer seems to have given up the ghost after I went flying across my desk. Frankly, I'd be happier to go back to just using pen and paper. And pens with proper ink, at that . . ."

Murphy was hearing Isis but his attention was already miles away, on the treacherous, icy slopes of Mount Ararat. Then suddenly he had an idea.

"Would you like to go?" he interrupted.

"What?"

"Would you like to be part of the discovery team searching for the ark?"

Isis was momentarily stunned. Murphy had seemed genuinely distraught about the attack. He even felt personally responsible. For the first time she was beginning to think he actually cared about her.

And now he was inviting her to go on an expedition to one of the world's most inhospitable if not downright dangerous places. All for the sake of a biblical artifact. Which, of course, made perfect sense. Because biblical artifacts were all he *really* cared about.

How could she have been such a fool?

"What do you say, Isis? If the ark really does have more secrets, we might well need someone with your linguistic skills to decipher the ancient texts."

Isis didn't need any more time to think about it. She'd show

Michael Murphy that she wasn't some softhearted female at the beck and call of her emotions. Blast him!

"Count me in. Apart from the skills you mentioned, you might need an experienced mountaineer along for the ride. My father and I used to spend every vacation in the Highlands, I'll have you know."

"Great. But you might need to start getting in serious shape once you're feeling better. We're going to be at high altitude in difficult conditions."

"Don't worry about me," Isis said sharply. "I've climbed more mountains than you've had hot dinners. Anyway, you've got some organizing to do. I'll let you get on with it."

Murphy grinned as he put the phone down, then let out a sigh of relief.

Mount Ararat might be a dangerous place, but at least if Isis came on the expedition, he'd be there to protect her.

They might find the ark. They might not. Ultimately it was in God's hands. But he was determined that he wasn't going to lose Isis.

SIXTEEN

IT WAS 6:00 A.M. when Murphy walked through the doors of the Raleigh Health and Fitness Gym. He liked to get an early-morning workout three days a week if he could, not just to stay in shape, but because physical activity gave him the space in which to think. A step machine was one of the few sanctuaries he knew where no student was likely to ask him about an assignment.

He changed and selected a machine. After forty-five minutes he'd built up a sweat and could feel his mind beginning to let go of the immediate concerns of the day. He stepped off and ambled over to the free-weights area to begin his routine.

He was working on the bench press when he heard a voice behind him.

"Would you like me to spot for you?"

Murphy looked up as he pushed the two hundred pounds

above his chest and let out some air. Hank Baines was standing behind his bench, dressed in baggy gray sweats that masked his muscular physique.

"Sure," he said as the bar came down and went up again.

Murphy finished his set and then sat up. He took a few breaths and turned and shook Baines's hand.

"I haven't seen you here before," said Murphy.

"To be honest, this is a little early for me," Baines admitted. "But I thought I might run into you. I was hoping we could talk."

"No problem. But you're going to have to wait until I get through my routine. It's kind of hard to talk when you're pushing a couple hundred pounds over your head."

Baines laughed. "Okay," he said. "Let's get to it."

Half an hour later, the two men were sitting on a workout bench, catching their breath between sets. "You really like to make it hard for yourself, don't you," Baines said.

"You've got to be kidding. I was just trying to keep up with you." Murphy grinned. "So what's on your mind? How's Tiffany doing?"

Baines smiled. "Great. Just great. I wanted to say thanks for the advice you gave me. I've tried my best to be less critical. To look for ways to say positive things, and, well, it seems to be having an effect. Going to church seems to have calmed her down. And whatever your friend Shari said to Tiffany, it's really changed her attitude. She actually apologized to me for her wild behavior." He shook his head, smiling. "That I thought I'd never see."

"That's great. You two obviously care for each other. You just needed to realize it." Murphy looked at Baines, and he could see he was still troubled. "And how's Jennifer doing?"

"Funny you should ask. As a father I seem to be doing better. As a husband, not so good. Now that Tiffany and I have stopped shouting at each other, I can really hear the silences between Jennifer and me."

Baines picked up some dumbbells and began a set of curls. Murphy joined him.

"You find it difficult to talk to each other?"

Baines shook his head. "Jennifer doesn't like any kind of conflict and just clams up and won't talk."

"What does her clamming up do to you?"

"It drives me nuts. I get so frustrated when she won't even yell and shout at me if she's mad, I just leave the house and slam the door."

"What happens when she does talk?" asked Murphy as he set the weights down.

"We'll be discussing a problem and I'll explain to her why her way won't work and why we should do it differently. I try to be real patient, to show her how she hasn't thought it through completely."

"Sounds like you might not be giving her a chance to disagree with you. Maybe that's why she withdraws," said Murphy with a firm smile.

Baines said nothing. Murphy could tell that he might have struck a nerve.

"How long has this been going on?"

"About a year."

Murphy made a calculated guess as he looked Baines in the eye.

"Are you seeing anyone else?"

Baines tensed and the color drained from his face. His nod was almost imperceptible.

"It's a little difficult trying to make two relationships work, isn't it?"

Baines's lips tightened and again he nodded his head slowly.

"You know, Hank, it's been my experience that people who have gone through a divorce end up with a lot of regrets. The biggest one usually is they didn't try harder to make it work. The excitement of an affair is only a fantasy. One day you wake up to the fact that the new person has just as many hang-ups and problems as your present spouse. Believe it or not, you can have communication problems with them too. Besides having to carry a load of guilt. It's just not worth the price."

Murphy could tell Baines needed to think about what he'd just said. "Come on, let's cool down with a jog in the park."

About fifteen minutes into the jog they began to walk. Baines still hadn't responded to Murphy's plea for marital fidelity, but Murphy felt he was receptive.

"Tell me something, Hank. What do you do when you come home after a day at work?"

"I usually change my clothes and sit down and read the newspaper or watch some TV before dinner."

"I used to do that when Laura was alive too. Then one day I realized that we weren't communicating. She wanted to talk at night and I wanted to go to sleep. I decided that instead of putting my feet up when I got home, I would spend that time focusing my attention on the most important person in my life. When do you and Jennifer usually have your talks about heavy issues?"

"Well, I haven't really thought about it. I guess it's usually late at night after Tiffany has gone to bed. Why do you ask?"

"You might think this sounds crazy, but studies show that marital discussions after 9:00 P.M. usually have a tendency to go downhill. Maybe it would be good to choose a different time, when you're both not so tired."

"Sounds like very practical advice. Now can I ask you a question?" said Baines.

"Sure."

"Did you and Laura ever have any big fights?"

"I guess we had our share. Being a Christian doesn't mean that you're perfect. But you have spiritual resources to draw upon, like I mentioned before. In the Bible."

"For example."

"There's a verse I committed to memory, because I wanted to be the best husband I could. It says, *And you husbands must love your wives and never treat them harshly*. There were times that I have to admit I treated Laura harshly."

Baines could sense the genuine regret in Murphy's voice. He wasn't just trying to make him feel better about his own behavior.

"I found that there were five things that were helpful during those times. The first was to learn to say 'I'm sorry.' That was hard for me, but the second thing was even harder. It was to admit I was wrong. That meant I had to swallow my pride. That was hard."

"Yeah. That's really hard for a perfectionist like me who always has to prove that I'm right."

"The third thing was to ask for forgiveness. That was hard

too. There were times when I didn't feel like it. But then I followed it up with two more things. Those were to say 'I love you' and that we would try and wipe the slate clean with the words *let's try again*."

"That all makes sense. But getting past your own pride, that's the hardest part."

"That's where being a Christian comes in. I couldn't have done all of that without the help of God. He gives us the strength when we turn our lives over to Him."

They walked back to the gym together.

"Hank, you mentioned that you thought that church was helping your daughter. Maybe you should consider that it could help you."

Baines looked doubtful. "Maybe."

Murphy left it there. He'd planted a seed. Now it was up to Baines.

SEVENTEEN

THE THREE-HOUR ROAD TRIP from Raleigh to Norfolk, Virginia, was one that usually brought back good memories. Often he and Laura had traveled north toward Weldon and then east past Murfreesboro and Sunbury, where they would find a place to eat. They would then drive up through the Great Dismal Swamp to Norfolk and then over to Virginia Beach near Cape Henry. As the familiar landmarks triggered little flashbacks to those carefree days, Murphy began to wonder why he wasn't feeling relaxed—why, in fact, his gut was churning.

Was it because he'd told Hank Baines his marriage to Laura had been less than one hundred percent perfect? Had that been a betrayal of her memory? No, that was ridiculous. He hadn't mentioned Laura's being in the wrong, only his own failings. And there was no merit in glossing over them—not if another person was being open and honest with him about his own marriage problems.

So what was bothering him?

Betrayal.

For some reason the little word stuck in his mind and wouldn't go away.

Then another little word joined it, and suddenly it all fell into place.

Isis.

He was feeling guilty because of his feelings toward Isis. Feelings he was only this minute admitting he even had.

He gripped the steering wheel tighter. Since Laura's death, the last thing on his mind had been another relationship. As far as he was concerned, he'd found his soul mate, his life mate, in Laura, and no one could ever replace her in his heart. He would wait patiently, alone, his aching heart nourished by memories, until they were finally reunited in heaven.

He didn't want to fall in love with someone else. He *couldn't* fall in love with someone else.

Stifling a curse, he tried to concentrate on the moving landscape. St. Paul's Church caught his eye. He focused on recalling every fact he could about the church. It had been built in 1739 and was one of the few buildings that had survived the British bombardment of Norfolk during the Revolutionary War.

Being the headquarters for the Atlantic Command, Norfolk was definitely a Navy town. Murphy saw ships and Navy personnel everywhere. Which thankfully reminded him what this trip was all about.

He headed to the west along the Elizabeth River.

It wasn't long before he turned in to the driveway of Vern Peterson's house. Vern was out in front mowing the lawn, and Kevin, his three-year-old, was playing with a toy lawn mower, trying to imitate his father. Kevin had Vern's red hair and green eyes, and seeing them together banished Murphy's blues instantly.

Vern turned off the mower, scooped up his son, and gave Murphy a mock salute.

Murphy put the car in park and returned the salute with a smile. Vern put his son down and the two men gave each other a bear hug while Kevin hopped excitedly at Vern's feet, wanting to know what all the fuss was about. Eventually Vern picked him up again with one brawny arm. "This is Michael Murphy. *Professor* Michael Murphy. Can you remember when you last saw him?"

The boy looked confused and Murphy helped him out. "It was a long time ago, Kevin. But I remember you. I seem to re-member you were dragging an old teddy bear around that was bigger than you were."

The boy giggled. "Tramps!"

"Those were the days," Vern laughed. "When all he needed was a raggedy old bear. Now it's video games and DVDs and goodness-knows-what."

Vern's wife, Julie, came running out the house and flung her arms around Murphy. She was a petite brunette with a pixie-like face that always wore a mischievous smile, and Murphy thought back to one of the last times he'd seen her. It had been his and Laura's wedding anniversary and the four of them had been celebrating in a downtown Raleigh restaurant fancier than any of them could afford, reminiscing about their wedding, when Vern had been his best man and Julie had been Laura's maid of honor.

He gave Julie a hug and stood back to look at her. "Julie, you seem to be the only person round here who hasn't gotten any bigger since I last saw you."

She grinned and put a hand to his cheek. "You say the sweetest things, Murphy. Now, come on inside the house. Dinner's about ready, and I know you and Vern have things to talk about."

Murphy waited until the last mouthful of apple pie had been washed down with homemade cider and the dishes had been cleared before strolling out onto the porch with Vern, where they settled into a pair of old rockers.

"Tell me, Vern, when was the last time you flew a chopper?"

Vern looked sideways at him. "I think you know the answer to that, Murphy. Not since Kuwait."

He didn't need to elaborate. Vern had been headquartered out of Kuwait when General Schwarzkopf began the advance on the Republican Guard. The Iraqi army had been crushed in about one hundred days. The thirty-eight-day air campaign had broken their morale. The Iraqi troops were tired, hungry, and weary after over a month of relentless bombing. They had surrendered by the thousands.

"I remember the statistics," said Murphy. "We lost four tanks and they lost four thousand. We lost one piece of artillery and they lost 2,140 pieces. They lost two hundred forty planes and we lost forty-four."

"We weren't so lucky with the helicopters," said Vern. "We lost seventeen and they lost only seven. In fact, the ship I flew was hit twice but didn't go down."

The talk about war faded out and Peterson looked at Murphy.

"Michael, you've got something up your sleeve, what is it?"

"I need your flying expertise. You have experience in flying at both high and low altitudes."

"So you want me to fly to Canada?" said Vern with a grin.

"A little farther than that." Murphy paused. "I want you to join my discovery team to search for Noah's Ark."

Peterson shot forward in his chair.

"You want me to fly over Ararat? You've got to be kidding!"

"Okay, Vern. Don't bite my head off." Murphy went on to explain how he needed Peterson to fly in supplies from the town of Dogubayazit, at the foot of Ararat, to the base camp high on the slopes of the mountain. He might not be able to land on the snow due to the steep slope, and he might have to air-drop supplies by cable. Peterson sat there and looked at Murphy.

"Well, I've done crazy things with a helicopter, but this would top them all."

Murphy assured him that the Parchments of Freedom Foundation would be funding the entire trip. He would make a very handsome salary and would be home in about three weeks after leaving. Peterson just shook his head in disbelief.

"You'll have to give me some time to think about it and talk it over with Julie. We haven't told you yet, but we're expecting another baby. I'm not sure how she'll feel about me leaving."

"That's great news about the baby, Vern. Congratulations. I'll understand if you don't feel you can do it."

"Not so fast," Vern said. "The baby coming means we need every cent I can lay my hands on. I could even build that extension Julie's always talking about. Anyway, Ararat's a pretty tough place to fly a chopper, but it's not like Kuwait. I mean, there won't be anyone shooting at us, right?"

"I hope not," Murphy said. "I hope not."

EIGHTEEN

THE LUSH GREEN FOREST *of Azer was a welcome sight after the long journey from the city of Noah. And when Noah, his sons, and their wives beheld the clear blue lake in the center of the forest, tasted its cool, refreshing water, and let their livestock graze on the rich meadow grass around its banks, many wondered why they had made so many sacrifices to defend the city in the dusty plain. Surely this was paradise, and this was where God meant them to be.*

Soon Noah and his sons began the process of cutting timber and erecting shelters. The women were busy with catching fish from the lake and preparing meals, as well as tending the horses, camels, sheep, goats, and cows that munched contentedly on the gentle grassy slopes.

During a time of rest, Noah at last opened the box that Tubal-cain had given him. Inside he found weights and measuring devices and instruments for surveying land. There were also three bronze plates with instructions engraved on them. But most intriguing of all was a golden chest with designs of leaves around the edges.

Carefully, Noah opened the golden chest. It was filled with various colored crystals, grains of what looked like sand, and small pieces of metal. He reached his hand in and scooped up the material. Instantly, he dropped the grains and pulled out his hand, which felt as if he had just put it into a furnace. He slammed the lid of the golden chest and ran to the lake, plunging his hand in the cooling waters. The fiery pain subsided gradually, but when he finally withdrew his hand, the skin was red and throbbing.

Returning to the box, he took out the three bronze plates and began to read. Each plate contained instructions for the use of the elements in the golden chest.

The first plate told how to identify rocks containing various types of metals. The second plate instructed how much of the elements should be used with each type of metal. And the third plate described the type of fire that would be needed to produce various metals.

Tubal-cain had a reputation as an inventor of metal artifacts and implements of warfare. And now, Noah realized, Tubal-cain had given him the secret of his singing swords.

During the next few months Noah and his sons built a forge and began to experiment with the instructions on the bronze plates. They collected various types of rocks and began a smelting process and added the elements from the golden chest.

They were amazed by the results.

Noah began to make axes, saws, and other tools for working with wood. He and his sons could not believe the strength of the metal and the keenness of its edge, and soon they had built fine, solid houses beside the lake.

But Noah knew Tubal-cain's gifts had another, more important use. One day he declared, "Now we must begin the ark of safety."

The loud snapping sound made Shem swivel around. It only took a split second to realize the danger.

"Look out! Run!"

Ham, Japheth, and Noah had also heard the fearful sound and had already started to move before they heard Shem's words. With a quick glance upward, they started running to the south.

It wasn't the first time they had heard the sound of a snapping rope giving way under the weight of the heavy beams. The horses were strong and could pull the weight, but the ropes would sometimes give out due to heavy use. It was becoming more and more difficult and dangerous to raise the beams as the ark grew in size.

Noah and his sons had begun their construction project in the middle of the forest of Azer. They had cleared a great space where the ark was to sit but had left the larger trees standing around the perimeter to use as hoists. By stringing ropes from tree to tree over the ark, and with the use of pulleys and horses, they could lift the beams into place.

But now one of the dark brown beams came crashing down to the floor of the ark. Besides putting a large gouge in the beams below, it knocked over two ladders and broke some of the bracing on the middle floor. If that weren't enough of a problem, it also knocked over the large barrel of pitch that they were using to help seal the cracks. The sticky liquid spilled everywhere, covering some of their hammers and a stack of wooden pegs that they used to hold the beams in place.

Noah's sons looked forlornly at the scene of destruction.

"What are we going to do?" exclaimed Japheth, his head in his hands.

"A whole day's work ruined!" joined Ham.

Shem just stood there and shook his head.

Only Noah seemed to be unaffected by the accident. "Well, sons, no one was hurt. The Lord has protected us."

"At first I wondered why the Lord gave us one hundred twenty years to build the ark," said Japheth. "But even with Tubal-cain's amazing tools, it's going to be a lifetime's work."

"That may be part of it," Noah said. "But the real reason God is giving us such a long period to build the ark is to give us time to get His message out to as many sinners in this wicked world as possible. They, too, can be saved from the coming flood if they will only turn from their evil thoughts, their corruption, and their worship of false gods."

No sooner were the words out of Noah's mouth than the harsh sound of laughter reached them. The forest of Azer was far from any major settlements, but the rumors about the ark had spread far and wide, and many people had come to see Noah and his sons laboring to build a huge sea-going vessel over one hundred miles from the ocean in the middle of a forest. Some simply stared in awed amazement, but most entertained themselves by jeering at them or even physically harassing them.

"You'll never get that thing built!"

"It doesn't look like your God is helping you now! Perhaps a different god would help you more!"

More laughter.

Noah waited until they had finished. "You can laugh now, but the day is coming when laughter will cease. God will punish evil men and women with a judgment of water," he said calmly. "The sky will break forth with rain, and wells of water will spring out of the ground. Every living creature that has the breath of air will die. The only place of safety will be the ark of God's protection. Please listen and turn from your wickedness!"

The peals of laughter resumed and a few pieces of rotten fruit were aimed in Noah's direction.

One man in particular decided to challenge Noah. "You have been building that ark for years, Noah. You have been preaching to us for years. Nothing has changed. People are born and people die. Living a life of goodness does not pay as well as stealing for a living."

At this the laughter turned to cheers.

Noah turned his back on the hecklers with a sigh. "Back to work, sons. We need to repair the damage and continue. Some people only live for the moment and do not think about the future, but we know better."

"I'm tired of their ridicule. I'd like to give them some judgment before floodwaters come!" said Shem.

"Like we did to Zattu and his army," added Ham.

Japheth nodded in agreement.

Noah looked each of them in the eye and said, "We will leave judgment in the hand of God. Within the next two weeks we must try to finish the structure for the third floor. We will then need to spend the next month cutting down more trees. We still have a long way to go. But God will give us strength."

Naamah and her daughters-in-law had come running when they heard the commotion of the falling beam. Fear had struck all of their hearts, for they knew the dangers of working so high off the ground. Had one of their men been injured or killed?

They were relieved to see that no one was injured, but the sarcastic comments of the spectators were deeply painful.

Bithiah broke into tears. "This is more than I can bear."

The other women gathered around to comfort her.

"Everywhere we go, people call us names and make fun of us. I can't go to the market without men making crude and suggestive comments. I'm afraid that they might attack me as they do the other women. My friends have left me and talk about me behind my back."

"I know it is hard," said Naamah as she gave her a hug. "Living a godly life is not an easy task. But when the devastation comes, they will not be laughing anymore. Whereas you and your sons will be saved."

Bithiah wiped the tears from her eyes. "But how much more will we have to endure before the flood comes? How long must we survive this torment?"

Naamah looked at Noah before replying. "Do not wish the day of devastation to come before its appointed time. Even for us, it will be more terrible than you can imagine."

NINETEEN

WHEN THE BUS finally came to a halt at the end of the winding mountain road, Tiffany Baines and her friends Lisa and Christy practically exploded off it. "This better be good, Tiff," warned Christy, shaking out her jet-black waist-length hair. Tiffany took one look at the lake and felt certain it was going to be. The mile-long finger of emerald-green water was nestled in a small valley surrounded by pines and oaks, and the mountains rose on all sides, making the setting incredibly dramatic. How could anyone not have a good time here?

But even though Lisa and Christy were her two closest friends, Tiffany was beginning to wonder if bringing them here had been a good idea after all. When she first told them about the retreat, she deliberately didn't add the word *church*. She figured there was no point in frightening them off before they got here, and she just trusted that once they did, the experience would be so different from their normal lives that they'd quickly find themselves caught up in it.

After all, a month ago Tiffany wouldn't have believed she could be going to church regularly—but now she found herself looking forward to it all week.

Dismissing her doubts, she put her arms around her friends and they ran down toward the main building on the lake shore. Finding their dorm, they unpacked quickly, then started exploring.

"The cute boys you promised us must be round here somewhere, right?" said Christy with a grin.

Pretty soon they had teamed up with another busload of students and together discovered the recreation room with its table tennis and pool tables. By the time they heard the bell summoning them to dinner, Lisa had beaten just about all comers on the pool table, and the girls high-fived their way into the main refectory.

After the meal, a young man in faded jeans and a gray sweatshirt stood up and introduced himself. "Hi, everybody, and welcome to Lake Herman. My name's Mark Ortman and I'm the youth director here. You probably all have different reasons for coming here today, but I'm going to tell you something that may surprise you. I hope it will also inspire you."

The talking and joking faded out as everybody waited to hear what he was going to say.

"You didn't arrive here by accident. God has a purpose for our lives—whether we've been paying attention to Him or not—and I sincerely believe He brought us all together now in this place at this time so He could reveal that purpose to us.

Being young nowadays means you've got messages being beamed at you twenty-four-seven from every direction. You've got TV, magazines, music, video games—all trying to grab your attention. Sometimes it seems there's no time and no place to just be quiet and tranquil and listen to God's voice talking to you. Well, that's what Lake Herman is all about." Quickly he put his hands up, palms out. "Okay, Okay, there's going to be a lot of crazy fun stuff too. But in this beautiful setting, away from all that noise, we're going to see if we can find the time to close our eyes and listen. Just listen. And see what God says to us. Because, believe me, He has a message for you, and it's the most important message you're ever going to hear." He clapped his hands. "All right, guys. Enough of listening to *me*. Remember, lights out at ten o'clock. Breakfast starts at eight, and our first meeting is at nine. Looking forward to seeing you all there."

Christy and Lisa turned toward Tiffany, and she could feel a death stare directed at her from both sides.

"Okay, guys. Maybe I forgot to mention this was a *church* retreat, but—"

"You didn't forget," Christy said, cutting her off. "You knew if you mentioned the word *church* it would have taken a bunch of, like, totally wild horses to drag us here. So what is it with you, Tiffany? What's *happened* to you?"

Tiffany could feel herself blushing, and she suddenly felt completely tongue-tied, but she really wanted her friends to understand what she'd been going through.

"You know I told you my dad was making me go to church on Sundays with my mom?"

"Uh-huh." They nodded.

"Well . . . he wasn't exactly *making* me. I mean, it wasn't my idea at the start, but after a couple times I sort of got into it and started really listening to what the pastor was saying—this guy Pastor Bob—and actually it was kind of, well, cool."

"*Cool?*" they chorused in disbelief.

Tiffany nodded. "Yes. Cool. About looking at the big picture, and what's going to happen in the future, and why we're here."

Lisa rolled her eyes. "The big picture. Have some fun and then you die, girlfriend. *That's* the big picture."

Tiffany knew she might be losing her best friends, but strangely she felt more sure of herself the more they mocked.

"No it isn't," she insisted. "There's more to it. A lot more. And if you don't listen, then you're not just going to waste your life, but you're risking everlasting damnation. I don't want that to happen."

Christy and Lisa just looked at her, and Tiffany hoped against hope they weren't going to burst out laughing. But they didn't. They both put their arms around her and Christy said, "Listen, Tiff, *just* because we're best friends and we love you, we're going to overlook the fact that you brought us here on totally false pretenses, and we're going to tough it out and stay here through the weekend and do this quiet listening thing, and then, when we get back to Preston . . ."

"Boy, are we going to get wasted!" said Lisa.

They all laughed and hugged one another and Tiffany closed her eyes as she felt the tears come and she said a quick prayer that Christy and Lisa would hear the voice before the weekend was out.

———

At the Saturday morning meeting Mark Ortman challenged everybody on their relationships with others. Did they have anyone in their life that they hated? Was there anyone that they needed to forgive? Were they obeying their parents and contributing to their families? Or were they just taking and never thinking to give back?

Tiffany was relieved that Lisa and Christy seemed to be listening intently, and afterward neither of them made fun of what Mark had been saying. Even so, all three gladly took the opportunity of burning up some energy in physical activity for the rest of the day—kayaking on the lake, playing volleyball on the beach, and hiking on the wooded slopes.

By the time they'd showered and got ready for the evening meeting, their minds were open to new ideas and new challenges to the usual way they thought about things.

This time Mark Ortman delivered a stirring talk on how Jesus suffered and died in our place. He did it because of His great love and forgiveness for all men and women, Mark told them. Something about the way he talked of Jesus as if He was a real person whom Mark knew personally made them feel that He really had sacrificed Himself for each one of them.

"Tonight, we are going to have a Discipline of Silence," said Ortman finally. "After the meeting, I want you to go outside and get alone for fifteen minutes. Just you and God. Without any of your friends. I want you to ask yourself this question: Who is running your life? Either you are or God is. Maybe tonight you need to do some business with your Creator. Please leave the building quietly."

Everyone silently filed out of the meeting hall. Tiffany lost sight of Lisa and Christy as they walked into the woods beside the lake, found a log by a stream, and sat down.

This is not a hard question to answer, she thought as the quiet sounds of the forest seeped into her consciousness. *I've been running my life and it's gotten to be a mess.*

Hesitantly, feeling a little awkward even though she knew she was alone, she began to talk aloud.

"God, I don't really know how to talk to you. I'm not really sure what it means to ask you to come into my life. But tonight, I want you to come into my life. It is a mess. Please forgive me for my sins. Change my life. Please help me to learn to live for you. I believe that you died for me. I believe that you rose from the grave to make a home for me in heaven. I invite you in. Please come."

Tiffany couldn't say any more. Suddenly she was overcome with tears. The sobs shook her body. She cried until there were no tears left. For a few minutes she just sat there and stared at the magnificent star-studded sky.

Then a thought came to her. *I need to call Mom and Dad.*

She walked out of the forest and back inside the main building to the lobby area where the public phones were located. She was surprised to see it was filled with other young people doing the same thing. All of them, it seemed, had a burning need to talk to their loved ones. After waiting in line for about a half hour, she eventually got hold of her parents. Her tears started all over again as she tried to tell them what had happened and how she was feeling and how she wanted to change her life. By the end of the conversation all three of them were crying.

But as she walked away from the phone booth, she felt happier than she had ever been in her life.

TWENTY

DEEP WITHIN THE subterranean vault, the Seven had moved to the cavernous dining room. An oversize crystal chandelier hung from the ceiling with the lights dimmed, turning it into a place of shadows whose limits seemed to extend far beyond the walls. A deep recess in one wall housed the fireplace, where giant logs were crackling fiercely. In the surrounding blackness it looked like the mouth of hell.

The candles on the large round walnut table flickered on the seven faces as they sat across from one another. The main course of wild boar stuffed with quail had been finished, and they were sipping wine from crystal goblets.

Mendez was the first to break the eerie silence.

"Do we know any more about what might be discovered on Ararat?"

The somber voice of Bartholomew responded.

"Only that there has been some discovery regarding potassium forty and the possible extension of life. We do know that Murphy is planning an expedition in search of the ark. Talon knows what to do."

"And what will become of Professor Murphy?" asked the hatchet-nosed man with gray hair.

"We are allowing Professor Murphy to do some . . . *spadework* for us," Bartholomew replied. "Of course, when he has outlived his usefulness he will be eliminated."

Everyone again lifted their glasses in a toast.

Bartholomew surveyed the smiling faces as they seemed to float happily in the semidarkness and said, "Do not become overconfident, my friends. There is still much to be done. Many steps yet to be taken on the road to ultimate control. We must institute a system of universal commerce, for one thing."

Then the Englishman spoke. Sir William Merton looked like a harmless, slightly portly English cleric. Especially with the white collar around his neck and his black shirt. But, as he continued to speak, his English accent began to disappear. His voice became deeper and echoed strangely in the chamber. Those across the table could see a slight red glow in his eyes in the flickering light.

"But make no mistake, progress is being made. Great strides toward our goal. The leaders of 138 nations have joined together endorsing the establishment of a World Court. The European Community gets ever nearer to becoming a single nation. The seeds for the transfer of the United Nations to Iraq have been planted. Soon oil money will be filling their coffers. All is moving as planned!"

Merton's voice became stronger as he warmed to his theme.

"Christianity is under attack in America and throughout the world. Through our influence it will soon by a byword for intolerance and cruelty. Its death knell has been sounded, I tell you. And our one world religion will be ready to take over!"

Then a woman in a green dress spoke in a faintly Germanic accent. "I agree, William, we are making progress on all fronts. Through Barrington Communications and our access to cable-TV news channels, our agenda is gaining ground in the media. The evangelicals are in retreat, without a doubt. And our plans to bring all commercial activity under control of a single authority are well advanced. One world government, one world religion. It is all within our grasp." She nodded toward Bartholomew. "Though, of course, we must take nothing for granted. We must continue to work at maximum efficiency toward the goal."

She paused and contemplated her wine goblet for a moment, seemingly lost in thought. Then she turned back toward Bartholomew.

"But I'm sure I am not alone among us in wondering about . . . the one who will come to lead us. You must know, John. You must know something! When is he coming? Where is he now?"

Even though the woman was one of the most powerful bankers in Europe, a woman used to making billion-dollar decisions without turning a hair, she was beginning to sound desperate, almost childlike. Bartholomew took pity on her, knowing that indeed she was not alone in her desire to know.

He steepled his hands in front of him. "I understand your eagerness, of course. Each one of us yearns for the day when we shall see him face to face and hear his voice. And that day will come. Soon! But until that time, we must possess ourselves in patient readiness." He smiled. "We shall not know the day, nor the hour . . . but rest assured, his journey has begun. He is on his way to us, even now!"

He stood up, raising his goblet, and the others followed suit. They drank a silent toast, each of them contemplating the word he had deliberately left unspoken.

Antichrist.

Then they turned as one and hurled their goblets into the fireplace. The echoes of glass shattering and wine hissing in the flames sounded like the end of the world.

TWENTY-ONE

SHARI WAS RIGHT in the middle of placing an Egyptian papyrus scroll into the hyperbaric chamber for rehydration when the phone rang.

Carefully she laid it down on the worktable in front of the chamber and walked to Murphy's desk. "Hello, this is Professor Murphy's office, may I help you?"

There was silence on the other end of the line. "Hello, is there anybody there?"

More silence. But Shari had the uncomfortable feeling that someone was there, listening. As the silence lengthened, almost unbearably, the feeling grew stronger. She found herself rooted to the spot, the phone glued to her ear, unable to speak or to cut the connection.

Then suddenly she knew, without a trace of doubt, who was

on the other end of the phone. Putting the phone down carefully on the desk, she walked into the next room and coughed to get Murphy's attention.

"Was that the phone? Someone I need to talk to, Shari?"

She nodded.

"Who is it?"

She looked down at her shoes. "Um, he didn't say."

Murphy gave her a quizzical look, picked up a rag, and wiped his hands as he walked to the phone.

"This is Michael Murphy."

There was a slight pause on the other end of the line. "Well, well, Murphy. Dried out yet? Or are you still feeling a little damp?"

"Methuselah!" Murphy gripped the phone tighter. "I almost died in that cave!"

"Tsk, tsk. I do wish young people would take more responsibility for their own actions. It was your choice, Murphy. You know the risks. You know the rules." He chuckled. "But maybe I was a little harsh on you this time. In fact, I was more than a little surprised you made it out of that place—and with those two adorable little puppies too. Your soft heart is going to be your undoing one of these days, you know."

"At least that's not something you have to worry about," Murphy growled.

"Temper, temper, Murphy. Where would you be if it wasn't for me? You certainly wouldn't be in possession of that rather interesting piece of wood, now, would you?"

Murphy didn't say anything, and Methuselah began to chuckle that low, rasping laugh of his.

"Don't tell me you've gone and lost it, Murphy. After all the trouble you went to. After all the trouble *I* went to!"

"It's no joke, old man. People have been killed. A friend of mine was almost—"

"I know, I know," Methuselah cut him off. "Most regrettable. Most regrettable. Look, you fool, why do you think I'm calling? It's not to check on your health. I've got better things to do. I heard about the break-in at the museum and it didn't take a genius to put two and two together. Our little piece of driftwood is gone, and all its secrets. Which means you might be in need of a little extra help. A couple of extra clues to help you on your way."

The idea of being helped on his way by Methuselah was not a very pleasant prospect, Murphy thought. But beggars can't be choosers, and right now Methuselah seemed to have all the cards. "All right, Methuselah. Go ahead. I'm all ears."

"You could sound a little more enthusiastic, Murphy. Grateful, even. This is a freebie, no risking of life and limb involved."

"You're all heart," grunted Murphy.

"By my watch it is almost ten o'clock, Murphy. You should be receiving a FedEx delivery momentarily. If you want to get back on track, just follow the directions. Good luck, Murphy."

Murphy was determined to make Methuselah tell him what was going on, but the line was dead.

He looked up and Shari was at his shoulder. Her eyes were wide and she was nervously fingering the crucifix at her throat.

"What did he want?"

Murphy looked at his watch. "Hard to say with that old coot. But we should be getting another surprise package any minute."

Shari had her arms folded. "I really don't think you should—"

A knock at the door cut her off. Murphy raised his eyebrows and Shari sighed and went to the door, where the FedEx guy was waiting. She handed Murphy the package with a frown and watched nervously as he opened it. A three-by-five card slid out.

IN A CIRCLE IS A SQUARE . . .
THE ANSWERS YOU SEEK WILL BE FOUND THERE.
7365 EAST WATER STREET
MOREHEAD CITY

Murphy handed the note to Shari to read.

"What does it mean?" she asked.

"Only one way to find out," he said, grabbing his jacket.

It was about a 130-mile drive from Raleigh to Newbern and then on to Morehead City. During the two hours, Murphy had time to think about Methuselah's note.

Why would Methuselah choose a place like Morehead City?

Murphy racked his memory of the history of North Carolina's Crystal Coast. He remembered that John Motley Morehead was governor in the early 1840s. Morehead wanted to develop the seaport town into a great commercial city. It was ideally situated where Shepherd's Point intersected with the Newport River and Beaufort Inlet. However, the Civil War interrupted and destroyed his plans. Then Murphy remembered that Morehead City had a section known as the Promised Land. It was settled by refugees from the whaling communities on Shackleford Banks.

The Promised Land! His clue must have something to do with the Old Testament. Well, at least that's a start, Murphy thought to himself.

At about a quarter to two Murphy found the address. It was an old round warehouse building that looked as if it had been constructed around the time of the Civil War. Set within the redbrick walls were a number of loading docks with large wooden doors. Teams of horses with wagons must have backed up to the loading docks before trucks were invented, Murphy thought as he explored the cavernous space.

There were no cars or trucks in the deserted loading area. The only light that he could see was a single bulb hanging over a door with wooden steps leading up to it. That lonely light in the midst of darkness was his invitation to enter.

Murphy got out his flashlight and walked around the circular building. Nothing looked strange or out of place— just old. He stopped before the lighted steps and looked around. He then took a deep breath to let off some tension and started up. With each step a loud creaking echoed through the building. He reached down to the door handle and turned it. It was unlocked.

As Murphy opened the door he found himself in a large

warehouse room. In the center was a boxing ring with a single light hanging above. Folding chairs were set up on each of the four sides. The rest of the room was dark.

Murphy shined his flashlight around through the empty darkness. No one was there. He caught a glimpse of several doors that looked like they must lead to some type of offices. The doors were closed.

I guess they must be using this old place for illegal fights, he thought.

Murphy approached the boxing ring cautiously. In the center of the ring was an envelope. He set his flashlight on the edge of the ring and crawled through the ropes. Inside the envelope was a delicate line drawing of an angel with outspread wings.

Murphy was pondering its meaning when he heard a cough from somewhere in the darkness.

"Plenty of time to wrestle with that!" Methuselah's grating laugh reverberated around the room.

Murphy then heard a noise behind him and turned. Climbing through the ropes was a huge man. As he stood up straight and took a step forward, Murphy felt the vibrations under his feet. The huge man was dressed in a form-fitting striped leotard that showed off his impressive musculature. With his long, waxed mustache and shaved head, he looked like an old-fashioned circus strongman. As if reading Murphy's thoughts, he grinned and flexed his biceps.

This isn't a boxing ring, this is a wrestling ring! Murphy thought to himself. *There's too much give in the platform.*

"You said this was a freebie, old man!" Murphy protested as the giant took another step toward him.

"There's no such thing, Murphy! You should know that by now," Methuselah cackled. "TV is such a bore these days—we need to make our own entertainment, don't you think?"

Murphy was about to frame a sarcastic retort, when the giant lunged at him, three hundred fifty pounds of muscle and bone slamming into his chest like a souped-up steamroller. Murphy bounced into the ropes and hung there for a moment, gasping for breath, while the giant turned and paced the ring with his hands above his head, as if acknowledging ghostly applause from the empty seats.

Murphy desperately tried to think. How could he turn his martial-arts training to account against this behemoth? One body slam or bear hug and he was a dead man. If he let the giant get close to him, it would all be over in seconds—but if he kept out of his reach, how was he ever going to beat him?

Suddenly he didn't have any more time to figure it out, as the giant let out a roar and all Murphy could see was a mass of rippling stripes hurtling toward him.

Instinctively, Murphy pivoted on his left heel and sent a roundhouse kick flashing toward the giant's temple. But as he braced himself against the impact, he felt his foot being swatted away by a huge forearm, then a hand grabbed the front of his shirt and suddenly he was spinning through the air like a rag doll.

As he landed on the canvas with a thud, he could hear Methuselah's demented cheering. "Bravo! Bravo! Come on, Murphy, on your feet. Give me my money's worth! I'm afraid if you continue to lie there, my supersize friend will be obliged to squish you like a bug!"

Murphy looked up, and the giant was swaying across the ring toward him as if that was exactly what he had in mind. He staggered to his feet, clutching his left shoulder as if it was broken. The beginnings of a plan were forming in his mind.

He just had to hope the giant would be content to spin it out for his master's pleasure.

The giant grinned, like a cat eyeing a bird with a broken wing, and that gave Murphy some badly needed encouragement. *If he thinks I'm too badly injured to be a threat, maybe he'll lower his guard long enough—*

Murphy had no time to finish the thought as the giant scooped him up effortlessly and hoisted him above his head. Holding Murphy's body like a barbell, he displayed his prize to the four sides of the ring and Murphy could almost hear the raucous catcalls and jeers of a drunken mob ringing in his ears.

Then the floor rushed up to meet him as he was slammed mercilessly to the canvas. Violent as it was, the impact barely winded him, since he'd already prepared himself, allowing his body to go as limp as possible. It was a hard technique to put into practice, because instinct made every muscle tense against impact, but it was one Murphy was grateful he had taken the trouble to learn.

Five years earlier, on an archaeological dig outside Shanghai, Murphy had befriended a young Cantonese archaeology student named Terence Li. Murphy had been happy to share his knowledge of the latest archaeological techniques with the young man, and to show his appreciation Li had taught him his family's style of kung fu—a rare honor for a *gweilo*, a foreigner.

On their first day of practice, Murphy had been surprised to see that Li wasn't adopting the pose of a crane or a tiger but was staggering around like a drunk as he invited Murphy to try to land a punch on him. Murphy had been amazed to find how difficult it was—and then was even more amazed when Li sent him crashing to the mat with a well-aimed heel strike to the temple.

The secret of drunken-man fighting, Li explained with a smile, is that his opponent thinks he has already won before the fight has begun. When the drunken man falls, he is soft, like a rag. He does not hurt himself. When he stands up, he is hard to hit, like a sapling swaying in the wind. And when he strikes, no one expects it.

Now Murphy was putting the drunken-man techniques to the ultimate test as he swayed about the ring like a man who could hardly put one foot in front of the other. And by rights the pounding he'd already had *should* have turned him into jelly. But by willing his body into total looseness, he was surprised to find how easy it was to absorb the punishment the giant was handing out.

"When you go out, get very drunk, you don't know how you get home. You keep falling down, bump into lampposts, walls, everything. But when you wake up next day, everything fine! No broken bones! Maybe just a bad headache. This is the secret of the drunken man," Li had told him.

"I'm afraid I don't drink anything stronger than root beer," Murphy had responded. "So I'll just have to take your word for it."

But if I get out of this alive, Murphy thought to himself, *dinner's on me next week, Terence, that's for sure.*

Murphy got slowly to his feet, reaching out to grab one of the ropes to steady himself, his other hand hanging limply at his side. The giant was beaming as he slowly circled the ring, striking bodybuilder poses and waving to the nonexistent crowd. *Quite an act*, Murphy thought. *Let's hope he's bought mine. Next time I figure he's in for the kill.*

As if reading Murphy's thoughts, the giant spun round and fixed him with an evil leer. Murphy swallowed hard. Away to his right, he could hear a slow hand-clap.

This is it.

Murphy groaned theatrically as the giant pushed back against the ropes on the far side of the ring, filled his lungs, and began his charge. One, two, three enormous strides and he was speeding like a runaway train. Murphy held his breath, waited for the last possible split second, then danced to his left and spun around, his right leg whirling in a wide arc so that his heel connected with the back of the giant's head. Not expecting any resistance, the giant was taken completely by surprise, and the perfectly directed kick added just enough momentum to his headlong charge to lift him off his feet and out of the ring. As he sailed over the ropes, Murphy could tell that he'd already lost consciousness.

The thunderous crash as he landed in a pile of chairs was just the icing on the cake.

There was a screech as Methuselah scooted away from the crash site and made for one of the exits.

With his last breath Murphy shouted after him, "These things are always faked, Methuselah! Didn't you know?"

A door slammed and Murphy sank to the canvas. This time

he wasn't pretending. Note to self, he thought: The next time one of Methuselah's packages landed on his desk, it'd be Returned to Sender, Address Unknown. He didn't know how many more of the old man's surprises his body could take, but there had to be a limit. Especially since this time he'd been suckered into performing purely for Methuselah's entertainment.

On the way back to his car, Murphy was amazed to find that the drunken-man technique really had spared him any major injury. He knew he'd be hurting for a day or two, but at least there were no actual dislocations, just a few muscle pulls and bruises.

On the drive home, Murphy had plenty of time to think about the strange wrestling bout. It did seem as if Methuselah had finally stopped playing by even his own twisted rules. After all, Murphy had won the bout fair and square—something Methuselah obviously hadn't been expecting since he didn't hang around to give Murphy his prize. Weird. Very weird.

Unless Murphy had already been given it.

He started to go over every detail again in his mind. The Promised Land. So they were talking Old Testament. Then what? Of course—the sketch. An angel with outspread wings. Okay, an Old Testament angel. That didn't narrow it down much.

So what else did he know?

He drummed his fingers on the steering wheel in frustration. Maybe the drawing meant something else. He should have kept it, looked at it more closely. He'd gone ten rounds with a homicidal giant, and all the time—

That was it! Of course! The wrestling match. Who'd wrestled with an angel in the Old Testament?

Jacob.

And what did Jacob have to do with Noah's Ark? Murphy's mind was in high gear now. What else could it be but the Monastery of St. Jacob, the one at the foot of Mount Ararat?

Murphy pulled over at a gas station and called Isis on his cell phone.

She seemed pleased to hear his voice. "I've been training hard, Murphy. You better watch out when we get to Ararat. I'll race you to the top—loser buys dinner."

Murphy grinned. "I seem to be buying everyone dinner now."

"How come?"

"Never mind. Listen, could you go over to the National Archives and the Library of Congress and see what you can find out about St. Jacob of Nisibis and the Monastery of St. Jacob in Turkey?"

"No problem. Why?"

"I'm not sure," Murphy replied. "But it could be important."

When he got back to his office Shari had already left. Murphy began to pore over his books and manuscripts relating to Noah's Ark, searching for any references to St. Jacob. He already knew that the monastery had been destroyed by the earthquake of 1840. It had been buried by a landslide from the Ahora Gorge. All of the ancient books and manuscripts, as well as the artifacts, had been destroyed.

It was late in the afternoon when his phone rang.

"Michael! I did a search on St. Jacob and the monastery. There wasn't much, I'm afraid."

Murphy's heart sank. Had he followed the wrong clues?

"But I did find one rather interesting book on the travels of

Sir Reginald Calworth, written in 1836. In one chapter he mentions visiting the Monastery of St. Jacob and talking with a Bishop Kartabar. It seems that the bishop allowed him to look at the ancient manuscripts in their library. He also was taken to a special room where what he calls *the treasures from Noah's Ark* were kept. The book mentions that there were over fifty items that the priests claimed came off the ark."

Murphy whistled, trying to imagine what the items could possibly have been.

"But that's not the best part," Isis went on. "Calworth makes a passing comment that caught my eye. He says, and let me quote, *After we left the room of treasures, the Bishop told me he had sent some of the manuscripts and artifacts to the town of Erzurum in the care of priests.*"

"Is that it? He doesn't say where in Erzurum?"

"No. From there Sir Reginald goes back to describing the local flora and fauna, the culture of the local people, the weather, et cetera."

"Erzurum," Murphy repeated. "Maybe the secrets aren't on the mountain at all."

TWENTY-TWO

"OKAY, YOU GUYS. Hand them over. And no funny business."

There was a ripple of laughter as the students filed past Murphy and handed in their assignments before going back to their seats in the lecture hall. He was impressed. Everybody seemed to have written something. Perhaps the subject of Noah's Ark and the Flood really had stirred their imaginations.

"Did any of you discover anything of interest that you would like to share with the group?"

A hand went up to the right of Murphy.

"Yes, Jerome!"

"Professor Murphy, I learned that Noah was the best financier in the Bible. He floated his entire stock while the whole world was in liquidation!"

Murphy smiled. Joking around was fine with him, as long as they could focus on the serious stuff as well. He was about to gently steer the conversation in that direction when Clayton, the class clown, piped up. If people were telling jokes, he wasn't going to get left on the sidelines.

"Professor Murphy, I found out that they didn't play cards on Noah's Ark. That was because Mrs. Noah sat on the deck!"

The whole class groaned.

"Well," Murphy said. "If you spent as much time and effort on your assignment as you did on your jokes . . . we're in trouble!" He waited for the laughter to die down. "Does anyone have anything on more of a serious nature? Yes, Jill!"

"Professor Murphy, I was amazed to discover that around the world scientists have found fossils of sea creatures high in the mountains. This gives credibility to the concept of a universal flood that covered all the mountains of the earth."

He nodded. "Sam, you have a comment?"

"Yes. In my research I found out, like Jill, that sea fossils were found in the mountains near Ararat at the ten-thousand-foot level. That's over three hundred miles inland from the Persian Gulf."

Another hand went up.

"I read that fossils of sand dollars and clams have been found behind the Dogubayazit Hotel at the five-thousand-foot level. Dogubayazit is the town at the foot of Mount Ararat. The article went on to say that the ministers of the interior and defense of Turkey say that fossils like sea horses, and other fossils of ocean origin have been found as high as fourteen thousand feet on Mount Ararat."

"Professor Murphy! I found some information that Nicholas Van Arkle, a Dutch glaciologist, took pictures of fish and seashells near the ark rock on the western rim of the Ahora Gorge on Mount Ararat."

Hands were beginning to be raised all over the lecture hall. Murphy nodded to himself in quiet satisfaction. Their imaginations had been stirred, all right.

Don West raised his hand.

"Professor Murphy. I tried to follow the various flood stories that are mentioned around the world. I was amazed to find that there are over five hundred different stories about a worldwide flood. I think that *The Epic of Gilgamesh* is the most famous."

"You're right, Don, it is. It's amazingly similar to the biblical account of the Flood. In fact, I have prepared a paper for you that gives a comparison."

Shari passed out the sheet to the students.

	Genesis	Gilgamesh
Extent of flood	Global	Global
Cause	Man's wickedness	Man's sins
Intended for whom?	All mankind	One city & all mankind
Sender	Yahweh [God]	Assembly of "gods"
Name of hero	Noah	Utnapishtim
Hero's character	Righteous	Righteous
Means of announcement	Direct from God	In a dream
Ordered to build boat?	Yes	Yes
Did hero complain?	Yes	Yes
Height of boat	Several stories	Several stories

Compartments inside	Many	Many
Doors	One	One
Windows	At least one	At least one
Outside coating	Pitch	Pitch
Shape of boat	Rectangular	Square
Human passengers	Family members	Family & few friends
Other passengers	All species of animals	All species of animals
Means of flood	Ground water / rain	Heavy rain
Duration of flood	40 days & nights	Short 6 days & nights
Test to find land	Release of birds	Release of birds
Types of birds	Raven & 3 doves	Dove, swallow, raven
Ark landing spot	Mount Ararat	Mount Nisir
Sacrificed after flood	Yes, by Noah	Yes, by Utnapishtim
Blessed after flood	Yes	Yes

As they read, Murphy continued. "The Epic of Gilgamesh was discovered by a British bank clerk named George Smith in 1872. In his spare time he translated four-thousand-year-old cuneiform tablets that were dug up in the old Assyrian capital of Nineveh near the Persian Gulf. During his ten years of labor he discovered the Gilgamesh story about a character named Utnapishtim. As you can see, it was very similar to the biblical story.

"Now, in addition to the Gilgamesh story, there are many, many countries throughout the world where the story of a global flood has been passed down from one generation to another. While the specific details of these traditions may differ, there is no escaping that each of these cultures holds to a belief in a global flood occurring at some point in the past. I have made a partial list of the countries and peoples and ancient writers where these flood traditions exist. Shari, would you please pass this out?"

MIDDLE EAST & AFRICA
Babylon
Bapedi
Central Africa
Chaldea
Egypt
Hottentots
Jumala Tribe
Lower Congo
Masai Tribe
Otshi Tribe
Persia
Syria

PACIFIC ISLANDS
Alamblack Tribe
Alfoors of Ceram
Ami
Andaman Islands
Australia
Bunva
Dutch New Guinea
East Indian Island
Engano
Falwol Tribe
Fiji
Flores Island
Formosa
Hawaii
Kabidi Tribe
Kurnai Tribe
Leeward Islands
Maoris
Melanesia
Micronesia
Nais
New Britain
Otheite Island
Ot-Danoms
Polynesia
Queensland
Rotti Tribe
Samoa
Sea Dyaks
Sumatra
Tahiti
Toradjas
Valman Tribe

FAR EAST
Bahnara
Bengal Kohl
Benua-Jakun
Bhagavata
China
Cigpaws
India
Karens
Mahabharata
Matsya
Sudan
Tartary Mongols

EUROPE & ASIA
Apamea
Apollodorus
Athenian
Celts
Cos
Crete
Diodorus
Druids
Finland
Hellenucus
Iceland
Lapland
Lithuania
Lucian
Megaros
Norway
Ogyges
Ovid
Perirrhoos
Pindar
Plato
Plutarch
Rhodes
Romania
Russia
Samothrace
Siberia
Sithnide
Thessalonica
Transylvania
Wales

NORTH AMERICA
Acagchemens
Aleutian Indians
Algonquins
Appalachian Indians
Araphos
Arctic Eskimos
Athapascans
Blackfoot Indians
Cherokees
Chippewas
Cree
Dogribs
Eleuts
Flatheads
Greenland
Iroquois
Mandans
Nez Perces
Pimas
Thlinkuts
Yakimas

CENTRAL AMERICA
Aztecs
Antilles
Canaries
Cuba
Mayas
Mexico
Muratos
Nicaragua
Panama Indians
Toltecs

SOUTH AMERICA
Abederys
Achawois
Arawaks
Brazil
Caingans
Carayas
Incas
Macusis
Maypures
Orinoco Indians
Pamarys
Tamanacs

"As you can see, there are many groups around the world that have a flood tradition in their culture."

As Murphy was speaking, several people entered the lecture hall. He recognized two of his students, who were late and were entering sheepishly. The third person he thought he recognized. He was a tall man with very strong features. He was wearing a well-cut blue pinstripe suit. Murphy followed the athletic figure as he moved to the back of the auditorium. He leaned against the wall and faced the front. When he took off his sunglasses, Murphy could see his gray eyes even at a distance.

I know him. What's his name?

Murphy's attention was brought back to the front row. Paul Wallach had his hand raised. Shari looked a little apprehensive.

"Yes, Paul."

"Couldn't these different people have gotten similar stories from their relatives who may have traveled to another country? Or perhaps, couldn't some missionary have told them about the Flood and that is the reason they have flood stories?"

Murphy nodded. "I suppose that could be possible, but that would be a pretty big stretch, Paul. It is difficult to imagine that people from, say, the jungles of Papua New Guinea, had relatives who traveled very far. There are over 860 languages in that country alone. Missionaries have translated the Bible into only about 130 of those languages, and yet the newly discovered tribes still have a flood story.

"Let me give you an example. In the western district of Papua New Guinea, there is a tribe called the Samo-Kubo. When the missionaries arrived at this remote tribe, they found a flood tradition. The tribesmen believed that if you make lizards mad, they will bring another flood and destroy the world again. If previous missionaries had been there, they certainly would not have taught the tribesmen that lizards would destroy the world with a flood."

Murphy had Shari turn on the projector.

"Let me show you one slide of how the story of the Flood could have been passed on. You will see the arrows running away from the Mideast to all parts of the world. It is believed that after Noah landed on Ararat and the people began to multiply, they built the Tower of Babel. God then confused their languages and the people dispersed throughout the world. They could have taken the flood story with them. Over time, as the story was passed down, it was changed in each location. This seems a more logical conclusion as to why there are over five hundred flood traditions around the world. I believe that they came from one source. They had a common origin."

Murphy could see that Paul was trying to figure out the weak point in this argument. He could also see that Shari was beginning to have a difficult time with Paul. She looked uncomfortable as he frowned in concentration beside her.

"If what you are saying about the Flood is true," Paul said at last, "it contradicts the theory of evolution. They can't both be true."

"I agree," Murphy said.

"So on the one hand we have a bunch of myths and stories," Paul said. "And on the other a proven scientific theory relying on fossil evidence." He smirked unpleasantly. "I think I know which one I go for."

Shari looked as if she wanted the ground to swallow her up,

but Murphy smiled at Paul, trying to show Shari he wasn't fazed or annoyed by Paul's argument.

"You have a point, Paul. Evidence is evidence. Do you remember last semester when I demonstrated that there had been more than twenty-five thousand archaeological digs that had unearthed evidence confirming the authenticity of the Bible? And that there had never been one single artifact unearthed contradicting any biblical reference? I might also point out that every one of your proofs for evolution, the so-called missing links, have all turned out to be either fraudulent, misidentified, or simply a case of wishful thinking. Even evolutionist Dr. Colin Patterson, former head of the British Museum of Natural History, has admitted there is not one single transitional fossil in existence anywhere that could be used to prove the theory of evolution. So tell me, Paul, what would you think if someone discovered the remains of the Ark? You'd have to give up your theory of evolution then, wouldn't you?"

Paul shrugged. "Sure. I'd eat my hat too."

Murphy wagged a finger at him. "Don't make any promises you can't keep, Paul. I'll let you off eating your hat, as long as you promise to look at the Bible with an open mind and think about what it teaches." He turned to the rest of the class. "Let's imagine someone does find the remains of the ark. It would be the most important archaeological discovery ever made. But even more awesome, it would be the proof that God *did* judge the wickedness of the world with the Flood. And if the Bible was accurate in predicting the flood judgment, it must also be accurate in predicting the next judgment—the judgment of the Son of Man that Jesus talks about!"

Paul didn't seem to have an answer to that, much to Shari's obvious relief, and Murphy began to shuffle his notes into order.

Then some instinct made him look up at the stylishly dressed man leaning against the back wall of the lecture hall.

But he was gone.

TWENTY-THREE

MURPHY HURRIED OUT of the amphitheater, but all he could see were students leisurely making their way to and from classes or the cafeteria. No sign of the man in the blue suit.

He turned back to retrieve his notes, and there he was, standing by the door, his hand held out. "Professor Murphy, I'm Shane Barrington. Interesting lecture."

I knew the face was familiar, thought Murphy.

"I just flew in to Raleigh," he said, as if that explained everything. "The search for Noah's Ark, eh? Interesting topic. Have you been researching it long?"

"This is my third class on the subject," said Murphy guardedly. It seemed bizarre to be having a conversation about Noah's Ark with the head of Barrington Communications, one of the world's most powerful businessmen. What did he want to do—buy advertising space on the ark? He'd be disappointed when Murphy told him it hadn't been seen for several thousand years. "The students seem to be quite interested."

"Yes, I can see that. I'm interested too."

"You are?" said Murphy. "No offense, but I don't think there's a lot of money to be made from biblical artifacts like the ark. When they're found, they belong to everybody. And their value is way beyond mere money."

For a fleeting second Barrington's eyes darkened, then he suddenly laughed. "Excellent. I admire your passion, Professor Murphy. In fact, that's why I want to talk to you. Do you have some time right now?"

Murphy was still suspicious, but it was hard not to be swayed by Barrington's charm. And it couldn't hurt to talk, whatever Barrington's real motives. "You're in luck. I have half an hour before my next lecture."

Murphy led the way across the campus to the student center, where they ordered iced teas and found a quiet table.

"First, let me say how sorry I was to hear about the death of your wife. What a shocking, terrible event. Did they ever catch the man who was responsible?"

"Not yet," Murphy replied grimly. He wondered why Barrington had brought it up, and Barrington seemed to sense his curiosity.

"My son was also murdered—around the same time as your wife."

Murphy nodded. "I heard about that. I'm very sorry."

"Thank you. So, you see, Professor Murphy, we have something in common after all. We've both suffered the loss of loved ones. I know the loss of Arthur has given me a different perspective on life—on what's important." He smiled. "You're looking skeptical, Professor Murphy. Well, maybe we don't have exactly the same outlook, but I think it's true to say that each of us, in his own way, is trying to use his influence to make a difference in the world. And I think maybe we'd have an even bigger influence if we worked together."

His well-rehearsed patter tripped easily off his tongue, but despite himself, Barrington found he was transported back to the day when his son had died—and when he had failed to save him. But the truth was, he hadn't loved Arthur at all, just as his own father hadn't loved him. He really didn't have anything in common with Murphy.

Except for one thing. Murphy's wife and Barrington's son had both been killed by the same man.

Talon.

And that was a fact he wasn't about to share.

"There's so much violence and disorder in the world," Barrington continued. "So much crime and violence. I'm trying to use Barrington Communications to fight that."

"How?" Murphy asked, sipping his tea.

"Information. Communication. The more we know about the world, about one another, the less reason there is for conflict. Does that make any sense to you?"

Murphy nodded. "Sure. As long as what you tell people is the truth. Sometimes truth does lead to conflict. Sometimes truth is what you have to fight about."

Barrington looked thoughtful. "I see what you're saying. And what's your particular battle in this great conflict?"

"I try to prove the truth of the Bible," Murphy said simply.

"And why is that so important?"

"For a number of reasons," Murphy replied. "But let me give you just one example. If we can prove that Noah's Ark really existed, then we know for sure that God really did punish the evildoers in Noah's time. So when the Bible tells us that there's another judgment coming, it would be smart to take it seriously and try to change our lives in accordance with His will."

"Saving people's immortal souls," mused Barrington, stirring the ice in his tea. "What could be more important than that, right? So the more people you can communicate that message to, the better."

"Of course," Murphy agreed.

"Then I guess if you had the chance to utilize one of the world's most influential cable-TV channels to spread the word, that would be a—how can I put it?—heaven-sent opportunity, wouldn't it?"

"I guess it would," Murphy said.

Barrington grinned like a poker player who had just scooped the pot. "That's what I was hoping you'd say. You see, Murphy, I'd like to offer you a job. I'd like you to come to work for the Barrington Communications Network."

Murphy's mouth opened but no words came out. He truly didn't know what to say. Barrington kept on talking. "I want to develop a new department of special interest. I would like you to head up a team to produce documentaries in the field of archaeology. I think our more scientific and serious-minded viewers would enjoy this discovery type of format. You could select your own staff. We would provide the filming and editing crew. You'd be completely in charge. You can make any program you want—any subject. Money's no object. How does that sound?"

The truth was, it sounded incredible. Instead of standing in a lecture theater, talking to a hundred students, Murphy could talk to millions of people, all around the world. And instead of battling with Dean Fallworth on a daily basis over the content of his lectures, he'd have a free hand to go in any direction he wanted.

"I'm not sure what to say. I'm just an archaeologist."

"Trust me," Barrington insisted, leaning over the table. "You've got star quality. Charisma. Call it what you will. That's why you're a great teacher. People respond to you. Trust you."

And why should I trust you? Murphy wondered. *What's really going on here?*

It was as if he'd suddenly snapped wide awake after a particularly vivid dream.

"I appreciate the offer, Mr. Barrington, but the answer will have to be no."

That dark look clouded Barrington's features again. Clearly he didn't like people saying no to him.

"Don't be hasty. Give yourself time to think about it. If there's something else you want, ask. I'm sure we can figure it out."

Murphy could feel his temper rising. He didn't like people assuming he could be bought.

"The answer is no. Thank you."

"Would you do me the courtesy of telling me why?" Barrington asked, not bothering to keep the venomous edge out of his voice.

"Because I don't want to be a part of your sleazy organization. Your late-night shows are nothing but pornography. Your prime-time shows are filled with sexual innuendos, distasteful language, and an assault on morality. Your comedy shows make fun of everything that is decent in America. Your reality shows don't even touch reality. And you support political leaders who are corrupt. If I've left anything out, I apologize. To quote a verse from the Psalms, *I would rather be a doorkeeper in the house of my God than dwell in tents of wickedness.*"

Barrington sat quite still. Murphy had a sense that Barrington wanted very badly to reach over and grab him by the throat. But something was holding him back. Something more powerful even than his own rage. Murphy wondered what it was.

Slowly, Barrington got up and straightened his tie. He smoothed the front of his jacket and held out his hand, his expression of barely suppressed fury unchanging.

"Until we meet again, Murphy. Until we meet again."

Murphy held his eye and remained seated, his hands on the table. Barrington turned on his heel and walked quickly away.

Murphy watched him go. He still wasn't sure what had just happened. *I need to think about this,* he thought. But at that moment his cell phone began to ring.

"Murphy."

"Michael, this is Vern. I was calling about our conversation. I told you I was going to give you an answer about flying the discovery team to Ararat."

"Right. What did you and Julie decide?"

"The answer is yes."

"How does Julie feel about it?" Murphy asked.

"I won't kid you. She's concerned. She doesn't like the thought of me being gone. She knows that Turkey is not the safest place for Americans right now."

"She's right, Vern. You don't have to go."

"I realize that, but this will be an opportunity to help make a better life for my family. Sometimes you've got to take risks if you want to do that. Besides," he chuckled, "you can't do this without me. I've seen you in action, remember. You need someone smart to watch your back."

Murphy grinned. "And I can't think of anyone I'd rather have do it. Good to have you aboard, Vern."

He cut the connection and looked off toward the lake. A cold shudder passed slowly through him.

He was sure Barrington's offer had been a poisoned chalice. Tempting, but dangerous. And now he'd just made his old friend Vern an offer. An offer Vern had found equally tempting. Tempting, but possibly fatal.

And if it was, how would Murphy feel about that?

TWENTY-FOUR

PAUL WALLACH WAS IN the library, deeply absorbed in taking notes from a book about archaeological digs in the Valley of the Kings. He didn't notice the man standing behind him until he reached for the chair next to Paul and pulled it out.

"Do you mind if I sit down?"

Paul didn't look up from his notes. "Sure. Whatever." Then something made him turn.

"Mr. Barrington! What are you doing here?"

Barrington smiled and stuck out his hand. "I came to check up on my investment, Paul!"

"Your investment is doing great," Paul gushed, closing the book. "Thanks to you and the scholarship. It was a great honor to have you come and visit me in the hospital after the bomb explosion at the church."

Barrington waved a hand dismissively. "That was a tough time for everyone, even me, Paul. After I lost Arthur I was devastated. Probably like you were when your father passed away. I guess since losing Arthur, I've begun to think of you a little bit as a son. I hope you don't mind."

Paul just smiled a puppy-dog smile, as Barrington knew he would. His emotional buttons were easy to press.

"Could you possibly take a break from your studies and go for a walk with me?"

"Of course. I was just finishing up here, anyway."

As they left the library, Paul was aware of the other students talking and pointing. He concentrated on looking casual and relaxed, but inside he was glowing. One of the world's most recognizable businessmen had come to Preston to see him. Paul Wallach.

They found a bench shaded by azaleas and dogwoods and sat down.

"Paul, I would like to propose an idea. Something for you to think about. I want you to consider working for me when you graduate. You're smart, you're a hard worker, and you're a team player. That's a pretty rare combination."

Paul tried not to let his excitement show.

"I don't know what to say, Mr. Barrington. It would be an incredible opportunity."

"You see, here's what I was thinking, Paul. I think you have real leadership potential. I would like you to join BCN and work as an apprentice. I would like to take you under my wing and mentor you. I think you can go far in our media organization.

You already have a background in media with your father's having been in the printing business. I'm sure that you learned some of his skills."

Paul just nodded.

"Here's what I'd like to see happen, Paul. I would like you to continue to stay in school. I'll take care of all of your school expenses. But I want you to begin to develop your skills as a writer. To begin with, I would like you to give me samples of your writing on a weekly basis. For example, take your class on biblical archaeology. The one that Professor Murphy teaches. Let's start by having you give me a four-page report of what is taught in his class. I'll read your material and come back to you with suggestions. What do you think?"

"That's one of my most interesting classes. That would be great. I'm sure I could learn a lot from you."

"Good. Then we'll start with that. By the way, I forgot to mention, not only will you have a scholarship, but it's only fair to pay you for the tasks I assign you. How does twenty dollars an hour sound, is that acceptable?"

Paul couldn't believe his ears. His schooling was going to be paid. He was going to get a part-time job for twenty dollars an hour. And then he was guaranteed a high-paying job upon graduation. It didn't get any better than that.

"Paul, before you give me a final answer it is important that you think it over. I wouldn't want to push you too hard or rush you into a decision. I'm asking you to take on responsibilities beyond your course work. I want you to be comfortable and happy. So you don't have to worry about what I'll say if you turn me down. Like I say, I think of you as a son. I only have your interests at heart."

Paul was about to speak, but Barrington held up a hand.

"Oh, one other thing. Are you free this weekend? I've got tickets to *The Phantom of the Opera*. How would you like to fly up to New York and join me? You can stay at the penthouse."

"That would be great, Mr. Barrington. And I could do some writing on the plane."

Barrington clapped him on the shoulder and stood to go. "Excellent. I'll have my limo pick you up and take you to the airport on Friday afternoon." He made a show of looking at his watch. "Which is where I've got to go right now. Important meeting. Keep up the good work, Paul."

"Yes, sir. Thank you, Mr. Barrington," Paul called after him. He sat back in a daze, imaging himself in Barrington's office in New York, learning important stuff about the business, being privy to confidential information, seeing multimillion-dollar decisions being made.

"Sorry, Shari," he muttered. "I'm going to have to take a rain check on that Bible study meeting this weekend. You see, I'm going to New York. Shane Barrington's personal—"

"Hey, Paul. Are you talking to yourself?"

Paul looked up, embarrassed. "Oh, hi, Shari. Er, no, I was just going over something in my mind."

She sat down next to him. "Wasn't that Shane Barrington I saw you with just now?"

Paul looked uneasy. He knew Shari was suspicious of Barrington. He knew she felt his interest in Paul since the explosion had something insincere about it, but she could never quite say what it was. He didn't want to have another one of their arguments about it. Especially now.

"Yes, it was," Paul said guardedly.

"What did he want? Did he come here just to see you?"

Paul had intended to steer the conversation in another direction, but Shari's tone was getting under his skin.

"Why shouldn't he? He takes an interest in my work, that's all."

"Why should the head of Barrington Communications be interested in your work? You're a student, Paul, not a world-famous professor."

Paul felt himself going red. "Oh, that's right. I don't have crazy ideas about proving that fairy stories in the Bible really happened. Not like world-famous Professor Murphy."

Shari felt her anger rising to match Paul's. "They're not fairy stories! How can you say that? I thought you were interested in biblical archaeology. I thought you liked Murphy's classes."

Paul realized the conversation was getting out of hand. "Okay, okay. Murphy's classes are very . . . stimulating. I'm just not sure he's living in the real world, that's all."

Shari nodded, like she finally understood what this was about. "And Barrington is? Why? Because he has money? Because he's successful? Look how he makes his money, Paul. By peddling trash."

"You don't even watch TV," Paul countered. "Maybe if you took your nose out of your Bible once in a while, you'd get a different perspective on things."

"You agreed to join me in a Bible study group this weekend, Paul. Are you telling me you're no longer interested?"

Paul took a deep breath. He couldn't look Shari in the eye.

"I was going to tell you. Something's come up. I can't go."

"Something to do with Shane Barrington?"

"Yes, if you must know. He's invited me to New York for the weekend. To show me around his business. It's a great opportunity, Shari. How could I say no?"

Shari looked at him. They had argued before. About the Bible and about evolution. Sometimes bitterly. But at least they had been honest with each other. And however bad the fights got, she felt, if they could still be honest with each other, then there was still hope for them.

But now Paul had told her a lie. She was certain of it.

And for the first time she felt him slipping away.

TWENTY-FIVE

"MICHAEL, THIS IS HANK BAINES. I hate to impose on you like this, but I need to see you."

Murphy caught the undertone of anxiety in Baines's voice.

"I'm just walking out the door now. I'm on my way to the State Department of Archives and History. I could meet you there around eleven A.M. How does that sound?"

There was an audible sigh of relief on the other end of the line. "I'll see you there."

By the time eleven o'clock rolled around, Murphy was so engrossed in his research, he didn't notice Baines approaching.

"What's so interesting?" Baines asked.

Murphy looked up and motioned for Baines to sit down at the secluded table in the library section.

"The Lost Colony."

"What's that?"

"In 1587, Sir Walter Raleigh sent a group of one hundred seventeen settlers to colonize Virginia. They landed on Roanoke Island on the way to Chesapeake Bay. There were ninety-one men, seventeen women, and nine children. The first English baby to be born on the continent was named Virginia Dare."

"I've heard of her," Baines said, nodding.

"The supply ships for the colonists weren't able to return from England until 1590 due to the Spanish War. When they did return, everyone in the colony had disappeared. No trace of anyone. The only thing they found was a tree with the letters CRO carved on it, and a second tree with the word CROATOAN carved on it. No one's ever figured out what it means or what happened to them."

"So you think you'll have a crack at it?" said Baines.

Murphy smiled. "Solving mysteries. That's what rings my bell. But you didn't come all the way over here to talk about that. What's on your mind, Hank?"

"Have you heard about Tiffany?"

Murphy sat up in his chair. "No. What happened?"

"She was in a head-on collision with a truck two days ago. The car rolled and the driver was killed. Her friend Lisa."

"What about Tiffany?"

"Just some scrapes and bruises. It seems like a miracle she wasn't more badly hurt. But she's pretty cut up about her friend."

Murphy could see Baines was close to tears.

"Tiffany almost . . . That was a real wake-up call, I can tell you. I don't want to lose my daughter and I don't want to lose Jennifer. I don't know, but I get the feeling somebody's trying to tell me something. There's something I need to do. The trouble is, I don't know exactly what it is."

"Maybe you know more than you think," Murphy said.

Baines looked at him quizzically. "What do you mean?"

"You know how we were talking about listening? Hearing what other people in your family have got to say?"

Baines nodded. "Uh-huh."

"Maybe it's time to listen to that small voice within. You know, Hank, we all have this yearning, this emptiness inside that can only be filled by God. Pascal, the great French philosopher, taught that there was a God-shaped vacuum in the heart of every man that could only be satisfied by God Himself through having a relationship with Jesus Christ, his Son."

Hank looked down at the desk. "Boy, it's hard to talk about this. But I hear what you're saying. I've had a feeling the last few days that I need to . . . make a commitment. I just don't know how to do it."

"Well, the important thing is you have to want to do it. Then it's like jumping off the high board. You just close your eyes and go for it!"

Baines laughed. "You make it sound easy, Michael. But here's the thing. I never had much religious teaching. There's so much I feel I need to know."

"Like what?"

Baines frowned in concentration as he tried to order his

thoughts. "Okay, here's a for-instance. You talk about God, and Jesus, and the Holy Spirit. Three different things. What's going on there?"

Murphy smiled. "I know that sounds a little confusing. Let me try to explain. God is the Father, and the Son, and the Holy Spirit. They are three in one."

"Three in one?"

"It's sort of like three responsibilities. For example, you have a wife and daughter. As Hank Baines, you are a husband to your wife, a father to your daughter, and a professional in the FBI. You display different functions at the appropriate time."

"Okay, I'm following you."

"Let me give you another example from nature. Water, H_2O, can exist as a liquid, as a solid, or as a vapor, but it's still H_2O."

"All right, but I've heard a lot of talk about Jesus Christ as a man. How can he be a man and God at the same time?"

Murphy laughed. "A lot of people smarter than me have wrestled with that one over the last couple thousand years, but let me give it a try. How's your Shakespeare?"

"I read some stuff in college. But I don't remember a whole lot, to be honest."

Murphy laughed. "Me neither. But you remember who Macbeth is?"

"Sure. The Scottish guy. Had a doozy of a wife."

"See, you remember more than you think. Anyway, could the character Macbeth ever meet the author Shakespeare in person?"

Baines looked confused. "I would say no."

"Ah, but he could meet him," Murphy went on. "Shakespeare could write himself into the play, as a character named Shakespeare, and introduce himself to Macbeth."

"I guess."

"Well, that's what God did. He is the author of the universe. He wrote Himself into the play of life in the bodily form of Jesus Christ. God took on the form of a man. Jesus even said, 'I and the Father are one.'"

Baines was silent for a moment. Murphy let him think about what he'd just said.

Finally Baines said, "I guess the important question is, if I accept the fact that Jesus is God in a human body, is it going to make a change in my life?"

"You'd better believe it. Let's take this a step further. Do you know anyone who's perfect?"

Baines shook his head.

"God is perfect. And He wants mankind to spend eternity with Him in heaven. There is, however, a problem. We are not perfect. If we were to enter God's presence in our imperfect state we wouldn't be able to endure it. Why? Because God is Holy. Remember when you were a kid and you did something bad? You didn't want your parents to find out, right? Imagine your Creator forever being aware of every single bad thought or deed you committed during your lifetime. You wouldn't want to spend five minutes in His presence, let alone eternity. But if your sins had been paid for and erased by the acceptance of Jesus Christ as your personal Lord and Savior prior to your entrance into heaven, there wouldn't be a problem, would there?"

"That makes sense," Baines agreed.

"God took on the form of the Son—Jesus—to die for our imperfection, our sins. He then covers us with the perfection of Christ, so that we can enter His presence. All a person has to do is to believe and accept this great substitution."

"It sounds too simple. Isn't there something else we have to do?"

Murphy held up his hands. "That's it. Anything else we would try to do would be imperfect."

"It seems like it should be harder than that."

"Don't take it from me. Let me quote you something from the Book of Romans, Chapter Ten, Verses Eight through Thirteen: *The word is near you; it is in your mouth and in your heart, that is the word of faith we are proclaiming; That if you confess with your mouth, 'Jesus is Lord,' and believe in your heart that God raised Him from the dead, you will be saved. For it is with your heart that you believe and are justified, and it is with your mouth that you confess and are saved. Everyone who calls on the name of the Lord will be saved.*"

When Murphy finished, Baines was deep in thought. Murphy had done all he could, had explained his faith to the best of his ability. Now it was up to Baines. He wasn't sure Baines was listening to him anymore, but he wanted to add one more thing.

"Remember, Hank, you can ask Christ into your life at any time. Any place. You don't have to be in church. It could be while you are driving your car. Walking to the store. Anywhere. You just have to say a prayer and ask Him in. He will be there to answer you, I guarantee it."

Murphy slowly gathered his books, laid a hand gently on Baines's shoulder, and walked away.

He said his own silent prayer as he went.

TWENTY-SIX

WHEN ISIS REACHED the terminal, she stopped and looked at the arrivals monitor for American Airlines. On time. She found a vacant chair by the window of the arrivals hall and sat down to wait, hoping her heartbeat would steady to something like normal by the time he arrived. The last thing she wanted to do was let him know the effect he had on her.

Murphy spotted her, sitting demurely, hands in her lap, almost as if she was meditating. It looked as if her eyes were closed. He stopped, drawing out the moment. As soon as he greeted her, it would be all business. That was the way he'd decided it had to be. So this sight of her was an unexpected gift. Her flame-red hair looked wind-tossed, even here, a violent contrast to the porcelain serenity of her face, tapering to an elfin chin he suddenly had an urgent desire to touch with the tip of a finger.

As if she'd divined his thought, her lids snapped open and her blazing green eyes found his across the hall. Then just as quickly she looked away. He raised a hand in greeting, took a deep breath, and made his way through the crowd.

By the time he was standing before her, she'd composed her features into her usual sphinxlike half-smile.

"Murphy," she said.

"Isis. You're looking . . ." He stumbled for a moment. Dressed in combat pants and a tight-fitting green T-shirt, sneakers, no makeup, she looked like a supermodel trying to blend into the crowd. And failing. Big time.

She looked stunning.

" . . . well. You're looking well," he managed finally.

She jumped out of her seat and started marching toward the taxi stand. "I told you. I've been training."

Murphy trailed behind her. "Good," he said. "Great."

In the cab Murphy was relieved to be able to concentrate on checking that he had everything he needed in his briefcase, and Isis kept her eyes out the window until they arrived at their destination, nestled in the quiet community of McLean, Virginia. The original grounds had been purchased in 1719 by Thomas Lee. He had named the property Langley after his home in England.

After passing all the security stations, they were soon walking on the collegelike campus grounds. The landscaped courtyard, the large grassy lawn, and the flowering plants and trees added to the impression of an Ivy League university.

It was only when they stopped in front of the Kryptos monument that they remembered that this was no idyllic seat of learning. Murphy remembered the first time he had stood before the S-shaped copper screen, which looked like a piece of paper coming out of a computer printer. On it, several enigmatic messages challenged the reader to decode them. He'd tried and failed before, and glancing sideways at Isis, he wondered if some mysteries were never to be fathomed.

Soon they entered the modern glass-enclosed headquarters and walked over to the receptionist.

"May I help you?"

"Michael Murphy and Isis McDonald. We have an appointment with Carlton Stovall."

Murphy and Isis were soon joined by a short, slightly overweight, and balding man with a bland smile. He invited them into his office.

Stovall waited until they were seated in front of his desk. "I mentioned to you over the phone that I didn't really think I could be of much help. I hope you haven't made this trip in vain."

"We'll see," Murphy said evenly. "As you know, I'm interested in copies of documents relating to Noah's Ark."

Stovall's laugh was shrill. "I'm sorry, Professor Murphy, all our files were damaged in the Flood!" He laughed again. "You'll have to forgive me. We get a lot of crazy requests—you know, people wanting to see the file on where Elvis is living, how the Secret Service murdered Marilyn Monroe, that sort of thing. But this! This really takes the cake. You're sure you don't want the file on Jonah and the whale?"

He took out a white handkerchief and began to dab at his forehead.

Murphy waited until he was sure Stovall had no more jokes. "Maybe you call it by another name. Let me see . . . how about the Ararat Anomaly File? That ring any bells?"

Suddenly Stovall wasn't laughing anymore. The blood drained out of his face. He began to stutter in reply, but Murphy cut him off.

"I know for a fact that on June seventeenth, 1949, a U.S. Air Force plane was making a routine flight over Mount Ararat. I know that photographs were taken and that an object was spotted at the 15,500-foot level. I've been told that this object was called the Ararat Anomaly within the CIA. I also know that in 1993, under the Freedom of Information Act, the Anomaly File was finally declassified after over forty years of secrecy. How am I doing?"

Again, Murphy didn't give Stovall time to reply.

"I am also aware that Porcher Taylor, a scholar at the Washington-based Center for Strategic and International Studies, made some interesting discoveries. He found out that a U-2 spy plane took pictures of the same anomaly in 1956. Taylor also discovered that the CIA snapped some shots with their high-resolution KH-9 military remote-sensing satellite in 1973. And not to be outdone, the KH-11 satellite photographed the same spot on Ararat in 1976, 1990, and 1992."

Murphy paused, but Stovall seemed to have nothing to say now.

"If I am not mistaken," Murphy continued, "the IKONOS satellite even identified the secret coordinates of the Mount

Ararat Anomaly at thirty-nine degrees, forty-two minutes, and ten seconds north longitude and forty-four degrees, sixteen minutes, and thirty seconds east latitude."

Stovall's eyes darted back and forth between Isis and Murphy. He looked like a trapped rodent trying to find a way out. Finally he said, "I don't have the authority to grant access to those files. I'll have to talk to my superior."

"That's just fine," Murphy beamed. "We have all afternoon, Mr. Stovall."

Stovall left the room, and Isis grinned at Murphy despite herself. "Wow, you really gave him both barrels. Was all of that true?"

"That's what we're here to find out," Murphy replied.

They were just settling themselves in for a long wait when the door opened and two men walked briskly into the room. Stovall looked a little more composed. Behind him was a man Murphy knew only too well.

Instantly Murphy was assailed by flashbacks to the bombing of the church and the aggressive investigations of an FBI agent convinced that Christians like Murphy, Laura, and Pastor Bob Wagoner were responsible.

Agent Burton Welsh.

The man Hank Baines had told him was now working for the CIA.

Small world, Murphy thought.

"Well, well, Professor Murphy." Welsh scowled. "It seems I can't get away from you, however hard I try."

"Just what I was thinking," said Murphy. "But we'll be happy to leave you alone so you can get on with whatever it is you do here. Just give us the files and we'll be on our way."

"I'm sorry, but that's not going to be possible," Welsh said, not sounding sorry at all. "You see, all of those items have been reclassified as secret documents."

"That's impossible," Murphy said, getting out of his chair and standing toe to toe with Welsh. Isis put a restraining hand on his arm, worried that he was going to lose his temper, but he didn't seem to notice. "All of those materials come under the Freedom of Information Act. You don't have the right to deny us access."

Welsh stood impassively, arms folded. "There's nothing more I can tell you."

Murphy jabbed a finger at him. "You've told us plenty, Welsh. You've told us we're right. The CIA has all this information but they don't want it to get out into the public domain. It's a cover-up!"

Welsh shrugged. "What can I say? Maybe you should write to the President. Take it up with him. Have a pleasant trip home." He spun on his heel and walked out, slamming the door behind him.

TWENTY-SEVEN

MURPHY WAS STILL quietly fuming as they left the building and walked back through the grounds toward the exit.

"That guy Welsh. First he tries to smear Evangelicals over the bombings, now he turns up here, shutting the lid on the Ararat files. What's going on?"

Isis put her arm through his, telling herself she was just trying to calm him down. "I think you're being a trifle paranoid, Murphy. I mean, if the CIA has evidence that the ark exists, why would they be trying to keep it secret? You and Welsh have a history. I just think he's stonewalling because he doesn't like you."

"Maybe you're right," Murphy said. "Maybe I am just getting paranoid."

"So what do we do now?" Isis asked. "Since the files thing

has been a bust, we have a few hours to kill before you have to be at the airport. Do you want me to give you a tour? See some of Washington's sights?"

Murphy wasn't really paying attention. "Sure. There's no way we're going to get those files now."

"Listen, if you don't want to, that's fine with me. I've got plenty of work to do back at the museum," Isis pouted.

Murphy forced a smile. "I'm sorry, Isis. Let's grab that cab and do the tour. You lead the way."

"What a piece of luck. You don't usually see cabs waiting here," Isis said. "We'd like to go to the Washington Monument," she told the driver as they climbed in.

The driver nodded and they joined the traffic. For a while they didn't speak. Murphy was still going over his confrontation with Welsh in his mind, while Isis looked down at her hands resting in her lap. She was beginning to wonder if this was such a good idea.

After a while she looked up and was surprised to see unfamiliar streets. "Hey!" She tapped on the glass partition separating them from the driver. "I said we wanted to go to the Washington Monument. This isn't the right way!"

Murphy stiffened in the seat beside her. "What's the problem, Isis?"

"I don't know where we are. But we're definitely heading in the wrong direction." She rapped firmly on the glass.

The driver didn't respond.

Murphy could feel an adrenaline rush kicking in. This wasn't right. Not right at all.

He shook the door handle, but it wouldn't budge. Then suddenly the cab started to slow, and it looked as if the driver was going to let them out. Isis sighed with relief as they pulled up to the sidewalk. Murphy took Isis's hand and they prepared to leap out.

Before they could move, the doors opened and two men got in, squeezing Murphy and Isis uncomfortably between them. Murphy started to twist in his seat, and found himself looking down the barrel of a silenced automatic. The man was dressed in a dark suit with a white shirt and red tie. His dark hair was slicked back and he showed even rows of teeth as he smiled.

"You want a tour? No problem. But this is going to be a special one. Places the tourists never see. If they're lucky," he added with a smirk.

Murphy turned his head and caught Isis's eye. She was shaking visibly as the other man—lean and blond—pressed a similar automatic against her forehead. He wasn't smiling.

As the cab moved off, the possibilities raced through Murphy's mind. Was this a carjacking? A kidnapping? A case of mistaken identity? The whole operation had a professional feel. A word Levi had used sprang into his mind.

Spooks.

Which meant he would need to be careful. Professional or not, he felt he had a reasonable chance of disarming the man pointing a gun at him. But that would leave Isis. He couldn't risk it. They would have to wait until they got where they were headed and see what opportunities presented themselves.

There was a squeal as the blond man roughly stuck a length of duct tape over Isis's mouth and then slipped a blindfold of dark material over her eyes.

"Hey!" Murphy instinctively reached out, but before he could do anything the butt of a gun whipped across his forehead. Momentarily stunned, he felt plastic cuffs pinning his wrists together, then a length of tape being fastened over his own mouth, and finally the blindfold.

His world went dark.

He sensed the man on his left relaxing. "Just sit back and enjoy, folks," he said. "We'll be there before you know it."

Unable to do anything else, Murphy concentrated on memorizing every detail about their assailants. Had the man on his left spoken with an accent? Was there a hint of a southern twang? There was a faint smell of aftershave but Murphy couldn't name the brand.

He shook his head beneath the blindfold. He knew he was clutching at straws. For all he knew, he was about to get a bullet in the brain. Isis too. He strained against the cuffs, suddenly convulsed with anger, and felt the gun being shoved hard into his ribs.

He slowed his breathing, trying to channel his anger into something more positive, trying to prepare himself for whatever was going to happen when they arrived at their destination. Trying to figure out the beginnings of a plan.

It seemed to Murphy as if only seconds had passed since the two men got into the cab, but it must have been longer. They were slowing again, and the sounds had changed. He couldn't hear any other traffic. Then the car stopped, and all he could hear was the click of the engine cooling, the hammering of his heart, and Isis's muffled sobbing.

Strong hands grabbed him and pulled him out of the car, then a sharp prod of the gun in the small of his back sent him lurching forward. More hands took his arms and he stumbled down a flight of steps. He felt himself falling, then being shoved upright. As he regained his balance, the tape was roughly torn from his mouth and the blindfold pulled off.

He found himself standing alongside Isis in a long, bare, concrete room with a low ceiling. A single bulb hung down, illuminating the only piece of furniture, a gray steel table. The man with the slicked-back hair was leaning against it, his gun laying to one side.

He looked at Murphy contemptuously. "Considering how many important people you've riled up, you don't look like much," he said.

"Which important people would that be exactly?" Murphy asked, trying to keep his voice neutral.

The man scowled. "Correct me if I'm wrong, but I believe I'm the one with the gun. That means I get to ask the questions."

Murphy forced a smile. "Ask away." Beside him, he could see Isis trembling.

"In actual fact, there's only one thing I need to know," he said. "Which one of you wants to go first?" He picked up the gun and pointed it first at Murphy, then at Isis. "I mean, I'd understand if you didn't want to see your girlfriend get a bullet in the brain. On the other hand, perhaps letting her go first would be the gentlemanly thing to do. Mr. Enson, what do you believe would be the correct etiquette in this situation?"

In his peripheral vision, Murphy could see the second gunman and the driver standing a couple of paces behind.

The driver chuckled. "Hard to say. I reckon it all comes down to personal choice."

"Tsk, tsk." The first man shook his head. "How can people find direction in this godless world of ours if there are no proper rules of behavior? It's a wonder our children don't all grow up to be savages. What do you say, Murphy?"

Murphy was trying to figure out a reply that would keep the conversation going, give him some more time, when he heard a choking sound. Isis was bent over, having some sort of convulsion. Then she took a step and collapsed on the floor, her eyes rolling back in her head.

For a second everyone looked in her direction. "I hope you're doing what I think you're doing," Murphy muttered under his breath before turning to his left, taking one quick step, and launching a powerful kick between the driver's legs. He groaned and clutched his hands to his groin, and Murphy snapped a second kick that sent his gun skittering across the floor. As the first gunman drew a bead on him, Murphy threw himself into a forward roll in the opposite direction and heard the *phut* of silenced rounds behind him.

Then there was a strangled scream as Isis sprang up and looped her plastic handcuffs over the second gunman's neck. As the improvised garrote cut into his windpipe, he dropped his gun and tried to pry her hands away, but she hung on, snarling like a wolverine, forcing his head farther back.

Murphy knew he only had seconds to take advantage of the situation. He scrambled past the prostrate body of the driver until his fingers closed around the handle of the gun. With his hands still cuffed, it took him a moment to get a decent grip.

It was a moment too long. The first gunman was crouching in a marksman's stance, the barrel of his automatic pointed at Murphy's chest.

"Don't even think about it," he warned.

Then he seemed to flinch, and a spray of blood blossomed from the side of his head as he fell to the floor.

Murphy turned, incredulous, to see Isis holding the automatic, a wisp of smoke slowly curling out of the silencer. "Don't just stand there," she said. "Help me out of these handcuffs. There's a penknife in the front pocket of my trousers." Murphy quickly found it and slashed through the plastic cuffs around Isis's wrists before doing the same for himself.

He looked down at the body of the second gunman, who didn't look as if he was breathing.

"Look out!" Isis screamed.

Murphy whipped round to see the driver launching himself at him like a linebacker. Without thinking, he dropped into a fighting stance and powered his knee sharply up into the driver's jaw. There was a horrifying crack, and a limp body dropped at his feet.

For a moment they stood frozen, looking at the grotesquely splayed bodies on the floor. Then Murphy gently eased the gun out of Isis's hand and said, "I think we should get out of here. There may be backup on the way."

Isis looked as if she hadn't heard, then she shook her hair

out of her eyes and nodded. "You remember I said you were being paranoid? Well—"

"Later," Murphy said, steering her toward the door.

They retraced their steps at a jog, up the stairs and into a garage. Murphy opened a door and then they were standing in the street, the sunlight blinding them for a moment. At the end of the street they could see cars, people walking, safety.

Without a word they started running.

TWENTY-EIGHT

ON THE DRIVE HOME, Baines played the phone conversation with Murphy over in his mind, trying to make sense of what had happened. After flagging down a cab—a real one this time—Murphy and Isis had been driven to the nearest precinct house. Cops being cops, they'd been skeptical at first but eventually agreed to send two squad cars to the address where Isis and Murphy had been held, while more cops took detailed statements.

Murphy was not entirely surprised when the squad cars returned and the captain told them not a single word of their story checked out. There were no bodies. No weapons. Not a trace of blood anywhere.

Spooks, Murphy thought. *Boy, these guys are professionals.*

Eventually the cops let them go, but not without a lecture about wasting police time. Isis was furious, but Murphy didn't see the point in arguing. Even if they could convince the cops their story was true, what good would it do? They were dealing with forces too powerful for ordinary law-enforcement agencies.

Which is why he'd called Baines. And why Baines was now turning over in his mind everything he knew about Burton Welsh.

When he got home, he was relieved to find that Jennifer wasn't home. If his suspicions proved correct, he was going to have to send her and Tiffany away. Somewhere safe.

He took the sensor equipment out of his gym bag and began with the most obvious place—the phones. All three housed tiny silver-colored bugs. His computer would be the obvious place to look next. Bingo.

By the time he'd swept the house from top to bottom, he had quite a collection. And he couldn't even be sure he had them all.

If they're prepared to bug the house of an FBI agent, they must be serious, he thought. He was going to have to be careful.

Murphy was driving in to the Preston campus when his cell phone rang.

"Michael, this is Hank."

"Hi, Hank, is everything okay?"

"Don't talk, Michael. Just listen. Do you remember where we talked about Jennifer and me?"

"Sure."

"I'll call you there in about twenty minutes."

"Okay."

Murphy punched off his cell phone and turned the car

around. Fifteen minutes later he pulled up outside the Raleigh Health and Fitness Gym. He told the receptionist he might have a phone call coming in shortly, and she indicated an empty desk. He didn't have long to wait. She picked up the phone on the first ring and said, "Yes, he's here." She pointed to the blinking light on the phone at Murphy's desk.

"Murphy."

"Michael. Sorry for all the cloak-and-dagger. I had to get out of my office and use a public phone in a shopping mall. All of my phones have been bugged. Cell phones aren't secure either."

"Hank, is all this related to the spooks who attacked us in Washington? Are they targeting you too?"

"We can't talk about it over the phone. Are you familiar with Mount Airy Park on the south side of town?"

"I know where it is."

"Good. Let's meet there, say, about 4:00 P.M. I'll meet you by the old carousel."

"I'll be there."

"And, Michael, try to make sure you aren't tailed."

Murphy called Isis at the Smithsonian before he drove back to the university. They'd agreed it was the safest place for her to stay, with the extra security and police patrols following the break-in. But he could tell she was never going to feel a hundred percent safe anywhere ever again. And it was all his fault.

He felt a renewed determination to get to Ararat and find what was there, to get to the bottom of the mystery and confront whoever was trying to stop them.

When he entered his office he found a very angry Shari Nelson.

"Look at this! Just look at this! Somebody's come in here and broken the Egyptian papyrus manuscript I was working on. They must have knocked it on the floor and put it back on the counter. I can see small pieces under the table. Look, there's—"

Murphy made a circle with his lips and placed a finger over them. Shari stopped in mid-sentence with a quizzical expression. He then went over to the radio on the file cabinet and turned it on to a loud rock station, and whispered in her ear, "The place may be bugged." Shari nodded, though the questioning look remained. Murphy tore a sheet from a pad and wrote:

Let's look around and see if anything is missing.

It didn't take Murphy long to find that all of his files on Noah's Ark were gone. They'd even taken his class notes. Years of research—gone. He looked at his watch. No time to do a thorough search if he was going to make his meeting with Baines. He motioned to Shari to follow him outside.

Murphy turned in to a parking lot that was filled with the burned-out remains of a car, worn-out tires, cans, and trash. An old van covered with graffiti was half on the dry lawn and half on the pavement. It looked as if it had run into a tree. Murphy could see that the carousel was in disrepair and hadn't been used in years. The park itself was run-down, and there was quite a bit of graffiti on the slides and other playground equipment. Many of the animals on the merry-go-round were damaged and painted oddball colors. Some of them had gang signs on them.

As far as he knew, he hadn't been followed. He'd pulled over several times to let any tail go past, but he never saw the same car twice, and nobody followed him when he doubled back. He was certainly alone in the parking lot. If Baines was here he must have parked somewhere else and come the rest of the way on foot.

Calmly, quietly, and gently, the silencer was screwed onto the Russian Dragunov SVD gas-powered semiautomatic sniper rifle. All ten rounds were loaded in the magazine. Slowly, he focused the sights of his powerful telescope. It wasn't long before the crosshairs were hungrily looking for the target.

"Patience, patience!" he whispered to himself.

Murphy got out and ambled through the debris. He looked at his watch. Ten after four. He began to worry about Baines.

"Michael!"

The voice had come from the direction of the carousel. He turned to where Baines was leaning on a green and gold horse. Baines motioned him over. "Sorry about the setting. This is the only way we can get some privacy."

They shook hands.

"How's Tiffany doing?" asked Murphy.

"Great. She's out of the hospital—she's been home for about a week."

Baines was relaxed, but his eyes never stopped roaming the park.

"And how about you and Jennifer?"

"We're doing much better, thanks to you. But listen, we may not have much time. Is there anything else you can tell me about what happened in Washington—any details you may have left out?"

Murphy thought for a moment, then shook his head. "I pretty much told you everything, I think."

He adjusted his sights one more time. The barrel moved from one target to the other. The targets were in deep discussion and did not move very much. "Sitting ducks," he said to himself. "Yes, sitting ducks in the midst of a stampede of motionless horses." Encased in its latex glove, one of his fingers began to gently squeeze.

Baines nodded. "Okay. Well, I may have found out a couple of things. I used my FBI clearance to get into some of the computers at Langley. They can trace any incoming requests, but I know a trick or two to cover my tracks. I got some information, but you have to have a special access code to get into the main file on Ararat."

"So what did you manage to find out?" Murphy asked, trying to keep his voice steady.

"As you know, in the 1980s, Apollo astronaut Colonel James Irvin made three trips to Ararat in search of the ark. He was convinced that there was something on the mountain.

There were references to that and to some other information he must have had access to. I also ran across a memo that said there was *a boatlike structure on the mountain.* It went on to say that *it looked like the heavily damaged bow was sticking out of the snow* in the photos taken. The men who examined the photos said that the object was definitely *man-made, due to the ninety-degree angles.* They were certain it was—"

Murphy heard the bullet a split second after Baines had been driven back against the carousel horse by the force of the impact. He made a gurgling sound, clutched at his chest with one hand, and slid down to the floor, leaving a vivid splash of red against the green-painted horse.

"Hank!" Murphy crouched down and cradled Baines's head. Hank was staring ahead, trying to form words, a horrible sucking sound coming from his chest.

Murphy was frozen there for a second, then instinct kicked in and he rolled to the side as another bullet clanged noisily off one of the horse's legs, sending up a shower of sparks. He wormed his way under another horse, trying to put as many obstacles as possible between himself and the shooter. Trying to buy some time to think. He glanced back at Baines and saw he had his automatic in his hand. Something must have warned him in the split second before the bullet hit. Murphy crawled back and eased the gun out of Baines's grip.

Did the shooter think they were both hit? Or was he going to wait for another clear shot? Murphy had already figured out where the shots came from—the graffiti-covered van. He crawled a few yards to his left, away from Baines. Taking a deep breath, he jumped to his feet, braced his shoulder against a carousel pole, and squeezed off four shots before ducking down again. A crash of glass told him he'd hit one of the windows. No way of knowing whether he'd taken out the shooter, but at least he was making him worry. He stood up again and sighted on the van, but before he could get off another shot there was a squeal of tires and it bumped off the grass, onto the tarmac, and screeched toward the parking-lot exit.

Murphy lowered the gun and ran back to Baines. Murphy placed the palm of his hand on the pumping wound and pressed down, trying to stop the flow, but he knew it was hopeless. Baines had already lost too much blood. Blood seemed to be everywhere.

"Hang on, Hank!" Murphy yelled.

With his other hand he was reaching for his cell phone. His bloody fingers were pushing 911.

Baines was trying to talk. Murphy put his ear close to his mouth to try and catch the words.

"Tell Jennifer . . . I'm sorry . . . wasted so much time. Tell her . . ."

Murphy felt Baines buckle under his hand, his body spasming. Then he fell back and everything was still. He was gone.

TWENTY-NINE

STEPHANIE LOOKED AT HERSELF in the long mirror and sighed. The dress looked good, no doubt about it. The material clung to her every curve, accentuating her slim waist and full breasts, but somehow the cut was stylish enough to keep it classy. It was the kind of dress you might see being paraded on Oscar night, the kind of dress you see only on film stars or the ultrawealthy.

Or the mistress of one of the world's most powerful media magnates.

She carefully unzipped it and slipped it off, and prepared to put on something more suitable for a crusading TV-news reporter—a cream-colored suit that buttoned up to the neck, still stylish but much more sober, allowing just a suggestion of the hot body beneath the cool exterior.

That was the Stephanie Kovacs her millions of fans identified with. The tough-as-nails journalist, fearlessly chasing down bad guys to get the big story.

She looked in the mirror and saw the old Stephanie, the one who had carved out a career in the dog-eat-dog world of TV news through talent and guts and sheer determination. Before Barrington had called her to his private suite on the thirtieth floor and made her an offer she couldn't refuse. Before she'd sold out.

Before she'd sold her soul.

She looked down at the shiny black material of the cocktail dress, lying in a dark pool at her feet. It felt good to be a reporter again, but the truth was, it felt good to be Barrington's bedmate too. It made her feel more powerful than any politician or film star. It made her feel untouchable. She could do whatever she wanted, have whatever she wanted.

As long, of course, as she did whatever her master commanded.

And right now her master had commanded her to forget about dinner at the best table in the city's swankiest restaurant, exchange her Gucci purse for a reporter's notepad, and get down to Raleigh, North Carolina.

An FBI agent named Hank Baines had been shot at a deserted amusement park by a gunman who had fled the scene, leaving no clues as to his identity or motive. With her detached reporter's eye, she could see that it had all the elements of a prime-time story. An odd, slightly creepy setting. A violent death. And a big mystery.

But more important, it had Professor Michael Murphy. And that was undoubtedly the reason Barrington had broken their dinner engagement and ordered her to get to the scene as quickly as his private Gulfstream jet would allow.

Forty-eight hours later she was busy choosing the best camera position, as close to the graveside as possible without upsetting the mourners *too* much. As her cameraman set up the live feed, she replayed her report from the day before, the one that had once again given Barrington Network News the jump on all the competition.

"This is Stephanie Kovacs reporting live from Raleigh, North Carolina, outside a Raleigh Police Station. Late yesterday afternoon, FBI agent Hank Baines was gunned down in what seems to be a random drive-by shooting. Police and FBI officials have been working all night to investigate this senseless murder. Baines, along with Professor Michael Murphy from Preston University, was in Mount Airy Park when the incident took place. The police and FBI have not released any information at this point, but the police are said to be looking for an old Dodge van covered with multicolored graffiti. We will keep you up-to-date as more details become available. This is Stephanie Kovacs reporting live from Raleigh, North Carolina, for BNN."

Stephanie nodded to herself in satisfaction. Not bad, not bad at all. And not another news crew had been in sight. As usual, Barrington seemed to know what was happening before even his best reporters did, and Stephanie had long ago stopped asking herself how that was possible.

It made her look good, and that was all that mattered.

Smoothing her skirt and checking her hair, Stephanie was impressed to see how many had gathered for Baines's memorial service. Several hundred people filled the chairs on the lawn. Around the edges of the crowd she could see plainclothes officers wearing dark glasses and earphones. Clearly FBI agents on high alert. There were also dozens of uniformed police.

Were they expecting the person who killed Baines to make some sort of move at the memorial service?

Other news services were scurrying around preparing for their telecasts, some checking Stephanie's team out nervously, wondering what scoop she had up her sleeve now to make them look foolish. She smiled. Let them wonder, she thought, as Pastor Bob Wagoner walked up to the graveside podium and prepared to read the service.

As he began to speak, she looked at the mourners seated in front of him.

Baines's wife, Jennifer, was in the front row, sitting very still, her expression unreadable beneath a black veil. Next to her was Tiffany, wiping her eyes with a handkerchief as a girl-friend beside her squeezed her hand. Kovacs spotted Professor Murphy and his assistant, Shari Nelson, seated behind the grieving family. She hadn't seen Murphy since the Preston Community Church bombing, and she couldn't help noticing that he was looking good, tanned and fit, with an air of quiet power about him like a sprinter waiting on the blocks. She waited until he caught her eye.

We meet again, she thought, and felt a little jolt of adrenaline.

Pastor Wagoner finished, and a police officer in full Highland regalia began playing "Amazing Grace" on the bag-pipes. The eerie wailing sound of the pipes floated over the grass as an American flag was ceremoniously folded and handed to Jennifer Baines. It was impossible to see her reaction, but Tiffany was moved to fresh tears by the gesture.

As soon as the sound of the bagpipes had faded away, Stephanie started to work her way through the crowd. Jennifer Baines, with Tiffany clutching her arm, was making for one of the waiting black limousines, but Stephanie was on course to cut her off, her cameraman trotting behind her, ready to start filming at a moment's notice.

Suddenly a dark shadow crossed Stephanie's path, stopping her in her tracks. She looked up and Murphy was scowling at her.

"Can't you leave Mrs. Baines and her daughter alone? They've been through enough without the press hounding them."

Stephanie smiled her sweetest reporter's smile and put a microphone in front of Murphy's face. The camera was already rolling.

Murphy realized he'd fallen for her ploy. She hadn't been after Jennifer Baines at all. It was him she wanted to interview, and now she'd got him exactly where she wanted him. There was no way out now without making a scene, and that would play right into her hands.

He gritted his teeth and waited for whatever was coming. He didn't have to wait long.

"Here at the memorial service for FBI agent Hank Baines, I'm talking with Professor Michael Murphy of Preston University. Professor Murphy, you were the last person to see Hank Baines alive, is that right?"

"I was present when he tragically lost his life, yes," he said.

"Would it be correct to say you were friends?"

"Yes."

"Then can I ask you what you were doing meeting with your good friend Hank Baines at an abandoned carousel at Mount Airy Park? Kind of a strange place to meet up for a chat, isn't it?"

Murphy started to reply, but Stephanie ignored him.

"Unless you were concerned that people shouldn't witness this meeting, of course." She lowered her voice, the familiar sign to her viewers that she was moving in for the kill. "What was it you and Agent Baines were discussing, Professor Murphy? Have you told the police? Have you told his grieving widow? Tell me, do you feel any sense of responsibility for his death? Do you think it was appropriate for you to be here today? Can you explain why your fingerprints were on a gun found at the scene?"

Murphy was momentarily stunned. He'd seen her do the exact same thing in dozens of interviews, but that didn't make it any easier to deal with. She'd fire a series of questions at the interviewee without pause, each one more provocative and outrageous than the last, until they were in such a state of shock that they couldn't muster any sort of reply. Standing like a deer in headlights, they'd look just the way she wanted them to look.

Guilty.

And then quick as a flash she'd cut back to the studio and they'd be left high and dry.

Murphy was determined that wasn't going to happen. "I've come here to pay my respects to a fine man and a good friend. I think it would be tasteless and inappropriate to speculate about the perpetrator of this tragedy at his graveside, don't you? I have given the police and FBI the fullest possible statement. Perhaps you should ask them. Thank you very much."

He turned to go, satisfied that he'd ended the interview on his terms, but she had one more round left and she aimed it at his back.

"Professor Murphy, is it possible that Hank Baines's death had anything to do with the clandestine expedition you're planning to search for the remains of Noah's Ark on Mount Ararat? Would you like to comment on that?"

Now Murphy really was stunned. How had she found out about that? Had one of the team leaked the information? Did she have a source within the CIA?

He tried not to looked fazed by the question. "Like many archaeologists, I've been fascinated by stories of the ark since I was a boy," he said. "It would certainly be a great adventure to try and find it. Now I'm afraid I have to go."

He turned away again, wondering how Stephanie would wrap up the interview before heading back to the studio.

"Good luck, Professor Murphy" was all he heard her say. "Good luck."

THIRTY

ONE THING STEPHANIE KOVACS had wrong: During the memorial service Murphy wasn't thinking about Mount Ararat. He was thinking about Mount Rainier in Washington. Or to be exact, the Mount Rainier Mountain Climbing School.

It was the perfect place to train for the ordeal that lay ahead.

Levi and Murphy had chosen it because Ararat and Rainier are both volcanoes. Ararat is 16,854 feet high and Rainier 14,410. Both have glaciers with large crevasses and snow bridges, and both have steep terrain.

Murphy and Levi flew from Raleigh to Seattle together. The rest of the team members were to meet them at the school. Murphy had selected Vern Peterson and Isis—the rest were up to Levi, and Murphy was keen to know who they were.

"Picking a team like this, it's all about balance," Levi explained as they buckled in prior to takeoff. "You have to have the right mix of skills. Personalities are important too. You have to remember you may be relying on one another for your lives." He glanced at Murphy disapprovingly.

"Isis is going to make a valuable member of the team," Murphy insisted, correctly interpreting Levi's veiled remark. "We'll need her to translate any writing we may find on the ark, and she's a very experienced mountaineer."

And, he might have added, *she's already saved my life once.*

Levi grunted. "First, security. Two guys, very highly recommended. The first is Colonel Blake Hodson. Ex–Army Ranger. The other is Commander Salvador Valdez. Ex–Navy SEAL. Very tough, but he has a sense of humor too."

Murphy nodded. "Sounds like security's covered. Who's next?"

"Professor Wendell Reinhold. PhD from MIT in engineering. Knows all there is to know about building structures. He'll be able to assess the state of the ark and advise on all scientific matters. He's a bit of an action man too. Good on mountains."

"I've heard of him," Murphy said. "I read his book on the construction of the pyramids in Egypt and Mexico. A brilliant man. It's great he's on board."

"I thought you'd approve," said Levi with a smile. "Now the political stuff. The next two members will be representing the governments of Turkey and the United States. Mustafa Bayer is a former member of the Turkish Special Forces. Since his retirement from the military, he's been working with the government in the Department of Natural Resources and Environment. He is also an expert on Turkish history and archaeological artifacts. His counterpart for the United States is Darin Lundquist. He presently serves as Special Assistant to the Turkish Ambassador."

"You're sure he doesn't work for the CIA?"

Levi just smiled. "It's imperative we have a Turkish member on the team, and the Turkish government insisted on an official U.S. representative. But Lundquist is no desk jockey. He's climbed a lot of mountains in Turkey. He'll be useful. The last member of the team is Larry Whittaker. He'll be your cameraman. He'll film the entire trip. You've probably seen his stuff from the Gulf War. There's no one better at taking great pictures under tough conditions."

Levi handed him a slim file on each member of the team, and Murphy settled down to read. By the time he finished, they were touching down in Seattle.

Twelve hours later the team was climbing a steep boulder field on the slopes of the mountain, and Murphy was beginning to realize what the training exercise was all about. Undoubtedly they would all learn valuable skills, or hone existing ones, but more important, he would have a chance to observe each member of the team in an extreme environment, under stress, and in difficult conditions.

It was the only way to find out who these people really were and whether he could rely on them.

At the first team meeting Murphy had introduced himself and explained the goals of the expedition—as well as the risks. Then he asked for questions. Valdez was the first to raise his hand. The ex-SEAL was solidly built, with a square jaw and an iron-gray buzz cut. So far Murphy hadn't seen him smile.

"You need someone who can climb a thousand-foot vertical face in the dark with a blizzard going, you've come to the right guy. But something tells me you picked me and Hodson for something besides our mountaineering chops. Just what kind of bad guys are you expecting to find on Mount Ararat?"

It was a good question. And the bad news was that Murphy didn't have a good answer.

"Mount Ararat is situated in a dangerous part of the world, period. We could be facing bandits, wild dogs, or just local tribesmen who are suspicious of strangers."

Valdez narrowed his eyes. He didn't look convinced. "So take some dog chews and a few bucks to hand out to the locals. You don't need us." He pushed his chair back and stood up to go.

"Okay!" Murphy held his hands out in front of him, palms up. "You're right. There could be other . . . dangers. I want to make sure the team is properly protected, and Levi tells me you guys are the best. The problem is, I can't tell you exactly what those dangers are."

Valdez remained standing, his thick forearms folded over his chest. Murphy realized he'd have to level with him before he could go any further.

"Look, you probably heard about that FBI agent, Hank Baines, who was shot. He was standing next to me at the time. And the day before that, Dr. McDonald and I were abducted and threatened in Washington."

He could see Isis raise an eyebrow. Clearly she didn't think "abducted and threatened" described their experiences accurately.

"The fact is," Murphy continued, "somebody knows about this expedition and doesn't want it to succeed. Right now I can't tell you who that somebody is. But I can tell you that they are ruthless and will stop at nothing to get whatever it is they want."

"And that is?" asked Professor Reinhold. He was a surprisingly boyish figure, with an unruly mop of blond hair he was forever pushing out of his eyes and old-fashioned round spectacles. Unlike Valdez, he always seemed to be grinning.

"We have to assume it's the same thing we want—the remains of the ark and whatever's in it."

Reinhold scratched his chin thoughtfully. "If they're willing to kill for it, it must be something pretty awesome. More than a few fragments of soggy wood, I'll bet." The prospect of somebody trying to kill him for a biblical artifact seemed to please him immensely.

Hodson, the ex-Ranger, seemed to like Murphy's answer too. With his mirrored shades and constant gum-chewing, it was hard to read his expression, but he was nodding vigorously, as if meeting some serious bad guys was his idea of a great vacation. He turned to Valdez and grinned. "I'm sure me and the professors can handle any trouble, if you want to sit this one out, Commander."

Valdez sat down, but not before fixing Hodson with a steely stare. "I'm in," he grunted.

Murphy breathed a sigh of relief. At least so far no one had walked out. But the fireworks weren't over quite yet. At the back of the group, Mustafa Bayer was leaning back against his chair as he smoothed out his dark mustache with an elegantly manicured finger. He addressed Isis, who was sitting next to him, her legs and arms crossed in what looked like a fiercely defensive posture.

"Luckily also, Mr. Levi was wise enough to ensure a Turkish military presence, so you will be safe, Miss McDonald, even if Mr. Valdez and Mr. Hodson decide to start shooting each other."

Leaning across Isis, Lundquist, a tall figure dressed in a well-cut charcoal-gray suit, decided to join in. "Hey, Mustafa. Let's not forget who foots the bill for all those planes and missiles you people are so proud of!"

Murphy jumped in before things could escalate. "Hey, guys. Let's focus on the goal here. You have each been selected because of your very special skills and accomplishments. But our only hope of success is if we pull together. Anybody has a personal beef, leave it at base camp or we're all going to be in trouble."

No one spoke. Valdez, Hodson, Bayer, and Lundquist all glared at each other, Isis glared at Bayer, and Reinhold just seemed amused by the whole thing. Then Murphy noticed Whittaker, standing against the wall, aiming his camera at the group.

Click.

Great team photo, Murphy thought ruefully. He had two days on the slopes of Mount Rainier to turn these people into a tightly knit unit. Only God would know if it was going to be enough.

THIRTY-ONE

THE DRIVE FROM ANKARA to Erzurum was long and dusty, and Isis had slept most of the way. Murphy wasn't surprised. The training on Mount Rainier had been hard—even for the ex-Special Forces guys—and they all had the sore muscles and bruises to prove it.

He looked in the rearview mirror and caught a glimpse of her red hair, fiery in the late-afternoon sunlight. Her mouth was slightly open, giving her an innocent, childlike look. But he now knew it was an illusion. He thought back to their ordeal in Washington. She certainly hadn't looked innocent or childlike with an automatic in her hand and a dead man at her feet.

And to think I brought her along to keep her safe.

The Land Rover bumped over a pothole, and Murphy looked in the mirror again to see if Isis had been wakened, but her eyes remained closed. *She must be exhausted*, he thought.

Ahead, the empty road wound through low, dusty hills. On each side, biscuit-colored fields stretched into the haze. It felt to Murphy as if he were utterly alone. The sound of his own voice, barely audible over the hum of the engine, surprised him.

"You've got me all confused, Isis, you know that? I thought I knew what I was doing, but now . . . You know why I asked you to come on the expedition, to help me find the ark? To keep you safe! That was my stupid plan. After Talon tried to kill you, I knew I had to protect you, but how could I do that with you in Washington and me in Preston? I had to find a way to keep us together, even if it meant exposing you to more danger. I was dumb enough to think that I could keep you safe. I guess I still felt so bad that I wasn't there when Laura got killed . . . I couldn't let it happen again. Some plan, huh?" He shook his head. "But you know what? After you shot that guy in Washington—after *you* saved *me*—I finally realized I'd been kidding myself all along. I didn't want you with me so I could protect you. I mean, I *do* want to protect you, but that wasn't the real reason. I could have told Levi to keep a watch on you. No, the real reason was because . . . because I couldn't bear to be apart from you. Because . . ." His voice lowered to a whisper. " . . . I'm in love with you."

Curled in the backseat, Isis's eyelids flickered briefly, but they remained closed. A single tear slowly made its way down her cheek.

An hour later they pulled up at the shabby-looking hotel Levi had recommended. "Here we are," Murphy said, turning to Isis.

She sat up in the backseat and yawned, avoiding his eyes.

"We better get a move on, then," she said matter-of-factly. "The museum will be closed in an hour. Just enough time to shower and change."

Twenty minutes later they were standing at the front desk of the Museum of Antiquity and Ancient Relics. A young man in a threadbare gray suit greeted them. "Welcome. I take it that you are Professor Murphy and this is Dr. McDonald, yes?"

They nodded. "It's good of you to let us look around," Murphy said.

"It is my pleasure." He stood up and gave a shallow bow. "Now, what exactly is it that you are looking for?"

Murphy explained about the Monastery of St. Jacob and Sir Reginald Calworth's account of his travels there in 1836. The guide knew nothing about the writings of Calworth and little about the monastery. As for relics, he shrugged as if to say, "How would I know?" It seemed an odd attitude for a museum guide.

Then his face brightened. "Just a minute! We have one of our former curators here today. He is eighty-three years of age, and occasionally he comes and helps us out for a few hours. He is in the basement. I will get him."

Murphy doubted the old man would know any more than the young guide, but when a frail, white-haired figure emerged from the basement a few minutes later he seemed sprightly and alert. The guide explained what Murphy and Isis were looking for, and after a minute's thought, the old man nodded vigorously and spoke excitedly to the guide in Turkish.

"Come!" said the young man, and they followed the old man

down a flight of steep wooden stairs and into an Aladdin's cave of antiquities. In the light of a single bulb hanging from the ceiling, they saw ramshackle piles of boxes, papers, and objects scattered in all directions.

"How are we going to find anything in this mess?" Isis muttered.

"He seems to know what he's doing," Murphy replied as the old man made his way through the chaos toward the far end of the room. Reaching a tottering pile of antique trunks, he ran his fingers over the worn labels, seeming to read what was written there by touch rather than sight.

Murphy and Isis held their breath and waited.

Eventually the old man rapped on one of the trunks and smiled broadly.

"This is the one! This is what you are looking for, I think," announced the guide, and they quickly moved the other trunks aside. Murphy pulled out a flashlight and Isis peered at the label.

"Monastery of something," she said. The old man nodded some more.

Opening a penknife, the guide slid the blade under the lid of the trunk and pried it open. A puff of sour-smelling dust made him lean back, coughing.

Murphy shined the light into the trunk. Then he reached in and gently pulled out what looked like an old copper kettle, blackened with grime.

He held it up to the light and Isis snorted. "Try rubbing it, Murphy. Perhaps there's a genie inside who'll give us three wishes."

The old man didn't seem disheartened. This was obviously

what he had hoped to find in the trunk. He jabbered something to the guide.

"Sir Reginald! Yes, it is his, I think," said the young man, grinning proudly.

Murphy carefully placed the kettle back in the trunk. "That's it?" he said. "Nothing else?"

The guide conferred with the old curator. He shook his head sadly. "He says that is the only relic we have left from Mount Ararat." He shrugged fatalistically. "Thieves. It is the way of the world."

Back on the street, Isis and Murphy wondered what to do next. He was surprised when she took his arm and steered him down a narrow street. "Come on, let's find a café and get some coffee. Although a cup of tea might be more appropriate," she giggled. He let her lead him past rows of dusty-looking shops, most of which were shutting up for the day as the call of the muezzin drifted down from the minarets on the other side of the town.

Something made Murphy look back, and he saw a large man duck quickly into a doorway. "Don't look around," he said, "but I think we're being followed."

Isis's lighthearted mood changed in an instant, nightmare visions of their ordeal in Washington flooding her mind.

They quickened their pace and Murphy led her down a side alley. They broke into a run, hoping to emerge at the other end before their pursuer could see which way they'd gone. The way was suddenly blocked by a thickset, unshaven man dressed in a shabby leather coat.

He smiled broadly, showing a row of gold teeth. "Please. No need to be afraid. I understand you are interested in relics from the Monastery of St. Jacob. Come this way." He turned his broad back and started walking down the alley.

Murphy and Isis looked at each other, then followed.

Ten minutes later they were sitting cross-legged on a threadbare carpet, sipping tea from little glasses in which cubes of sugar slowly dissolved. The man in the coat held out a tray of pistachios and they each took one.

"How did you know who we were and what we were looking for?" Murphy asked.

The big man laughed. "Erzurum is not so big place. Easy to know everything."

Murphy was about to press him further, but Isis knew they were wasting time. "Have you really got relics from the monastery? Things that came from Noah's Ark?"

The big man touched his hand to his chest with an offended look. "You think I lie to you? Maybe it is better if you go. Perhaps somebody else will appreciate what I have."

"Forgive me," Isis said quickly. "Please, will you show them to us?"

He grunted and went to a pile of carpets against one wall of the little shop and reached behind them. He lifted out an ornately carved box about three feet long and set it down in front of them.

A rusting metal plate was inscribed in Turkish. Isis translated for Murphy.

"Bishop Kartabar," she said.

Murphy's heart started racing. "Kartabar was the bishop in charge when Calworth visited in 1836!"

They quickly opened the box and peered in. On the top were five booklike manuscripts with ancient leather bindings. The language seemed to be Latin. Underneath the manuscripts was a bronze plate with some strange markings on it that already had Isis puzzled. Below that were several small vases containing what looked like crystals, and some curious instruments that looked somewhat like sextants or theodolites. Murphy picked one up. "Whatever these are, Calworth must have brought them with him. They look too modern to have come from the ark."

Isis started reading through the Latin manuscripts. Murphy continued to examine the other contents of the box, while the big man's eyes flitted impatiently between his two guests as if he was trying to measure how interested they were—and how much they'd be willing to pay.

Eventually Isis said, "This is relatively straightforward stuff. Latin mixed occasionally with some Turkish and Armenian. Most of it describes life at the Monastery in the fourth and fifth centuries. But this is interesting—a letter addressed to the curator in Erzurum from Bishop Kartabar. It says the items in the box were taken from the *sacred ark* by a monk named Cestannia in A.D. 507. A very hot summer had melted snow from the ark, and this Cestannia entered and took these items and many more. The rest of the items are stored at the monastery."

"What about the bronze plate? What did you make of the markings?"

"I've never seen anything quite like it," she admitted. "It looks a bit like Hebrew—perhaps some type of proto-Hebrew. All I can tell you with any confidence is that it's talking about metal and fire."

"What do you mean, 'metal and fire'?" said Murphy.

"It just talks about different types of metal and what kind of fire you need to make them. It doesn't make much sense."

She flipped some more pages. "Hmm. The bishop mentions that Cestannia saw *large writings* carved on the walls inside the ark, but that's about all he says about it."

Murphy turned to the big man. "Is this everything you have?"

His offended look returned. "Is it not enough? Ah, perhaps you would like some hairs from Noah's beard!"

Murphy laughed. "That won't be necessary. This is all very interesting. How much do you want for it?"

The big man stroked his chin. "One hundred thousand American dollars," he said finally.

"What? You have to be kidding!" Murphy said, shaking his head. "I'm not even convinced any of these items came from the ark. Like I said, it all looks too modern." He got up, dragging Isis with him.

With a panicked look, the big man put his hand on Murphy's arm. "Okay, how much are you willing to pay? Maybe I give you a discount."

Murphy pretended to think about it. "Ten thousand dollars. That's my final offer. Take it or leave it."

The big man scowled. "Okay, I take it. Give me the money now," he said, holding out a grimy hand.

"We don't carry that kind of cash around with us," Murphy

said. "We have to go to a bank. We'll be back in the morning—say, ten o'clock?"

"Ten o'clock," the big man agreed. "Don't be late. Maybe I have other customers, you know."

Murphy shook his hand and ushered Isis out into the street.

The big man sat down and carefully put the items back in the box before picking up a glass of tea and sipping the sweet, lukewarm liquid with a satisfied smile.

After a few minutes he looked at his watch and started to get up.

Which was when the high-velocity round punched a hole through the window and entered his forehead at several hundred feet per minute, blowing the back of his head and most of his brain out in a cloud of blood and bone.

THIRTY-TWO

SHEM WAS BARTERING FOR lamp oil when he heard a faint cry. He knew instantly it was Achsah. He turned and began running, pushing people out of the way.

Neither Shem nor Achsah had thought there would be any danger in the crowded marketplace in broad daylight, but they were wrong. He had left her talking with a spice merchant when he went to look for lamp oil.

A group of three men had spotted Achsah unaccompanied, quickly grabbed her, and were dragging her away from the market. She had started to yell when one of them struck her across the mouth and she fell. They ripped her robe and exposed her as they lifted her off the ground. Some in the marketplace turned and looked, then went back to their business.

Just another rape. Nothing out of the ordinary.

With a yell, Shem charged the three men holding his wife. They turned to see a wild-eyed madman launching himself bodily into their midst. With as much force as he could muster, Shem hit the man to the right of Achsah with his shoulder. He went sprawling into a stack of pottery.

He then struck the man on the left with his fist, and blood gushed as the man staggered backward, holding his hands to his shattered nose.

The man in front began to reach for his dagger. Shem saw the move and started drawing his sword, but they were jammed too close together for him to use it effectively, so he jabbed the sword handle into the man's mouth, sending fragments of teeth into the air. There was a cry of pain.

The three men picked themselves up, cursing, and prepared to attack, when they saw the glittering steel in Shem's hand. The thought of facing an angry husband wielding one of Tubal-cain's singing swords was too much. They quickly ran back to the market and disappeared into the crowd.

Shem held Achsah, who was crying uncontrollably. He still clutched the sword and kept one eye on the staring bystanders. He was filled with anger. "Let the flood come, O Lord," he said to himself, "so we do not have to endure such things any longer."

Japheth was walking on the roof of the ark when it happened.

Suddenly, in the middle of the morning, it was starting to get dark. Turning around, he gasped. The entire eastern sky was filled with a vast flock of birds, like a huge locust swarm blocking the sun.

"Where are they going?" he wondered. Then the first birds started landing on the ark. First a lark, then an egret, a bright blue parakeet, a mourning dove. Soon they covered the roof, birds of every size and shape and color.

Japheth was speechless; he couldn't move. He could only stare at the strange sight. Birds he couldn't even put a name to were twittering and cooing around him. Even more amazing was the fact that the birds seemed not to be afraid of him. He held out his arm and a dozen finches, sparrows, and hawks alighted on it as if it were the branch of a familiar tree.

Soon he found himself walking among the birds, looking at their fantastic colors. These were birds he had seen only at a distance. Now they were only a few inches from him. He saw small birds like the canary, thrush, and warbler. There were woodpeckers, owls, and kingfishers. He was amazed by the multicolored toucans, macaws, and pheasants. Peregrines brushed wings with pigeons as if they were the best of friends instead of deadly enemies. The ducks waddled around with the pelicans and the flamingos. He was overwhelmed.

It took a few minutes before the reality of what was happening struck him.

For 120 years he had helped his family build the ark. It had seemed like a never-ending task. Would there ever really be a terrible rain and a great flood? Would all the animals really gather together and come aboard the ark?

His smile of understanding began to fade. What about those who would be left behind? They would be facing God's judgment. They would be destroyed. His father's warnings were now coming true.

Japheth's thoughts were interrupted by a harsh yelling. He went to the edge of the roof and looked down. His brothers and Noah were shouting and pointing toward the forest. As his eyes lifted, his breath stopped.

Coming over the hill, and through what was left of the forest of Azer, were the animals.

They were making their way to the ark in a great herd, a milling crowd of beasts that was so huge he could hardly tell one animal from another. Straining his eyes as his mouth opened in astonishment, he could make out bears, lions, an elephant amid the torrent of smaller creatures.

As they neared the ark, he could see wondrous animals he had no names for and whose weird shapes he had never dreamed of–kangaroos, rhinoceroses, giraffes. The deer and the monkeys wandered with the leopards. The elephants looked huge as they lumbered among the skunks and porcupines, somehow managing not to crush a single one.

"Come down and help us," cried Shem.

Japheth climbed off the roof to the walkway and then to the third floor. He went through the door and down the large zigzagging ramp to the ground.

"What should we do now?" said Ham.

"God has brought the animals here. He will show us what to do," said Noah. He climbed up on part of the scaffolding supporting the ramp and looked over the animals.

He began to notice that the animals were sorting themselves into pairs. Soon they were standing next to their mates. His heart leaped with joy as he realized what God was doing.

"We will begin taking them up the ramp into the ark. Lead the larger and heavier animals in first. Take the elephants, hippopotami, and rhinoceroses down the inside ramp to the bottom floor. It will help to keep us from capsizing. Put the bear, moose, elk, and tapirs with them. We will bring in the large cats next."

They set to work, amazed at the docile way even the fiercest animals let themselves be led aboard the ark and into their stalls. Noah and his *family were too busy to notice the crowd of people who had gathered at a safe distance to watch this incredible sight. No one spoke—either from astonishment or from fear that the animals might attack them. Or perhaps the terrible truth had finally dawned on them.*

The flood was coming.

THIRTY-THREE

"THEY WERE PROBABLY FAKES," Murphy said as he and Isis caught their first glimpse of Dogubayazit. "I mean, that bronze plate—it's hard to believe something like that was really on the ark. I think our man got cold feet. He probably thought we'd show up with the police in the morning. That's why he made himself scarce."

"Those documents were genuine. I'm sure of it," Isis countered. "And ten thousand dollars is a lot of money. I find it hard to believe he wouldn't stick around to collect."

Murphy sighed. "Well, we'll never know now. So let's just put it behind us. What do you think of Dogubayazit?"

Isis snorted. "If you'd been prepared, if you'd had the money with you—"

"Isis, please!" Murphy almost shouted. "I've had a lot more experience than you with these things. Trust me, we were about to be taken for a ride. And now we're within striking distance of Ararat. Let's look forward, not back. Okay?"

She snorted again, but didn't say anything. They continued in silence along a highway running east on a large, flat plain between two ranges of desolate, craggy mountains. The road had slowly risen to an altitude of 6,400 feet as it got nearer to the Iranian border.

Now they could see Ararat in the distance about fifteen miles away, the top third covered in snow. It seemed incredible that the resting place of the ark was there in plain sight, as it had been for thousands of years, so clear they felt they only had to reach out to touch it. And the wonder of it banished all thoughts of what might have been in Erzurum.

They entered the town between clusters of shabby concrete houses and headed for the Hotel Isfahan, a favorite among climbing teams.

Dogubayazit had grown to a town of forty-nine thousand people, and Murphy wondered what they all did for a living out in the middle of nowhere. He had been told by Levi that the main source of income for the town was smuggling, which made sense.

When Murphy and Isis walked into the lobby, they could hear raucous laughter coming from farther inside the hotel. The receptionist, a thin man with an outsize mustache, seemed to know who they were before they had a chance to introduce themselves and simply pointed toward the dining room. They hefted their bags and followed his directions.

Inside the dining room, the Ararat team seemed to have pretty much taken over. There was no sign of any other guests.

And Murphy wondered whether the sight of Hodson and Valdez—dressed in army fatigues and with handguns slung in shoulder holsters, loudly downing shots of the local raki—had sent them scurrying for cover. They certainly looked like a dangerous crew, and Murphy was very glad they were on his side.

Also sitting at a long table spread with a red-checked tablecloth were Professor Reinhold, holding a book in one hand and a breadstick in the other, Bayer and Lundquist, engaged in a fiercely whispered debate over something, and Vern Peterson, who was chatting amiably with Whittaker. Vern was the first to spot Murphy and Isis, and he quickly got up from the table and intercepted them. "Murph, I've got some bad news. The Turkish government is giving us a hard time about the helicopter. I was able to fly it into Dogubayazit, but they say I don't have permission to go any nearer to Ararat."

Murphy looked over at Mustafa Bayer.

The Turk put his glass down and sighed theatrically. "I know! I know! I am working on it! I got the permits to climb the mountain, and we had permission to fly, but the man who was in charge of the military area was reassigned to a different post. The new colonel does not know about our arrangement. It's just typical Turkish bureaucracy. I'm sure I can clear it up soon."

"I hope we can by tomorrow evening," said Murphy. "If not, we'll need to hire horses to carry our gear up to Camp One. Then we will have to carry the other supplies to Camp Two and Camp Three by backpack. That won't be fun."

Peterson continued, "I sure want to get a chance to fly this thing, Murph. It's a twin-engine, four-rotator-blade Huey. It'll fly six people and some gear up to about twelve thousand feet.

If we go higher we'll probably have to drop it down to about four people. The four blades will help in the thin air, but the higher we go the less efficient we are."

"What happens if it starts snowing while you're flying at a high altitude?" asked Professor Reinhold, putting down a forkful of salad.

"That shouldn't be a problem. The Huey comes equipped with de-icing equipment. I think wind would be more of a problem. Strong gusts are difficult to deal with. Especially if you're too close to the mountain. We wouldn't be the first plane to flip. But don't worry, you're in good hands!"

"I'm relieved to hear that," Reinhold said, sounding anything but.

Hodson spoke up. "Isn't it possible that the wind from your blades could start an avalanche?"

Vern shrugged. "It's possible. You'll have to be sure you're not under a cornice or a steep face when I pick you up. I won't be able to land on most of the mountain. It's too steep. We'll have to use the winch and pull you up."

The group was silent for a moment, focusing on the fact that the helicopter pilot could be their savior—or could condemn them to an icy grave.

Then Lundquist waved Murphy and Isis over. "Come on, you two. Have a drink and something to eat. It's not bad, you know, and it may be a while before we see real food again."

Murphy decided it was time to establish his authority. "No thanks. We need to get things moving. I want you and Valdez to help me check all the climbing equipment and supplies." He nodded toward the other end of the table. "Hodson can check the first-aid equipment and radios. Isis has a list of food supplies we're going to need. I suggest Professor Reinhold go with her to the market."

Plates were reluctantly pushed aside, drinks downed, and everyone got moving. Bayer was left lounging in his chair.

"And what would you like me to do?" he smiled.

Murphy didn't return his smile. "We need that permission to fly over Ararat. Who do we have to talk to?"

Bayer frowned. "Do not trouble yourself. Trust me, it will be done."

"Then do it," Murphy insisted.

Bayer slunk off with a scowl. Whittaker watched him go and gave Murphy a wink. "Way to go, Murphy. I hope you haven't made an enemy there."

Murphy turned on him. "There's no room for prima donnas on this team, Whittaker. The sooner Bayer realizes it, the better."

"Then I guess I better go upstairs and check that all my film's loaded," Whittaker said, making for the door. "I don't want to get chewed out by the boss."

When everyone else had left, Murphy sat down with Vern and reviewed their plans, trying to make sure he had thought of everything. The way the rest of the team had seemed so relaxed was bothering him. Two hours later a disconsolate Bayer arrived back at the hotel.

"Is he going to release the Huey?" asked Peterson.

"I think so," Bayer said. "But it will not happen for at least two days. We will have to make other arrangements to get the equipment to the mountain. You will not be able to fly the team to Ararat, but you will be able to pick us up and bring us home."

"Let's go!" said Murphy, slapping the table with his palm. "We can't waste time here. We have to find someone with horses who can pack us in."

It was 5:00 A.M. the next day when the team assembled in front of the hotel and began loading their gear into a truck. Valdez got in the cab next to Bayer, while the rest of the team piled into a van. Peterson waved them off.

"We'll keep in touch by satellite phone," Murphy assured him, winding down the passenger-side window. "God willing, we'll see you on Ararat!"

Vern saluted and watched the van disappear around the corner.

The back of the van was fitted with rough benches on each side, and as the team settled themselves, Murphy was reminded of paratroopers waiting to be dropped over enemy territory. "Last chance to bail out," he said. "Next stop, Ararat."

"Next stop, Noah's Ark," Reinhold grinned.

Up front, Bayer was talking. "We'll head east on the main highway toward Iran, until we come to the Dogubayazit Commando Post. You will all need to have your passports and climbing permits ready for the military guards. About one kilometer past the post we will turn left and go north toward Ararat. It is a fairly good dirt road. It should not take too long."

Isis watched out the window as the sun rose over two small

villages. Some of the early-morning shepherds were already out rounding up their flocks.

Soon they began to climb the slopes toward a house. When they reached the 6,600-foot level, they stopped and unloaded their gear. The horse-packer and his two sons were waiting, huddled around a fire. They loaded the equipment onto the horses and the team began the trek to Camp 1. As the sound of hooves on the rocky trail replaced the grinding of gears, and goat-herder settlements replaced villages, they began to feel they had entered a different world—a world that still had links with the ancient past.

Murphy dropped back to watch his team as they progressed up the mountain. Valdez and Hodson had each taken a flank, scanning the trail ahead and periodically turning one-eighty to check behind. Machine pistols were slung round their necks, but their hands never left the stocks. Murphy didn't want to know how they'd got the weapons into Turkey. Bayer had taken point, no doubt an issue of pride, and was striding ahead up the trail. Occasionally he would slow and look up toward the snowline as if he was waiting for something. Lundquist walked behind him, his eyes never straying from Bayer's back, as if he was determined to keep him in sight at all times.

In the middle of the group, Reinhold was trying to read a book balanced on the back of one of the horses. Every now and then he would stumble against a rock, cursing, and the book would fall to the ground. Murphy shook his head. For a man who seemed to share many of his own interests, Reinhold was curiously uncommunicative. He was clearly as fascinated by the possibility of finding the ark as Murphy was, but Murphy suspected he was put off by the spiritual underpinning of their quest and preferred to keep his thoughts to himself. Fair enough, Murphy thought. Plenty of time for talking later.

Just ahead of Murphy, Isis was keeping up a good pace with her easy, economical stride. She looked as if she was on a Sunday morning stroll up a gentle hillside, and Murphy marveled again at her reserves of strength and endurance. He also marveled at her wild, natural beauty, which perfectly complemented the awesome landscape around them.

And he wasn't the only one to appreciate it. For every shot of the mountain Whittaker took, he surreptitiously snapped off two of Isis. Despite himself, Murphy felt a pang of annoyance. Or could it be jealousy?

It was mid-afternoon, and they seemed to have been climbing for hours when the clouds grew dark and it began to rain. By the time they had unpacked their rain gear, it had begun to pour. Thunder roared and lightning flashed, and slippery mud quickly made the going treacherous. But the horse-packer and his sons didn't slow down for the weather. They trudged on until the clouds broke up and the sun peeked through.

At about ten thousand feet the team reached a small grassy meadow. Streams of crystal water flowed from under a nearby snowbank, and the horse-packer and his sons helped to set up camp. Bright-colored nylon tents soon covered the ground, the horses were hobbled, and the evening meal was bubbling in pots over a brushwood fire.

As everyone hungrily devoured the meal of rice and beans,

Murphy explained the plan for the following days, a series of treks up to Camps 2 and 3, ferrying supplies back and forth while they acclimated themselves.

There was little conversation. Everyone had their own thoughts about what was to come, and there was a palpable sense of energies being conserved. The easy part was over.

The sun had gone down and a breeze was picking up. The horse-packer and his sons tied blankets over the horses and went to their tent, while the rest followed suit.

Isis curled up in her sleeping bag and pulled the drawstring tight against the cold air. In the darkness she could hear the nylon flapping in the breeze. She couldn't help thinking that Murphy was only a few feet away. Then exhaustion took over and she began to fall asleep, her mind filling with a jumble of violent images that would feed her dreams through the night.

Murphy lay with his eyes open, listening to the sounds of the night. He could hear the noise of weapons being field-stripped. And the rustle of pages—probably Professor Reinhold studying his research materials on the construction of the ark.

Then all he could hear was the sound of the wind on the mountain.

He began to pray.

THIRTY-FOUR

"YOU'RE SURE EVERYTHING will be safe?"

It was early in the morning and Murphy and Bayer were standing on a patch of ground away from the tents, by the horses. Behind them, the rest of the team were busy making breakfast and cups of hot tea.

Bayer touched his hand to his chest. "Of course, I will watch over them. There will be no problem." He patted the automatic holstered at his waist.

"Okay," Murphy said. "We're going to cross the Araxes Glacier and explore the area around the Ahora Gorge. If nothing else, Whittaker should get some good footage on the glacier."

Bayer sat down on a rock and lit a cigarette, staring off into the distance, while Murphy went back to the tents to help pack the rucksacks with ropes, carabiners, ice screws, crampons, and ice axes.

Leaving Isis, Reinhold, and Bayer, along with the horse-packer and his sons, the rest of the team checked their GPS equipment and headed toward the glacier, their plan being to traverse east at relatively the same level around the mountain. They would save the strenuous upward climbing for later.

The morning air was crisp and exhilarating. The sky was bright blue and not a cloud could be seen. But as Murphy knew, appearances on Ararat could be deceptive. Within an hour a clear sky could deliver a raging blizzard.

The team moved at a good pace across the rocks and occasional snow drifts on the shady sides of the mountain. Even though it was early in the morning, they began to unzip their jackets and open them up. It was important to let out body heat and reduce the sweating to a minimum to keep their clothes dry and reduce dehydration.

We're getting closer, Murphy thought excitedly, adrenaline surging through him as he entered a rock-strewn gully.

Isis watched the little group as they disappeared into the snowfield. The ache in her legs felt good, and despite a night of feverish dreams, the clear mountain air had invigorated her. She felt herself beginning to relax for the first time in weeks. Or was it simply that she felt better when Murphy was around? She looked for a sunny rock with a good view of the mountain where she could enjoy a few more minutes of leisure before cleaning up the pots and pans, and saw Professor Reinhold sitting on a rock at the front of the meadow where it began to drop down the mountain. He, too, liked the sun, but he also liked the slight breeze. The only thing he didn't like was having to hold the pages of his book down while he read. The breeze kept trying to turn them for him.

Bayer was nowhere to be seen.

When the team reached the Araxes Glacier, they unloaded their spiked crampons and put them on. They each hooked on to a rope for safety, with about forty feet between each climber, and began to cross a sea of white snow covering the glacier. Murphy was leading the team, with Valdez behind him. Next came Lundquist, and Hodson brought up the rear. Whittaker had a separate rope tied to the main rope between Lundquist and Valdez, allowing him the freedom to move forward or backward to take pictures.

Despite Valdez and Lundquist's suddenly dropping to their armpits in the snow as they fell into small crevasses covered by snowdrifts, crossing the glacier was relatively easy.

Descending the east side of the glacier was more difficult. The snow had turned into ice. Murphy was pounding in some ice screws when he slipped and fell a few feet before catching himself. He hooked onto the belay ropes to drop the seventy feet to the rocks below, aiming to leave the ropes in place for the climb back up on the return trip.

He hoped they'd still be there.

"Beautiful, aren't they?" Reinhold said, pointing to the horses. The horse-packer's sons were feeding them hay and talking to them. Isis wondered whether the horses understood Turkish.

"Yes, they are. And the boys look after them well. You don't always see that out here," Isis replied. "This is the first time I've seen you with your nose out of a book," she laughed.

Reinhold smiled. "You can never learn too much. When we find the ark—or I should say *if* we find the ark, whatever's left of it—I want to make sure I know what we're looking at, how stable the structure is. And, of course, if it really *is* the ark. There's been plenty of time for someone to plant fake remains on the mountain."

"You mean like the Turin shroud?"

"Exactly. Although your Professor Murphy probably believes that's legitimate."

Isis was rather disconcerted to hear him referred to as *her* Professor Murphy. "I have no idea what he believes," she said airily. "But what about you? I find it hard to believe you'd leave your precious research behind to take your life in your hands on Mount Ararat if you didn't think there was something here."

Reinhold kept his smile in place, but his boyish eyes had hardened. "Oh, I think there's something up here, all right. The question is, what?"

Progress toward the Ahora Gorge was becoming more difficult as the team entered a large boulder field. Some of the rocks were as large as a small house. Climbing around the boulders or over them was beginning to eat up time and energy.

"Let's rest for a minute," Lundquist suggested, his face streaked with sweat.

"Come on, Lundquist, we don't have the time. We got a schedule here," protested Hodson, looking to Murphy for confirmation.

Murphy was about to speak, but Whittaker put a hand on his shoulder. Then he put a finger to his lips. He seemed to be listening for something.

"What is it?" Murphy whispered.

Whittaker didn't reply, but then Murphy could hear it too. A faint crackling in the distance, like waves dragging stones down a beach. He looked up the slope, back the way they'd come, and suddenly he could see it.

"Rock avalanche!" he yelled. "Take cover!"

Murphy and Valdez scrambled toward the house-shaped rock to their right. Hodson and Lundquist were trying to reach a similar rock twenty feet below them.

Whittaker for some reason started running toward the avalanche as if he had some sort of bizarre death wish. For a moment Murphy thought he was going to have to turn around and pull him back. Then he saw that Whittaker had spotted a perfect nook scooped into the boulder field just above them. *I guess he's done this more times than I have,* Murphy thought as he hurled himself to the ground alongside Valdez. He rolled just in time to see Whittaker squeezing off one last shot with his camera before the huge wave of dust and rocks surged over his position and crashed into the rock Murphy and Valdez were sheltering behind.

As the tremendous noise overwhelmed them and the dust forced them to close their eyes, Murphy tried to picture Lundquist and Hodson's last position. He had no idea whether they'd managed to get out of the avalanche's path in time. For several agonizing minutes Murphy clung to the rocks, waiting for the dreadful grinding and crashing noise to stop, signaling that the danger had passed. Eventually he pushed himself to his feet. Holding his scarf over his nose and mouth against the choking dust, he moved down the boulder field, trying to locate the other members of the team. Valdez and Whittaker were soon at his side.

"Hodson!" he shouted. "Lundquist! Where are you?"

There was a muffled "Here!" and Murphy saw movement in the rubble. Hodson was staggering to his feet and then Lundquist, too, began to emerge.

Hodson put a hand to his forehead and it came away bloody. "I was making for that rock over there when this guy trips me up. Luckily we fell into a hole. Otherwise that would have been it."

"You never would have made it," Lundquist protested, brushing himself off. "You were lucky I grabbed you in time."

Hodson glared at him and spat into the dust. "Whatever."

"Look, the main thing is we're all okay," Murphy said. "Thanks to Whittaker's sharp senses."

"You never know who's going to save your life, do you?" Whittaker grinned, snapping off a shot of the disheveled and dusty mountaineers.

Then they heard another sound and their heads all jerked up at the same time. Was it the sound of another avalanche starting? They listened, readying themselves to dive to shelter if they needed to. But it was too far away. A steady *pop-pop-pop* back from the direction of the camp.

Gunfire.

The only ones to hear them coming were the horses. Their
ears went up first. Then their nostrils flared as they began to
sniff the air. They snorted a couple of times and whinnied softly.

The noise of the horses made the dozing horse-packer open
his eyes. He looked at his horses to see what was wrong. Could
they smell a pack of wild dogs?

The horse-packer sat up just in time to see a figure stepping
out from behind a rock. He had a rifle in his hand and a scarf
covering his face. He was heading for Professor Reinhold, back
on the rock with his book.

The horse-packer was about to shout a warning when he
heard another sound. The sound of a round being chambered. It
came from his left and he turned to see another masked gunman, his rifle pointing straight at the horse-packer's heart.

He raised his hands and slowly turned his head to see a third
gunman moving quickly toward Isis's tent. Beside him, his sons
were awake, and the horse-packer put his hands on their shoulders to keep them still, but they needed no prompting. They
had lived long enough in these mountains to know that when a
rifle was pointed at you, you simply trusted in Allah and waited
to see what would happen next.

Reinhold was still deep in his book when he felt the hard jab
in his back. He turned and looked into the barrel of a rifle held
by a man with a scarf over his head. He slowly raised his hands.
He could see Isis emerging from her tent as another gunman
grunted something to her in Turkish.

This doesn't look good, he thought. *Not good at all.*

The gunmen herded everyone into the cooking area. One of the men held them at rifle-point while the other two searched the tents. They came out holding a few items that they wanted.

The leader of the gunmen spoke to the horse-packer in what sounded like Kurdish. Reinhold couldn't understand the words, but his meaning, emphasized with hand gestures, was clear enough. They wanted him to take his horses and sons and leave. As long as he kept his mouth shut and didn't alert the authorities to what had happened, they wouldn't be harmed. The horse-packer gave Reinhold and Isis a pitying look, then began leading the horses back down the trail.

The gunmen turned their attention to Isis and Reinhold, roughly tying their hands with old pieces of nylon rope. Jabbing at Isis with the point of the rifle, one man was asking her something urgently in Turkish.

Reinhold realized he had an urgent question of his own.

Where was Bayer?

Just then there was a clatter of rocks farther up the mountain, and the gunmen swung their rifles around instinctively. The leader shouted a few words in Kurdish, and he and one of the other gunmen started jogging down the trail in the direction the horse-packer and his sons had gone, dragging Isis between them. Reinhold was left alone with the third gunman. The gunman waved a finger at him and said something Reinhold didn't understand, but he was sure it was something along the lines of "Don't try anything." He wished he knew enough Kurdish to be able to tell him, "You've got to be kidding."

Then there was another clatter of rocks and the gunman

swung his rifle around in the direction of the noise. Out of the corner of his eye, Reinhold could see a dark figure approaching fast. The gunman saw it too, but too late. His head was jerked back by a powerful hand and a knife blade flashed. He clutched his side, made a retching noise, then collapsed to his knees as Bayer pulled the blade out and wiped it roughly on his fatigues. He looked at Reinhold fiercely, pressing his finger to his lips. Reinhold nodded. Then Bayer jogged away in the direction the other two gunmen had taken, and Reinhold was left staring at the bloody corpse as the last twitches of life left it.

After a while he walked a few feet away, toward the tents. He didn't know what to do. Eventually he went back to the corpse and pried the rifle out of the dead man's grip. He hoped he'd know how to use it if he had to.

Suddenly the camp had gone very silent. Even the wind had dropped to a whisper. He strained his ears to hear the slightest sound. He thought he heard a cry. Was it Isis? He dreaded to think what might be happening to her. Then he heard a crack. Then another. A noise like rocks falling down a steep slope. Then silence.

He waited, expecting at any moment to see the two other gunmen returning to camp. Then he'd have to use the rifle. He suddenly realized how foolish it was to be standing in the middle of the meadow, a sitting target. He started running toward the glacier, searching to find a boulder large enough to hide behind, when he heard a shout.

"Professor Reinhold! It is okay, my friend. No need for running!"

He turned and there was Bayer, grinning from ear to ear as he led a pale-looking Isis back into camp. She was clearly trembling.

"What happened?" Reinhold asked when they reached him.

Bayer shook his head. "Very bad men. Very bad." Then he grinned again. "But also very stupid. And now very dead."

He let go of Isis and she collapsed into Reinhold's arms.

THIRTY-FIVE

THE NEXT MORNING Murphy was sharing a mug of steaming tea with Isis while the rest of the team sat around the fire. It was all he could do not to hug her to him, but she seemed to be happy he was simply there. The high-speed trek back to camp from the glacier had been brutal, as they pushed themselves to exhaustion, not knowing what would be awaiting them. Now that they were all together again—and alive—for the first time there was a palpable sense of brotherhood.

"So who were they?" Murphy asked Bayer, realizing that, amid the euphoria of Isis's safe return, he hadn't inquired about the identity of the gunmen.

"PPK for sure," Bayer replied.

Isis looked at him quizzically and Lundquist stepped in, happy to show off his knowledge of Turkish politics.

"Kurdish rebels. The Worker's Party of Kurdistan, to be exact. They recently discovered that they can get money for their cause by kidnapping tourists and holding them for ransom. That is most likely what they were going to do with you."

Bayer nodded. "Exactly."

Murphy looked thoughtful. "You're probably right, but I want to be sure."

Bayer looked affronted, as if Murphy was questioning whether he really had saved Isis. "What do you mean?"

"I want to examine the other bodies. See if there's any identification."

Bayer shook his head, as if this was typical American craziness. "Rebels, that's all they were. What else could they be?" He got up suddenly. "But come, if you want to see them, I can take you." He grinned. "I don't think they will have gone anywhere in the night."

Murphy, Valdez, and Bayer hiked down the trail until Bayer motioned them to stop and pointed into a side gulley.

"There."

They walked to the edge and looked over. Before they even saw the bodies they heard the noise. Murphy motioned them to approach slowly. Valdez unslung his machine pistol and slipped off the safety.

They peered over the edge and Murphy gasped. A writhing, heaving mass of shaggy brown bodies was tearing at the corpses of the gunmen, the bloody remains of which were being tossed around like rags. A pack of maybe fifteen wild dogs snarled and growled as they fought for the tastiest morsels, but from the looks of the bodies, the best pickings were already gone.

"Holy—" Valdez spat and chambered a round. Bayer put a restraining hand on his arm, but it was too late. As one, the dogs pricked up their ears and turned in their direction.

Valdez shook off Bayer's arm. "You think I'm scared of a bunch of dogs?"

"You should be," Bayer said quietly, backing away. "These are not like dogs in your country. These are beasts."

The wolflike dogs were now eyeing the three men hungrily and nosing the air.

"Come on," Murphy said. "Animals that hunt in packs are basically cowards—and I'll bet these pooches prefer their meat already dead."

He started picking his way through the rocks and down the slope, and the dogs began to back off, snarling, snouts lowered to the ground. Reluctantly, Valdez and Bayer followed.

Valdez fired a round into the air and the dogs backed off a little farther. The three men knelt over the bodies, and while Valdez kept an eye on the dogs, Murphy sorted through the grisly remains, searching for anything that might give them a clue to the gunmen's identity.

"Hurry," Bayer whispered fiercely.

Valdez shot Murphy a panicked look and got to his feet. Then suddenly two dogs launched themselves out of the pack, and Murphy heard the stutter of the machine pistol as Valdez cut them down. As the bodies lay twitching at their feet, Murphy hoped that the rest of the dogs would retreat.

He was wrong. Their hunger was stronger than their fear.

With the instinct of true pack hunters, the rest of the dogs advanced as one. Bayer drew his knife from his boot, cursing the fact that he had left his pistol back at the camp. But at least he had a weapon. Murphy had nothing.

"How many rounds in that clip?" Bayer asked Valdez urgently.

"Not enough," came the grim reply. "And I think they know it. If they rush us, we're finished."

"And all because of what? To see if these men are KGB?" Bayer spat.

Murphy picked up a rock and hurled it at the nearest dog, hitting it squarely in the shoulder. The dog snarled contemptuously and took a step forward. It seemed to sense the men's fear.

Suddenly, the unexpected happened. From the other side of the gulley a tall, slim man walked slowly toward them. He was wearing a gray robe with a wide leather belt around his waist, and Murphy could see dark, piercing eyes above a ragged gray and black beard. He carried a twisted staff that was almost as tall as he was.

For a moment the three men forgot their dilemma, watching mesmerized as the man approached the dogs, half of whom had turned in his direction. The man seemed to be deciding on something, then he took a step forward and Murphy realized he was selecting the alpha male. The strange man fixed his gaze on the largest dog and the dog seemed to accept the challenge, easing itself out of the pack so that it stood alone.

It let out a fierce bark and leaped at the man's throat. With surprising agility he pivoted and swung the staff around, cracking the dog across the skull just as the jaws were about to close on his wrist. The dog fell to the ground but instantly snapped at the man's ankle. But the man was too quick. He wheeled the staff in a blur of movement, and they heard a sickening crunch as it impacted. The dog lay still.

The man raised his staff again and took a step toward the pack. As if with a single thought, they turned tail and ran back down the gully, yelping as they went.

Of course, Murphy thought. *Kill the leader.* He hadn't been thinking straight. They watched the dogs go out of sight, Valdez keeping his machine pistol cocked in their direction. Then Murphy turned to the strange-looking man.

But he was gone.

THIRTY-SIX

MURPHY DIALED THE NUMBER on his satellite phone and waited.

"This is Vern Peterson."

"Vern. This is Murph. It's good to hear your voice."

"How's it going with you and the team?"

He hesitated. "We've had our share of excitement. How's it going with you? Any news on the permission to fly over Ararat?"

"Two more days, it looks like," said Peterson. "They have to get formal written permission from the commander in charge. He's in Istanbul attending a meeting. They tell me he's signed the forms and they're on their way in a military transport, but don't hold your breath. I'll believe it when I see it."

Murphy knew Vern's time in the military had given him a fatalistic attitude toward paperwork. It would happen when it would happen. But even so, there was an edge to his voice. He wanted to be on the mountain, where the action was. That was why Murphy had spared him the details of the last couple days. It would only make Vern more frustrated.

"Don't worry, Vern. We'll move the supplies up to Camp Two by backpack."

"Where's that on the map?"

"On the East Plateau, at about thirteen thousand feet. Then we're going to explore the area from the East Summit over to Abich Two, above the Ahora Gorge. Some of the sightings of the ark have been in this area."

"I feel guilty, Murph. I'm staying in a nice warm hotel while you guys are freezing your tail ends off!"

"Don't worry about it. We'll call you if there are any problems or we discover something. Keep your satellite phone charged up. And, Vern, it's not over yet. You'll get your fair share of the excitement."

"Roger that!"

Murphy cut the connection. *Be careful what you wish for, Vern,* he thought to himself. *If Julie knew what was going on, she'd skewer me like a hog.*

The rest of the day Murphy and the team began the tiresome process of hauling their equipment and supplies from Camp 1 to Camp 2. The mountain was so steep that the team had to rope together and zigzag their way up the snowfield. In a couple of places the wind had drifted mounds of soft snow that they had to almost literally swim through. By the end of the three-thousand-foot climb, they were all sweating profusely, despite the cold.

Murphy looked at Isis as she scrambled onto the plateau. "How are you doing?" She nodded her head and gave a forced smile. She didn't have enough air in her lungs to speak.

The East Plateau leveled for about two hundred yards until it began to rise again toward the summit, almost four thousand feet higher. Lundquist, Reinhold, and Bayer began to set up the camp and anchor the tents.

"I may be colder up here, but I feel safer," Isis said to Murphy as they looked up at the majestic snowy summit, framed by an azure sky. "There's nothing for dogs up here."

"Except us," Murphy said.

She laughed. "Tempting morsel though I may be, I don't think they'd climb three thousand feet through snow and ice for the privilege."

"More fools them," Murphy said, and she blushed despite the chill.

Suddenly Murphy didn't know what to say, and he was relieved when Hodson signaled that he was starting back down for a second load of supplies. Murphy gave Isis an awkward smile and turned to join Hodson.

The trip toward the East Summit began at first light to allow a full day of exploration. Murphy had everyone put on their crampons and he took the lead with Hodson behind him. Following the colonel came Bayer, Isis, and Lundquist. Professor Reinhold and Valdez brought up the rear. Whittaker was anchored to the main rope and wandered around taking his pictures as usual.

It was about 11:00 A.M. when there was a yell as the team was crossing a ridge near the summit. They all turned in time to see Whittaker disappear.

He had wandered toward what looked like the top of the ridge. The rest of the climbers were slightly below in a straight line. But it wasn't the ridge. It was a cornice, and he had dropped straight through and was hanging in midair over a two-thousand-foot abyss. For once he didn't seem to be thinking about taking pictures.

All seven climbers instantly dropped to the ground and dug their feet into the snow. The rope played out and disappeared down the hole in the snow until it went taut. Murphy yelled orders and the team all began to slowly back away from the ridge. Eventually the snow-covered head and shoulders of Whittaker appeared. They kept backing away until he was on the solid part of the ridge. Whittaker sat there for a moment, a little dazed, but soon shook himself and stood up. Then he sat back down again as his knees gave out. Hodson made a square with his fingers and a clicking sound. Whittaker looked over and scowled, then his face broke into a grin. "You still got the lens cap on, you big ape!"

After a brief break to check Whittaker over, they started up the mountain again. Soon the climb became steeper and more difficult. Valdez noticed that Reinhold was weaving to the right and left as he was climbing. His pace was slowing. Murphy went back to see what the problem was.

"Altitude sickness," said Valdez. "He hasn't taken in enough water. You and the team go on. We'll catch up once he's hydrated."

Murphy nodded. "Just follow our tracks."

Twenty minutes later, Valdez hooked a thirty-foot section of rope onto the professor. "You go ahead and lead," said Valdez. "I'll follow. Go at whatever pace is comfortable. Use your ice ax like a cane if you need to."

A light snow had begun swirling around the two men, but the team's tracks were still clearly visible. Reinhold turned his head into the wind and started up the steep slope. They made good progress for half an hour, then suddenly the professor took a step and the snow gave way underfoot, catching him off balance. He fell to the side, and his body began to slide, quickly gaining momentum down the slope.

"Use your ax!" yelled Valdez.

Reinhold tried desperately to turn his ax into the snow so he could dig in with the wide blade, but before he could do it he hit the end of the thirty feet of rope and it snapped tight, jerking Valdez off his feet. Now both of them were sliding down the steep slope. Valdez rolled onto his stomach and put his body weight on the ax, instantly putting the brakes on his descent.

By now Reinhold had done likewise and they both came to a gentle stop. For a full minute neither of them moved, unwilling to loosen their ice axes' grip.

"Are you okay?" yelled Valdez.

"I think . . ." Reinhold took stock of his situation and realized he couldn't feel the ground beneath his legs.

"I'm in trouble! I'm hanging over a cliff!"

Valdez shouted back. "Hold on! Don't move! I'm gonna dig a snow seat."

Valdez kicked one foot at a time into the snow with his crampons, then slowly began to release his weight off his ice ax to see if his feet would hold his body weight. Nothing moved. He breathed a sigh of relief.

He began to dig a hole in the snow next to him with the ax. It had to be deep enough for him to sit in it like a bucket seat. He just hoped the snowbank was solid enough to hold the weight of both men.

When he finished, he again dug in his ice ax with a mighty blow and put his weight on it. It held. He slowly dislodged one foot and then the other and rolled into the bucket seat. Again he slowly released his weight while still holding on to the ax. Now the true test would come. Would it hold both of them?

"Valdez!" Reinhold screamed frantically. "I don't think I can hold on much longer!"

"You can and you will," Valdez replied.

Valdez tied a prussic knot onto the rope and then hooked it into the carabiner on his harness. He began to pull on the rope tied to the professor and slide the slack through the prussic knot for safety.

"Okay, I'm gonna pull you up!" Valdez was now yelling louder against the howl of the wind.

The professor tried to help by pulling on his ice ax. He moved up a couple of feet.

"See if you can kick your feet into the snow and stand on your crampons."

The professor did as he was told, and they held.

"Now take out your ice ax and dig it into the snow above you and see if you can start climbing up."

Reinhold got a new bite in the snow with the ax and began to step up the steep slope. As he pulled out one of the crampons and attempted to kick it into the snow, the one he was standing on broke out and he fell. He dropped a couple of feet and then the rope went taut.

The full body weight of both men pulling on the rope caused the seat Valdez was sitting in to compress about six inches. Valdez was sure they were both going to go over the edge when the snow stopped compressing. It was going to hold.

Valdez could feel the numbness in his fingers from cold and the effort of holding on to the rope, but he knew he wouldn't have to hold on for much longer. Reinhold was clawing his way nearer to the snow seat minute by minute. Just as Valdez felt the rope begin to slide through his fingers, Reinhold reached him and was able to cling on while Valdez dug another seat next to him. In another ten minutes they were sitting side by side, thirty feet above a cliff, in a snowstorm.

"You all right, Professor?"

Reinhold nodded, too exhausted to speak.

"Okay, Professor, here's the good news. About seventy feet above us is a rock outcrop. I'm gonna climb up to it and secure a rope. Then I'll lower a rope down to you, you hook it onto your harness, and you can climb up."

Reinhold looked horrified. He clearly wanted to stay in their snug snow seat as long as he could, and the prospect of another climb didn't appeal to him at all.

Valdez could see his willpower was nearly gone.

"Don't worry. I'm gonna be pulling you. You won't have to do nothing."

Reinhold nodded wearily and Valdez eased himself carefully out of the snow seat and began to climb. In the driving snow, it took him twenty minutes to reach the outcrop. He took the rope out of his pack and attempted to tie it to one of the rocks. His hands were now very cold, and he was having a hard time tying the knot with his gloves on. He put a glove finger in between his teeth and pulled the glove off. The tie was successful, but now his fingers were burning with pain. He knew frostbite was beginning to kick in, but there was no time to warm them. He put his glove back on, then tied onto the rope and lowered himself about twelve feet so he could get a better look. He began to lower the rope down to the professor.

He yelled to Reinhold, but there was no answer. The wind was too strong.

The professor was beginning to get cold just sitting in the seat. He couldn't understand what was taking so long. Had Valdez gotten into trouble?

Then something caught Reinhold's attention. It was a bright orange rope sliding down the slope about ten feet away from him.

The knife was gently taken from its hiding place. The hand slowly reached out and the blade lightly touched the taut rope. The orange rope exploded and disappeared. One frayed end blew frantically in the strengthening wind.

Reinhold watched the orange rope slowly descend and then suddenly pick up speed. What was happening? Then, horrified, he saw Valdez shoot by and over the edge below, followed by a small avalanche of snow.

Reinhold's mind was whirling. He couldn't move, couldn't believe what he'd just seen. *I'm going to die here*, he thought.

"Valdez! Reinhold!" Hodson yelled as loud as he could, then listened, trying to pick up any reply. But there was only the keening of the wind.

He continued down to the place where the team had left them.

Maybe the professor was too sick and they went back to camp, he thought to himself. *I'll go back and get the team. We should head back.*

On the way back up the trail, Hodson noticed a slight depression in the snow. As an Army Ranger he had been taught to notice anything out of the ordinary. Had someone fallen here? What if they had slipped and pulled each other down the slope roped together? He yelled their names a couple more times. Then he thought he heard a muffled cry in reply.

Hodson began to slowly move down the slope. He stopped and yelled again. It sounded like Reinhold. He looked around and spotted a cluster of rocks sticking out of the snow. He moved toward them with the thought of tying on a safety rope and lowering himself toward the sound below.

Reinhold had heard someone yelling. He cupped his hands together and yelled up toward the sound. After about ten minutes he saw a red rope descending the slope about ten feet away from him, where the orange rope had appeared.

Then he saw Hodson rappelling down the rope. A sense of peace flooded over him and he closed his eyes.

When Reinhold regained consciousness, Hodson was feeding him a glucose drink and the rest of the team were huddled around.

Murphy was the first to speak. "Where's Valdez?"

"He's gone," said Hodson simply.

"What do you mean gone?"

"He died trying to save the professor."

Murphy winced. "I don't know what to say."

"No, you don't understand," Hodson said, his voice choking with emotion. "Someone cut his rope. He was murdered."

THIRTY-SEVEN

THAT NIGHT, MURPHY TOOK the first watch. Hodson would relieve him after an hour, followed by Bayer. Then they would start the cycle again. Murphy cradled Hodson's machine pistol in his lap, staring into the dark, the icy wind biting his face. But he hardly noticed the cold. The treacherous weather on the mountain was proving to be the least of his worries.

At dawn the others struggled out of their tents. It didn't look as if anyone had had much sleep. They slowly gathered together in the cooking area and shared mugs of steaming tea, waiting for Murphy to address them.

"Okay, listen up. I've got some bad news to share with you. Hodson thinks Valdez's death was not an accident. Somebody deliberately cut his rope. He was murdered."

There were gasps from around the campfire. Lundquist dropped his mug in shock, splashing tea into the fire, where it hissed noisily. "But that's incredible . . . I mean, who?" he spluttered.

"Are you sure?" Whittaker asked. "I mean, couldn't the rope have just snapped?"

Hodson shook his head grimly. "I checked. It was sawed through with a knife."

Whittaker turned to Bayer. "Rebels, do you think? Some sort of revenge for the three you took out?"

Bayer shook his head. "I do not think they would climb this far up the mountain. And why just kill Valdez? It makes no sense."

"None of it makes any sense!" exclaimed Reinhold, jumping to his feet. "We're on a mission to find an ancient historical artifact. Why would someone want to kill us?" He was clearly in shock. Isis sat him back down and made him drink some more tea.

"I told you before," Murphy said. "There *are* people who want to stop us from finding the ark. Or maybe they want us to lead them to it, and then . . ." He trailed off. "Look, if any of you wants to stop right now and call it quits, I'll understand. I'm willing to risk my life to find the ark, but I have no right to ask you to do the same. You all knew there would be dangers to face on Ararat, but this is something different." He glanced over at Isis, who was looking at him resolutely. "Dr. McDonald and I have had some experience of what I can only call evil forces at work in the world. Powerful, ruthless people who will stop at nothing to get what they want. I believe they could be responsible for Valdez's death. And I have no reason to think they'll stop there," he added grimly.

288

There was silence around the campfire as they all tried to process what Murphy had said.

"Let's take a show of hands," Murphy said after a while. "Who wants to go back to Dogubayazit?"

No one raised their hand. Murphy was surprised when Reinhold spoke up.

"You can count me in, Murphy. It may sound corny, but a man died while saving my life, and I don't want his sacrifice to have been for nothing. If we do find the ark, I'm going to take a piece of it and give it to Valdez's family."

Hodson looked at Reinhold as if seeing him in a new light. "Way to go, Professor." He turned to Murphy. "I'm in too. I know Valdez would want it that way."

Murphy looked at the rest of the faces around the fire. One by one they nodded.

"We've made it this far. Might as well go the distance. We all want to be famous, don't we?" said Lundquist with a forced laugh.

"Okay," Murphy said. "I appreciate it. But from now on we have to be extra vigilant. We have to be on the watch for strangers."

And maybe not just strangers, he thought.

The transfer of supplies from Camp 2 to Camp 3 took most of the day. The move from thirteen thousand feet to fifteen thousand feet could be felt in everyone's lungs. It was a steep climb in powder snow.

The team was about five hundred feet below Camp 3 when they heard the sound of the helicopter. In the distance they

could see Peterson coming from the south. The sound of the ro-
tator blades lifted their spirits. They stood still and waved and
yelled. As Peterson circled the group, Murphy's satellite phone
rang.

"Hey, Murph. I flew over the coordinates that Hodson gave
me. I spotted the cliff. Reinhold was right. By my altimeter, I
estimate the drop to be twenty-nine hundred feet. I couldn't
see anything but fresh-fallen snow at the bottom. It would be
impossible to find him."

Murphy's heart sank. The last fragile hope of finding Valdez
was gone.

"Roger that!"

"Murph, I'm going to head back. There's not much I can do
here. Keep in touch. I'm praying for you guys. If you find the
ark, let me know!"

"Thanks, Vern. It's good to see you flying. We're looking forward to a comfortable ride home in a few days. Over and out."

The team watched as Peterson disappeared into the brightness.

At Camp 3, Murphy left Isis, Reinhold, Lundquist, and
Whittaker to set up the tents. Along with Bayer and Hodson,
he started down the hill for a second load. Isis felt an ache seeing Murphy walk away.

"You guys be careful!" she yelled.

Murphy turned and waved.

The wind had begun to pick up a little as Murphy, Hodson,
and Bayer finished packing the supplies. Gusts of powdered
snow were swirling around the tents left at Camp 2.

Murphy and Hodson were zipping up the last tent when Bayer let out what sounded like a curse in Turkish. He started pulling out his pistol.

Turning around, they saw someone trudging purposefully up the slope from Camp 1.

He had a pack on over his robelike coat with the leather belt. He was wearing a fur-lined leather hat with two flaps that hung down, covering his ears, and snow was starting to collect on his beard.

No one spoke as they watched him getting closer, but Bayer kept his pistol at the ready.

About thirty feet away he stopped and looked them over. Then he stepped forward and began to speak in a deep, resonant voice. They were surprised to hear him speaking in broken English.

"You go higher up the mountain?"

"Yes, we are moving up about two thousand feet," Murphy replied. "I'm glad to see you. You saved us from the dogs the other day. I wanted to convey our thanks."

The stranger made a slight bow. "It is nothing. My name is Azgadian. I live on the mountain."

Hodson had moved a couple of paces to the stranger's left, anticipating any move he might make. The man no longer carried his staff, but who knew what else he had in that coat. Even if he had saved them from the dogs, Hodson was taking no chances.

The stranger pointed to the summit. "You go there?"

"No," said Murphy. He paused, searching the man's face. "We are searching for the Ark of Noah."

The stranger's dark eyes flashed for a moment but he said nothing. He held Murphy's gaze, as if weighing him in the balance. Eventually he seemed to see what he was looking for, and looked away.

"Have you heard stories about the ark?" Murphy asked.

The stranger nodded. "Since I was a small boy, my father used to bring me here, on Agri Daugh. It is a sacred mountain." His tone suddenly hardened. "And why do you look for it, the Ark of Noah?"

Murphy replied carefully. "It would be a great thing for our faith. Faith in Jesus Christ. And the word of God."

The stranger seemed satisfied.

"We were looking for the ark past the glacier over by Abich Two but had no success," said Bayer, clearly becoming impatient with the way the conversation was going.

Surprisingly, the stranger laughed. "Ah, no—it is much higher up!"

"What!" said Murphy, with his eyes wide. "Higher up?"

"Yes, it is resting on the side of a valley. There is much snow."

"Then you've actually seen it?" said Hodson incredulously.

"Oh, yes," said the stranger. "I have climbed there many times. It has been a mild winter this year on the mountain. Almost half of the ark is there for you to see. The rest of it is in a glacier. Most times the whole boat is covered with snow."

Murphy couldn't believe what he was hearing. This man was talking as if the ark was an everyday sight.

"You must look above the glacier to the northeast," the stranger continued. "You will climb a ridge and then you will see it on the far side of the valley by some rocks." He bowed. "I must return to my home before nightfall. I wish you good fortune in your quest." And then, without further word, he started trudging back down the slope.

The three men watched him gradually fade into the distance. When he disappeared behind a rocky outcrop, it was as if they had just woken up from a dream.

"Is he for real?" Hodson asked, hands on hips.

"Only one way to find out," said Murphy.

THIRTY-EIGHT

EVERYONE WAS UP before dawn preparing for the trek to the ark site. Murphy had instructed them to pack a three-day supply of food and water and to take their polar bags. Hodson was already packed and studying the maps, and excitement was in the air. Everyone seemed to feel that the appearance of the man calling himself Azgadian, so soon after they had made their decision to continue the quest, was a good omen. The ark actually seemed to be in their sights.

For Murphy, the excitement was tinged with worry. Since Valdez's death he had started to look at every member of the team critically, with the exception of Isis. They had all proved themselves by now, physically and mentally. But he couldn't get rid of the nagging suspicion that at least one of them was not what he seemed.

Take Bayer. He had demonstrated all the deadly skills of an

elite Special Forces commando when dealing with the rebels who had taken Isis, and by rights Murphy ought to have felt nothing but gratitude. So why did he find himself wondering why Bayer hadn't been anywhere near the camp when the rebels had attacked? Had he known in advance that they were coming? Was it all a setup of some kind? He dismissed the thought. Why would Bayer let the rebels take Reinhold and Isis hostage and then go to the trouble of rescuing them? It didn't make sense.

At least Bayer couldn't have been responsible for cutting Valdez's rope, sending him to his death. Only Hodson had had the opportunity to do that, and despite their rivalry, Murphy was certain Hodson would never have done such a thing. His grief over Valdez's death seemed utterly genuine.

As for Reinhold, he seemed to spend most of his time in near-death situations himself. Which left Whittaker and Lundquist. The hard-bitten photographer was always at the edge of the group, never quite part of it, but Murphy suspected that was just his professional persona. If you were going to take pictures, you had to be on the outside looking in.

Lundquist was the enigma. He seemed to have the weakest motivation for volunteering in the first place, and the most reason to turn and run after Valdez was killed. So why didn't he? What was it that drove him onward?

Murphy remembered asking Levi whether Lundquist was CIA, and he tried to recall Levi's reaction. He certainly hadn't denied it outright. So if Lundquist *was* CIA, what was his mission? Just as Welsh had made it his job to keep Murphy from getting his hands on the Ararat Anomaly File, was it Lundquist's job to make sure he didn't get his hands on the ark itself? Or was that paranoia? Was Lundquist just an observer, making sure that the CIA ended up knowing everything Murphy knew about the ark?

He closed his eyes, trying to still the chaos of thoughts in his head. There was no way he could figure it out now. He would just have to watch everybody like a hawk. And from now on he wasn't going to let Isis out of his sight. He put the last items into his pack and fastened the straps.

Time to focus on what we've come for, he thought.

By the time the sun was up it was clear it was going to be a perfect day on the mountain. Blue sky, no wind. And since Camp 3 was already at fifteen thousand feet, the team didn't have to do any serious uphill climbing. They only had to traverse the mountain and eventually drop down about five hundred feet to get to their goal. For about four hours they trudged slowly through the snowfields on almost a level course. It was only about ten-thirty when the slope they were crossing became steeper and more dangerous. Murphy, in the lead, was the first to notice that the soft snow was getting harder and turning to ice. Looking up, he could see some exposed rocks. They were headed toward an ice wall. Water dripping from the rocks above had created large fluted icicles that hung above a straight drop of about a thousand feet. They couldn't climb up and they couldn't climb down.

They were going to have to traverse it.

The ice wall seemed to stick out on a corner, and then it disappeared out of sight. Somewhere on the other side, Murphy figured, they would again meet snowfields. But they couldn't be sure until they reached the outer edge of the corner.

Murphy thought it best to break the group up into three smaller teams. It would give them more flexibility as they moved in and out of the icicle flutings.

Murphy took the lead team, comprised of himself, Isis, and Whittaker. Hodson and Reinhold were second. Lundquist and Bayer would be last. They hooked together on shorter safety ropes with about ten feet between them.

Murphy began by hammering in an ice screw and attaching a carabiner and a rope. He then pounded in his ice ax, getting a solid hold. Pulling his weight up on the ax, he kicked the points of his crampons into the wall and began to move sideways across the ice.

About every fifteen feet Murphy pounded in another ice screw for safety and hooked in the rope. The team members following held on to the rope with their left hand and planted their ice axes with the right. Then they kicked in the points of their crampons in the same way Murphy did and slowly worked their way in and out of the large ice flutings.

Murphy was the first to round the corner. He was right. The ice wall ended after about fifty feet, where it met the snowfield again. The steepness began to taper to about thirty degrees, much safer than the vertical wall they were on.

Murphy, Isis, and Whittaker made it to the snowfield and unhooked from the ice screws. Isis seemed relieved to be off the ice wall and back on the snow.

Hodson was climbing behind Reinhold, gently encouraging him, knowing that after his nightmare experience on the cliff, the thousand-foot drop from the ice wall would be preying on his mind. Murphy watched intently as Reinhold eased himself off the ice wall and onto the snow.

From around the corner, they heard a sudden shout.

As Lundquist swung his ice ax to get a new bite, his crampon broke loose and he began to fall. Because he was reaching out at the time, he couldn't hold on with his left hand. His entire body weight hit the end of the ten-foot tether rope, jerking Bayer off the wall. Their combined body weight then popped the ice screw out of the wall behind Bayer, and the two men dropped another fifteen feet. For a moment it looked as if the second ice screw would stop their fall, but then it, too, popped out and they dropped again.

Lundquist was screaming at the top of his lungs when they came to a sudden stop. The third ice screw had held.

Bayer's carabiner was hooked on to the safety rope and Lundquist was hanging ten feet below him. Bayer was close enough to the wall to reach it with his ice ax, but he couldn't focus properly. Blood from a collision with an ice flute on the way down seeped into his eyes, blinding him, and he felt disoriented. Both were dangling in midair above a dizzying drop.

Hodson, who was still hooked on to the safety rope, felt it go tight as Bayer and Lundquist fell. He waited to see if he, too, would be pulled off the wall, but all of the ice screws on his side of the corner held.

Quickly, Hodson unhooked the ten-foot safety rope that was attached to Reinhold. He yelled to Murphy, who had already started to move toward the rope.

"Give me all your pulleys and an extra rope. I'll hook a pulley on each of the ice screws as I go back to the corner and run the rope through them. You guys dig snow seats and get ready to pull on the rope when I give the signal. You can help lift them. I won't be able to do it by myself."

Hodson then moved back across the ice wall toward the corner, hooking in the pulleys and rope. Now he could see them. Lundquist was twisting in a circle below Bayer, who had managed to embed his ice ax in the wall just above him and was trying to pull them both up.

He must be crazy, Hodson thought. *Nobody has the strength to do that.*

Hodson yelled and tossed the coils of rope down to them. Lundquist was still twisting too violently to be able to grab hold. Hodson pulled it back up and tossed it three more times until eventually Lundquist made a lunge and held on. Hodson then attached the end of the rope to his harness. He could see the look of agony on Bayer's bloody face. His strength was fading.

Hodson hooked in the last pulley at the corner of the flutings. He then drove in two more ice screws for safety and hooked himself on to them. He signaled to the rest of the team on the snow to pull. He, too, grabbed on to the rope and helped lift Lundquist, easing some of the strain on Bayer.

It took about five minutes of pulling to get Lundquist to the point where he could use his ice ax to help lift his own body weight. This allowed Bayer to rise enough to kick his crampons into the wall and help with the climb.

Lundquist was the first to get to Hodson's position. He had to unhook and rehook on the other side of the pulley. They then both helped to pull Bayer up as the rest of the team held the rope tight.

Forty-five minutes after Lundquist had first fallen, they were all resting, exhausted, on the snowfield, eating energy bars and drinking water to restore their strength.

Lundquist looked as if he now realized what a big mistake he'd made, agreeing to continue their journey. But it was too late to go back, and he knew it.

"How far are we from where the ark's supposed to be?" he asked.

Murphy was gazing across the snowfield with a strange look on his face. "Can't you feel it? We're almost there."

THIRTY-NINE

ENERGIZED BY MURPHY'S SENSE that they were closing in on their goal, the team began to move forward across the snowfield. But there was another reason for Murphy's urgency. He knew they had to make quick progress because the clouds were coming in and the temperature was beginning to drop sharply. Even if they didn't find the ark, they would need to get off the snowfield and find a protected spot to camp for the night. They were right in the middle of avalanche territory, and the wind was beginning to pick up.

Everyone zipped up tight and buried their heads in their hoods. They could feel the biting wind force its way into the smallest openings. Soon it brought with it tiny snowflakes.

By late afternoon it had become very dark and the flakes had become larger, making visibility difficult. Murphy told the team to break out their headlamps, in case they lost someone in the whiteout.

"We can't keep moving forward," Murphy yelled to Hodson, the wind taking away some of his words. "We can't see what's ahead in this blizzard. I don't want us walking off the top of some cornice. We're going to have to dig snow caves. We're right beside a big drift. This is about as good a spot as any."

Hodson and Reinhold began their cave immediately. Murphy, Isis, and Whittaker started to dig a cave large enough for three. Bayer and Lundquist nodded at each other and began theirs.

First they carved out a small doorway with their ice axes. Then one of them began to dig forward into the snowbank and push snow out the doorway. This carving and pushing of snow took about forty-five minutes, until the hollowed-out room in the snowbank was large enough for two or three sleeping bags. To be sure there was enough air in their snow rooms, a couple of holes were poked through the outer wall of snow.

The three groups then crawled into their hollows and laid out their sleeping bags. Each group set up a small propane stove in the entrance and started to make a hot meal. Before long they all felt surprisingly cozy. After the meal, rucksacks were stacked in front of the entrance to keep out the wind, and they crawled into their polar bags. Outside, they could hear the low rumble of avalanches on the snowfield they had just crossed.

Murphy tossed and turned throughout the night, his mind filled with strange dreams. He dreamed he was laboring through a dense snowfield, but the more he struggled the less progress he made, until he was stuck, unable to go forward or back, the snow reaching up to his chest. Then he saw an angel descending. A slim, red-haired angel with sparkling green eyes. She hovered in front of him and held out a hand. He grasped it and instantly felt himself being pulled free of the snow. Then he was floating through the air, hand in hand with the red-haired angel, the wind caressing his face, the lazy beats of her downy wings brushing his shoulders. Then she turned her face toward him, smiling, and he knew she was going to kiss him.

There was a loud crack, like a rifle shot. She screamed. He felt her hand being plucked from his own. Then they were both falling.

He woke up, panting. For a moment he didn't know where he was.

He saw the light filtering through the cracks in the entrance and pushed the rucksacks aside. He stepped out onto the snow, shielding his eyes from the sudden brightness, and took a deep breath. Gradually his eyes became accustomed to the glare, and he found himself looking down across a shallow valley toward a cluster of rocks.

His breath caught in his throat.

There it was.

The ark.

He could see the prow, jutting out of the snow. It was un-mistakable. Although he was smiling—a big stupid grin he couldn't control—he could feel tears running down his cheeks. He felt a huge mix of emotions he couldn't describe: joy, won-der, awe, gratitude, humility. He fell to his knees in the snow to give thanks, but he found he couldn't close his eyes to pray. He couldn't bear to tear his gaze away from those ancient fragments of wood, sailing on a sea of snow. He thought of how many millions of men and women through the centuries had imagined the ark, had seen it in their dreams, and now it was right there in front of him.

All he had to do was walk over a few hundred feet of snow and he could touch it.

He felt a hand on his shoulder. It was Reinhold.

"My God, Murphy, you found it. There it is. Noah's Ark."

Reinhold began laughing uncontrollably, rousing the others from their snow caves. One by one they stumbled out into the light until they were all there, huddled together, struck dumb by the sight that greeted them. Isis knelt down and put her arm around Murphy. She put her head on his shoulder. There was nothing to say.

Then the clicking of Whittaker's camera broke the silence and people started whooping and hugging one another.

Murphy took out his satellite phone and dialed a number.

"Vern, are you sitting down? We found it!"

"Are you kidding! I can't believe it! What does it look like? Have you been on board yet?"

"Not yet. I've only just seen it. We're still some distance away. When you fly up, you can take a look at it. We'll probably need you to take away some samples, okay?"

"Roger that," Vern replied. "Roger that and God bless you."

Murphy put the phone into a pocket of his parka. Everyone was waiting for him to make the first move. He grinned. "Come on!"

InstantIy the whole team was zigzagging down the slope toward the ark, while every few yards Whittaker stopped to take more pictures. Lundquist fell and started rolling down the slope and everyone laughed. Reinhold threw a snowball at him, evoking more laughter.

It's like Christmas, Isis thought with a smile. *And we've just been given the best present ever.*

As they got closer, Reinhold brushed himself off and began to study the outline in the snow. He estimated that between one seventy-five and two hundred feet of the superstructure was sticking out of the glacier. He remembered that the Bible said the ark was about four hundred fifty feet long and seventy-five feet wide. *It's incredible,* he thought. *I imagined there would be just scattered fragments. But it's here, the whole ark. We are actually going to be able to go inside.* He couldn't help imagining how jealous his university colleagues would be if they could see him now. He was about to become the most famous scientist in the world.

Lundquist wasn't thinking at all about science. But he was thinking about fame. As one of the first people to actually stand on Noah's Ark, he would become the most celebrated diplomat in America. He might even become the ambassador. Perhaps he would write a book about his adventures on Ararat. *Hey, not a bad title,* he thought. *Adventures on Ararat.* His terrible experience hanging from the ice wall was already beginning to seem like a great anecdote.

Bayer strode toward the ark, his head held high. He was proud to be representing his country on this historic occasion.

Proud also that he had saved the lives of two of his teammates along the way.

Isis wasn't sure what was more thrilling—to watch Murphy's lifelong dream being realized or to finally come face to face herself with a piece of the Bible. A strange, unfamiliar feeling started to seep through her. She remembered Murphy saying once that there is a vacuum in everyone, a God-shaped vacuum that only He can fill. As she looked across the few yards separating her from the ark, she began to feel that empty space in her heart filling.

But was it filling with love of God or just love of Murphy? It was all too confusing.

But it was also incredibly exciting.

Now they were all standing by the prow, its dark wood smooth and glistening in the bright sunlight. They looked to Murphy, waiting for him to step onto the ark. No one was going to deny him this special moment.

He closed his eyes in prayer for a moment.

God, thank you for the privilege of seeing your great ark. May I be a faithful teacher of right, living like Noah.

Then he reached out a trembling hand and touched it.

FORTY

TRY AS HE MIGHT, Noah couldn't sleep. God's words echoed and re-echoed in his mind. One hundred and twenty years ago he had started building the ark. The thought of how many hours, days, months he and his sons had spent on the task overwhelmed him. For one hundred and twenty years he and his family had been cursed by enemies, jeered at by strangers, and made fun of by friends. For one hundred and twenty years he had warned everyone of God's coming judgment for their wickedness. He had begged them to turn from their evil thoughts and imaginations and come to the ark of safety.

Not a single man, woman, or child had heeded him.

And now God had spoken directly to him once more.

"Seven days from now, I will send rain on the earth for forty days and forty nights, and I will wipe from the face of the earth every living creature I have made."

Noah knew it was true. It was God's word, and it would surely come to pass as He had told him. But he still couldn't quite believe it.

The next morning Naamah found him sitting alone. "What are you doing up so early? Is something wrong?"

"They have only seven days," Noah said in a troubled voice.

"What are you talking about?"

"Seven days!"

She still didn't understand what he was talking about. "Who?"

"Our neighbors! Everybody! They have only seven days before God will close the door to the ark of safety. I must warn them again before it is too late!"

Naamah sighed. "You have warned them so many times. They never listened before. Why would they listen now?"

Noah stared at her with a wild look. "But they must! Tell Ham, Shem, and Japheth to finish loading the supplies. I must try one more time. Tell them I will return in six days."

Noah hurriedly put on his cloak. He packed a few items into a sack and grabbed his staff. He bent over and hugged Naamah and kissed her.

"I must go."

She sighed deeply. "I know. I will be praying for you."

She watched her husband disappear out of sight.

Ham was working on one of the window coverings when he looked up and saw someone in the distance coming toward the ark. It didn't take him but a moment to recognize the strong, powerful, and determined gate of his father.

"Father is coming!" he yelled down one of the large air vents in the floor.

Everyone came out to welcome Noah back home.

Japheth was the first to speak.

"Well, were you successful? Did anyone listen? We were all praying for you."

Noah's normally bright and sparkling green eyes were dark with sorrow as he turned to his family. He shook his head. "No one. Not one would listen. They just laughed and jeered as they have in the past. I pleaded with them until they took up stones and started casting them at me."

They could see some fresh cuts and bruises on their father.

"I told them that tomorrow was their last chance. Then it would be over for them all. Maybe someone will come."

"Did you see my parents and family?" asked Bithiah with a tremble in her voice. "I heard that they had come to visit relatives."

Noah put his arm around her gently. "Yes. I told them the time was short. I told them to come."

"And?"

Noah hugged her tightly. He couldn't find any words.

Bithiah began to cry.

It was noon the following day when Noah and his family slowly walked up the ramp and entered the ark, but it might as well have been night. They had never seen the sky grow so dark before. Black clouds massed in the distance, squeezing out the light. Every minute seemed to bring them nearer.

Their hearts were heavy with foreboding.

They lined the top walkway, just under the roof, and looked out the windows. There was nothing to do but wait.

"Look," said Shem. "People are coming."

They could see what looked like fifty or sixty people coming to the ark. They recognized some of their friends and neighbors. There were also many that they did not know.

"My parents and brothers and sisters!" cried Bithiah.

"Let us hope they are coming to the ark for safety," said Achsah with a smile.

They all prayed that it was true.

Noah walked out the large door and stood on the platform at the top of the zigzagging entrance ramp.

"Welcome, friends, I'm glad you've decided to come. Please come up the ramp and enter before it is too late."

In his heart of hearts he knew what would happen next. They began to laugh. A few people picked up stones and threw them in Noah's direction. The rocks rattled off the side of the ark like hail.

Bithiah called desperately to her parents and brothers and sisters to come in to the ark.

"Don't be a fool, Bithiah! Noah is mad! Don't listen to this nonsense about the end of the world! Come back to us," they answered.

For a moment she was torn. But she knew in her heart that she couldn't leave. She was overwhelmed with tears as she turned to her husband. Ham put his arm around her and drew her in.

Noah entered the ark and stood with his family at the windows, looking out sadly at the crowd.

The next event shocked everyone. The huge door slammed shut with startling force and a deafening noise.

"What happened?" shouted Noah. "Did one of you remove the brace?"

"No!" they chorused back, but Noah already knew the answer. God had shut the door.

It was time.

Noah and his family couldn't believe their eyes. Water was falling out of the sky. It had never rained on the earth before, and the sight was awesome to behold.

A streak of light flashed in the sky and a great roar terrified them— the first lightning and thunder. Then they saw springs of water shooting out of the ground, making fountains to the sky.

By now the mood of the crowd gathered below had changed abruptly. They were yelling and screaming and running in all directions, seeking shelter from the incredible storm. A dozen or more of Noah's neighbors sprinted up the zigzagging ramp.

Noah could hear them pounding on the large door.

"Noah! Let us in, Noah!"

"We believe you now, Noah!"

"We were wrong, Noah! Please let us in."

Ham, Shem, and Japheth rushed to the door. They pushed and shoved with all their might. They were soon joined by Noah, Naamah, Achsah, Bithiah, and Hagaba. Everyone was yelling and pushing and trying to open the door.

It would not budge.

Bithiah could hear her family yelling and pounding on the door. She collapsed on the floor, weeping hysterically.

Noah held her, sobbing himself. "The door that God closes, no man can open," he said softly.

For several hours they could hear the screams and cries . . . and then it was quiet, except for the rain.

FORTY-ONE

POWERFUL EMOTIONS FLOODED Murphy when he climbed off the snowbank onto the roof of the ark. *It's true! It's all true!*

He could hear in his mind the words of Jesus: *As in the days of Noah, so will it be at the coming of the Son of Man. For in the days before the flood, people were eating and drinking, marrying and giving in marriage, up to the day Noah entered the ark; and they knew nothing about what would happen until the flood came and took them all away.*

He tried to imagine what it must have been like to build a boat with these incredible dimensions. What a sight it must have been to see God bring all of the animals to the ark. How awesome and terrifying to encounter the rain for forty days and forty nights.

Then Murphy was sobered when he thought about how Jesus Himself warned that there was another judgment coming.

Murphy's elation at the discovery turned to anxiety. *How can I warn people? How can I convince them? Maybe this discovery will help the world to realize that they need to turn to God and run to Him for safety from the coming judgment.*

"Look over here!" said Hodson, who was down on his knees looking over the edge of the roof. "It's a row of windows about three feet high."

Reinhold clambered over. "Ventilation, I should think. Let's go in!" he said with a grin.

"That's what we're here for!" responded Murphy, tearing himself from his somber thoughts as he tied a rope to one of the window posts. "This is just for safety. We don't know if there are any steps or ladders on the other side. I don't want anyone falling three stories after what we've been through to get here."

After tying on the rope and hooking it to his harness, Murphy took out his headlamp and put it on. "You all better put these on. The ark is a miracle of construction, but I doubt there are any electric lights inside."

Murphy then crawled through one of the windows and shined his light around in a slow arc. Directly below the window was a walkway. He crawled down on it and looked over the edge. There was an immediate drop into the darkness. He shined his light down and could make out what looked like three floors below.

The center of the boat seemed to be open from there to the bottom, forming a vast chamber.

Soon the rest of the team was climbing through the windows and down to the walkway. Reinhold began to immediately wander down its length.

"Be careful!" cautioned Murphy.

"Look!" said Reinhold. "There's a ramp that goes down to the floor below."

Murphy took the lead, followed by Hodson. They stepped carefully, checking out the safety of the ramp as they descended, but the wooden planks seemed sound. At the bottom was a large room. A railing was attached to supporting beams to keep anyone from falling into the shaft in the center of the boat. Here and there were bridge walkways that crossed over the shaft to the other side.

"Noah and his family probably used this large room as their meeting place," said Isis. "Perhaps we can find their sleeping quarters."

As they moved through the darkness of the ship, their headlamps began to reveal cages and stalls of various sizes. Reinhold and Murphy were amazed to find metal bars in front of the cages. "Incredible. How on earth did they come by such advanced knowledge of metalwork?" asked Reinhold in wonderment.

Whittaker joined him and started taking pictures, the flash of his camera like little bursts of lightning illuminating the incredible scene.

"Look up there!" shouted Lundquist. He was pointing to what looked like birdcages hanging from the ceiling in each stall. "This must have been how they were able to get so many animals in the ark."

It wasn't long before the team encountered the ice and snow from the glacier, making a wall that prevented them from exploring any further. They turned back and crossed one of the walkway bridges to the other side of the ark. As they worked their way back toward the large room, they found more cages and stalls. In many of the stalls were structures that looked like feeding troughs.

Near the large room they found what seemed to be living quarters, with beds and storage places with shelves. Past the great room were more rooms containing remnants of broken pottery and damaged baskets. "I'll make a guess that this is where they stored some of the food," said Bayer, holding up a pottery shard under his headlamp.

After most of the first floor was explored, they moved on to the second. As they moved slowly through another large chamber, Lundquist stopped and yelled.

"Look!"

The six turned in the direction he was pointing and shined their headlamps on the wall.

"There's something carved into the side of the boat."

Murphy and Reinhold came running down the ramp.

Isis stepped forward and ran her fingers over the symbols. "It looks like a story, written in a form of proto-Hebrew. Perhaps the story of the building of the ark." She gasped as the implication hit her. "This could be the oldest writing ever recorded!"

She dragged herself reluctantly away and they continued on. Soon they were in a room full of tables—or perhaps workbenches—and shelves. Under a collapsed beam was what looked like a chest. With a lot of effort they dragged it free, and Murphy began to pry it open with his ice ax. With a loud crack, the wood gave way and Murphy opened the chest.

Murphy peered inside and saw a cloth-covered bundle. The

cloth turned to dust in his hands, revealing bright metal. Craning over his shoulders to see, the others were amazed at the sight of an elaborately engraved sword with a companion dagger. The metal shone in their headlamps as if it had been forged yesterday. Murphy then pulled out some bronze objects and handed them to Reinhold. "What do you make of these, Professor?"

Reinhold held them up the light and examined them from every angle. Finally he said, "I believe that these items together form some type of surveying equipment."

"That would make sense," said Murphy, nodding. "Josephus wrote in his book, *Life and Works,* that Cain determined property boundary lines and built a city with fortified walls. He also said that Cain moved into that city with his family and called it Enoch. My guess is that these surveying instruments were passed down from Cain to Tubal-cain, his son. It's thought that Tubal-cain's sister, Naamah, was married to Noah."

Murphy began to lift other items out of the chest. He pulled out an ax and a short saw that seemed to be made out of the same material as the sword and dagger.

Reinhold was shaking his head in disbelief. "I would swear that this is tungsten steel." He tapped the blade of the sword on one of the beams, and it emitted a high-pitched ringing sound. "It has the highest melting point of all metals. It also has the highest tensile strength and makes the metal more elastic. The finest cutting tools are made with tungsten. But it's simply not possible they mastered that process in Noah's time."

But if the tungsten blades astonished him, there was more to come. Murphy was slicing open a pitch-covered cloth to reveal a curious-looking bronze machine with dials, pointers, and interlocking gears and wheels.

"This is impossible!" exclaimed Reinhold. "This bronze had to precede the Bronze Age. Look at the extreme precision of this instrument!" They all passed it around and examined it.

Underneath the machine were two metallic tablets inscribed with ancient markings. Murphy handed them to Isis to see if she could translate them. While she examined the tablets, they took a box out of the chest containing what seemed to be weights and measures.

"Josephus mentioned in his writings that *Cain was the father of weights and measures and cunning craftiness,*" mentioned Murphy as he picked up one of the bronze weights.

"I think I've got it!" said Isis, startling everyone. "I believe that this first tablet describes how to use the bronze machine. These markings look like the positions of the stars and planets."

"That sounds right," said Murphy. "Josephus also said that *Seth and his children were the inventors of wisdom which was concerned with the heavenly bodies and their order.* He also says that the children of Seth inscribed their discoveries on a pillar of brick and a pillar of stone. The stone was to remain if the Flood washed away the pillar of brick. He said that the stone could still be seen in the land of Siriad. I'll bet that that machine was used to determine the motion of the sun, moon, and planets. Probably even the movements of the tides. This is incredible! What about the second tablet?"

"It seems to be talking about Adam and how he predicted two destructions of the world. One would be by flood and the other by fire."

Murphy nodded, deep in thought. "The New Testament writer Peter, in his second book, not only talks about Noah and the Flood but also mentions that the heavens and the earth would be destroyed in a judgment of fire. Josephus says almost the same thing when he says, *Adam predicted that the world would be destroyed one time by water and another time by fire.* God must have also revealed these judgments to Adam."

A last box was pulled out of the chest and opened. It contained a beautiful golden casket with designs of leaves around the edges and two bronze plates. There were also small samples of various rocks, each containing different elements of metal. The golden box glittered in Whittaker's flash. Again, the bronze plate was given to Isis to translate.

Murphy carefully opened the lid to see various colored crystals, elements that looked like sand, and small flecks of metal.

"What is it?" asked Bayer, reaching a hand in to scoop up some of the crystals, before jumping back, his fingers scorched.

"I don't know," laughed Murphy. "But whatever it is, it still seems to be working!"

Isis pulled at the sleeve of Murphy's parka. "Michael, I don't mean to keep harping on it, but these bronze plates look remarkably like the one that was supposed to come from the Monastery of St. Jacob. The one you were so sure was a fake," she added pointedly.

"Of course," Murphy admitted. "You're right."

"What are you both talking about?" asked Reinhold impatiently.

Murphy's voice was grim. "I believe there were originally three plates. One ended up in the Monastery of St. Jacob in the

1800s. It was sent to Erzurum for translation, and I think it was then stolen—possibly quite recently. I'm pretty certain the three plates are separate pieces of a puzzle, and you need all three to figure it out."

He brought his fist down on the table with a crash.

"I had the third one in my hands—but I let it go!"

FORTY-TWO

MURPHY, HODSON, AND REINHOLD watched the helicopter disappear down the valley, then turned and reentered the ark. It had not been easy to persuade the rest of the team to go back, but Murphy had been adamant. They had achieved what they had set out to do. They had all the evidence they needed to prove the existence of the ark, and much else besides. After all they'd been through, he was determined not to expose them to any further risk.

The three men made their way back to the room holding the large wooden chest to figure out which items to pack and haul out. Hodson's curiosity got the best of him and he picked up one of the small vases. Looking inside, he saw some of the crystals Bayer had burned his hand on. Sticking out were two small pieces of metal. While Murphy and Reinhold were deep in conversation about Isis's translation of the bronze plates, Hodson pushed one of the metal rods against a beam to see if it would move. As the rods came closer together, there was a sudden burst of flame and a bright light.

Murphy and Reinhold turned to see Hodson backing away from the vase, which he'd dropped on the floor. An intense glow emanated from it, lighting up the whole room. For a moment they didn't move.

Murphy slowly reached out his hand and grabbed the bottom of the vase, then set it on one of the beams. They all put on their snow glasses because of the glare and to get a better look at it.

Reinhold was the first to speak. "Amazing! The combination of the crystals and the metal rods are forming some type of battery energy source. How on earth did they discover how to do that?"

Murphy was silent as he studied the object.

"What do you think, Michael?" asked Reinhold.

"I was just thinking about some ancient history and mythology. It's all making sense. Josephus mentions that Tubal-cain was the father of metallurgy. I wonder if he discovered some secret process for working with metals and various elements like the crystals in the vases and the chest. Some scholars believe the name Vulcan, the Roman god of fire and father of metalsmiths, came from the name Tubal-cain. As the story goes, Vulcan was thrown out of heaven. When he landed on earth he taught men metallurgy."

"It sounds like the combined story of Cain and his son Tubal-cain," said Reinhold. "Cain was cast out of God's presence. And Tubal-cain became the father of the smelting process."

Murphy continued. "We get the word *volcano* from the name Vulcan. The ancients believed that volcanoes were the natural chimneys of subterranean smithies deep in the earth."

"The light in that vase came on when I pushed the two pieces of metal together," said Hodson. "I wonder what would happen if we separated them?"

"Try it," said Murphy.

Hodson found a small splinter of wood and separated the two metal rods. The light went out. He then pushed them together again and the light went on. "It's like a switch," he said.

"It all makes sense!" shouted Reinhold suddenly.

"What are you talking about?" asked Murphy.

"The Philosopher's Stone! Throughout history, men of science have been searching for the Philosopher's Stone. Oh, it's not really a stone as much as it is a process. It was believed that all metals have or come from the same basic source. The bottom line is this: If you mix certain chemicals together, you can change any base metal into gold. In other words, lead could be turned into gold if you had the right chemicals and the right heat."

Reinhold was pacing excitedly.

"One bronze plate talks about different types of rocks and metals. Another mentions the amount of crystals needed for each type of metal. I'll bet the bronze plate you saw in Erzurum talks about the type of fire needed. Tubal-cain discovered the Philosopher's Stone!" Reinhold started rubbing his chin. "Of course, if someone had the Philosopher's Stone today, they wouldn't waste their time turning lead into gold."

"They wouldn't?" said Hodson.

"No, no," said Reinhold, shaking his head vigorously.

"Platinum! That's the most valuable metal in the world right now."

"Platinum? Why?"

"To make hydrogen fuel cells work! Let me explain. Hydrogen is the most abundant of all elements in the universe. It's estimated that hydrogen makes up ninety percent of all atoms. If we could convert hydrogen into energy, we could stop using fossil fuels, which lead to pollution. And hydrogen would never run out. By using the electrolysis of water, hydrogen would create a clean-burning renewable resource."

"Okay, I'm following so far. Water can be turned into energy. But what does that have to do with platinum?" asked Hodson.

"Right now, Daimler-Benz, the Ford Motor Company, Chrysler, Motorola, Westinghouse, Toyota, 3M, and many others are already working on hydrogen energy cells." Reinhold continued, "Even the U.S. Army is building a backpack-size fuel-cell generator. It will be able to power a soldier's electronics gear. That would include laptop computers, night-vision goggles, and infrared heat detectors."

"Yeah. I heard something about that before I left the Rangers."

"You see, Colonel, fuel cells have no moving parts. As hydrogen feeds into the cell, it passes through a thin layer of platinum. The platinum induces the gas to separate into electrons and protons. The protons mix with oxygen and produce water. The electrons that cannot pass through the platinum membrane are channeled and harnessed to power an electrical motor. Fuel-cell cars would be two-point-eight times more efficient than the internal combustion engine. The Ballard Company is already in the process of developing a two-hundred-fifty-kilowatt hydrogen generator. It will be able to power a small hotel or a strip mall. Colonel, the only reason the fuel-cell industry is moving slowly is because platinum is rare and extremely costly."

Murphy was already way ahead of him. "So if the Philosopher's Stone could convert base metals into platinum, whoever controlled it could control the world's supply of renewable energy. They would have the power to do whatever they wanted."

The two men looked at each other as the implications of what Reinhold was saying became clear.

Murphy was the first to move. "I'm going to pack some of this stuff into my rucksack and hike down to the pickup site. Then I'll come back and we can pack up the rest."

Hodson saluted, and Reinhold went back to carefully examining the crystals, while Murphy collected some of the larger items, hefted his pack, and marched back up to the top of the ark.

After a few minutes Hodson spoke. "Do you think once you had them, you could make more of those crystals?"

"I think so," answered Reinhold. "Why?"

"Because I think that's the first thing my controllers will want to know. And I think you just gave me the right answer."

"Your controllers? What are you talking about?"

"I might as well tell you, since you're not going to live to repeat it. I'm employed by certain people within the CIA who have believed for a long time that the ark might contain some useful technology. Technology that must at all costs be kept in the right hands. We've been planning our own clandestine expedition to find the ark, but our information has never been good enough to pinpoint it. Then up pops Murphy, and we decide the smart thing to do would be to piggyback. Let him lead the way."

Despite the terror that had begun to grip him, the professor's brain was still working swiftly. "You killed Valdez, didn't you? Why?"

"He was pro. He was on to me. I couldn't risk him fouling things up. So when I saw the opportunity to get rid of him, I took it."

Reinhold was starting to shake. "Why didn't you kill me too? Or just leave me there to freeze to death on the ledge?"

Hodson smiled. "Good question, Professor. I still needed your expertise in case we did discover something on the ark. But in case you're wondering, I did try to take care of Bayer and Lundquist on the ice wall. I was ahead of them and loosened the two ice screws. I thought their combined weight in the fall would pull them both to their deaths. However, I have to hand it to him, Bayer is one tough guy. He really hung in there. So in the end I had to go back and rescue them so that the rest of the team wouldn't get suspicious."

"But they've already gone back!"

Hodson shrugged. "It's not important. Before they left, we'd discovered nothing of importance. The Philosopher's Stone— that's the important thing. Anyway, I still have plenty of time to eliminate them. When Murphy comes back, I'm going to have to kill him too. Then when Peterson arrives with the helicopter, I'll just tell him that the both of you will come on the next trip. When we land, I will eliminate him. I'll let Isis freeze to death at Camp Two. That leaves only Bayer, Lundquist, and Whittaker. They should be easy to dispose of. It's a fairly tidy package, wouldn't you say, Professor?"

Reinhold had been using the time Hodson took to explain his plans to figure out one of his own. He was confident he could handle himself in normal circumstances, say, a drunk getting obnoxious in a college bar. But these weren't normal circumstances. And Hodson was no drunk. He was a trained killer, with no doubt dozens of scalps to his name. Killing Reinhold would be no big deal—just as killing Valdez hadn't been.

Reinhold was going to have to be smart if he was going to live through the next few minutes.

They were about ten feet apart, the box containing the crystals on the floor between them. If Reinhold could distract Hodson long enough to grab a handful of the crystals and throw them in his face, he could then grab the dagger on the table behind them and maybe—

While Reinhold was still calculating the times and distances involved, Hodson took two quick steps forward and launched a vicious side kick that caught Reinhold squarely in the solar plexus and sent him crashing into the table. He crumpled into a heap, knees drawn up to his chest, groaning feebly. Hodson came and knelt over him, grabbed a handful of hair with one hand and his jaw with the other, and twisted.

There was a crack, and Reinhold went limp.

"I guess we could have talked all day, Professor, but I gotta keep things moving along, you know?"

Hodson stood up and looked around, figuring out if he could get everything he needed into one backpack.

Suddenly he heard a noise. It was the sound of someone clapping. The sound came from the darkness over by the ramp.

He turned to see a man in dark clothing jumping down from a beam. He landed almost soundlessly, like a cat.

"What the—"

"Nice technique," the black-clad man said. "But it was all over a little fast for my taste. I was hoping for more entertainment, to be honest."

Hodson quickly went for his pack, but as he was still fumbling to get his machine pistol out, the other man kicked it out of his grasp. Hodson rolled to the side and came up in a fighting stance, trying to ignore the pain in his forearm.

"Who are you? What do you want?"

"My name is Talon, and I want exactly what you want. And before I take it I'd like to thank you for doing my dirty work for me. Once you and I are through, I just need to take the crystals and the two bronze plates and my job is done."

After the initial surprise, Hodson now had his focus back. Years of intensive training had made him react instantly to changing circumstances, and he was even beginning to see an upside to this. Talon had made no move for the machine pistol and seemed to carry no weapon of his own. If he was one of those supermacho types who wanted to go at it hand to hand, that was fine with Hodson. And if Hodson could defeat him, then Talon would make a handy-dandy fall guy for Reinhold and all the other deaths.

Perfect. The power of positive thinking. He smiled to himself. Talon caught the expression and grinned back.

"I think this is going to be fun," he said.

There was a pause as each waited to see who would make the first move, then Hodson exploded forward with a jumping front kick aimed squarely at Talon's temple. He felt his foot connecting with air and landed in a panic, expecting a retaliatory blow to his exposed back—but nothing came. He spun round to see Talon standing casually, his hands at his sides.

Okay, this guy is better than I expected, Hodson thought to himself. *No more flashy moves. Let's see what he's got and try to react to that.*

He resumed a fighting stance and waited.

Talon didn't move. Not a hair. Almost like one of those guys pretending to be robots. As the seconds grew into what seemed like minutes, Hodson began to find it mesmerizing. He shook his head to maintain focus.

"You're a student of martial arts," Talon said suddenly. "I'm sure you've studied all that kung fuey stuff. You know, the way of the crane, the tiger, the monkey—whatever." As he spoke, he went through a rapid series of moves while standing in place—kicks, blocks, punches—that seemed to mimic the movements of different animals.

Hodson focused on Talon's eyes, trying not to get distracted.

"All very pretty," Talon continued. "But how many animals have you ever seen that could do this?"

Before the words were out of his mouth, Talon took two quick steps and lashed out with a reverse punch aimed at

Hodson's jaw. Without thinking, Hodson parried, raising both arms to make an *X*, which would trap Talon's arm and allow Hodson to twist it around.

But Talon's arm wasn't there anymore.

Instead, both of his arms shot forward again, palms out, to deliver a double blow to Hodson's exposed rib cage. Hodson grunted as the wind was knocked out of him, instantly knowing that several ribs had been crushed as if by some sort of human sledgehammer.

He also knew he was about to die.

He took up a shaky defensive stance through a blur of pain, pure instinct making his body take up the posture.

Talon had stepped back, out of range, with a thoughtful expression on his face.

"It would be fun to draw this out a little more," he sighed. "But as you said yourself, we've got to keep things moving. Sometimes we have to take our pleasures in little sips, like a cat, don't you think?"

Hodson tried to speak, but no words would come. He could feel a wave of nausea rushing over him. *Not just my ribs,* he thought. *He's damaged some internal organs. I'm bleeding inside.*

As his thoughts began to disconnect, he wondered if Talon would teach him the move. It would probably take a lot of practice. But Hodson enjoyed that. In fact, he was looking forward to it. He tried to picture how Talon had done it. *I guess you pull the right arm out of the punch at the same time as—*

He slumped forward onto his knees, then toppled sideways. He was dead before he hit the floor.

Talon turned and walked over to the wooden chest. He picked up Tubal-cain's sword, swinging it slowly from side to side as he approached the corpse.

"Now," he said, with a dark smile. "Let's see if this little beauty is as sharp as they say."

FORTY-THREE

ISIS HAD TWO OF THE six tents packed away when the wind began to pick up. She zipped up her jacket and tightened the strings on her hood to help keep in her body heat. Strong gusts blew powdered snow in her face.

She knew that she would not be able to take down the other four tents without having them blown off the mountain—and maybe her with them. She decided to consolidate the equipment and supplies into two of the tents. In just a couple of minutes the wind had become so strong that she had to stop hauling and simply climb into one of the supply tents for safety.

She moved the equipment and supplies around the edges and cleared out a place in the center of the tent for her polar bag. She climbed in to wait out the wind.

Her mind began to drift to the first time she met Murphy, in the emergency ward at Preston General. He was sitting in a chair next to Laura's bed as she lay dying. He had looked so tired and grief-stricken. Isis had come with a piece of Moses' Brazen Serpent—offering the hope that this mysterious artifact had healing powers.

But Murphy had rejected it. It would be a sin, he said. He put his faith in God and God alone. Not relics or magical talismans.

And Laura had died.

At the time Isis had not understood how Murphy had just let it happen. If you really loved someone, wouldn't you try anything? Why did it matter if it was a sin? He'd seemed heartless—putting his faith before the life of his wife.

But here on the mountain, alone in her tent and surrounded by a raging blizzard, she was beginning to understand. She felt so isolated and helpless, so powerless in the face of the elements, so utterly dependent on forces beyond her control, that it was easy to believe her fate was no longer in her own hands. She felt herself give something up—the pretense that she could control things, that she was in charge—and at the same time she felt herself inviting something else in.

She wasn't quite sure what it was, but in the cold and the dark, it was a comforting presence.

She found herself thinking about what they had discovered. Her mind was reeling from everything they'd found on the ark. And she still couldn't quite believe that she had actually been standing where Noah had stood, on the very same planks of wood. But the excitement was slowly being replaced by different thoughts and deeper feelings. She knew that for Murphy, the discovery of the ark was more than just a spectacular archaeological find. It was proof that the Bible was literally true. And not just the story of Noah and the ark.

It was proof that one judgment had come.

And that another was surely coming soon.

If it came now, she wondered, *would I be one of the ones on the ark? Or would I be one of the foolish ones who stayed outside, jeering and laughing until the floodwaters swept them away into oblivion?*

As a wave of exhaustion overcame her, her last thoughts were a prayer. *If the judgment comes now, God, please look kindly on Murphy. If I can make a difference by praying about it, please spare him. . . .*

Isis didn't know how long she had been asleep. It was still dark in the tent. The wind had stopped blowing and it was eerily silent. She reached around until she found her rucksack and opened it. She moved her hand through the various items until she found her headlamp and turned it on. She glanced at her watch, but the hands weren't moving. *The battery must have died.*

She unzipped the tent and a pile of snow fell in on her. About six inches of fresh snow lay on the ground, and it looked like more would be coming. She realized that no one would be coming for her. Not in the middle of a snowstorm.

Isis began to think back to the mountain-climbing training she received on Mount Rainier. *I must eat and drink. I have got to keep up my strength, stay hydrated.*

She began to rummage through the supplies until she found a small cooking stove and a bottle of propane. It didn't seem that there was much in the bottle. She scooped up some snow from outside before zipping the tent closed again. Then she began the slow process of melting snow for drinking water and some soup.

After her meal, Isis tried to busy herself by checking the equipment and preparing to spend a cold night on the mountain. She tried not to think about how scared she was. She didn't want to imagine what would happen if no one came for her. Could she possibly get down the mountain by herself? She really hadn't paid attention to how they got to Camp 2. She had just followed the other members of the team. What would happen if she had to cross a crevasse by herself or fell through a cornice?

"Oh, no!" she exclaimed. The light on the headlamp was beginning to fade. Her battery was going. Quickly, she laid out important items where she could find them.

And then it went dark.

FORTY-FOUR

AS MURPHY ZIGZAGGED his way up to the ark, he was thinking about Noah and how he must have begged people to come aboard and escape God's judgment. And yet, only eight people were saved in the Flood.

He was imagining the awesome sense of responsibility, and Noah's sadness at his failure to convince more people of the truth of his message. And he began to feel some of the same weight of responsibility himself. *When the next judgment comes, we have to make sure more people heed God's warnings,* he thought to himself.

Murphy climbed up the snowbank next to the ark and stepped onto the roof. He bent down and examined the wood, amazed at the preservative qualities of the pitch.

He crawled through one of the window openings to the

walkway, put on his headlamp, and proceeded down the ramp to the middle floor. The ark was strangely silent.

"Colonel Hodson! Professor!" he called out. But there was no reply. Just a ghostly echo.

He continued down the ramps until he came to the bottom floor. He yelled several more times. Where could they be?

All of Murphy's alert buttons were flashing red. Slowly he entered the room that contained the large wooden chest. He took a quick glance around, his light following his turning head. He didn't see anything. He was looking the other way when his feet hit something on the floor. He shined his light down into the face of Professor Reinhold.

Quickly bending down, he felt for a pulse. Nothing. Looking more closely, he noticed that Reinhold's neck seemed to be at an odd angle, as if he'd broken it.

Or someone had broken it for him.

Suddenly things started to click into place. So Hodson *had* killed Valdez. And now Reinhold. Hodson had seemed extremely interested in the Philosopher's Stone. With Murphy out of the way, he'd taken the opportunity to get rid of Reinhold and take the crystals for himself.

Murphy looked around. The box seemed to be gone.

So was Hodson already making his way down the mountain with his booty? Or did he have a rendezvous with someone else? Another chopper, perhaps?

Or was he waiting in the shadows for Murphy to return?

Murphy shined his headlight around the room in a wide arc. He couldn't see anyone. And surely Hodson would have just taken him out with his machine pistol by now, knowing that Murphy was unarmed. There was no reason to skulk in the dark.

Then the beam of his light caught something, and his breath stopped in his throat.

Perched on a crossbeam was Hodson's head.

Before he could react, he heard a voice.

"You know, Murphy, these singing swords really live up to their name. That Tubal-cain was one smart guy. Poor old Hodson's head just dropped like a ripe peach. Even if he'd been alive I'm sure he wouldn't have felt a thing."

Suddenly one of Tubal-cain's crystal lights flashed on, and Murphy saw a black-clad man lounging against the far wall.

"Talon!"

"Got it in one," Talon said gleefully, stepping forward. "For a professor of biblical archaeology you're surprisingly sharp." And he swung the singing sword in a wide, lazy circle in front of him. Behind him, Murphy could see a bulging rucksack.

For a moment, Murphy was too full of rage to register fear. All he wanted to do was close the distance between them and tear Talon apart with his bare hands.

Then there was a flash as the sword was launched through the air like a missile. Murphy ducked instinctively, but the throw had been aimed in a different direction. The sword point penetrated deeply into a wooden wall to his left with a noise like a cleaver chopping through a carcass.

"Fair's fair," said Talon. "You don't seem to have your bow this time, and I really wouldn't want an unfair advantage." His bright teeth flashed in a grin. "You know what a gentleman I am at heart."

Murphy fought to control his emotions. Anger could lead to bad judgment. He needed to be cool. He had to push thoughts of Laura out of his mind. Otherwise, Talon was going to win.

And it was imperative that Talon not win. He couldn't be allowed to walk off with the marvels of the ark.

He looked into the eyes of the man who had crushed Laura's throat . . . the man who had shot Hank Baines . . . the man who had tried to murder Isis. And who now had killed Hodson and Reinhold.

And he felt nothing.

As they began to circle each other, the light from the vase on the floor made their shadows huge on the walls. It looked like some weird dance. A dance of death.

"After I finish with you, I'm going to bury your precious ark with an avalanche. You will be able to enjoy it forever, as your tomb." Talon laughed suddenly. "Ironic, isn't it—to meet your end on the ark of safety."

Murphy didn't react to Talon's goading. He was filled with a pure, white-hot intensity that was beyond rage, beyond emotion. He tried to imagine he was a weapon being wielded by a force greater than himself.

Then Talon struck. He covered the distance between them with a jump kick to Murphy's face. Murphy leaned to one side without changing his stance. He felt the wind of Talon's foot as it creased his face, and struck out with a back fist to the shoulder blades as he passed by, making Talon stumble when he landed. He quickly recovered and turned to face Murphy.

"My, my, Professor. You've been practicing."

But Talon's first attack had not been serious. He was just

testing Murphy's reactions. The next moment he dropped low with a leg sweep, and Murphy found himself tumbling to the floor. He managed to turn the fall into a forward roll, but as he got back to his feet, Talon delivered a solid side kick to his ribs, sending him crashing against the table.

Murphy rose and deliberately held what little breath he had left. His body screamed for air. Slowly, he forced the rest of the air out of his lungs, closed his mouth, and sucked air in through his nose. Both of his feet were planted solidly on the ground. He didn't feel any pain.

Talon advanced, smiling.

He launched a vicious spinning back kick. Murphy waited until the last millisecond before ducking under the kick and driving a palm heel into Talon's jaw, sending him sprawling. Talon picked himself up, rubbing his jaw and frowning.

"Perhaps I've been underestimating you, Murphy. You're a lot sharper than I remember. So let's stop messing around and cut to the chase."

He reached behind him and pulled two throwing knives from his belt.

Talon smirked. "Not exactly the Marquis of Queensberry's rules, but who's to know?"

He raised his arms and in a single motion threw the blades. Murphy had time to register a silvery blur of motion, and then without thinking he dived to his right, connecting with the safety railing guarding the central air shaft. The ancient wood shattered like matchsticks and he tumbled down into the darkness. Talon raced over to the edge to hear a muffled thud as Murphy hit the floor below. He shone the vase down the shaft until he could see Murphy's body lying crumpled on the wooden floor. He wasn't moving.

For a moment Talon considered jumping down after him, but it was too risky. Murphy clearly wasn't going anywhere, and even if he wasn't dead, he soon would be when the avalanche struck.

Talon grabbed the rucksack, went up the ramp to the top level, and crawled out one of the windows. He stood on the roof and looked around. He wanted to survey his escape route after planting the explosive charge to set off the avalanche. He figured that it was about fifteen hundred feet of steep climbing before he could place the device.

He began to work his way up the hill behind the ark.

"Good-bye, Murphy," he said to himself.

FORTY-FIVE

BAYER, LUNDQUIST, AND WHITTAKER sat in the
Huey and watched the snow-covered landscape unfold below
them. It had taken three days of tough hiking to get to the ark.
The journey back to Dogubayazit—where hot showers, comfortable beds, and plentiful food awaited them—would take
only an hour and twenty minutes. For the first time in days,
they allowed themselves to relax. The hard work was over.

"Hey, Vern, can you land this thing on that level spot next to
the gorge?" Whittaker was pointing down to the right.

"What for?"

"I want a shot of the helicopter with Ararat in the background. All I would need is a couple of flybys. Ten minutes,
max."

"Sure. Not a problem. That is, if I can have a nice big print
for Julie and Kevin."

Whittaker laughed. "I think that can be arranged. I'll take the other satellite phone with me. I'll call you from the ground and give you directions, so I can get the best possible shot."

Whittaker crawled in back and explained the plan to Bayer and Lundquist. They nodded and smiled. Whittaker rummaged through his rucksack, removing items he wouldn't need, while Peterson gently landed the Huey on the level patch of rocky ground.

"Give me about two minutes to set up and then make a pass by from the south at about a hundred feet off the snow. I'll call you and tell you what would be the best shot after that."

"Roger!" said Peterson, giving Whittaker the thumbs-up sign as the photographer jumped out.

Whittaker watched the helicopter rise again, then sweep off to the south. He waited until it was out of sight before pushing the buttons on the satellite phone.

"Hey, Vern. Can you hear me?"

"Loud and clear, Larry."

"Great. Make your first pass by, then go out about a half mile and turn around and come back. I'll film you all the way."

"Roger that!"

Peterson made the first pass with Ararat in the background. The air was so clear, Whittaker could see the smiling expressions on the faces of Bayer and Lundquist. Both were waving.

Whittaker took several more shots on the second pass, then picked up the phone again.

"Can you take her down into the gorge, out of my line of sight, and then come straight back up? It would make a spectacular shot, having the helicopter rise out of nowhere with the summit of Ararat in the background. Keep rising 'til I tell you to stop and then just hover."

"Piece of cake," Peterson replied.

The Huey turned and disappeared over the lip of the gorge. There was silence, then Whittaker could hear the sound of the blades getting louder again. The Huey looked as if it were rising straight out of the snow.

Awesome, thought Whittaker. *That shot has award-winning written all over it. Such a shame no one will ever see it.*

"Good-bye, Vern, thanks for the ride."

Peterson sounded confused. "What did you say, Larry?"

Whittaker didn't reply. He put the satellite phone back in his pack and pulled out a small control box.

He looked up and saw the helicopter turn in a tight circle before dropping back toward the gorge.

"You got good survival instincts, Vern," Whittaker muttered to himself. "But not good enough."

He pressed the red button just as the Huey disappeared into the gorge.

The thunder of the explosion was followed a moment later by a mushrooming orange fireball, and then blackened debris began raining down.

Whittaker jogged twenty yards farther away from the gorge until he was out of range of the falling debris. He quickly packed his camera gear and rearranged everything in his rucksack. He took out an energy bar and chewed for a while as he looked at the beauty of the snowcapped summit, then tossed the wrapper on the ground and watched it blow away in the breeze.

He sighed. "It really would have been nicer to get a ride

down to Dogubayazit," he said to himself. "But what the heck. A job's a job."

He dialed another number on the satellite phone.

"Whittaker here. It's done." He listened for a moment. "Survivors? No way. That baby went up like the Fourth of July."

As Whittaker started trudging down the trail toward Dogubayazit, the charred remains of the Huey sank deeper into the snow lining the side of the gorge, sending a cascade of rocks rattling down into the abyss. Thirty yards away, Vern Peterson lifted his head and opened his eyes. He tried to turn his head to see if Bayer or Lundquist had managed to jump in time, but he knew in his heart they had perished in the fireball. It was the sixth sense of a combat veteran that had saved him—and only by a hair's breadth.

He fell back into the snow again and closed his eyes. His thoughts turned to Vietnam. He imagined he was lying in a rice paddy, trying to keep still to conserve energy. Waiting for them to send another chopper to get him.

But this was Mount Ararat.

Who was going to save him now?

FORTY-SIX

AZGADIAN STOPPED IN HIS TRACKS when he heard the noise. He had lived on Ararat from the time he was a small boy and had become accustomed to the sounds of the mountain. But that sound was different. It wasn't a rock or snow avalanche. It was a sound he had never heard before.

Still, he instinctively knew what it was.

He looked in the direction of the echoing boom but could see nothing. Then he caught sight of what looked like smoke in the distance, toward the gorge.

He had seen the helicopter fly toward Camp 2 and then toward the gorge as he was climbing to the ark by a different route. Surely if it had fallen into the gorge, no one could have survived.

Azgadian quickened his pace. He wasn't far from the plateau at the bottom of the valley below the ark. Soon he reached the level ground and looked up at the ark. He could see no one, but something didn't feel right.

He was about halfway to the ark when his sharp eyes detected movement in the snowfield above it. He squinted at the sea of white. Then he saw someone in a white polar outfit zigzagging up the steep slope. *What is he doing up there?* An avalanche could be set off at any time. He would not survive, and the ark would be covered with tons of snow.

Soon Azgadian reached the base of the ark and climbed up the snowbank before stepping onto the roof. He glanced up the hill above him. The man in the white suit was still moving up the snowfield.

Azgadian reached into his pack and pulled out a flashlight. He climbed through one of the windows and disappeared into the ark. He paused for a moment and listened. Everything was silent except for his breathing. He walked down the ramp to each floor and looked about.

Reinhold's body was cold when he found it. Hodson's was still warm, as it lay in a cooling pool of blood. Then he looked up and saw the head.

Gasping in shock, he made the sign of the cross and muttered an ancient prayer.

Did the man in the white suit kill them? What evil is this?

As he was hurrying from the room he saw the broken rail by the air shaft. He approached cautiously and shone his torch down into the blackness. At the bottom, he could see another body. He was about to turn away when he saw the man's chest moving.

He's still alive. I've got to get him out of here before he freezes to death.

Azgadian climbed down to the lowest level and examined the injured man. He recognized the man who had spoken to him about the ark. With a huge effort, he hefted Murphy onto his shoulder, then carried him up to the top floor, shoving him gently out the window onto the roof. He then ran down the ramps back to the room with the wooden chest. He found Hodson's and Reinhold's rucksacks and grabbed a sleeping bag, a rope, and both ice axes before hurrying back up the ramps.

On the roof, Azgadian again searched the snowfield above the ark. The man in the white suit was still climbing intently, as if he knew exactly what he was doing.

He was going to start an avalanche.

Azgadian quickly tied the rope around Murphy's chest, then tossed the ice axes off the ark along with the sleeping bag. He dragged Murphy over to the edge, grabbed the rope, and began lowering him to the snow below.

Azgadian climbed down the snowbank, took out his knife, and cut the rope into two pieces. He cut a hole on each side of the sleeping bag and ran ends of the two ropes through before tying them to the bag. Then he took the other two ends and tied each of them to an ice ax.

He dragged Murphy over to the sleeping bag and eased him inside. He drove the two axes into the snow and pushed Murphy to the top of the snowfield. The sleeping bag slipped over the edge and started sliding down the hill. When the bag hit the end of the ropes, the ice axes held.

Azgadian then pulled one of the ice axes out and drove it into the snow two feet below the other ax. He repeated the process with the second ax. Gradually he began to lower Murphy down the valley.

When Azgadian had reached the plateau at the bottom, he looked up at the snowfield above the ark. The man in the white suit had stopped.

Azgadian dragged Murphy across the plateau and began to lower him down the other side of the mountain. By the time they heard the explosion and the distant rumble of the avalanche, they were safe.

He stopped briefly to listen to the last sounds of the avalanche. He imagined the snow filling the empty ark and piling on top of it. In his heart, he knew he would never see the ark again.

It was growing dark by the time Azgadian reached the cave. He lit his torch and placed it in a holder on the wall, then began to heat some soup on his propane stove. Soon the air in the cave began to warm. He unzipped the sleeping bag and checked Murphy's body temperature. He couldn't detect any broken bones.

Azgadian placed several thick furs over the sleeping bag before eating his soup and a hunk of dry bread. When he had finished, his brow was creased in thought. He had some hard decisions to make. If Murphy regained consciousness during the night, he needed to get some warm liquid into him or he would surely be dead before morning.

But he knew now the sound he had heard had been the helicopter crashing into the gorge. If anyone was still alive on that mountainside, they wouldn't be able to survive much longer without help.

He put his hands together in prayer and asked for guidance.

After a few minutes he heard a noise at the entrance to the cave. As quietly as he could, he took his staff from where it was leaning against the wall and crept forward. Anyone coming in would have to bend down as they squeezed through the narrow entrance, and that would give him his chance.

Azgadian held himself in readiness as someone pushed aside the furs sealing the entrance, then he raised the staff above his head. One more step and—

As the staff whooshed down, he caught sight of a pale, pointed face surmounted by a wild mop of red hair.

The face looked up at him and screamed.

He diverted his swing just in time, the staff clattering harmlessly against the floor. It was the woman. He smiled reassuringly and held out his hand. Still trembling, Isis took it and followed him into the cave.

Azgadian pointed down to Murphy.

"It is good you have come. God has heard me and answered my prayers." Azgadian briefly explained to Isis about the helicopter crash and how he had found Murphy. "I must go now. Stay with him. If he wakes, he must drink. There is soup by the fire. I will be back in the morning, God willing."

He wrapped his cloak around him and hefted his pack. He turned before slipping out of the cave. The woman was kneeling over the unconscious man, a look of infinite tenderness on her face.

If anyone can save him, Azgadian thought, *she can.*

FORTY-SEVEN

ISIS SPENT THE NIGHT talking gently to Murphy, praying that the sound of her voice might wake him from the coma.

"I'll admit it, I was more afraid of staying in that tent than of anything. I thought I'd go mad. So when the wind died down and the snow stopped, I thought I'd see how far down the mountain I could get." She laughed. "Completely crazy, I know, but I probably had lost my wits a little by then. If another blizzard had come and I'd lost my way, I can't imagine what I would have done. Anyway, it wasn't long before I saw this light up on the mountainside. At first I was terrified. I thought it might be a cave used by more of the rebels or . . . or, I don't know what I thought. But *something* made me climb up here." Isis looked at him as his chest gently rose and fell, and she brushed away a tear. "I'm so glad I did."

"Me too."

"Murphy!"

His eyes were open and he was trying to smile.

Isis grabbed one of his hands and squeezed it tightly between her own.

"You're awake. Oh, thank God!"

She was laughing and crying at the same time, then she let go of his hand and forced herself to be practical. He wasn't out of the woods yet. She went over to the fire and brought back a canteen of soup.

Murphy started to mumble and she put a finger to his lips.

"Don't talk. Just try to eat some of this. Azgadian told me it has healing herbs in it. He's the one who found you in the ark. He carried you back here to the cave."

She started spooning the liquid into his mouth but he waved her hand away. "Where's Azgadian?" he asked hoarsely. "Why isn't he here?"

She sighed. "The helicopter—there was a crash. He's gone to see if there were any survivors."

Murphy groaned.

"He has another cave, a bigger one, farther down the mountain nearer the gorge. When you're strong enough we're going to try and get down to it. Now shush. There's nothing we can do. Try and eat."

Murphy lay back. He suddenly felt too weak to think, let alone speak.

Gradually, through the night, the herbs did their work. By morning, Murphy felt as if he had a massive hangover and had gone ten rounds with Mike Tyson, but otherwise he felt remarkably good. He was determined to get down to Azgadian's second cave to see if anyone had survived the helicopter crash.

Two hours of strenuous hiking later, Isis spotted a wide opening in the mountainside, thirty yards or so above the trail.

"This has to be it," she said.

The cave entrance was only slightly larger than the one where they had spent the night, but inside it seemed huge. It was also filled with supplies. There was a small kitchen area with a propane stove, a roughly made table, and a couple of chairs. Furs were spread on the ground like rugs, and a number of curious paintings hung on the walls. They were ancient with grime but seemed to depict the building of the ark, then the ark floating on the Flood, and finally the animals being led out onto dry land, with a rainbow in the background.

"Azgadian!" Murphy called out. "Are you here?"

A fur was pushed aside, revealing a sleeping area. Azgadian stood, smiling.

"It is good you are here. Your friend, she has looked after you well."

Murphy took Isis's hand in his. "Yes, she has. But you are the one who saved me from the ark, I believe. I owe you my life."

Azgadian bowed slightly and said nothing.

"Were there . . . ?" Murphy asked hesitantly.

Azgadian gestured for them to come. They walked over to the sleeping area and saw a figure curled up on a mattress of straw.

It was Vern Peterson.

"Is he okay?" Murphy asked, kneeling down.

"He will be. He has some bad cuts, and a sprained ankle, I think. I do not know how he survived the explosion."

"It's a miracle," Isis said with a smile. "I think I'm beginning to believe in them."

Just then there was a shout, followed by a peal of raucous laughter that ended in a sustained bout of coughing.

Azgadian smiled. "I think your friend from the helicopter has woken up."

Murphy was hugging Peterson, tears streaming down his face.

"I can't tell you how relieved I am to see you, Vern, old buddy!"

"Likewise," said Peterson, before subsiding into another fit of coughing.

Murphy waited until his friend was breathing easier. "So what happened, Vern? Are you the only one who made it?"

Peterson nodded sadly. "We were on our way down the mountain and Whittaker asked me to put her down so he could take some more pictures. We were talking on the satellite phones, and something he said just didn't seem right. Then he took out some sort of control box and I guess my instincts just took over. I tried to take the chopper down into the gorge so an electronic signal wouldn't reach it, but I figured it was going to be too late and I just jumped." His voice choked with emotion. "There wasn't time to explain to Bayer and Lundquist. I was hoping they'd just follow me out, but I guess they . . ." He couldn't go on.

Murphy's jaw was clenched in anger. "*Whittaker.* I was looking in the wrong place the whole time."

"What about the rest of them?" Vern asked, trying to sit up. "Where are Reinhold and Hodson?"

"Dead," said Murphy.

"How?" asked Peterson incredulously.

Murphy had difficulty saying the word. "Talon. He's pure evil, and he must have been tracking us all the way to the ark. He almost killed me too. I'd be buried under an avalanche right now if it wasn't for Azgadian here. Whittaker must have been working with Talon. They were trying to wipe out the whole team." He turned to Isis. "Thank God you did leave the camp and manage to find the cave. Otherwise I'll bet Talon would have come looking for you too."

Isis paled, imagining another confrontation with Talon.

Peterson was trying to make sense of it all. "But I don't understand, Murph. Why did this Talon guy want us all dead? What was he after?"

"The secrets on the ark," Murphy said simply. "Reinhold figured out that the bronze plates we found were a set of instructions—instructions for what he called the Philosopher's Stone."

Peterson looked puzzled.

"A method for turning one element into another. Say, lead into gold. Or platinum. According to Reinhold, anyone who had the trick of making unlimited supplies of platinum would be able to control the world's energy supplies. That's a secret some people would be willing to kill for, I'd say."

Peterson was trying to absorb what Murphy was saying. "And this Talon character—he wants to take over the world?"

Murphy looked grim. "I don't know what motivates Talon,

apart from a love of killing for the sake of it. But the people he works for, yes."

"And who the heck are they?"

"I wish I knew, Vern. I wish I knew. All I'm certain of is that they're evil and they have to be stopped."

Murphy stood up and turned to Azgadian, who had been listening with an interested expression. "Azgadian, you have saved my life twice now, and my friend Vern's too. We can never repay you for what you have done. But tell me, why have you chosen this strange life on the mountain? Why are you here?"

Azgadian looked at them seriously. "It is right you should know. I am one of the guardians of the sacred ark. For centuries my family has been doing this. It goes all the way back to a monk named St. Jacob. He charged my Armenian ancestors with the task of guardianship over the Ark of Noah. My relatives and friends from the village below keep me supplied. I will watch the mountain for two years and then someone will replace me for a while. Then I will come back again."

Vern was shaking his head in disbelief. "Now I really have heard it all."

"Have there been many who have found the ark and taken relics?" asked Murphy.

"A few, over the centuries," Azgadian replied. "But we were able to get most of the sacred objects back."

"Why did you tell us where the ark could be found? Why didn't you just let us search like all the other explorers?" Isis asked.

Azgadian turned to Murphy. "There was something about you and your . . . sincerity. Your strength of purpose. I could tell you were not here to plunder the ark. For some years now we have been waiting for the right man to come seeking the ark. It is written that there is a coming evil in this world. It will be so wicked and ungodly that many will be led astray." He nodded to himself. "This man you call Talon. I believe he must be a part of it. We think that it is God's time to unveil the ark to remind the world of His judgment against wickedness. We think you might be the man to do this."

Michael suddenly didn't have any words. He felt like Moses when God told him to lead the children of Israel. Moses had asked God to choose someone else. At that moment Murphy very much wanted to believe someone else, someone better and stronger than he, could be chosen.

"But the ark is gone, Azgadian, isn't it?"

Azgadian shook his head sadly. "The avalanche buried it under many tons of snow. But its resting place was always unstable. I believe the remains may now be lost in a crevasse created by the glacier. Perhaps no one will ever see it again."

Isis gasped. "Then how will we prove it was there? What about the artifacts?"

Murphy groaned. "My rucksack! I left it near the ark where Vern could pick it up. Maybe it's still there!"

He started to make for the cave entrance, but Azgadian put a gentle hand on his shoulder. He shook his head. "It is gone," he said.

Murphy put his head in his hands. "Then Talon has the bronze plates. He has the secret!"

"And the proof of the ark's existence," added Isis.

Murphy thought for a moment. "Azgadian, you have already

done so much for us. If you could look after my friend Vern here until he is well enough to return to Dogubayazit, you will have my eternal gratitude. I wish I could repay you in some way for your courage and your kindness."

Azgadian waved him away. "It is the guardians' duty to look after the seekers if they are pure in heart. You owe me nothing. But I would ask one thing of you. When God calls on you to be His messenger, do not disregard Him."

Murphy held his gaze. "I'll do my best to do God's will, whatever it is." He turned to Isis, taking her gently by the shoulders.

"You stay here too, Isis. I'm sure Azgadian could do with some help looking after Vern."

She narrowed her eyes. "And what exactly will you be doing all this time?"

Murphy paused. "I'm going after Talon."

A cocktail of emotions flashed through her green eyes. "Blast you, Murphy. You think you can do everything on your own, don't you? Well, not this time."

"What do you mean?"

She had a defiant look on her face. "I'm going with you, of course."

FORTY-EIGHT

SHANE BARRINGTON raised his antique crystal goblet and proposed a toast.

"To us. And to many more moments like this."

They clinked glasses and each took a mouthful of the vintage champagne.

"Well, I must admit I was disappointed when you canceled our dinner engagement, but I guess this makes up for it," Stephanie said with a dazzling smile.

In fact, the setting Barrington had chosen was far more impressive than the most glitzy of downtown restaurants. The top floor of the Barrington Communications building had been transformed into a florist's fantasy. Every surface seemed to be covered with flowers. Huge sprays adorned every corner, there were rose petals scattered over the floor, and the whole room was awash in their scent.

Barrington smiled back. "I just wanted to show my appreciation for all your hard work, Stephanie. And more important, for your loyalty. I know how you like to ask questions all the time—it's your job, after all. But you never question anything I ask you to do. That's important. That's why I can trust you."

Stephanie chose her next words carefully. "I'm sure there's always a good reason for your decisions. I don't need to ask why all the time. You're the boss, after all."

He raised his glass again and drained the rest of his champagne in one gulp. "Right. But I know deep down you must find it tough to hold that reporter's tongue of yours. So as a special treat tonight, I'm going to let you ask me anything you want. And I'll tell you the answer."

Stephanie tried to keep her smile in place, but under the surface she was worried. When she'd first agreed to become Barrington's mistress and do whatever he commanded, she'd naturally been curious about a lot of things. Why was he pursuing his aggressive campaign against evangelical Christians? Why was he so interested in Michael Murphy? And how did he appear to know some stories were going to break before they'd even happened? But she'd gradually learned to suppress her curiosity. That was the price she had to pay, after all.

But there was also another reason for not asking questions.

She was afraid of the answers.

She was smart and experienced enough to know that people like Shane Barrington didn't get to the top of the corporate pile

by playing by the rules. She had no doubt he had a few skele-
tons rattling around in his closet. Perhaps even literally. That
wasn't what bothered her.

What bothered her was her growing conviction that
Barrington was doing something more than making money,
more than just accumulating power for himself. He was doing
something . . . evil.

She surprised herself by even thinking the word. It wasn't
part of her vocabulary. Sure, she'd used it plenty of times in her
more sensational TV reports when describing rapists or serial
killers, but she hadn't meant it literally. It was just a word you
used to spice things up.

But the more time she spent with Barrington, the more she
thought it really meant something.

And the more she wondered how she was going to ever get
away from him.

"Okay," she said finally. "Here's a question. How did you
know Michael Murphy was planning an expedition to find
Noah's Ark? And how did you know before any of the other
networks that FBI agent, Hank Baines, had been shot?"

Barrington's face darkened. "That's two questions, Stephanie."

He looked at her intently, his eyes boring into hers, and she
suddenly felt she'd gone too far. But then his expression light-
ened, and he laughed.

"Well, they're connected, so I guess I can count it as one
question. But before I answer, you have to promise me something, Stephanie."

She gulped. "Sure."

"Promise me you won't do anything foolish, so I'd be forced to . . . dispose of you. I've grown very fond of you, Stephanie. I'd hate our relationship to end in tragedy."

Now she really was scared. "Look, if you don't want to tell me, that's fine. I was just making conversation."

"No, no," he insisted. "A promise is a promise." He laughed again. "Even from me. I'll tell you what you want to know. And then," he added ominously, "you'll be part of the family."

"Okay," she whispered, hardly able to speak.

Abruptly, Barrington stood up and walked to the window, looking down over the brightly lit streets many stories below.

"I was going out of business," he began, still looking out the window. "My company had massive debts, which I'd managed to hide with some creative accounting, but I wasn't going to be able to do it for much longer. And there was some other stuff I could have gone to jail for too, if anyone found out. Well, someone did find out. And they put a gun to my head and made me one of those offers you can't refuse. They'd inject five billion into the business to make it the biggest communications company in the world. To put me where I am today. And all I had to do in return was help them in their enterprise."

The words were out of Stephanie's mouth before she could stop them. "And what enterprise was that?"

He turned back to her and smiled grimly. "Why, to take over the world, of course."

He sat back down opposite her, filled his glass, and quickly drained it.

"And what has all that got to do with Murphy and Noah's Ark? You see, these people I work for, these people who *own* me, are hell-bent on establishing a one-world government. A one-world religion too. And people like Murphy, they see it all coming, in the Bible. So they have to be stopped. Before they can persuade people to resist."

"And the ark?"

"Ah, yes, the ark. If the ark was found sitting on Mount Ararat, that would be a blow to my friends. It would show that the Bible was true. It would make people think what the Bible said about the one-world government was true too. You can see why they wouldn't want that."

Stephanie nodded, not sure what to say. Her brain was reeling from Barrington's bizarre confession. Was incredible stuff like this really happening in the world? And was she really caught up in the middle of it?

"And Baines? What was their problem with him?"

"I'm not sure. I think my employers had a connection inside the CIA and Baines was about to expose it. So they dealt with him."

Stephanie felt as if she was in free fall, as if she was stuck in an elevator hurtling toward the ground—except there *was* no ground. This elevator was going to keep on falling until . . . until it reached hell itself.

But then, unexpectedly, she started to hear a voice at the back of her mind. A voice of hope. A little voice telling her that maybe this was her chance for redemption. Her chance to prove that she wasn't all bad. If Barrington was going to trust her with his secrets, if she could keep his trust so he didn't *dispose* of her, then maybe she could make a difference after all.

Already she was forming a plan in her mind. The first thing she needed to do was to contact Murphy.

But where was he?

FORTY-NINE

MURPHY STOPPED IN THE middle of a narrow street crowded with tiny shop fronts and put his hands on his hips.

"They all look the same to me, Isis. How are we ever going to find the right place?"

"It can't be far away," she said. "We were near the museum when that guy accosted us, and then we followed him for about five minutes. It has to be within a one-mile radius of the museum."

"One mile. That's a lot of alleys, a lot of buildings that look exactly the same. It could take forever."

Murphy suddenly winced.

"Is it your leg?" Isis asked, looking concerned.

"It's nothing," he said, rubbing his thigh. "I'm fine."

Isis tutted. "You must have fallen thirty feet, and onto a hard wooden floor. It would be amazing if you didn't have some injury to show for it. Why can't you men just admit it when you're hurt?"

"That's a discussion for another place and another time. When we've found the bronze plate. And when we've found Talon."

"Have it your own way," Isis said. She turned in a slow circle. "This way," she suddenly pointed. Gritting his teeth as he limped after her, Murphy followed farther down the street.

"We were walking south, then we doubled back to try and shake him off, then he took us off in another direction . . . west. So . . ." She took a hairpin left, Murphy struggling to keep up, then a right into an alley choked with carts laden with oranges and limes. They squeezed their way through and then they were in a wider street lined with ancient-looking wooden doorways.

"This is starting to look familiar," Murphy said.

"I think so too," said Isis. "Which means round that corner should be an archway, and through it . . ."

They hurried around the corner. There indeed was a low arch. They exchanged glances and ducked under the arch, entering a tiny courtyard littered with rusting motorcycle parts.

"Did I ever tell you you're a genius?" Murphy exclaimed.

"Not nearly often enough," Isis replied with a grin. She pointed at a door that had once, many years ago, been painted blue. "Come on, this must be the one."

Murphy rapped on the door, then stood back and waited. He rapped again, louder. Still there was no sound of anyone inside the house.

Then he heard the unmistakable noise of a gun being racked and he looked upward. A blond man with a thin beard was leaning out of a second-story window, pointing a pump-action shotgun. Murphy knew there was no chance of escape. The field of fire was too wide.

"What do you want here?" the man shouted.

Murphy walked in front of Isis. If the man fired, perhaps he could at least shield her from the blast. "We're looking for someone. A big man. Gray hair, wears a long leather coat."

"My brother, Amin."

"Yes, do you know where we can find him?"

"Sure. But you'll need to take a shovel if you want to talk to him. I buried him a week ago."

Isis gasped. She had experienced too many deaths in the last few days. "I'm sorry. We didn't know."

"How do I know it wasn't you who killed him?" asked the blond man. "Maybe I should take my revenge now."

Murphy held his hands up. "Look, if we'd done it, why would be looking for him now? We had no idea."

The blond man thought about it for a moment, then disappeared back inside. A few moments later the door opened and he beckoned them across the threshold at gunpoint.

The room was exactly as they remembered it. The only difference was the dull reddish stain against one wall. Isis tried not to think about what it meant.

The blond man gestured for them to sit.

"Why are you looking for my brother?"

"He had some artifacts, some things he claimed were taken from Noah's Ark. They came from the museum," explained Murphy. He was careful not to say *stolen* from the museum. "He offered to sell them to us, but when we came back the next day he was gone. Or that's what we thought."

"Gone, yes, and to hell probably," said the blond man, spitting noisily on the floor. "Someone else wanted these things, I think. Someone who didn't want to pay for them."

"They're gone?" Isis asked.

The blond man waved his arm. "See for yourself."

With one eye on their host, Isis and Murphy carefully searched the room. There was no doubt about it. The bronze plate was gone.

"So now he has all three," Murphy said forlornly.

"Who? You know the man who did this?" asked the blond man, his voice urgent.

Murphy nodded.

"Can you tell me what he looks like?"

An image of Talon's long, pale face with its dark eyes suddenly sprang into Isis's mind, as sharp as a photograph. "That won't be a problem," she said.

"But what good would it do?" Murphy asked. "He isn't in Erzurum any longer, you can bet your bottom dollar on that."

"Our family, it is very big. I have cousins all over Turkey. If this man is still in the country, we can find him."

Murphy thought he knew what kind of "family" the blond man was referring to. "I understand. Let's make a deal. If we give you a description of this man, you must promise to tell us if anyone in your . . . *family* finds him. I want to deal with him myself."

The blond man stroked his chin for a few moments, cradling the shotgun in his lap. "Then you must make *me* a promise. If you catch him, you must kill him."

Murphy bit his lip, contradictory emotions flooding through him. Isis looked at him, wondering what he was going to say. She knew how powerful was the instinct for revenge when a loved one had been killed, but could he make such a promise as a Christian?

"I promise," Murphy said.

FIFTY

IT WAS EARLY *in the morning when they first heard the sound. Dressing quickly, Noah's family gathered on the walkway above the third floor. They forced open one of the windows, only to be blown back by a fierce wind. The window slammed shut in their faces.*

"What is happening, Father?" asked Ham. "The waters have been calm ever since the tops of the mountains disappeared under the waves. Is God angry about something? Have we done something wrong? We've worked hard to look after the animals."

"I don't know," Noah answered. "We are in God's hands. Surely He will tell us if we have failed to do His will."

The whole family closed their eyes in prayer as they listened to the wind howling outside the ark.

———

The winds continued unabated, day after day. Then one morning Noah heard Japheth call out excitedly, "Father, come quickly. Look out the window. Over there. Do you see the top of the mountain?"

Noah stroked his long beard and nodded. "I think I know why God has sent the strong winds. He is drying out the sea. The waters are receding."

As the days went by, more land emerged from the waters, mountaintops peeking through in all directions. They began to hope that they would soon set foot on dry land again.

Then one day they heard a massive grinding sound, and the ark came to a halt.

Rushing to the third-floor walkway, they crowded around one of the windows. The sight took their breath away.

"Look!" shouted Ham. "We're not floating anymore! Look outside! We're on a mountain." And indeed, the great boat was wedged at the bottom of a gulley on a rock-strewn mountainside. It seemed as if they only had to reach out their hands and they could touch things they'd only dreamed about for so long: earth, rocks, dirt.

"The waters have indeed greatly receded," said Noah with a smile. He put his hand on Japheth's shoulder. "But we must be sure the earth is ready again to receive all the animals."

"How will we know?" asked Ham impatiently.

"We will send out a raven to see if it can find a resting place," replied Noah.

Japheth fetched one of the ravens from its cage. He held his hand over its eyes until he was leaning right over the deck, then flung it into the air. The raven squawked loudly, as if it had forgotten how to fly, then with a few strong beats of its wings it disappeared up into the sky.

They waited eagerly, some unable to take their eyes from the horizon. Then a few hours later the raven returned. It had not found land.

A week later Noah sent out a dove, but it returned even more quickly than the raven.

"We've been on this boat for almost a year," cried Naamah. "How much longer must we endure this?"

"Have patience," said Noah. He knew this was the most difficult time, when the end seemed so near.

Another week passed, and Noah again sent out a dove. This time the dove returned with a freshly plucked olive branch in its beak.

Everyone looked to Noah. Was this the sign they had been waiting for? "It won't be long now," he said. "Just a little longer, I am certain of it."

The third time Noah released the dove, it did not return.

"Now we can leave the ark," he announced. "Try the door and see if it will open." Ham, Shem, and Japheth eagerly put their shoulders to the door and pushed. They were determined to finally escape the confines of the ark that had been their home for so long it now seemed like a prison.

To their surprise it opened easily. As the light flooded in, they could see green trees in the valley below. The fresh air was the most wonderful thing they had ever tasted.

As they laughed and hugged each other, it was Shem who brought them back down to earth. "We will have to rig up the pulleys and lower each other down, along with our tools," he said. "We are going to have to build another ramp to get the animals out of the ark."

The days passed quickly as they worked at fever pitch, constructing a ramp to the third floor. Then the incredible exodus began. Noah's sons ran along the stalls, opening cages, and two by two the vast sea of living things charged, scurried, flew, scampered, wriggled, and slithered out of the ark and into a fresh new world.

Only the sacrificial animals remained. Noah and his family stepped out onto the sweet-smelling earth and immediately built an altar. They thanked God that their ordeal was over at last and their new life could begin.

They walked around slowly at first, unused to having solid, unmoving ground beneath their feet, not quite believing that it was real.

"What's that in the sky?" asked Achsah, pointing to the east.

Everyone turned and looked. Their mouths opened in wonder as they beheld the multicolored beauty of a great arc framing the sky.

Noah smiled. "That is a rainbow. It is a promise to us from God that He will never again bring a flood to cover the earth. It will be a reminder to all of our generations of His faithfulness and mercy."

"Father, should I bring the things from the chest?" asked Shem.

"No, son. Not yet. We must first see where we shall live. We need to explore the new country below. But we will return someday soon for the golden box of Tubal-cain and the bronze plates."

"What shall we call this place, Father?" asked Japheth.

Noah thought for a moment, looking out over the majestic landscape of rock and stone, with trees and grass farther down in the valley. "We will call it Ararat."

Hagaba leaned over to Naamah and whispered in her ear.

"We shall also call it the place where you found out that you will soon become a grandmother."

FIFTY-ONE

JOHN BARTHOLOMEW KNEW he was breaking one of his own unwritten rules, but the circumstances seemed to demand it. Most of the time, each member of the Seven led a perfectly normal life, whether as a banker, lawyer, churchman, or general. No one would guess that they were part of a conspiracy that aimed to destroy the word monetary system, the rule of law, the Christian church, and the military power of sovereign nations. When they came together, it was only at the castle, and only their most trusted lieutenants witnessed their meetings or even knew they were taking place. It was imperative that no one associated these seven people with one another. So outside the confines of the castle they were forbidden from ever meeting, unless by chance their business brought them together fleetingly.

But they were getting so close to their goal, so close to total triumph, he felt he could relax the rules a little. Surely whatever happened, no one could stop them now.

He planted his ski poles firmly in the snow and looked back down the gentle slope. General Li was quickly closing the distance between them with firm strides, closely followed by Mendez, red-faced and sweating but clearly determined not to be beaten by his much fitter fellow conspirator. Sir William Merton's portly frame was unmistakable at the back of the group, gliding effortlessly over the snow as if by some diabolical magic. Another man and two women trudged along in front of him, completing the Seven.

Bartholomew waited until they had all caught up with him on the ridge. The thin-faced, red-haired woman was about to make a comment about wasting valuable time, not to mention effort, when there were still important things to be done—when she glimpsed the view.

In front of them a vast glacier stretched down into the valley below, and beyond that a towering fortress of dark stone thrust up into the clouds, like a skyscraper built by an ancient race of giants.

"Magnificent, isn't it?" Bartholomew intoned.

"Sure, sure," came a harsh Brooklyn accent. "Very pretty. Now, what's this all about?"

Bartholomew smiled indulgently. "I have brought you all here because I wanted an appropriate setting for what I have to announce."

There was a hush as they waited for more. Then a heavyset woman with blond hair broke the silence impatiently.

"It's true, then! They have found the potassium forty. We have the key to eternal life in our grasp!"

Bartholomew shook his head. "I'm sorry to disappoint you, my dear. I know you were hoping to preserve those lovely features for future generations to admire. And perhaps it shall be so. But that was not what Talon found on the ark."

"Then what did he find?" asked Merton, intrigued.

"Something that will be of incalculable value in the next phase of our operation. A technology that will enable us to control all of the world's energy supplies—that will make oil a thing of the past. Imagine the power that will give us. It could bring forward the achievement of our goal by years!"

"And this was on the ark?" said General Li incredulously.

"Indeed," said Bartholomew. "It would seem our friend Noah was much more than just a zookeeper. He was the master of some ancient but highly sophisticated technologies. Processes that were lost when he left the ark."

"And Talon now has them?" said Merton.

Bartholomew nodded. "He is on his way back."

"How soon will he get here?" said Mendez.

"He is taking a cautious route. He cannot risk being intercepted. He was forced to terminate one of our friends from the CIA. We must anticipate that they will use all of their resources to track him down." He turned to the red-haired woman. "You will rendezvous with him in Romania."

She nodded. "What about the other members of the expedition team? Who else knows about this technology?"

"Talon reports that every member of the team has been eliminated, with one exception—the woman, Isis McDonald. But she is no threat to us. He will deliver the ark's secret to us before tying up that particular loose end."

Merton looked thoughtful. "Murphy's dead, then?"

"And buried. Under a thousand tons of ice and snow. Along with Noah's little boat, I might add. Talon has done exceptionally well, don't you think? The ark has been destroyed."

Merton smiled. "And the story of Noah will perish with it."

"Amen to that," the red-haired woman laughed.

FIFTY-TWO

THE FAT MAN SCRATCHED his stubble and carefully unfolded the crumpled sheet of paper, revealing a pencil drawing of a long-faced man with thin lips and intense, dark eyes. It was only a sketch, but the contained ferocity of his expression burned off the page.

On the other side of the table in the smoky back room of the bar, Murphy and Isis waited patiently.

The fat man looked at the drawing closely, then held it at arm's length, as if it was one of those optical illusions that reveal a different picture if you look at them a certain way.

Finally the fat man slapped his palm on the table, almost knocking over a half-finished glass of raki. "My cousin has seen him. And another man. They travel together, I think. In a boardinghouse near the docks." He peered again at the sketch. "This is a very dangerous man. It is best if you let us take care of him for you."

Murphy looked at him steadily. "Amin's brother promised that you would leave him to us."

The fat man shrugged, as if it was of no concern to him. "As you wish. But a man like this, he is like a wolf that must be killed quickly. Show him mercy and he will tear your throat out."

Murphy nodded solemnly. "We know what he is. And what has to be done. So where do we find him?"

"He will not be in Istanbul for very long," the fat man said. "He and his friend have booked passage on the *Arcadia* sailing to Constanta, Romania. The ship is leaving this afternoon. It will sail through the Strait of Bosporus and into the Sea of Marmara. It will eventually reach the Black Sea and sail on to Romania."

Isis was puzzled. "Why is he taking a pleasure cruise? Why doesn't he just get on a plane?"

"Because that's what we'd expect him to do," Murphy said. "Who would think of looking for him on a boat?"

"Maybe there's some significance about Romania too," she added.

"Maybe. Whatever it is, we have to make sure he doesn't get there and hand over the bronze plates to his masters." Murphy leaned across the table. "How can we get on the boat?" he asked.

The fat man smiled, showing a mouthful of gold teeth, then pulled an envelope out of the pocket of his leather jacket and put it on the table.

"Your tickets," he said. "Have a pleasant trip."

———

The sun was going down as Isis and Murphy approached the docks, turning Istanbul into a romantic realm of minarets and winding alleyways. For a moment, Isis imagined what it would be like to spend time there alone with Murphy. It would be a perfect place for them, a city brimming with history, just asking to be explored. They could discover its treasures together, and then perhaps they'd be able to find each other too.

Seeing the ship suddenly looming in front of her, Isis snapped out of the fantasy and back to the present. They were not about to go on a romantic vacation. They were about to step onto a boat where two killers were waiting for them.

The last passengers were hurrying up the gangplank, and Murphy broke into a jog. "Come on, Isis, we have to hurry."

As they stepped onto the deck, Isis brought her sun hat lower over her face. Her red hair was tucked out of sight and a pair of sunglasses covered her eyes, but she was still desperately afraid that Talon would recognize her before they spotted him. As for Murphy, as far as she could tell, he was trusting mostly to the fact that Talon was convinced he was dead. "He's arrogant," he explained to her. "He won't believe that he might have messed up." Even so, she insisted he wear his baseball cap low over his face until they got to their cabin.

Once inside, she bolted the door, then stacked a chair against it, just in case. Murphy looked at her quizzically. "*We're* looking for *him*, remember?" he said, trying to brighten her mood. But it didn't work. She went and sat on one of the twin beds.

"So what do we do now?"

Murphy sat on the other bed and put his hands behind his head. She had an awful feeling he was preparing to take a nap.

"We wait," he said.

"Wait? Until when?" She could hear her voice beginning to sound slightly hysterical.

"Talon's a hunter," Murphy said quietly. "And like most hunters, he's more at home in the dark. I think that's when he feels most comfortable. He's also a loner. Crowds aren't his style. I think he'll stay in his lair until most of the passengers and crew are asleep. Then he'll come out to play."

Isis looked at her watch. It was going to be a long wait. She watched as Murphy pulled a battered leather-bound Bible out of his rucksack, turned to the front, and began to read.

When she felt the hand shaking her, she had no idea where she was. The gentle motion of the boat riding the swell had soothed her into a deep sleep, and she was currently imagining herself striding through the thick heather with her father, on their way to climb some favorite Highland peak.

Then she saw Murphy's face, and his expression of icy determination brought her back to the present.

To Talon.

They opened the door of the cabin and stepped out into the corridor. Apart from the noise of the engines, all seemed quiet. They climbed a steep flight of steps leading up to the main deck and Murphy poked his head out of a narrow doorway. After a few moments he motioned to Isis to follow him onto the deck.

"No sign of them."

It was the middle of the night, but a few couples were strolling hand in hand or leaning against the railings and gazing out into the darkness. A sudden laugh made Isis clutch Murphy's arm. One of the couples swayed drunkenly against the railings.

Murphy pushed her forward gently. "Still too crowded for Talon, I reckon. Let's see if we can find a quieter spot."

They walked back along the rail, Isis starting at every little sound, until they reached the stern. The deck dropped down to a lower level, and a guardrail prevented passengers from going any farther. Murphy peered over at the lower deck. Empty. Isis breathed a sigh of relief. She prayed that Talon and Whittaker weren't on the boat at all, that somehow the Turkish mafiosi had gotten to them first. She didn't know what she would do if she had to come face to face with Talon again. All she was certain of was that she had to stay at Murphy's side, no matter what.

She was about to suggest that they go back to their cabin and make another plan when she felt Murphy's finger pressing against her lips. Her eyes widened as she looked in the direction he was pointing.

Thirty feet above them, perched on the very top of the ship's superstructure next to a radio mast, a dark figure was crouched like a cat waiting to pounce on a bird.

Her heart beating furiously, she waited for her eyes to adjust to the darkness. Gradually more detail came into view. Talon was facing to starboard, looking out over the sea. He didn't seem to have spotted them.

Murphy motioned for Isis to stay where she was. He pointed upward.

She shook her head vigorously. *No!* she wanted to scream, her eyes wide with fear. Murphy gave her an intense look, one that seemed to penetrate deep inside her, and she knew there was no point arguing. After a few moments she nodded. Tears welled up and she let them fall as she watched him moving stealthily around to the other side of the ship and disappearing up a ladder.

She closed her eyes, trying to make herself invisible, not daring to move a muscle in case a sudden noise alerted Talon to their presence. Leaning back against the guardrail, she could feel her whole body begin to shake.

Come on! Get a grip! she told herself angrily.

She willed her eyes to open and looked up.

Talon was gone.

She gasped, then quickly put her hand over her mouth. He must have seen them. She had to warn Murphy somehow. She thought of following him up the ladder but felt too shaky. Maybe she should just scream as loud as she could. Or was that the worst possible thing she could do? She bit her lip, drawing blood. She couldn't think.

She heard a soft thud, like a cat landing on a carpet, and Talon was standing right in front of her, his gray eyes glinting in the darkness.

"Will wonders never cease," he purred. "I was just trying to figure out when I was going to catch up with you and shut your pretty mouth before you tell any silly tales about Noah's Ark—and here you are. Almost makes you believe in miracles, doesn't it?"

He took a step forward, and a shiver traveled through her body.

"If you don't know already," he continued, "I have bad news about poor old Murphy. He's rather more than six feet under,

I'm afraid. About sixty feet under, I would say. Still, he got to see his precious ark in the end, so perhaps he died happy. Let's hope so, eh?"

She swallowed hard. Where was Murphy? Was he watching at this very moment, waiting for his chance to act? Or was he still trying to sneak up on Talon's original position? If she screamed a warning, would it simply alert Talon to the fact that Murphy was still very much alive? Would it put him in more danger?

She had to keep Talon talking while she tried desperately to figure out what to do.

"Where's Whittaker?" she said in a trembling voice.

Talon laughed. "Oh, I wouldn't worry about him. I sent him on a special assignment. Underwater photography." He narrowed his eyes. "So you saw our little accident with the helicopter, did you?"

She gulped, trying not to imagine Whittaker sinking down into the murky depths. "What about the bronze plates?"

He gestured behind him with his thumb. "Up there. Safe in my rucksack."

"Think again!"

Talon shoved Isis out of the way as he rushed to the guardrail and looked down. Murphy was sitting on the rail at the stern, holding on with one hand as he dangled a rucksack over the churning wake.

"Murphy!" Talon growled. "I should have known you'd come crawling back. I should have put one of those magic swords through your guts when I had the chance!"

He leaped over the rail onto the deck below and began advancing on Murphy.

Isis craned forward, her hand to her mouth. What was Murphy doing?

Murphy held his position, a confident smile on his face. "I guess your employers would be pretty ticked off if you came home empty-handed, wouldn't they? I'd say that would be your end-of-year bonus up in smoke, don't you think? Maybe they'd even terminate your employment." He shook the rucksack, and Talon could hear the bronze plates scraping together.

Talon was just a few paces away now and advancing more cautiously as Murphy leaned back and dangled the rucksack farther over the abyss.

Talon stopped and put his hands on his hips. "You wouldn't dare. You know the significance of what's in that rucksack, and you aren't going to throw it overboard. Not after all you and your friends went through to get it."

"Try me," said Murphy. He loosened his grip and the strap started to slip from his grasp.

Talon gasped. "No!"

He rushed forward. Murphy turned his back on him and swung the rucksack, as if he was preparing to hurl it overboard. Talon leaped at Murphy's back, a knife suddenly in his hand.

Isis screamed.

Then at the last moment Murphy let go of the strap. Talon changed course and hurled himself over the rail as the rucksack flew out of Murphy's hand. Talon grunted as he got a hand on it, ready to haul it back. Then gravity took over and Isis could see the look of horror on his face as he realized he was going over.

There was a rush of air, and Talon and the rucksack were gone.

Isis scrambled down a ladder and buried herself in Murphy's

arms, sobbing uncontrollably. They were both shaking. He hugged her hard, overcome with relief. They stayed like that for what seemed an eternity, until eventually she pulled away, smiling through her tears.

"Were the bronze plates really in the rucksack? Are they really—"

"Yes," he said. "They're gone."

She stared at him, eyes wide with shock.

"There was no other way. He had to know it was for real. Look," he said, gently brushing away her tears.

The first pink tinges of light were brightening the horizon.

They stood together, arms around each other, and watched the new dawn.

Return to where the adventure begins . . .

BABYLON RISING

Tim LaHaye

and

Greg Dinallo

Read on for an exciting excerpt from the
first book in the Babylon Rising series.

On sale now

THE *NEW YORK TIMES* BESTSELLER
BOOK 1   A NEW ADVENTURE BEGINS
From the Creator of
THE LEFT BEHIND® SERIES

TIM LAHAYE
AND
GREG DINALLO

BABYLON RISING

BABYLON RISING
On sale now

EXACTLY THIRTY-THREE HOURS and forty-seven
minutes after he had last been in church, Michael Murphy was
hurtling through a terrible dark abyss. Prayer had never seemed
more necessary to him than at that moment. In pitch blackness,
with the only sound the *whoosh* of his body falling through the
air, Murphy had no idea where he was heading.

Except down. Quickly. All six feet three inches of him.

Just a moment ago, Murphy had been standing on the rooftop
of what appeared to be an abandoned warehouse on a desolate
street in Raleigh, North Carolina. It was an unusual place for
him to be on a Monday night during the university semester,
when he normally would be preparing for his next day's lecture.

Yet it took only one word to make him drop all normal
activities and race to this dank and deserted height. Granted,
that word was in Aramaic, one of the many ancient languages
Michael Murphy could read with some fluency.

The Aramaic letters had been penned with elaborate style in
a bright blue ink that had seeped deeply into a thick, expensive
ivory-tinted paper stock that had been wrapped with great care
and tied up by a translucent ribbon around a heavy stone.

A stone that came crashing through the lower window of
Murphy's campus office late that afternoon.

Whoever threw the stone into his office had disappeared by
the time Murphy got to the window. As he unwrapped the

paper and translated the single word that appeared there, he first stared, then began to count.

Thirty seconds until his office phone rang. He knew what voice he would hear at the other end of the line, although he had never seen the face to go with that voice.

"Hello, Methuselah, you old scoundrel."

There was a high cackling laugh in answer, a sound Murphy would recognize anywhere. "Oh, Murphy, you never disappoint me. I take it I've piqued your interest."

"And cost me a replacement window." He looked down again at the single word on the paper. "Is this for real?"

"Murphy, have I ever let you down?"

"Nope. You've tried your weird best to kill me several times, but let me down, never. When and where?"

The cackling now was replaced by a tongue-clucking. "Now, don't rush me, Murphy. My rules. My time. My game. But trust me, this will be the best ever. For me, anyway."

"Then, I assume that, as before, no sane man would take you up on this challenge?"

"Only an eager lad like yourself. But as always, you have my word. You survive, you get what you came for. And trust me, you'll want to survive for this prize."

"I always want to survive, Methuselah. Unlike yourself, to me life is a precious thing."

The old man snorted. "Not so precious that you won't come sniffing like an eager dog after this bone I've just tossed you. But enough chatter. Tonight. Nine-seventeen. Be on the roof of the warehouse at Eighty-three Cutter Place in Raleigh. And take my advice, Murphy boy. If you do come, and I know you will, make the most of these last few hours."

With another cackle, the line went dead.

Murphy shook his head, put down the receiver, and picked up the paper. He double-checked his translation. This time, the name he read set his mind racing even faster than before.

For Michael Murphy, a scholar who could not confine himself to library stacks of dusty, ancient tomes, an archaeologist dedicated to hunting and rescuing artifacts that could authenticate events from the pages of the Bible, this was the name of the prophet who was guaranteed to intrigue him more than any other:

DANIEL

For the rest of the day, Murphy could think of little else besides speculating about his nighttime rendezvous with Methuselah. It had been approximately two years since Murphy had first been contacted by this eccentric figure. Each time, without warning, and without ever showing his face, Methuselah would get a message to Murphy, always a single word in an ancient language that would turn out to be the name of one of the books of the Bible.

This would be followed within a minute by cryptic directions, always to some deserted location, where Methuselah would watch from a secure hiding place and taunt him while Murphy would try to survive some very real, very deadly physical challenge.

The risk of death was very high and very real each time. Methuselah was seemingly as serious about his sadistic games as he was about the scholarship behind his finds. And apparently he had enough money not only to sponsor the acquiring of the artifacts but to indulge his wildest ideas to lure Murphy into the most elaborate death traps. Would he actually allow Murphy to die if it ever came to that? So far, each time Murphy had come extremely close to losing his life, and each time he had no doubt that Methuselah would have let him die.

Yet, despite two broken ribs, a fractured wrist, and too many scars to recall, Murphy had so far somehow managed to muster all of his considerable abilities to stay alive long enough to claim his prize.

And what prizes they had been. Three artifacts Murphy never would have seen in any other way. Each proven with laboratory tests to be genuine, yet Methuselah never uttered a word about his sources. There were lots of issues that plagued Murphy about these mad, whirlwind chases, but each time Murphy went public with the artifacts, no organization, government, or individual collector had come forward to claim they had been stolen.

So, however and from where Methuselah was getting his occasional treasures, they had proven to be just that.

Methuselah remained a complete mystery to Murphy. To say he was eccentric would not begin to explain his actions. The man was clearly a scholar of ancient artifacts, yet Murphy could find no trace of where he came from or how he found these artifacts that any archaeologist would drool for. It was especially mystifying why Methuselah did not keep these treasures for himself, or for a museum, or why he chose his really strange games to give Murphy a chance to claim them.

As a man of high integrity, Murphy believed he could overlook some potential gray areas regarding the source of these artifacts. Some wealthy, connected, but truly mad collector was as close as Murphy could come to an explanation of who Methuselah was. However, there was the troubling religious aspect.

Methuselah was clearly not a religious man. Quite the opposite. A good deal of the pleasure Methuselah seemed to get from these challenges was to taunt Murphy about his faith. So far, Murphy had been up to every challenge, and he had to admit that in addition to getting the artifacts, part of what drove him was the chance to defy Methuselah's nasty verbal insults about Murphy's faith.

Which was hardly a justification for his risking his life, Murphy realized. However, pride, temper, stubbornness were all high on the list of Michael Murphy's imperfections. Probably Murphy's greatest reservations about his Methuselah adventures were a result of his deep religious faith, which made it far more difficult to justify the extreme risk to his life and limb.

Justify the risk not merely to himself, but to his wife, Laura.

So far, his passion for the quest for artifacts had been a real test of Laura's passion for Murphy. It certainly helped his cause that she held a degree in ancient studies herself. However, there were many arguments after the fact, many pledges that he would try to resist the next Methuselah temptation, but Laura knew there would always be another insanely dangerous Methuselah trap. All he had to do was to dangle another artifact before her husband.

It was that understanding that caused Murphy to dash off a quick note to Laura before he left for Raleigh that evening. She was at a conference in Atlanta and would not be home for another night, and Murphy wrote down what little he knew about where he was going. He left the note on the mantel in their living room. Just in case.

Murphy kept a light touch on the accelerator all the way from Preston to Raleigh to make sure he did not get a speeding ticket. That was one risk he could definitely avoid for the night. The address Methuselah had barked at him was for an eight-story building on an empty street in a deserted neighborhood. When he got to the rooftop, Murphy looked for some sign for a next move.

Without warning, the very roof beneath his feet opened, and that was when he found himself dropping through the building.

Free-falling.

In the fleeting seconds after he started his descent, his multitasking mind flashed on how beautiful Laura had looked yesterday afternoon before she left for her plane, he offered up a quick prayer, and he forced himself to focus on his years of martial arts training, specifically on the best position for his body to be in when he finally landed.

Assuming he had to land eventually, it would not be pretty.

He settled on the combination he had come to call Cat's Last Gasp, his own poor interpretation of a Tibetan landing maneuver. He thought of it as the moves a cat in its ninth life would make to land safely. Murphy loosened every muscle, fighting the natural instinct to tense up in anticipation of what was bound to be one fearsome impact.

Instead, he bounced. In the pitch-black space his body hit

what felt like a huge net, and Murphy bounced up and down, rapidly making him more disoriented than the falling had.

Feelings that were intensified by a blast of bright light that completely blinded Murphy.

"So good of you to drop in, Murphy."

Methuselah. Though Murphy still could not see, there was no mistaking the cackling laugh that filled the space. Murphy also knew that even if he could see clearly, Methuselah would be well hidden, as he always was.

"You're probably still getting your bearings, eh, Murphy, so you can't appreciate what a great old building this is. They built that chute to go through all the floors so they could drop things from the roof down to the main work floor here. I had my people set this up especially for you, but I took pity on you at the last minute and provided the net. I'm getting soft. Let's hope you're not."

Murphy finally stopped bouncing and rolled himself to the edge of the net. His sight was beginning to normalize, but there did not seem to be much to see inside this building. There were white walls enclosing one giant floor space. The ceiling, if there was one, must have been several stories high, but the combination of gloomy darkness and now the piercing glow from spotlights mounted on the walls made it impossible to be certain.

The netting was strung up at one end of the floor space. It was made of thick rope in a crosshatched pattern. The net had been stretched between four heavy wooden poles that were bolted to the floor and stabilized by heavy bags of what Murphy guessed was sand. At the opposite end of the vast room, what looked like a sliding door of shiny silver corrugated metal stood closed.

Surrounding the floor was a raised work area that was protected by heavy glass. That was where Methuselah must be, Murphy thought, but he could not make out any specific figure up there. His head was clearing and his breathing was starting to normalize.

"That was certainly worth the trip from home, Methuselah. Now, may I claim my prize and get back there?"

"You call that earning your keep, Murphy? That was just my special way to get you inside the tent. Get ready for the real show. Right now."

For the first time, Murphy heard an ominous sound, a low rumble that filled the empty space, but he was not sure what he was hearing. "Aaah, I see, Professor Murphy, by your perked-up ears, that you are ready to meet your match."

Murphy sighed. *So, now it really begins,* he thought. Then came a second, much more ominous sound. Something crashed against the metal door from the other side. Something that Murphy suddenly realized was about to come shooting out that metal door, heading directly for him. "Say, um, Methuselah, aren't you going to tease me first with a look at your latest artifact? So I at least know what it is that will make you try so hard to kill me."

"Yes, you do know I love to have my sport with you, Murphy. I actually wish you could live to get this one. It's hot stuff. Tell me, what made you so excited about seeing the word 'Daniel' from me today?"

Before Murphy could answer, there was another, even louder banging against the door. Murphy could not help but flinch where he stood and looked anxiously at the rattling metal.

"Up to now you've put into play some amazing artifacts from Biblical times, Methuselah. I don't know how you got them, but I never would have found them on my own. And Daniel, well, you know he was the most important prophet of all. I have studied him for years. Let me at least get a good close look at whatever Daniel artifact you've gotten your hands on."

"No. Enough talk, Murphy. You're about to get a closer look than you'll want. Because tonight you're not going to *study* Daniel, you are going to *be* Daniel."

With a metallic clang, the sliding door at the other end of the room was raised.

A full-grown lion stood roaring in the doorway. Murphy could not help but marvel at the tawny color, the tensile muscles along its flanks, its full mane, and the way the bright floodlights from the walls made the claws practically sparkle.

The lion, however, was wasting no time admiring Murphy. With a roar that echoed from every wall, and a propulsive spring of all four powerful legs, the lion bore down on Murphy as if he were an easy meal for the taking.

On pure instinct, Murphy threw himself to the floor, landing with a jarring thud just to the left of where he had been standing but close enough to smell the full hot blast of foul breath from the lion's mouth.

"Come on, Murphy, don't run. Make a fight of it, be a man."

The lion's claws braked on the wooden floor as his roaring head swept from side to side. Angry flecks of saliva pelted Murphy. After the first landed on his face, Murphy was already moving again, rolling twice and scrambling to his feet. Without stopping, he reached one of the wooden poles of the netting and swung himself back up into the net. The lion was in close pursuit and swiped his front paw within an inch of Murphy's leg. Having missed once, the lion swung the razor claws again without resting, and again just missed. The third swipe ripped Murphy's left sleeve to shreds.

Before he could get raked again, Murphy bounced up from the net. He landed a few feet away, back on the ropes, and without stopping, he bounced up again. The lion swatted at the rope again and again, but looked frustrated and confused by this bouncing prey.

Between the wooden floor, which was slippery to his back claws, and the netting, which was tangling his front claws, the lion writhed and roared in frustration. Murphy kept bouncing as far from the lion as he could get each time because he knew that the moment the lion connected with him, even with a glancing blow, it could be his last moment on earth.

"Murphy, stop playing popcorn and come down and give the pussycat a chance to really play with you."

I'll come down, Murphy thought, *but not the way you're thinking.* He reached into his pocket and pulled out his army knife. He did not wish to intentionally take another creature's life, even though the beast had four paws full of blades to his one. Instead, as the lion clawed and tried to jump up toward him, Murphy stumbled to one of the poles in four bounds. There he slashed the rope holding the netting to the pole.

"Murphy, that's not fair," Methuselah screamed.

"Don't talk to me about fair, you maniac."

Murphy was bounding to the next pole. The lion swung furiously but seemed to be tiring, much like a heavyweight boxer in a middle round. Or maybe that was just wishful thinking, Murphy realized, but the lion definitely looked confused by Murphy's rapid movements.

As the second side of the netting fell away from Murphy's

knife, the lion realized too late that he should have moved out from under it. His two front paws were now hopelessly tangled in the heavy rope. Murphy slid more than jumped to the floor, careful to stay out of range of the lion's claws.

Or so he thought, until an intense pain seared his left shoulder when a back claw struck him as it jerked free from the ropes. Murphy forced himself to run toward one of the two remaining ropes holding the netting, able to run faster on the floor. Best case, he had maybe another ten seconds before the lion pulled himself free of the ropes that had already fallen around him.

The pain in his shoulder told him he would have to lift himself back up with only his right arm, and he was grateful for the hundreds of pull-ups he forced himself to do in the gym each week. He raised himself up and swung around, then bounced again to grab the pole and slashed the third thong just as the lion was twisting away from the heap of ropes he had torn away from his body.

Now with this new batch of netting entrapping him, the lion momentarily collapsed on the floor. He roared through ragged, heaving breaths, still trying to slash free with his claws. Murphy rolled to the floor but made sure to stay completely out of the range of the lion.

"Aw, Murphy, you spoiled everything." Methuselah was fairly sputtering. "But you got fight in you, boy. For a useless Bible teacher, you got moxie, I'll give you that."

Murphy was breathing almost as rapidly as the lion. He managed to gasp, "How about giving me my artifact instead?"

"Well, you earned it, I guess. Only it's not going to be what you think."

Murphy straightened and looked up at the platform. "What are you trying to pull here, Methuselah?"

"Shut up and listen. It's right there in front of you. You just have to grab it."

"Grab what? Where?" Murphy was getting a bad feeling.

"Oh, your body's still prime, Murphy, but I swear all those digs have turned your brain to dust. Look at the lion's neck." Sure enough, Murphy noticed for the first time that there was a thin leather strip tied around the lion's neck. Attached to the strip was a red tube approximately the size and shape of a very large cigar holder.

"Oh, no, Methuselah. You think I'm going to fight this lion again just to get at that thing around his neck? That's too crazy even by your standards." Murphy paused, sensing his opportunity slipping away. "Besides, what's in the tube?"

Methuselah started his cackling laugh again. "Oh, Murphy, I've put the fever in you good tonight. You can't resist. I know you too well. You'll go back at him; you can't stop yourself. And this time . . . heh-heh-heh, your curiosity's going to get the cat to kill *you* for sure."

Murphy looked at the knife in his hand and was tempted, but he folded it back and pocketed it.

"Ooh, ever the good Boy Scout, Murphy. Going to make it a fair fight."

Murphy shook his head as he walked over to the pole nearest the downed lion. "No, Methuselah, not exactly fair, but I can live with it. I'd never kill that lion any more than I'd kill you tonight, and Lord knows you've given me more pause for thought than he has. But that won't stop me from taking advantage of him when I get the chance."

He picked up the heavy bag that was weighting down the nearest pole. He needed both arms to hoist it, but his bleeding shoulder made him shout with pain, and he almost dropped the bag on his foot. Instead, he dragged the bag over to where the lion was still tearing at the rope netting that hopelessly tangled his paws.

"This is definitely going to hurt you more than it hurts me," Murphy grunted, and he dropped the heavy bag right on the lion's head. The lion dropped in an unconscious heap.

Murphy watched the stilled beast take several shallow breaths before he reached slowly for the leather cord that held the red tube to his neck. He held his own breath and yanked the tube free of the lion's mane.

He grasped his prize. It was so light, he feared it was empty. "What gives here, Methuselah? This better be something besides a cigar."

At first, Methuselah did not say anything in response. Then the metal door rolled up. "You won, Murphy, now get out. Enjoy your spoils of this war on your own time. However, I will tell you these three things, because a warrior in victory does deserve some respect. First, like I told you, this one is hot, really hot."

"Hot as in stolen?"

"Never mind how I got it. Like the others I've given you, there's no angry owner going to come hunting you. But there is somebody who will want to come after you once they know you have it. I don't know who they are or why they're so interested, but I cover my tracks very well, as you know, and I've picked up several hints that somebody is desperate to get this, and will stop at nothing—and I mean nothing—to get it."

"But get what? What's in here?"

"That's the second thing. The tube doesn't have the artifact. The tube has the key to finding the artifact. And what the key is and what the artifact is you'll have to figure out for yourself. But I think you're maybe one of a handful of people alive who can figure it out. And I also know that if you do figure it out, it will get you the find of your life. If you live."

"But Daniel, it's got something to do with Daniel?" Murphy was getting exasperated now.

"That's number three, and then that's all I'll say. The connection's not going to be obvious to you, but I swear to you, I'm certain it's the real thing, and it will make you the reigning king of your precious Bible circle. I guarantee it. Now get out."

"Come on, Methuselah, you can't leave me hanging like this. What is it?"

"Can and will, Murphy. Get out. I'm a sore loser and you know it."

Wincing with one last painful look over his wounded shoulder at the lion, Murphy walked toward the door, clutching the tube tightly. "Good-bye, then, you crazy coot. And thank you, I guess."

Just before Murphy was through the doorway, Methuselah growled, "Murphy, don't get overconfident with your Bible-boy heroics. I'm telling you to be careful with this one. If somebody's going to kill you, I want it to be me in one of our little contests."

Murphy looked up at the platform. "Ever the sentimentalist, Methuselah. Thanks for the warning, but so far, the way I'm scoring, it's Christians one, lions zero."